Sing For Your Supper

Rosie
HARRIS

Sing For Your Supper

WILLIAM HEINEMANN : LONDON

Published by William Heinemann 2007

2 4 6 8 10 9 7 5 3 1

First published in Great Britain in 2007 by
William Heinemann
Random House, 20 Vauxhall Bridge Road,
London, SW1V 2SA

www.randomhouse.co.uk

Addresses for companies within The Random House Group Limited can be found at: www.randomhouse.co.uk/offices.htm

The Random House Group Limited Reg. No. 954009

A CIP catalogue record for this book
is available from the British Library

ISBN 9780434016167

The Random House Group Limited makes every effort to ensure that the papers used in its books are made from trees that have been legally sourced from well-managed and credibly certified forests. Our paper procurement policy can be found at: www.randomhouse.co.uk/paper.htm

Printed and bound in Great Britain by
Mackays of Chatham plc, Chatham, Kent

For Alan, Maureen and Carina Bloxham
Mario and Rhona Caretti

Acknowledgements

All the wonderful people at Heinemann and Arrow, especially Georgina Hawtrey-Woore, for all their help and support. Also to Caroline Sheldon and Krissy Lloyd.

Chapter One

'Out of your mind you must be, Enid Pryce, you and your Owen, letting your young Karyn go ahead with this silly idea. Spoiled little madam, she is; always has been! Everyone in Pen-y-llyn knows that, but I thought that the two of you would have seen sense and put your foot down long before now, indeed I did.'

'And what about you, then, Bronwen Morgan? Couldn't you manage to bully either your Madoc or your Tudor into listening to your stupid ranting this time? Don't like it when you can't get your own way, do you now!'

Watched by their neighbours, and oblivious of the cold March winds, the two women stood on their respective doorsteps in Clydach Street, facing each other over the low brick wall that divided their front paths as they gave vent to their feelings. They'd been next-door neighbours for over twenty years, and their children Karyn and Tudor had grown up together and played together since they'd been toddlers.

Tudor, two years older than Karyn, had held her hand, proudly protective, when she'd started going to the infants school. Later, when

1

she'd joined him at senior school half a mile away, the two of them had ridden there on their bikes each day, side by side.

'Been on the cards for years,' a neighbour commented. 'We all knew that, lovely to watch them, mind! Pigeon pair, those two, like a couple of cooing doves.'

'Takes two to make such an agreement, you know. Always headstrong, your Tudor,' Enid Pryce sighed.

Lifelong friends, the two women were completely different in looks and build. Enid was short and plump with light brown curly hair, creamy skin and hazel eyes; Bronwen was big and bulky with dark hair, deep-set dark eyes, and sallow skin. Now they stood with arms akimbo, eyes flashing, staring accusingly at each other, both of them intent on justifying the actions of their two children.

Like their offspring, who were the centre of their heated dispute, there were only a couple of years between them in age. Bronwen was the eldest and, throughout their lives, Enid had looked up to her. Bronwen had protected her smaller friend from being teased and bullied when they'd been young schoolgirls and had staunchly defended her ever since.

The unusual sight of the two of them bickering had brought other women out on to their doorsteps. Everyone knew that Tudor Morgan and Karyn Pryce were in love. They always had been, so none of them could see what all the arguing was about. If they didn't marry now, they would marry next year or the year after, so why make such an enormous fuss about it all?

True, Tudor was out of work again, but then he had never held a job down for more than a couple of weeks. Tall, devastatingly handsome with his mother's deep, dark eyes and dark, straight hair, he had his father's tall, lithe frame and infectious smile. He was a heartbreaker of the first order with a melodious baritone voice that melted your bones when he started singing.

In contrast, Karyn was like her mam; petite and curvy, with light brown hair, hazel eyes, and a round face that dimpled prettily when she smiled – which was more or less all the time. Karyn had a sunny nature and was friends with everyone. No one had a word to say against the girl. Industrious, too, so Mrs Lewis, who ran the corner shop and who had employed her since the day she'd left school, said. She was always saying that Karyn was a cracking little worker, one of the best she'd ever employed.

Karyn's family were well aware that for all Tudor's handsome looks, he was a bit of a wastrel, but, since they didn't seem to let it worry them, no one could understand why his own mam was so opposed to the marriage.

'Bronwen should be cheering at the thought of getting him off her hands, not putting up a fight,' one neighbour commented. 'I know I would be, if he was mine.'

'Perhaps Bronny doesn't like the idea of her son being a kept man because that's what he'll be when he marries Karyn unless he changes his ways. Maybe that's why she wants to keep him tied to her apron strings until he grows up a bit and sees sense.'

'Let them get wed I say,' Janys Wilson interposed. 'It might be the making of him.'

'Let Tudor Morgan get married at eighteen! Don't talk daft, he's just a kid.'

'Should have called them Hansel and Gretel,' another laughed. 'Live in fairyland the pair of them.'

'I still say it will be the making of him,' Janys insisted, her dark eyes flashing. 'Karyn might only be a chit of a girl but she's no fool. She'll have him toeing the line in no time at all.'

One by one the neighbours seemed to be taking sides, throwing advice at either Bronwen or Enid, according to their viewpoint.

The more advice that was offered the more incensed the main protagonists seemed to become.

'For heaven's sake cut your cackle and have a cup of tea,' old Mrs Evans who lived next door to Bronwen, on the other side to Enid Pryce, told them.

'Never! I'll never have her over my doorstep again, not as long as I draw breath,' Bronwen declared.

Old Mrs Evans waved her walking stick at them menacingly. 'Stop talking such nonsense!

I'm going in to put the kettle on, so you'd best both come into my place and we'll see if I can talk some sense into the pair of you.'

'Let's get the air cleared before your men come home. Get those two boyos fired up and it will be blood and snot and broken bones, not just words. Come on now, no more argy-bargy.'

'Granny Evans is talking a lot of sense,' someone agreed.

'Do you want a couple of us to come in as well and help you sort it out?' another asked.

The wrinkled, grey-haired old woman looked challengingly at the women who were listening so avidly to what was being said. 'Please yourselves. Come in if you have anything useful to say, otherwise get back to your own homes and start getting a meal ready for your menfolk. They'll all be home within the hour so let's see if we can sort this matter out before then.'

'Come on then, Bronny, do as she says,' a voice urged.

'And you, Enid. Go and take the weight off your feet and see if the pair of you can be friends again.'

Enid Pryce shrugged her shoulders and spread her hands helplessly. 'What is there to say, I'm not the one objecting to my Karyn marrying her Tudor, now am I?'

'Then help old Granny Evans to convince Bronwen that it's all for the best.'

'Silly spat over nothing, if you ask me. I'm wondering now what it was all about,' one of the women commented as she picked up her toddler and walked towards her own house.

'Young 'uns will do what they want to do no matter what their families want,' another agreed.

'Those two should think themselves lucky that Tudor and Karyn want to get married in a proper manner and not just run off together and live in sin.'

'They still might do that if those two silly bitches go on creating such a fuss,' Janys pointed out.

'Not them. Mark my words; they'll get married even if the devil himself says no.'

'Well, there you are then, better for it to be done with their mams in agreement than fighting every step of the way,' Janys called over her shoulder as she headed home.

'Not sure I'd want my girl to be getting married to a bloke who can't hold a job down for longer than five minutes, mind,' Glenda Philips murmured worriedly.

'No,' another agreed, 'but you can see the attraction! That Tudor has only to open his mouth and the minute you hear that voice of his your heart lifts.'

'Yes, he's got a voice like rich, dark gravy,' one of the younger ones sighed.

'There you go, always thinking of your belly, Moira,' someone laughed.

'Well, so how would you describe it, then?' Moira Pearce scowled.

6

'God knows, but it's good, I'll give you that! If he worked down the pit, like most of the men around here, then he'd be in the colliery choir, there's no doubt about that.'

As Bronwen and Enid went into Granny Evans's house followed by Moira Pearce, the rest of the women began wandering back to their own homes still muttering amongst themselves as to what the outcome of it all would be.

Maggie Lewis turned the cardboard sign to 'CLOSED' and shut the shop door firmly behind Karyn. Then she stood there and waited for Karyn to give it a really hard push from outside to make sure that it was well and truly locked.

Karyn paused for a moment in the doorway, breathing deeply of the sharp, spring air. She loved working for Maggie Lewis, but it was good to get outside and breathe fresh air. The shop stocked everything from fresh bread to paraffin, from cheese to gobstoppers, and the resultant mix of smells was sometimes a bit overpowering.

She was just taking her second deep breath when she stopped, gulped, and stared in surprise when she realised that Tudor was sitting on a low wall on the opposite side of the road.

For a moment she stood admiring him. He was so good-looking. He was almost six foot, lean and lithe, with a handsome face, sloe-dark

eyes, black hair sleeked back from a broad forehead, a determined chin, and straight, dark
brows.

Sitting there, a cigarette dangling between
his long, sensitive fingers, Tudor looked every
inch the film star he hoped one day to be. Not
for him the blue-pitted face of a miner. Nor was
he dressed in a drab flannel shirt, shiny old
jacket, greasy cap and a muffler tied round his
neck like most of the boyos he'd known at
school. He was wearing smart grey flannels,
and a grey tweed jacket with a light blue shirt.
His grey tweed cap was set at such a jaunty
angle that it brought a smile to Karyn's lips.

Tudor was so different from all the other
chaps of his age. He was so astute and so clever.
That was what she loved about him. She'd
known him all her life, but it still sent a thrill
right through her when she walked into a room
with him, or walked down the street with her
hand tucked into the crook of his arm, watching
the admiring glances everyone gave them.

Very soon now they would be man and wife.
All her dreams would be coming true. They'd
both told their families last night that they'd
set the date for their wedding. They hadn't told
them why, of course. That was their secret.

Karyn sighed. Daft, really, that they'd let
themselves get carried away before they'd had
a chance to save up for a home of their own.
She didn't even have a bottom drawer ready!

It was all because of what had happened at

8

Christmas. They'd gone to a party at the home of a friend of Tudor's called Martyn Jones; a chap he'd become pals with when he'd gone down to Cardiff to look for a job. They'd missed the last train back and so Martyn had said they could sleep over at his place. There'd only been one spare bed, but both of them had assured her there was nothing wrong with her and Tudor sharing a bed as long as they bundled.

'Old Welsh custom, see,' Martyn insisted. 'Mind, by rights, you must have a bolster down the middle of the bed to keep you apart.' He grinned. 'That's how they did their courting in the old days.'

Karyn knew this as well as they did, but she was pretty sure that it was a custom that had died out years ago. She'd had a few port and lemons, though, so it had been easy enough to persuade her that it would be a giggle.

The trouble was it had turned out to be more than a mere giggle. Inflamed by drink, all their promises to each other about waiting until after they were married had been forgotten and they'd simply been carried away.

Now, her delight that Tudor had come to meet her from work dimmed as she wondered why. He'd never bothered before and she was puzzled as to why he'd done so now.

She didn't have to wait long to find out. The moment Tudor spotted her he stood up and strode quickly across the road towards her, dropping his half-smoked cigarette on to the road and not even stopping to stamp it out.

He broke the news even before he gave her a quick hug and a kiss.

'I thought I'd better come and warn you that your mam and mine are going at it hammer and tongs. What's more, most of the street are out on their doorsteps listening to them and taking sides.'

'Our two mams are quarrelling? They can't be! They're closer than sisters!'

'And they're fighting just as if they were sisters,' he said grimly. 'They're going at it like cat and dog.'

'What's it all about?'

'Us, of course.'

'You mean about us getting married?'

'It seems so,' he said dolefully.

Karyn's eyes widened. 'I can't believe it. They've known that we've been sweethearts since we were tiny tots.'

'Well, they're fighting about it now and with the rest of the street adding their two-penny-worth as well. The last I saw was the pair of them going into old Granny Evans's place to chew the fat over a cuppa. Oh, and that Moira Pearce went in as well to have her say, or else to act as referee.'

'So what are we going to do?'

Tudor's arm tightened around her shoulders. 'Go to the pub for a drink?'

10

Karyn pulled away and stared up at him, frowning. 'That's not a good idea, is it?'

'Why not? If you go straight home, someone will grab hold of you and march you in to join them. If that happens, what will you say? You don't want to face them with the truth, now do you, cariad? Not yet! Far better to wait until after we are married because they won't think that it is such a disgrace then,' he said in a cajoling voice.

'I don't know what to do for the best,' she murmured hesitantly.

'Yes you do, we worked it all out, girl. Remember? Our way and no one gets upset.'

Karyn nodded. She couldn't take it in that her mother and Tudor's mother were rowing. They'd always been such close friends that it didn't seem possible.

She looked up at him questioningly. 'You're not having me on, are you, Tudor? This isn't your way of getting me to go to the pub with you, now is it?'

'Of course it isn't, cariad. I suggested a drink because I thought that if you had a small port inside you, it would make you feel better about facing the music, see. Like it or not there's bound to be a row when we get home, now isn't there?'

Karyn spread her hands helplessly. 'I don't know. I don't know what to think. They've never said a cross word to each other in their lives so what's caused all this?'

11

Tudor shrugged. 'How would I know! Come on, we can talk over a drink. Do you want a straight port or a port and lemonade?'

Karyn sipped her drink in silence. Tudor didn't seem to be nearly as concerned as she was, she reflected. Yet he must think the row was pretty serious because he had come to meet her from work, to warn her what to expect.

In between swigs of beer Tudor kept telling her not to worry. 'They'll soon calm down and find something else to argue about,' he told her with a laugh.

'Surely you must have some idea what caused them to fall out,' she persisted. 'You were there . . .'

'Only for a very short while,' he interrupted quickly. 'The minute I realised what was going on I came to warn you so that you didn't walk straight into it.'

Karyn drained her glass. 'I think we should be going. My da and yours will be home soon, they're both on the same shift.'

'You're right. We ought to try and sort things out before they get back. We don't want them squaring up to each other as well.'

'Why on earth should they fight?'

'Over what's been said, of course.'

Karyn frowned. 'So you do know something that you're not telling me! Come on, Tudor, what was the row really about? You do know, don't you?'

Tudor sighed. 'Everyone seems to think we are too young and . . .' He paused and sighed.

'Go on, tell me the rest.'

'Well, they think I'm a wastrel, not good enough for you, see, cariad. You are so hard-working, according to what Mrs Lewis always says, whereas I don't seem to be able to hold any job down for more than a couple of weeks.'

'You earn money, though!' Karyn defended.

'You mean my singing!' He laughed. 'Folks around here don't really call that work. They look at it as something you do for your own pleasure in your spare time. Slogging your guts out down the pit, now that's what they call working.'

'You go and work down the pit!' Karyn gave a scornful laugh. 'Might as well ask the King himself to work a shift underground as ask you to do so.'

'True enough, but all the other boyos go down the pit and so does my da and yours, so they think I should be doing the same.'

'You're not like any of them!' Karyn defended. 'You've only got to look in a mirror to see that you are a different kind of man from all the others around here. You're destined to be a famous singer, you've said so yourself.'

Tudor gave a self-satisfied smirk as he squeezed her hand. 'You believe in me, don't you, cariad?'

'Of course I do! I always have, ever since you

used to sing at school. I knew then that your voice was special.'

He raised her hand to his lips and kissed it. 'Thank you, cariad. One day I'll prove to you that I can get to the top.'

'I know you will,' she agreed. 'One day everyone will know your name and what a wonderful voice you have!'

His eyes glazed over as he stared into space. 'I can see it now, my name up in lights outside the Prince of Wales Theatre in the very centre of Cardiff. Inside, it will be packed; every seat taken.'

'The audience will listen spellbound as you sing to them,' she enthused.

'Perhaps I'll become the new Caruso and sing all the old favourites as well as some of the popular new ones like "If You Were the Only Girl in the World" and "Look for the Silver Lining".'

He sighed and gazed down at her, his dark eyes full of confidence. 'One day, cariad; one day.'

Chapter Two

A noise like a tremendous clap of thunder sounded as Tudor and Karyn left the Miner's Arms. The ground beneath their feet trembled, windows cracked like shots from a gun, shop signs swayed dangerously, lights flickered, followed by a frightening stillness that seemed terrifying in the gathering dusk of the early April evening.

Karyn and Tudor looked at each other, their expressions a mixture of fear, horror and disbelief.

'An explosion!' they exclaimed in unison.

Without hesitation they hurried towards the pithead, joined by countless others, men, women and children. The men were struggling into their jackets as they ran; the women wrapping shawls around their shoulders. Children were being dragged by the hand or left to follow as best they could.

Like some enormous unkempt army they advanced towards the pithead, apprehension keeping them silent. All of them feared the worst. One shift was ending and another about to begin, which doubled the number of possible casualties.

Karyn and Tudor were amongst the first to arrive. Both of them were fearful, knowing that their respective fathers, Owen Pryce and Madoc Morgan, had been with the shift that was due to end and so they were bound to have been involved.

Everyone was expecting one of the mine officials to put in an appearance at any moment to tell them exactly what had happened. Everyone feared that there were would be fatalities, but how many would there be? There were also bound to be men injured, but how many and how badly? When the ambulances and fire engines arrived the crowd drew to one side to allow them access into the yard surrounding the pithead.

Karyn and Tudor were clutching hands, too scared to even speak, but both of them were grateful to the other for the strength and understanding that they shared. Like the rest of the huge crowd who were waiting in silence, their nerves were on edge. There were a hundred and one questions they wanted to ask, but they knew the futility of doing so until one of the mine officials came out and spoke to them all. None of them would do that until they had all concurred and were in complete agreement over what was to be said.

Hope flickered and wavered in every breast. Those patiently waiting were wives and mothers, sons and daughters, brothers and sisters. Everyone in the crowd had a relative or friend working at the pit, who were either about to end their shift or begin the new one.

Each time there was a pit explosion some of the men who worked there were either killed or maimed. Many were so badly injured that they were unable to work ever again. Sometimes it seemed as if nature was having its own revenge; wreaking justice for the way men desecrated the ground by hewing and hacking right down into the very bowels of the earth and scarring the surrounding countryside.

These thoughts were in the minds of many of those clustered at the pithead trying to anticipate the news.

The waiting seemed interminable. One minute they were filled with hope, the next they feared the worse, but no one expressed their thoughts out loud. Few spoke, most of them were afraid to disclose what was in their minds and hearts.

When one of the officials finally appeared there was a murmur that swelled into a rumble that reflected the agitation of the crowd.

'There's been a cave-in. We are not sure how many casualties there are, but as soon as we know, then you will be told,' the spokesman pronounced.

It was the standard announcement on such occasions and it conveyed no reassurance. The tension increased and became tangible. Another hour passed, many wondered if there would be any definite news that night.

Then there was a movement at the pithead.

As each man emerged from the cage, coal-grimed and shaky, his name was called out by the official standing there, and members of his family rushed forward to claim him and escort him home. Group by group the crowd thinned.

Soon there were only a dozen or so left, their faces grim and haggard, their eyes full of sorrow. The long pause signified that all the walking wounded had now been brought to the surface and claimed by their relatives.

Those who still remained at the pithead became disconsolate. If their man hadn't already been brought to the surface they knew it meant that either he was so badly injured that he needed to be stretchered out or, worse still, that he was dead.

Tudor and Karyn were amongst the ones who were still waiting.

The noise of the explosion made the china on Granny Evan's table dance.

Tea spilled over on to the tablecloth but none of the women there even noticed.

Bronwen and Enid both knew that their husbands were still underground, and fear gripped them like an iron fist. As one, they pushed back their chairs, grabbed their shawls and headed for the door. Moira Pearce followed in their wake, leaving Granny Evans to deal with the mess on her table.

Bronwen and Enid headed straight for the pithead, their disagreement over the coming wedding of their son and daughter forgotten in their urgency to find out what was happening.

Together they elbowed their way through the dense crowd, each of them asking about her husband as they did so, fearing the worst, but always hoping they wouldn't hear it.

They strained their ears to hear the names called out as the cage whirred to a stop and men were brought to the surface. As the crowd began to thin out as more and more small groups moved away supporting a dazed or slightly injured miner, the two women linked arms for comfort and reassurance.

They edged forward as the seriously injured began to be stretchered out. When they spotted Karyn and Tudor also waiting their fears increased as they joined them.

'No news of your da then, Karyn?' Enid asked.

'Not yet!' The girl's lips tightened and she blinked hard to keep back the tears which threatened.

'Madoc Morgan is still down there as well, is he?' Enid sighed.

'Yes, Tudor's dad is still down there,' Karyn sniffed, rubbing the back of her hand across her eyes.

'They're bringing some more of the injured up now, look,' Bronwen muttered as once again the cage came to a whirring stop and the gates were opened by men waiting at the top.

The two women moved closer to each other in a supportive manner, trying not to show their emotions or that they were shivering with almost uncontrollable anguish.

'Owen Pryce!'

The name rang out in the tense silence, followed by three others, but Madoc Morgan's name wasn't amongst them.

Enid squeezed Bronwen's arm. 'He'll be up with the next lot, you'll see, cariad.'

'Of course he will! You and Karyn get along and see to your poor Owen. I'll be all right. Tudor can wait here with me.'

'I'll come back and see how you are once we've seen my dad to hospital,' Karyn assured Tudor.

'Might even see you there,' he told her as he gave her a brief kiss.

'Any luck and he'll be brought up in the next cage.'

Karyn nodded and then followed her mother to where the stretcher with her father on it was being lifted up into an ambulance.

Tudor and Bronwen waited in silence, afraid to talk in case they didn't hear the names as they were called out.

Three more cage loads came to the surface and still Madoc Morgan's name hadn't been called. Ambulances came and went, their wailing sirens adding to the tension.

It was almost an hour later when the pit spokesman broke the news: the four men who still hadn't been accounted for were dead.

Bronwen Morgan refused to believe it. 'No,' she told Tudor when he tried to persuade her that they should go home out of the cold. 'You go if you want to but I'm waiting here until they bring the body up, even if I have to wait days.'

'What good will that do, Mam? Come on home and have a warm by the fire and a cup of tea—'

'Cup of bloody tea!' Her lip curled. 'You sound like old Granny Evans. If that's all you need then go and knock on her door, she's prob- ably got the kettle on the boil, she usually has.'

Tudor's mouth tightened and he let out a long breath. 'That wasn't what I meant, our mam, and you know it. I was thinking that you'd be better off at home, that's all I was trying to say. It would be better to wait there in comfort, not stand here shivering in your shoes.'

'No!' Bronwen declared obstinately, pulling her shawl tighter around her shoulders. 'I'm waiting here until they bring my man out. How the hell do they know he's dead, anyway? He might have only been knocked unconscious, or got a lung full of poison air. Bring him to the surface and he might be as right as rain.'

It was an unlikely hope and they both knew it.

'If you want to do something useful, then nip along and let your sister know what's happened,' Bronwen told her son.

'Olwyn's not bloody deaf. She'll have heard the explosion, it shook the whole town.'

'Then why isn't she here?'

'I don't know,' Tudor sighed. 'I suppose that if her Griff wasn't on the same shift she thinks everything is fine.'

'There's rubbish you talk! She would know that your dad might be down there. Go on, go and tell her. Make sure you get her to come back here with you.'

'What good will that do?'

'I don't know, but families should stick together, even after they have left home,' Bronwen declared emphatically.

Tudor hesitated uneasily. 'No, I think I'm better staying here with you, in case . . .'

'In case of what? You think he's dead, don't you! Go on, say it. You think that those four still down there are all dead.'

Suddenly, the realisation of what this meant seemed to penetrate her mind. Turning, she clung to Tudor, trembling so much that he had difficulty holding her as she shook with harsh sobs.

It was almost an anti-climax when the four bodies were eventually brought out. The small group who were still waiting made few outward signs of grief. Their nerves were already raw;

22

their minds had absorbed all the possibilities so it was no longer a shock when the pit spokesman announced their names.

Four bodies, four small family groups who submitted wordlessly to the catastrophe even though they knew their lives could never be the same again. Their man had endured his last shift in the bowels of the earth; the family bread-winner was dead. Now the responsibilities of being head of the household passed on to the shoulders of the eldest son; or to the dead man's wife.

Darkness was now shrouding the pithead scene as, one by one, the four bodies were claimed by their families in brooding silence. Not until they were back in their own homes, with the doors tight shut, would they give way to their tears. Only then would their grieving begin. Souls would be bared within the family group as they mourned their loss and tried to comfort each other.

Tomorrow there would be a funeral to be arranged, rituals to be observed, but for tonight, as they carried their dead away, their minds were blank and their hearts too heavy with grief to contemplate such matters.

Chapter Three

There were so many people in the reception area of the hospital anxiously waiting for news of men who had been brought in that it took Enid Pryce and Karyn well over an hour before they could manage to find out what was happening to Owen.

They'd been told on arrival that since Owen Pryce had only sustained minor injuries, they would have to take him home as soon as his broken arm and lacerations had been attended to.

'All our beds will be needed for the really seriously injured,' they were told. 'Call your own doctor if he needs any further treatment for shock or any other after effects.'

'So how long will it take for you to see to his arm, then?' Enid asked worriedly.

'Heaven knows!' the nurse told her with an impatient shrug. 'There're men who are much more seriously injured to be attended to first. You'll have to be patient. We'll call out his name when we're ready to discharge him.'

'That means we could be here for hours, Mam, so why don't we take it in turns? You go home and get some sleep and some hot food—'

'Don't talk daft, girl! I can't leave you waiting here on your own,' Enid snapped.

'Then call at the Morgans' and ask Tudor to come and keep me company,' Karyn suggested.

'There's rubbish you spout! Bronwen will be needing Tudor with her, have you forgotten that his da's just been killed!'

'I know that, but their Olwyn will be with his mam. They won't want Tudor there.'

Enid didn't even bother to reply. Shivering, she pulled her shawl more tightly round her shoulders and huddled down in her seat, rocking to and fro.

Karyn reached out and put her arm around her mother's shoulders in an attempt to comfort her. Her thoughts were concerned with how all this was going to affect her own future.

Already there was dissension because of her insistence that she was going to marry Tudor Morgan no matter what anyone said. It was going to be even more difficult now that her father had been injured. Both her parents would probably think she was just being selfish . . . unless she explained everything.

Karyn sometimes found it hard to believe that she had been so foolish as to let herself get carried away like that. Repeatedly she'd told Tudor that she wouldn't go all the way, not until she had a wedding ring on her finger.

He'd said he respected her for saying that because it showed she wasn't simply having a fling or that she was a free and easy floozy.

He'd also pointed out, though, that she couldn't expect him to go on waiting for ever.

'I'm a very passionate sort of chap, cariad,' he'd reminded her on more than one occasion when she'd put a stop to his more adventurous demands.

Their courting had become increasingly daring but, nevertheless, he'd respected her wishes and had always managed to stop short of the real thing. Well, he had until that night in Cardiff. She frowned, trying to remember which side of the bed the bolster had been on the next morning. Not that it mattered. The deed was done. She'd offered no resistance when he'd drawn her into his arms and his caresses had become so ardent that they were making love before she realised it. It had been pure bliss and she'd found that her passion was every bit as great as his so she could understand why he was so eager.

To give Tudor his due, he'd not tried anything again after that, though she knew he wanted to, and she'd tried to put it out of her mind. She told herself it was something to look forward to when they did decide to get married.

It had been around the end of February when she realised just how foolish they'd been. Tudor tried to laugh her fears away, but other signals made it impossible for her to do that. She was pregnant. She'd been shocked and scared, wondering if she dared tell her mother.

'It might be best if you don't do that, cariad,'

Tudor warned. 'You know the tongue-lashing we'll get from both your mam and mine.'

'They're bound to find out! It's not something I can hide,' she told him miserably.

'I know that, cariad, but it might be best if we box clever, not stick our necks in a noose,' he cajoled. 'We always intended to get hitched one day so why not now?' he went on, his dark eyes speculative. 'If we get married as quickly as we can arrange it, then no one need know about the baby until after we've tied the knot!'

'Don't you think they're bound to suspect?' she questioned doubtfully.

'Not unless you blab about it! Tell no one. I'll make all the arrangements.'

'How can we afford to get married? You're out of a job at the moment and we have no money saved up. Where will we live?'

He'd taken her into his arms at that point, covering her face with kisses, telling her how much he cared about her, how much he wanted her, and assuring her that everything would work out.

It had been exactly what she'd wanted to hear and so she'd gone along with his idea. They suspected that there might be opposition from their families because they were so young and, above all, because Tudor didn't have a proper job.

He kept reminding her that he earned enough each week by singing at the pubs and clubs to keep going on. The only problem was, the money was so irregular. He never knew how much he would get so it would be hard work trying to run a home on it.

When she tried to explain this to him he laughed. 'What are you worrying about, you've still got your regular wage packet coming in from Ma Lewis, now haven't you?'

'I have at the moment, but I won't be able to go on working once the baby arrives,' she reminded him.

'I'll have a job by then; something will turn up,' he assured her. 'If I don't, then I'll look after the babba while you work during the day and then when you come home at night I'll go out singing.'

It was late in the afternoon before Owen Price was discharged from the hospital. Enid and Karyn were tired out and hungry, but they rallied at the sound of his name being called and rushed to his side.

'Come on, you two, get me out of this place and take me home,' he exclaimed the minute he saw them.

'Oh Da, are you all right?' Karyn exclaimed, her eyes widening at the sight of his heavily bandaged arm supported in a sling and his face covered with lacerations which had been either stitched or covered with plaster.

'Right as I'll ever be, cariad. Bloody lucky, too, if you ask me. You should see the state some of the other boyos are in! At least I've only got a broken arm and the doctor says it will soon mend. Cheer up, the pair of you! Six weeks and it should be healed well enough for me to be able to throw away this sling.'

'Come on then, Owen, let's get you home,' Enid said tearfully. 'Do you think you can walk?'

'How else am I going to get there? Not going to try and carry me on your back, now are you, girl?'

'No, but I might be able to find someone strong to give you an arm to lean on.'

'Mam's right. Why not wait while I go and fetch Tudor to help us,' Karyn suggested.

'Tudor Morgan support me, that'll be the day!' Heads turned as Owen's laugh rang out.

Her face bright red with embarrassment, Karyn bit down on her bottom lip and said nothing. She'd hoped her da would be on her side, but it looked as though he agreed with those who didn't rate Tudor as highly as she did.

'If you let your da link his good arm through yours, Karyn, then I'll put my arm around his waist to steady him,' Enid suggested. 'That way we should manage all right, providing we take things slowly.'

'Get off, the pair of you, and stop panicking,' Owen exclaimed irritably. 'I've got a bloody broken arm not a broken leg. I can walk as well as the next man!'

'You must still be feeling a bit weak and dizzy,

so stop making such a fuss and let us help you,'
Enid insisted. 'Here, take my arm and our
Karyn can run on ahead and get the kettle on
so that you can have a hot drink.'

As they emerged from the hospital and into
the fresh air, Owen swayed a little and had to
lean against a wall to regain his balance.
Reluctantly, he grabbed hold of his wife's arm
and Enid's mouth tightened as she took his
weight.

Karyn walked beside them for a few yards
to make sure that her mother could cope, then,
seeing that Enid seemed to be able to manage,
she hurried on ahead to stir the fire into life
and have the kettle boiling before they reached
home.

Karyn waited until her father had enjoyed a
good nourishing meal and had warmed
himself in front of the fire and she had helped
to get him upstairs before trying to talk to her
mother.

By the time Enid came back downstairs again
after helping her husband to undress and get
into bed, Karyn had cleared away the remains
of their meal, washed the dishes, made up the
fire and had a cup of hot cocoa waiting for her
mother.

Enid was the first to speak as they sat in
companionable silence on either side of the
glowing fire sipping their drinks.

'There's no question now of you getting

married, Karyn,' she said quietly. 'Your da will be off work for weeks so we'll be relying on your wages to help out.'

'It's all planned, Mam. We've set the date; it's only a couple of weeks away.'

'Then you'll have to unset it, won't you?' Enid Pryce said tetchily. 'Folks will understand why you've called it off.'

'We can't call it off, Mam,' Karyn repeated stubbornly. 'You must try and understand.'

'What's there to understand? Your da's been badly injured and Tudor's dad is dead. He'll need to find himself some work and look after his mam.'

Karyn shook her head, tears spilling down her cheeks.

'Come on, girl! Grow up. You can't have everything your own way all the time.'

'It's not that, Mam, we must go ahead with our plans, we really must.'

Enid frowned angrily as she looked across at her daughter, but the words of recrimination died on her lips. 'Duw anwyl!' She drew her breath in sharply. 'No, don't tell me. Now I know why you're being so stubborn, I can see it in your eyes. You've bloody well given in to him, now don't try and deny it.'

'I'm not going to deny it. Perhaps you can understand now why we've got to go ahead with the wedding.'

'I never thought the day would dawn when I'd hear my own daughter admit to something like that,' Enid moaned. 'What got into you girl, you must have been out of your senses.'

'I'm not the first girl around here who's been caught out,' Karyn defended hotly.

'No, you're not. Olwyn Morgan was well and truly in the club when she walked down the aisle and look at her today: she's only just turned twenty and she's got three kids all under four hanging on to her skirts. The only difference between the two of you is that she married a bloke who has a job and works hard.'

'By that I suppose you mean he works down the pit!' Karyn said scornfully.

'That's right, and he brings home a steady wage packet each week. Not like her brother who's never done a proper day's work in his life. Well, things will have to change now, that's for sure. Bronwen will make certain of that.'

'Mrs Morgan can't expect Tudor to look out for her now. He's going to have responsibilities of his own in a few months' time,' Karyn reminded her tartly.

Enid shook her head from side to side in despair. 'As if we haven't had enough heartache today without you piling it on, girl,' she said bitterly.

'Will you tell my da?' Karyn begged. 'He might take the news better coming from you.'

'I doubt it! Broken hearted he'll be to think of you being in that state at your age. You're only seventeen! You've seen nothing of the world. Tying yourself down to the first boy who's asked you out and him a wastrel into the bargain.'

'Tudor's not a wastrel! He's very talented. He's got a wonderful voice and he can earn a living singing if he's given the chance.'

'There's rubbish you talk, girl. Earn a living singing! Pick up a few bob here and there round the pubs and clubs. Coppers chucked at him by men who are too drunk to know what they're doing. Money that they should be giving to their wives to provide grub and shoe leather for their kids.'

'That'll do, Mam,' Karyn said angrily. 'Stop slating him. In a couple of weeks' time he'll be your son-in-law, remember.'

'God forbid. We should have stopped you running around with him years ago.'

'You've always liked him. You've known how close we've been ever since we were little kids.'

'Not this bloody close!' Enid said vehemently. 'If I'd had any idea what was going on, I'd have got your da to tell him where to get off, or else punch his silly head in. How long has all this been going on? You'd better start explaining yourself, my girl.'

'It only happened once. At Christmas . . .'

'You mean when we let you go to that party down in Cardiff with him!'

'That's right.'

'You told us that you stayed with a friend because you missed the last train home, but

what you really meant was you were intending
to sleep together!'

'No, of course we hadn't planned for
anything like that to happen, Mam!'

'Duw! After all the warning me and your dad
gave you about behaving yourself if we let you
go to that damn party and then you go and let
him have his way with you.'

'No, it wasn't like that. We did stay with
Tudor's friend but there was only one spare bed.'

'So you decided to sleep together . . .' Enid
clapped her hands over her ears. 'I don't believe
this, I don't want to hear any more, you shameless little hussy.'

'No, Mam, hear me out,' Karyn pleaded. 'It
was never meant to happen like that. We've
always agreed that we would wait until we
were married.'

'Only he saw an opportunity and took it, the
scoundrel,' Enid declared. 'And you were too
drunk to know what he was up to until it was
too late, were you?'

'We had a bolster between us, honest to
God.'

'And that was supposed to make sleeping
together quite safe and acceptable, was it?'

'It was always considered to be all right in
olden times. They called it bundling, didn't
they!'

'The bolster was there to protect the girl's
honour! So what went wrong with it in your
case?'

34

Karyn looked shamefaced. 'I don't know, Mam. It was in place when we went to sleep but—'

'Somehow it got whipped away in the middle of the night by the fairies, I suppose,' Enid Pryce sneered. 'Fine tale that is for me to tell your da when he asks, isn't it?'

'It really is the truth,' Karyn muttered uneasily. 'I wouldn't have done something like that on purpose.'

Enid Pryce stared at her daughter in disbelief. 'You must think I'm a daft ha'porth and no maybe.'

'It is the truth, every word of it, and I know my da will believe me,' Karyn said defensively.

Enid shook her head wearily. 'Is Tudor going to tell his mam the same stupid story? I don't see her swallowing it, mind, any more than I am.'

Chapter Four

All the neighbours turned out for Madoc Morgan's funeral. They lined the street, every doorstep packed, as the hearse, drawn by a handsome pair of black horses, their heads festooned with black plumes, came to a standstill outside the Morgans' house. A murmur rippled through the crowd as the coffin was brought out and loaded. Then there were gasps of approval as one by one wreaths were piled on top of the coffin.

Bronwen, dressed in sombre black from head to toe, leaned heavily on Tudor's arm as she came out of the house, followed by Olwyn and her husband, Griff Baker.

As the chief mourners, they followed immediately behind the hearse. Behind them came the Pryce family, Owen, Enid and Karyn, also dressed in black. Owen's arm was still in a sling and his face was tense and drawn.

The hearse moved at a snail's pace and many of Madoc's friends and neighbours fell in behind the chief mourners to accompany the cortege the short distance to his final resting place. It was a long crocodile of black-clad figures, men and women who had known

Madoc Morgan all his life. Some had grown up with him, others had known him at school, or were colleagues from the pit.

Karyn felt numb as she walked with her parents behind the Morgans. When they reached the chapel all she could think about was that it was the same chapel where she and Tudor were to be married in less than two weeks.

Her heart quickened as her eyes rested on Tudor, standing beside his mother. Even in profile his handsome, sensitive face, thick dark hair, and tall lean figure sent a frisson of love and tenderness through her. Soon they would be together as man and wife; a whole new life stretching ahead of them.

She wondered if Tudor had told his mother yet that they were going ahead with their plans despite what had happened. If so, then how had she taken the news?

It must be so awful for her to have lost her husband and to know that in a sense she would also be losing her son as well. Leastways, Karyn reflected, that is how Bronwen Morgan would probably see it.

Still, Karyn reflected, she had Olwyn. She studied Tudor's sister and repressed a shudder. She could remember when Olwyn had been slim and carefree, always laughing, bubbling over with fun and high spirits. Now she looked fat and slatternly even in her funeral black. Her hair was long and straggly under the black cloche hat, and the hem of her black skirt hung unevenly beneath the black coat that was far too tight for her. Three children in four years had done nothing for either Olwyn's face or figure, Karyn thought sadly.

She wondered if Olwyn was happy with her life as a mother of three young children. Or did she regret the indiscretion that had resulted in a hasty marriage to Griffith Baker?

She was astonished that he wasn't there walking beside Olwyn, then she realised that along with some of the other miners he was acting as a pall bearer and had gone on ahead ready to receive the coffin when the hearse reached the chapel.

She wondered why Tudor wasn't doing the same. Probably his mother had decided she needed him close beside her to give her the courage and support she would need to see her through such a terrible ordeal. Did that mean that she still expected him to be at her side so that she could lean on him even after the funeral was over? Karyn pondered uneasily.

Now that she was widowed would Bronwen be willing to understand that Tudor's first duty was to provide a home for his wife and unborn child, and not for her? Karyn thought worriedly.

The only way that Tudor could do both was if they moved in with Bronwen after they were married. Karyn sighed; that was something she wasn't prepared to even contemplate because she knew that it wouldn't work.

She'd known Bronwen all her life, in some ways almost as well as she knew her own family. That was why she was so sure that the three of them living together was impossible. Bronwen would still boss Tudor around as if he was a young lad, not a grown man with a wife and child.

Anyway, she couldn't imagine him ever being able to earn enough money to support them all. And, even more important, all his lifelong dreams about one day earning his livelihood as a singer would be gone for ever.

Breaking the news to her da that she was pregnant had been one of the hardest things she'd ever had to do, Karyn reflected. She'd hoped her mam would tell him because she would have known how to do it without raising his blood pressure, but she'd refused.

'You got yourself into this mess so it is up to you to tell him yourself,' her mother had declared, her mouth tightening into a thin line of disapproval.

She'd put it off for a couple of days, telling herself that it wasn't fair to give him such a shock, not when he'd been so badly injured. She knew in her heart, though, that it wasn't the real reason for delaying it. She didn't want to see the hurt look on his face or the stark disappointment in his eyes when she told him. She was also very much afraid of what he would say.

As it happened, Owen Pryce had said very

little. He was already resigned to the fact that she and Tudor intended to get married. He also accepted that nothing any of them said would make Karyn change her mind.

He was well aware of how friendly she'd always been with Tudor, but that didn't mean he approved of him as a prospective son-in-law. He knew only too well how feckless Tudor was and that he didn't seem to be able to hold down a job for more than five minutes. He knew, too, that all Tudor was really interested in was singing, and in his opinion there was no future in that.

'Without a doubt he has a fine voice, but where will that get him?' he'd told Karyn time and time again. 'Plenty of chaps can sing and have their heart set on becoming stars and making money as entertainers but how many of them actually manage to do it?'

'Lots of them become very successful,' she'd argued. 'They sing on the stage, sometimes as part of a band; you hear about it happening all the time.'

'A few do! You can count on the fingers of one hand the number who really make it; ones who top the bill outside the theatres and whose names are really well known.'

'My Tudor doesn't want to become that famous,' she'd retorted. 'He just wants to earn a good living at it.'

'Well, he won't do that busking in clubs and pubs,' her father had pointed out. 'To get anywhere near the top you need to know the right people. You need an agent to get you bookings, you need to have your voice trained, and you have to be prepared to travel. He needs to go to Cardiff at the very least, or even to London, if he wants to be known as a professional singer.'

Her father's only comment when she finally screwed up the courage to tell him that they were going ahead with their wedding plans and why it was so important that they didn't put it off until later, had been, 'Then you'd better get on with it.'

He'd said it in such a flat, resigned voice that she'd wanted to cry because he'd sounded so disappointed. She wondered if she would have felt better about things if he'd been cross, like her mother, and had ranted and raved, or even slapped her. Not that she could ever recall him laying a finger on her in the whole of her life. He was not like some fathers who believed that a good hiding was the answer to everything.

In fact, his calm acceptance wounded her deeply; she felt that it was almost as if he had given up on her.

In the days leading up to his father's funeral Tudor had found it was impossible to talk to his mother about his wedding plans. He wanted to explain to her why it was so terribly important that he and Karyn couldn't put off getting married and why even postponing the date was out of the question.

Bronwen's grief was so great that she listened to nothing that anyone said to her. Most of the time she sat huddled in an armchair by the side of the fire, staring into the glowing embers as if in a trance. People came and went, cleaning her home, making her cups of tea and cooking food for her.

Olwyn tried her best to rouse her, but it wasn't until the day before the funeral that she managed to get through to her.

'Mam, you'll have to pull yourself together tomorrow,' she warned. 'The hearse will be here at eleven o'clock and you must be up and dressed and ready to leave by then.'

'Do you think I don't know that?' Bronwen said irritably. 'Make sure you and Griff are on time. Tell him I expect him to help carry the coffin,' she added with a touch of her old spirit.

'Have you got something black to wear, our mam?' Olwyn asked anxiously.

'Don't worry your head about me,' her mother snapped. 'I've got the black coat and hat I wore to your granddad's funeral. And some black gloves. I've a spare black skirt you can borrow if you need it. It's an old one of mine but it will probably fit you the shape you are now,' her mother told her critically.

'I'll take it home with me, then; it'll do under my black coat,' Olwyn told her.

'What are you going to do with your kids? A funeral is no place for them, you know.'

'I know that, Mam. Sari James from next door to me says she'll have them. Her sister is going to help her with them, so they'll be taken care of so there's no worry.'

'We need some beer getting in and some ham sandwiches making, you haven't forgotten, have you?'

'It's all in hand, Mam. Old Granny Evans says she'll come in and get it all set up while we're at chapel. She says she's too old to go traipsing along behind the hearse so she'll see to things here. Is that all right with you, Mam?'

'Have to be if that's what you've already arranged. And what about that lot next door? Is Owen Pryce going to help to carry your father's coffin?'

'I shouldn't think so, Mam. He's bruised and cut all over and his arm is in a sling.'

'Perhaps some of Madoc's other mates will do it, then. Griff had better ask them.'

'Is our Tudor going to be a pall-bearer?'

'He wanted to be, but I need him by me. I must have someone there to lean on in case I feel faint.'

'I'll be standing alongside you, Mam!'

'No, I need our Tudor to be there. He's the man of the house now, remember.'

Tudor waited until the last of the mourners had departed before he sat down to have a heart-to-heart chat with his mother. He knew it wouldn't be easy, but he had no idea just how difficult it was going to be to convince her that he couldn't look after her and the reason why he had to go through with his wedding plans.

She listened to him in silence, her breathing becoming more and more agitated by the minute.

'Fine time you've chosen to tell me all this, boyo. Bloody ashamed of yourself you should be, piling even more trouble and misery on to my shoulders.'

'I know, Mam, and I'm sorry about it all happening now, but I thought it was better to put my cards on the table and let you know exactly how things stood.'

'I thought you would have had more sense after seeing what happened to your sister. Brought shame on this family, the pair of you! Perhaps it's as well your da is dead and knows nothing about it.'

'Don't bring him into it, Mam.'

'Oh, and why not, indeed? Mind, it's enough to make him turn in his grave.'

'He can't do anything about it now, though, can he?' Tudor muttered morosely.

'No, I'm the one who's going to have to bear the brunt of it,' she muttered, dabbing at her eyes.

'I don't see that it will make all that much difference to you, Mam.' Tudor frowned.

'Of course it will! I was counting on having

44

you to look after me now your dad's gone. If you went and had a nice chat with the overseer then under the circumstances he'd be bound to give you a job and the pair of us could go on living here.'

'Mam, I've already made it clear that I have no intention of ever going to work down the pit.'

'If you don't then I'll be turned out! They own this house, boyo! Can't you get it into your head that they'll only let me stay here for a few months now your da is dead unless someone else in the family is working down the mine?'

Tudor scowled defiantly. 'Well, it won't be me, so stop yattering on about it. I'll find another job. Ever since I was a nipper I've always said that I'd never work underground. Nothing will make me go and work down the pit!'

'Time you changed your tune, then, since it's the best paid work you're likely to get round here.'

'Never! Mining is not for me,' Tudor told her stubbornly. He pulled out a packet of cigarettes, lit one and drew deeply on it, blowing out a cloud of blue smoke.

'It's the only thing that'll bring in enough money to support me and keep this roof over our heads,' Bronwen went on. 'You'd sooner see your old mam out in the street, bag and baggage, would you!' she sniffed, letting the tears roll down her cheeks.

'It won't come to that, Mam, so stop fretting about it,' Tudor said uncomfortably as he patted her arm reassuringly. 'We'll make some sort of arrangement to make certain that doesn't happen. Give me time and I'll think of something. But, I'm sorry, Mam, I won't go down the pit and that's final. And Karyn and I are getting married; we've made our plans, you know that.'

'That was before the explosion. Enid will need Karyn to stay at home now, and I need you to do the same. Enid will be depending on Karyn's wages to help them out until her Owen can get back to work again.'

'She'll be in for a shock if she thinks that is going to happen. Three weeks today, that's the date set for our wedding and nothing is going to stop it.'

'Don't you be so sure, boyo. When I've had a word with Enid Pryce she'll soon make her Karyn realise where her duty lies.'

'You won't stop us getting wed, Mam. There's nothing you or Enid can say that will make us change our minds. We'll go ahead even if neither of you approves. We don't care whether you give us your blessing or not; or whether you attend even.'

'Duw anwyl! What sort of son are you? Wait until our Olwyn hears what you are saying. Disgusted with you she'll be. What the neighbours will say I dread to think.'

'Who gives a damn about what any of them

think? It's our life, Mam, mine and Karyn's. We've got it all planned out and we can't change things, not now.'

Bronwen's eyes narrowed and her face creased with suppressed anger. 'Can't or won't?'

Tudor shrugged. Avoiding his mother's eyes he made his way towards the door.

'Slinking off out, are you?' Bronwen said acidly.

'No point in staying here if all we are going to do is row with each other, now is there?'

'Row? Who wants to row? I most certainly don't, not at a time like this. All I want is an assurance that you'll come to your senses and face up to your responsibilities.'

'That's just what I am doing.' Tudor glowered. 'I am complying with my commitment to Karyn.'

'Commitment to Karyn!' Bronwen mimicked. 'Those are fine words, boyo! You might be eighteen, but she's still not old enough to get married without her parents' say-so.'

'Don't worry your head about that, they'll give it,' Tudor told her with quiet confidence.

'I wouldn't be too sure about that! As I said before, Enid and Owen will be counting on her wage packet to help them out. Hardly likely to sign that away, not now.'

'Oh yes they will. What's more they won't need any arm twisting ... you'll see!'

As their gazes locked a gleam of apprehension came into Bronwen's eyes and every vestige of colour drained out of her face. Her mouth gaped. She struggled to speak, but the words wouldn't come, she could only gasp and shake her head in despair.

Later that night, when Tudor finally managed to escape from the confines of his own home and family and meet up with Karyn, he told her of his latest problem.

'I knew she'd try and find a way to stop us marrying,' Karyn said bitterly, struggling to keep back her tears.

'It's not so much the thought of us getting wed that's upsetting her,' he argued, 'it's the fact that she seems to think that I should step straight into my da's shoes. Mam even wants me to go up to the pit and ask the overseer if he will take me on so that she doesn't have to move out of the house!'

Karyn stared at him in disbelief. 'She wants you to go and work down the pit, but . . .'

'There's no need to go on about it, you know I'd never do that. Crawling around on me belly, hacking and hewing at bloody coal, that's not for me and well you know it.'

'So why bring it up, then?'

'I'm just trying to explain what my mam's asking me to do. She doesn't want to have to give up her home, see, but it's a pit house so they'll turf her out in a couple of months unless there's someone living there who works for them.'

Karyn chewed thoughtfully on her lower lip, trying to think of a solution.

'Would it work if she took in some young chap who already works at the pit?'

Tudor thought for a moment. 'No, that's not the answer, she'd never dream of doing anything like that.'

'Suggest it to her, you never know. She might rather have a lodger than be turned out of her house.'

Tudor shook his head. 'That would only have her nagging away at me saying that I was letting her down because I should be the one who went there to work . . .'

'Hold on a minute,' Karyn interrupted excitedly. 'I think I've got the very answer. What about if your Olwyn and her family moved in with your mam? Olwyn's husband Griff works at the pit so that would solve the problem.'

'Olwyn and Griff with their three kids?' Tudor looked doubtful. 'It would be a bit of a squeeze when it comes to sleeping. I can't see our mam giving up her big bedroom to Olwyn that easily, can you?'

'She wouldn't need to do so. The second bedroom's a fair size and big enough for Olwyn, Griff and the baby and the two boys could have your room.'

'Have them in with me! Don't talk bloody daft, Karyn. I couldn't stand that! I don't want to share a bedroom with a couple of rowdy little lads.'

'You wouldn't be sharing with them, though, now would you? By the time they moved in you would be moving out because by then we'll be getting married.'

'I think you might have something there.' Tudor grinned. 'It sounds like a great idea to me, providing I can get round our mam so that she'll go along with it.'

'You might also have to do some persuading when it comes to your Olwyn as well, mind,' Karyn warned. 'She mightn't like the idea of moving back in with her mam.'

'Damn sight better than living in two rooms like she has to do at the moment. The kids have the bedroom and she and Griff sleep in the living room. When he's on nights and needs his shut-eye in the daytime it's a right pandemonium, I can tell you. Usually he tries to kip in one of the kids' beds and Olwyn has to try to keep them all as quiet as possible in the living room.'

'So there you are, then, the problem is solved.' Karyn smiled.

'Yes, but if I manage to pull that one off then where does it leave us?' Tudor asked.

'We'll be able to find a place of our own just as we always intended to do.'

'Well, I did have an idea that perhaps we could move in with your mam and dad . . .'

'Never!' Karyn's cheeks flushed with anger. 'I wouldn't live with them come what may. They'd be running our lives for us in next to no time.'

Chapter Five

Karyn Pryce and Tudor Morgan were married
on Saturday, 29 April 1922. It was a very quiet
affair, not only because of Madoc Morgan's
death, but because of the strong disapproval
being voiced by both families.

Bronwen Morgan deeply resented the fact
that Tudor refused to comply with her wishes
and get himself a job down the local pit so that
he would qualify for the tenancy of the house
she lived in. Reluctantly, she had agreed to his
suggestion that she should ask Olwyn and Griff
if they would like to move in with her.

Olwyn had jumped at the chance and after
some discussion the arrangement had been
approved by the colliery management so
Bronwen at least knew that her home was
secure.

Griff had said very little about the arrangement, but even after the first week of living
with his mother-in-law he was wondering if
they'd been wise to give up their two rooms in
Morwen Street.

They'd been living in very cramped conditions there, but they had been free to live as
they liked. There had been no one constantly

51

nagging about how things should be done or complaining about the noise their three children made.

A further disadvantage he discovered was that Olwyn and her mother seemed to bicker with each other from the moment they got up in the morning until they went to bed at night. They couldn't agree over the domestic arrangements or about the way the children were being brought up.

The two eldest boys quickly cottoned on to the new arrangement and in next to no time they were adept at playing Olwyn off against Bronwen to their own advantage. Griff usually found that he was the one left to restore order and impose discipline.

Bronwen constantly bemoaned the fact that Tudor had gone off and left her in the lurch. It sounded as if he'd gone to Australia, but in actual fact he was only the other side the brick wall that divided their house from that of the Pryce's.

Although both families had attended the wedding there had been an uneasy atmosphere. The celebration afterwards, attended by most of the neighbours, was subdued. There were already rumours about why the wedding couldn't be postponed, but so far Karyn had managed to conceal the evidence so that suspicions were still little more than discreet whispers.

Enid hadn't been too happy about the newly

weds moving in with them, but it was the only thing they could do, and, as Tudor was quick to point out, it was only a temporary arrangement to give them breathing space to find a place of their own, as soon as he'd found a job. Also, it meant that Karyn could carry on working at the corner shop and with the baby due in September every penny mattered.

'We'll be fixed up long before the babba arrives,' Tudor promised. 'I've so many irons in the fire that it's going to be difficult to decide which job to take.'

For Karyn's sake they made him welcome, but right from the start it was easy to see that it disrupted Enid's life completely.

Owen Pryce who was still walking round with his arm in a sling, and knew it was likely to be at least another few weeks before he'd be able to leave it off, welcomed his presence.

Since Tudor hung around the house most of the day waiting for the postman to bring news about the many jobs he'd applied for, it was someone to talk to. So that they weren't under Enid's feet while she cleaned up and cooked dinner, the pair of them would saunter down to the Miner's Arms around midday for a quick half-pint.

By the time they got back home, eaten the meal that Enid had ready and had an afternoon nap it was time for Tudor to cut along to the corner shop to walk Karyn home.

When high tea was over it was time for Tudor

to smarten up and set off to one of the local pubs or clubs to sing. Although these stints brought in a mere pittance, it was better than nothing while he waited for someone to offer him a more permanent position.

Delia Morgan was born on Friday, 22 September 1922. She was only five pounds in weight, but even so, because Karyn was so petite, it was not an easy birth. The midwife insisted that Karyn must remain in bed for at least ten days afterwards and Enid fussed around her like an old hen the whole time.

Most of the time she was the one who cared for Delia, washing and dressing her because, as she was forever pointing out, she knew better than Karyn how to do such things.

Whenever Tudor tried to pick the baby up, Enid would push him to one side. 'Let me do it, you don't hold her properly. You've got to be so careful of her little head.'

'I know that!'

'Maybe you do, boyo, but you don't support it as you should,' she would chide and insist on taking Delia from him.

Her constant intervention infuriated Tudor, but Karyn was happy enough to let her mother take over. She had quickly discovered that much as she loved Delia, motherhood wasn't for her. The moment she felt fit enough she was eager to get back to the shop.

'It's not your place to go out and earn a living,

cariad,' Enid told her in shocked tones when she mentioned the idea of going back to work. 'Tudor won't like it; he's the one responsible for that side of things, not you!'

'Tudor doesn't mind,' Karyn assured her. 'He said if that's what I want to do then he'll pop along and ask Mrs Lewis how soon I can start back there.'

Owen didn't think it was right that Karyn should work and for the first time since they'd come to live there he and Tudor had a heated argument. Tudor didn't like his father-in-law's insinuation that he was a kept man.

Owen was now back at work himself, putting in a full shift underground and arriving home dog-tired. Seeing his son-in-law either lounging around in the house, or dressing up to go out singing began to irritate him.

He idolised his new granddaughter, but much of the novelty faded when he found that Enid was so busy caring for Delia that often his meal wasn't ready when he arrived home. Tired and irritated, his temper would flare and though he addressed his cutting remarks at Enid they all knew that it was really Tudor's presence he resented.

Christmas 1922 was so stormy, and there were so many arguments that in the end Owen said that it was time to tell Karyn and Tudor that they'd outstayed their welcome and that perhaps it was time they found a place of their own.

Enid bewailed the fact that if they moved out she wouldn't see as much of her granddaughter and that Karyn would be upset if it meant that she would have to give up working for Mrs Lewis in order to look after her baby full time, something she hadn't done since the day little Delia had been born.

Enid tried to remonstrate with Owen, repeatedly pointing out that Karyn and Tudor would never be able to manage. 'They haven't got a single stick of furniture they can call their own. What sort of place are they going to be able to afford if all they've got to live on is the pittance Tudor picks up from the pubs and clubs?'

'Then he'd better look around and get himself a proper job that does pay a decent wage,' Owen said firmly. 'It's certainly time for them to stop sponging on us.'

'They don't sponge. Karyn earns a tidy little wage, but she won't be able to do that if they move away and she hasn't got me to look after the baby for her.'

'That's another thing,' Owen argued, 'that babba is starting to take notice of what goes on around her and soon she won't know which of you is her real mam.'

'There's rubbish you talk,' Enid protested. 'Of course the little pet knows her mam from her nana. Bright as a button she is, you've only to look at her to see that!'

'Well, that's not the only reason I want them

gone from here,' Owen muttered, picking up his newspaper.

'Oh? And what's your other reason, then? We may as well have it all out in the open.'

'It's those bloody kids from next door.'

'You mean Olwyn's little ones? What on earth have they done to upset you?'

'They're forever running in and out of here as if the place was their own.'

'They only come in to look at the baby, or to see their Uncle Tudor. Nothing wrong with them doing that, now is there! In fact, I think it's lovely!'

'Snotty-nosed little urchins. They take after their fat slob of a mother.'

'Owen! I never thought I'd ever hear you say anything like that,' Enid exclaimed in a shocked voice. 'Whatever has got into you?'

'I need peace and quiet when I come home at night, that's what's got into me, and the sooner our Karyn and her husband find somewhere of their own the better pleased I shall be.'

'You can't be thinking of turning Tudor out,' Enid exclaimed in disbelief. 'What's come over you, Owen Pryce? It must have damaged your brain when you were knocked unconscious in that damned explosion down the pit. Talk sense, cariad; if we send Tudor packing, then it stands to sense that our Karyn and the baby go with him! We can't do it, Owen. Think of that poor little Delia. They've nowhere to go, now have they?'

'I didn't mean chuck them out tonight,' Owen protested indignantly. 'We'll tell them that we think it's time they had their own place and give them time to find somewhere else to live.'

'Where though, Owen?' Enid stopped ironing and faced him squarely. 'Where are they going to be able to find anyone to have them around here when they've got a young baby? The sort of woman who takes in lodgers wants a man she can fuss over and who keeps himself to himself, not a young couple with a squalling babba. Think about it, in next to no time she'll be running around and into everything.'

'Olwyn and Griff managed it. They had a place of their own until they came back here to be with her mam.'

Enid picked up the flat iron again, holding it close to her cheek to test if it was still hot. 'Yes, that was different, though. Her Griff had a decent job down the pit and he was earning regular money.'

'Then Tudor will have to do the same. He'll have to go out and find himself a decent job.'

'He's got ambitions, though . . .'

'Ambitions! Don't talk so bloody daft, woman! He's a lazy bastard who deludes himself that he can sing.'

'He can sing. He has a lovely voice. Ask anyone around here and they'll tell you the same.'

'A canary has got a lovely voice, but it doesn't mean it can earn a living by warbling away, now does it?'

'There's foolish!' Enid slammed the flat iron down on to the trivet. 'Nothing at all the same. Tudor is waiting for the right opening, waiting to be discovered.'

'That's what he's told you, is it?' Owen said scornfully. 'Or did he warble it to you in that melodious voice of his?'

'This is getting dafter and dafter, Owen. I've never in my life heard you talk like this.'

'I'm trying to make you see what I mean, woman, but it seems to be impossible to make you understand. They've been married for almost a year now, their babba is six months old, and he hasn't done a day's work in all that time. Not one job has he managed to get. Sponged on us all that time.'

'No, be fair, they've tipped up money each week as regular as clockwork to help towards the rent and their food and so on.'

'You mean our Karyn has! She's the one working her fingers to the bone, not him.'

'You've changed your tune,' Enid told him tartly. 'When Tudor first moved in you were happy enough to go to the Miner's Arms boozing with him every day.'

'Didn't last very long though, did it? Once I realised what was happening I soon put a stop to it.'

'Yes, but not until your arm was better and you had to go back to work,' Enid reminded him sarcastically.

'Look, woman, we're getting nowhere argybarging like this. Causing ructions between the two of us, all this is. They've got to go. I want our life back like it used to be.'

Enid sighed. 'Well, perhaps you are right, cariad. I'm not sure. I can't bear the thought of telling Karyn she must go . . . and that poor baby, it will break my heart to see her go. Who is going to look after her?'

'Leave it to me,' Owen said wearily. 'I'll sort it out, one way or the other. I'll take Tudor out for a quiet pint and have a man-to-man chat with him. I'll explain the situation and make him see that it will be better for him and Karyn to be on their own somewhere else like a real family. He'll understand.'

'Do it tactfully, then, Owen. It's a sensitive matter, you know. I wouldn't like him to have the impression that we think they're imposing on us or that we don't want them here with us.'

For all Owen's determination to be tactful, Tudor did take exception to his father-in-law's suggestion.

Enid tried to smooth things over with Karyn, but her daughter refused to be won round.

'I can't believe you don't want us here, Mam,' she sniffed. 'We would have found a place of our own months ago if we'd had any idea that you felt like this.'

'I understand that, cariad, but now it really is time to do something about it.'

'We only hung on here because we thought little Delia meant so much to you that it would break your heart if we took her away. That's the real reason why we haven't made other arrangements.'

'I do love having you here, my lovely,' Enid assured her. 'I'll feel lost without little Delia being around,' she added, wiping the tears from her eyes.

'I see, you'll miss Delia, but not me and Tudor,' Karyn flared, a furious look on her face.

'Of course I'll miss you as well, cariad,' Enid told her hastily. 'With any luck you won't move all that far away,' she added hopefully. 'Even if you aren't living here I can still give you a hand with Delia and take care of her for you from time to time,' she promised.

Karyn raised her eyebrows. 'You'll be lucky! You don't think we'll want to stay around here when everyone knows you've turned us out. Think what folks will be saying!'

'They won't say anything,' Enid defended. 'Most young people get a place of their own just as soon as they can manage to do so ... that's all you'll be doing.'

Karyn shrugged. 'I suppose so. It doesn't feel like that to me ... or to Tudor. He's cut to the quick. He said he couldn't believe his ears when Dad ordered him to find his own place.'

'Ordered? He didn't order him, he merely suggested that it was about time you stood on your own feet.'

'That wasn't what Tudor told me. He said Da gave him an ultimatum. He wanted us to be out in a month. How does he think we can manage to find a place in less than four weeks? It's absolutely outrageous!'

'I'm sure he didn't mean it quite like that. He was probably only making a suggestion and gently trying to stir Tudor into doing something about the situation as soon as he could. Tudor does tend to be a bit vague about getting to grips with things, now doesn't he?'

'What's that supposed to mean?'

'Well,' Enid hesitated, then, trying to put a brave face on things, she decided that perhaps the time had come to confront her daughter with the truth.

Karyn became more and more outraged as she listened to her mother explaining how all of them living together seemed to have changed her and Owen's life and that they didn't feel that things could go on in the same way any longer.

'Thanks for telling me what a burden we've been to you, Mam. Now that you've made it quite clear that you and Da are in complete agreement about how much trouble we've caused you we'll get out of your hair just as soon as we possibly can,' she stated coldly. 'It's a pity you didn't tell us all this months ago instead of suffering in silence,' she added acidly as she flounced out of the room.

Chapter Six

Tudor was reluctant to take any notice of Owen and Enid's plea for them to get a place of their own and stand on their own feet. He simply dismissed it as a passing whim on their part.

'Give them a couple of days and they'll have forgotten all about it,' he told Karyn when they went to bed that night. 'Something you've said or done has probably rubbed your mam up the wrong way, that's all. They'll soon calm down again if we keep quiet.'

'Oh no they won't,' Karyn told him heatedly. 'When my dad says something, he means it!'

'Maybe, but he won't turn us out though, cariad. Not his own daughter!'

'I don't want to wait to find out! I think we should start looking for somewhere else right away,' she insisted.

'Don't be daft! We're settled in here now, so why rush things? Like I said, sit tight and it will all blow over,' he repeated, reaching for her and holding her close.

Karyn pulled away. 'You mean take no notice and give them the chance to chuck us out into the street!'

'They won't do anything of the sort, cariad.

63

They think far too much of Delia to do that.'

'I'm not risking it. We're going. I've already told Mrs Lewis that I'm packing my job in.'

'You've done what?' Tudor's face darkened with anger. 'There's daft you are sometimes. Where the hell do you think we are going, and what are we going to live on without your regular wage packet?'

'We'll have to make do on what you earn singing,' she told him as she climbed into bed and pulled the sheet up to her chin. 'You've got a couple of regular bookings now, or so you keep boasting.'

'Yes, I have,' he admitted, as he started to undress, 'but not around here. They're at pubs down in Cardiff.'

'Then that's where we'll go and live.'

'Cardiff! That's almost thirty miles away,' he said with some exasperation. 'You won't be able to see your mam very often if we're living that far away.'

'Don't talk rubbish, there are trains and buses.'

'Yes, and it costs money to go on them,' he reminded her as he slipped into bed alongside her.

'You have to go down to Cardiff to sing, so think of the money you'll be saving by not having to pay out for fares to get there and back twice a week.'

'We'll need to pay rent, though, and places down there won't be cheap,' he told her cautiously.

'Then we'll draw our horns in. You can give up fags and beer for a start. Smoking so many Woodbines is probably no good for your voice, anyway.'

'I need some pleasures in life, girl!' Tudor growled, pulling her towards him suggestively.

Then you'll have to earn more to pay for them, boyo! I won't be working, mind.'

'You could be if we found somewhere around here to live,' he pointed out.

Karyn tossed her head defiantly. 'And have everyone talking about me behind my back and saying that my folks have kicked me out? No thank you.'

'They'll still talk whether you're still living around here or not,' he said ruefully.

'Yes, I know that and I want to be far enough away so as not to hear them. Understand?'

'No, cariad, I don't understand,' Tudor told her irritably. 'You're putting me in a very diffi-cult position.'

'How am I? Surely you knew that one day you'd have to provide a home for me and your little daughter,' she said indignantly, pushing him away and turning her back to him as she settled down to sleep.

Three weeks later, almost a year after getting married, their meagre belongings packed in a big fibre suitcase, or stowed under the bedding of Delia's pram, Karyn and Tudor left Pen-y-llyn for Cardiff.

Enid insisted on going to the station to see them off. She fussed in case they had forgotten anything, she expressed dissatisfaction with the corner seat Tudor found for Karyn and Delia on the train, and she was very concerned about whether or not Delia's pram and all its contents would be safe in the luggage van.

When the guard blew his whistle and she was forced to get out of the carriage she stood on the platform weeping copiously, almost as if she was afraid she would never see them again.

Handing Delia over to Tudor to nurse, Karyn lowered the window and leaned out to kiss her mother one more time. As the train gathered steam and began to slowly chug its way out of the station, Enid ran along the platform and thrust an envelope into Karyn's hand.

'Put this somewhere safe ... don't let Tudor know you have it ... it's for emergencies, cariad,' she gasped breathlessly.

Karyn took the envelope and pushed it down inside the front of her blouse. She guessed from the thickness of it that it contained money. She remained standing by the window, waving, until her mother became a mere speck in the distance and the passing breeze had dried her own tears.

'Our new life lies ahead of us now,' she murmured as she sat down and took Delia from Tudor. She smoothed Delia's dark curls back from her forehead and propped the child up

66

on her lap in such a way that she could see out of the window.

'Are you going to tell me all about our new home?' she persisted when Tudor said nothing.

'Not much to tell you,' Tudor said non-committally. 'A couple of rooms up over the pub where I go to sing, that's all.'

Karyn sighed contentedly. 'I can't wait,' she enthused, squeezing his arm. 'I've never been to Cardiff, see, so it's all going to be new and exciting.'

'Splendid place, so I'm told. The City Hall and all the buildings around it are in some sort of white stone that looks pink when the sun shines on it. And close by there's a park. Won't that be lovely?'

'Sounds fine,' he agreed evasively.

'You mean you haven't seen it?' she asked in surprise.

'No, not yet. I never have any time to go wandering around to look at things like that.'

'You've been going down to Cardiff a couple of times a week ever since Christmas,' she exclaimed in surprise.

'Yes, but I don't spend my time sightseeing. I go down there to work.'

'So this pub isn't anywhere near the City Hall or this park, then?'

'Of course it isn't,' he said in an exasperated voice. 'It's down the docks.'

'You mean it's by the sea?' she asked, her face lighting up again.

'Cardiff's a port, not the seaside,' he reminded her.

'I know that! It's one of the biggest and most important ports in the British Isles. We learned all about it at school, if you remember. There's more coal shipped out of Cardiff than anywhere else and it goes all over the world.'

'I don't know about that . . .'

'It's what we were told at school,' she insisted as she rummaged in her bag and found a bottle of milk for Delia who was becoming fractious.

Tudor took out a packet of cigarettes and opened it. 'We were told lots of things at school that seem quite different when you are grown up so don't get too carried away. Wait until you see it all for yourself.'

'A place of our own, though, Tudor. It's going to be so wonderful, isn't it?'

'We've got two furnished rooms up over a pub not Cardiff Castle,' Tudor said, scowling.

'What's the landlord like, is he nice?'

'No, he's a taciturn old bugger and he probably won't give you the time of day.' He struck a match and held it to his cigarette. 'He's my employer, not a friend of the family and the sooner you realise that the better. Don't expect him to be pally.'

Karyn pulled a face. 'Does he live over the pub as well?'

'Yes, he has the rooms immediately above the pub and we have the rooms up above that. He's not too keen on the idea of having a young kiddy living over his head, especially when she starts running about, so you'll have to make sure you keep young Delia quiet or else we'll find ourselves out in the street.'

Karyn looked taken aback. 'You never mentioned any of this before,' she exclaimed.

Tudor shrugged. 'I know, but I think it's as well for you to realise exactly what sort of set up it is.'

'Is there anything else I ought to know?'

'Not really, except that you'll have to use the side entrance, and go up the back stairs. Not go stalking through the pub.'

'I see. So what about Delia's pram, where do we keep that?'

'There's a lean-to shed in the backyard. It will have to go in there, I suppose.'

'Delia sleeps in it quite a lot during the day, though,' Karyn reminded him.

Tudor let out a lungful of smoke. 'Then you'll have to walk round the streets with her while she has her nap.'

'What happens if it's raining? We'll both get soaking wet if I have to do that!'

Tudor shrugged impatiently. 'Then she'll have to sleep in her cot.'

'Are you sure that there is a cot for her, Tudor?'

He looked uncomfortable. 'Well, no. I don't think there is, but we'll get one as soon as we've settled in.'

'Oh, Tudor!' she chided crossly. 'So where is she going to sleep until then?'

'In our bed with us, I suppose. Why don't you wait until we get there and you can see what's what and sort out the rest of the arrangements then?'

Karyn didn't answer. For the rest of the journey she remained silent. Delia slept, lulled by the motion of the train. Karyn studied her little daughter with pride. With her dark ringlets and winsome little face, her thick dark lashes resting against her pink cheeks, she was absolutely adorable. Bending forward, Karyn pressed her lips against the child's forehead. Delia stirred and let out a whimper.

'Let her sleep while she's quiet, we don't want her bawling her lungs out here on the train, do we?' Tudor warned.

'She never bawls her lungs out,' Karyn protested indignantly. 'She's as good as gold.'

'She is when your mam is there to fuss over her at every turn. She's going to miss all that attention.'

'She'll have both of us!' She sighed blissfully. 'We'll be a real family at last.'

He smiled indulgently. 'I'm going to have to work, have you forgotten about that?'

'You only go out singing at night; you'll be around during the daytime.'

'Don't count on it, cariad. I may have to look around for more than singing in the pub in order to make ends meet. We don't get these rooms for nothing, you know.'

Karyn tucked her hand through the crook of

his arm and squeezed it affectionately. 'We'll manage, you'll see,' she told him brightly.

Their arrival at Cardiff Central took Karyn by surprise. One minute it seemed they were racing through the countryside and the next the scenery outside the window changed first to dreary-looking factories then to row upon row of houses and before she could take it all in, the train was grinding to a halt.

The rest of the people in the carriage began fastening up their coats and then standing up and lifting down bags and packages from the parcel rack above their heads.

'Come on, we're there. Get all your things together, I'll go and unload the pram and our big case from the luggage van.'

'No, wait for me, I can't manage to carry Delia as well as all these bags and things,' Karyn said in alarm. She felt scared stiff by all the sudden noise and bustle.

'You'll have to, my lovely,' he told her impatiently. 'The luggage van is at the other end of the train so if I don't shoot off the minute we stop, there won't be time to collect our things and the train will move off with the pram and everything still on it.'

'So where do I meet you?'

'On the platform, of course. When you get off the train just stand still. I'll come back and find you.'

Before Karyn could say another word Tudor

had gone. She felt so frightened and so alone that tears came into her eyes.

The other people in the carriage hurriedly pushed past her, intent on completing their journey. Delia, who was now awake and scared by all the noise and rush, began to cry noisily.

Cuddling her close, Karyn struggled down on to the platform and then tried to reach back into the carriage, to collect the bags which she'd left inside on the floor. It was a struggle. Delia was wriggling and protesting and she found it difficult to hold her in one arm and pick up the bags at the same time. A passing porter who was checking that the carriage doors were all slammed shut ready for the train to move off pushed her to one side, reached into the carriage, and lifted the bags out on to the platform.

'Stand well back, missus,' he warned as the train began to belch out clouds of steam and then to move off.

Desperately she looked around for Tudor, wondering if he had managed to collect their other belongings. She wasn't sure which end of the train the luggage van was and she could see no sign of him. For one awful moment she was afraid that the train was going to pull away with him still on it.

As the steam cleared and the train vanished round a bend in the track she caught sight of Tudor coming towards her pushing the pram, with their big fibre suitcase balanced precariously on it.

With a sigh of relief she tried to pick up the bags by her feet, but Delia was having none of it. She screamed and wriggled so much that it took Karyn all her time to calm her.

'Duw anwyl, what the hell is she bawling about now?' Tudor said exasperatedly as he reached them. 'She's bringing the place down with all the noise she's making.'

'Oh, dear. I think that it might be because she's hungry,' Karyn said worriedly

'Why the hell didn't you give her another bottle before we got off the train?'

'I didn't know we were almost here and she was so fast asleep that I didn't know she was hungry.'

'You'd better sit on that seat over there, then, and see to her before we leave the station we don't want her bawling all the way from here to Pomeroy Street.'

'Where?'

'Pomeroy Street. That's where the pub is. I've told you all this before,' he said impatiently.

'Sorry, I must have forgotten,' Karyn said in a crestfallen voice.

'Well, try and remember, otherwise you'll be getting lost. The pub's called the Voyager and it's in Pomeroy Street. Got it?'

'Right!' Karyn repeated it twice to make sure she had committed it to memory.

'You going to stand there all day saying that over and over again, like some bloody parrot?' Tudor muttered. 'Get the kid's bottle out of

73

whichever one of those bags it's in and stick it in her mouth to see if it will stop her screaming.'

'There's no need for you to be so bad-tempered,' Karyn protested. Blinking back her tears she searched for it. Things were not going smoothly at all, she thought miserably, and she didn't understand why Tudor had to be so short-tempered.

Delia seemed to sense the discord. She refused her bottle, twisting and turning her head away and keeping her tiny mouth tightly closed.

'I thought you said she was hungry?'

'I'm sure she must be, it's well past the time she is usually fed.'

'Well, it doesn't look as though she's going to take it so come on, stick her in the pram and let's get going. It's a tidy walk from here.'

By the time they had manoeuvred the pram down all the steps and passageways and were out into Wood Street both of them were exhausted . . . and Delia was still screaming her little head off.

'Haven't you got a rusk or a biscuit or something you can give her to shut her up?'

Karyn rooted around in one of the bags; she finally found a packet of Farley's Rusks and gave one to Delia. For a moment she thought it had done the trick, then Delia threw it down and began screaming again.

'Oh, for heaven's sake let's get a move on.

Lie her down in the pram and perhaps she'll go to sleep.'

'I think she might be better sitting propped up ...'

'She can't sit up, we've all these bags to pile into the pram and I want to balance the big case on top as well.'

It took them quite some time to manage to get everything balanced and as soon as they started to push the pram they found that it was top heavy and in danger of tipping over if they weren't careful.

Tudor had another attempt at arranging everything then decided they would each have to take it in turns to push while the other steadied the load. Tudor walked so fast that Karyn had to take little running steps every so often to keep up with him.

'Is it very much further?' she kept asking anxiously as they walked along Taff Embankment with the river on their left and an endless row of buildings on the other side.

'No, we'll turn off soon, up one of the side streets and then we'll be in Corporation Road, that's a main road and that takes us almost to Pomeroy Street.'

When they did reach the main road, she found the noise of the traffic frightening. She'd never seen trams before and their noisy clanging as they went by in both directions startled her. The road seemed endless, but eventually they came to an enormous iron bridge.

'Not far now,' he added encouragingly. 'This is Clarence Road Bridge and it crosses over the River Taff and the Glamorganshire Canal. Once we go over this then we're in James Street. Pomeroy Street is on the right-hand side just two roads further on. Think you can last out until then, cariad?' he added sounding more cheerful.

'Having come all this way I'll make sure I will. I can't wait to see our new home!'

Chapter Seven

Karyn's first impression of the Voyager was the overpowering smell of beer and cigarette smoke as they went down the side passage of the three-storey building near the corner of Pomeroy Street and Clarence Place.

Tudor lifted the big case off the pram and told Karyn to stay there while he carried it up to their rooms, then came back down again to show her where to leave the pram.

If the smell was this strong in the alleyway, then what on earth was it like down in the pub itself, she wondered. Even more important, what was it going to be like up in their rooms! No wonder Tudor's clothes always smelled so disgusting when he was spending his evenings in such an atmosphere when he sang at clubs and pubs.

Yet it didn't have to be like that, she reflected. The Miner's Arms in Pen-y-llyn didn't smell. True, it was only half the size of the Voyager and probably had less than half the customers, but if the place was kept clean, it shouldn't make all that difference, surely.

She was still wrinkling her nose in distaste when Tudor came back. 'Come on, the landlord and his wife want to meet you. It will only take a few minutes because they're about to open up. Leave the pram here and I'll show you where to keep it after you've met Llew and Marged Parker.'

'They both seemed quite nice but the pub did have a terrible smell,' Karyn said to Tudor, after they'd meet the Parkers and returned to the flat upstairs.

'You won't notice it after a day or two,' he told her with a shrug. 'Anyway, you'd better not let the Parkers hear you saying anything like that,' he warned.

'It isn't the right sort of atmosphere for a baby to be in, though, is it?' Karyn persisted.

'She'll have to get used to it,' Tudor pronounced, looking up at the gaunt white-washed building. 'This is our home now. Give it half an hour and you won't notice the smell either.'

Karyn chewed her lower lip and said nothing. As he pointed to the lean-to wooden shed with its corrugated iron roof and told her that was where she was to keep the pram her feeling of gloom increased. It was dry inside, but the walls were festooned with cobwebs and there were piles of junk stacked in the corners.

'We'll have to take the bedding and the covers out of the pram; we can't leave them out here,' she protested when Tudor picked Delia up and told her to bring the rest of the bags.

He stared at her in surprise. 'What for, cariad?

The place is dry enough and no one's going to pinch them.'

'It's not that, but look at those droppings on the floor. There're mice out here and I don't want her bedding chewed up or the damn things nesting in it, now do I?'

He didn't argue; he simply picked up Delia and then tucked the cot mattress and covers under one arm. 'Come on, we use the side door.'

She followed him up the flight of stone steps to a green door at the top that led directly into their flat. She looked round the attic rooms critically. The furniture was not only shabby and broken down, but was also dirty. It was going to take a lot of elbow grease to get this lot sorted out, she thought grimly.

All the rooms had low ceilings and there was very little light from the dormer windows. The room they were standing in was obviously the main one and probably the largest, but it was still poky. Tentatively, she inspected the rest of the flat.

There were two bedrooms, one was a fair size, the other little more than a large cupboard. The kitchen was a long, narrow room with two small windows that looked down on to the yard at the back of the pub which was full of beer kegs and other paraphernalia. The last room she looked at had a flush lavatory, a washbasin and big cast iron bath in it. She'd never seen a bath so big, or so dirty, in her life before.

'Posh isn't it?' Tudor commented.

'It's filthy dirty, if you ask me!' Karyn retorted tight-lipped.

'We'll soon sort it out, though, won't we, my lovely,' he said confidently.

'We?' Karyn raised her eyebrows questioningly.

'I'll give you a hand! Though of course I'll have to fit it in with going to work.'

'Since you only work at night at the moment, you'll have all day to help get this place clean,' she told him firmly.

'Fair do's! We'll make a start on it tomorrow.'

'We're going to have to clean up the bedroom right now so that we can sleep there tonight.'

Tudor's mouth pursed up into a silent whistle. 'Have to make it quick, then, because I have to be down in the pub by seven o'clock. What about making a pot of tea first and—'

Before Tudor could finish speaking Delia let out a strident wail.

'You make the tea and I'll feed her,' Karyn told him, taking the baby from him.

'Feed her, again? You fed her while we were at the station, didn't you?' he quibbled.

'That was over three hours ago, and she's ready for her next bottle.'

'Then get on and give it to her. Anything to shut up that racket she's making.'

Karyn did her best, but Delia was upset by her strange surroundings. Constantly she struggled to push the bottle way, looking round and crying noisily.

'What the hell's the matter with her?' Tudor asked irritably.

'She's missing her nana. My mam always used to feed her, see. She's more used to being with her than with me.'

'Well, she'd better bloody well get used to you, then, because she won't be seeing her nana for a long, long time.'

'Stop talking such rubbish. Of course she will, why ever not?'

'I told you before, we won't be able to afford to go running to and from Pen-y-llyn every whipstitch. We've moved to Cardiff and this is where we are going to live so the sooner you settle down and make this your home the better.'

'It's your home as well, Tudor. We're in it together, you'll have to do your bit, you know, not just sit back and expect me to wait on you. I've got Delia to look after now and no one to help me.'

'Bringing up babies is woman's work,' he protested.

'Really! And making them is men's work, I suppose! Or is it just their pleasure?'

Tudor didn't answer. With a sigh, Karyn perched herself on one of the wooden chairs and concentrated on persuading Delia to take her bottle.

When she finally managed to coax her to do so Karyn looked round the room and took stock of her surroundings.

The iron fireplace was poky because it was a bedroom grate and she wondered whether the fire in it would give out enough heat to warm the room in winter. There was no fender or fireguard, the fire irons at the side of it were covered in rust, and the fireplace itself was badly in need of a coat of blacking.

There were two battered armchairs with home-made padded cushions. The covers were so dirty that it was impossible to tell what the pattern was. In front of the fireplace was a home-made rag rug. The rest of the floor was covered in linoleum that seemed to be in good condition and would probably come up quite bright when it was scrubbed and polished.

There was also a wooden table covered by a grubby red chenille tablecloth and three wooden chairs similar to the one she was sitting on. Against the longest wall was a Welsh dresser, packed with a miscellany of plates, cups and saucers and various dishes. She wondered what was in the drawers. Probably cutlery, she surmised.

She looked around for somewhere to lie Delia down now that she'd finished her bottle and had drifted into a satisfied sleep. It wasn't safe to leave her in one of the armchairs in case she rolled out, and the floor was too dirty to lie her down on it.

Cradling the sleeping baby in her arms Karyn made her way into the main bedroom. It was even more uncared for than the living room.

The double iron bedstead had a sagging mattress and there was a badly pitted oak dressing table, an oak wardrobe and a matching chest of drawers. Gingerly she opened the bottom drawer hoping it was deep enough to act as a makeshift bed for Delia.

It was empty and she tried not to shudder as she shook out the mice droppings from the bottom of it. It needed something soft for Delia to lie on but she couldn't bring herself to use one of the soiled pillows from the bed. Instead she laid the pram mattress at the bottom and settled her down on that. It was a tight squeeze for a seven-month-old baby, but it would do as a temporary measure, she told herself as she covered her over with her pram blanket.

By the time she reached the kitchen Tudor had made a pot of tea and was rinsing out two cups so that he could pour it out.

'There's no milk and I can't find any sugar either,' he told her as he passed her a cup of muddy-looking black tea.

Their first week living above the Voyager was fraught with problems. It wasn't simply a matter of cleaning up the rooms. Karyn and Tudor also found they had to make a great many adjustments in order to fit into their new lifestyle. It was the first time they had lived completely on their own and there was still a lot they didn't know about each other's ways.

Enid, like Tudor's mother, had waited on him hand and foot and he had always been used to finding his shirts and everything else washed and ironed and appearing like magic. He was also used to his meals being placed in front of him on the table without ever stopping to think about what went into providing them. Shopping, cooking and even washing up were all new to him.

Karyn was finding it difficult enough to cope with looking after Delia single-handed, as well as cooking and cleaning. It left her not only tired, but irritable. Nothing ever seemed to go right and Delia was very demanding. She was used to Karyn's mother nursing and cuddling her the moment she woke up and now she didn't take kindly to having to wait for attention.

They'd bought her a proper cot, because, as Karyn pointed out, it wasn't safe for her to sleep in their bed with them or to leave her for more than a few minutes in the makeshift bed in the drawer once she was awake.

Tudor had not been too pleased about having to pay twelve shillings for a second-hand cot, even though the sellers had thrown in the mattress and blankets as a bonus.

'We can't afford things like this, not on what I'm earning,' he grumbled.

'Then you'll have to earn more,' Karyn told him. 'Can't you work somewhere else?'

'If I do that, then we'll be out on the street.

The only reason we've got these rooms is because I sing in the Voyager every night.'

'I meant during the day. Couldn't you get a job in a factory or something as well? You'd be home in time to go and sing in the pub at night.'

'Rubbish! They expect you to do shift work in factories. Anyway, I'm not cut out for that sort of work.'

'Well, what about shop work, then?' she persisted.

'They stay open until nine or ten o'clock at night on Saturdays so how could I be in the pub by seven?'

'There must be some sort of day job you could do,' Karyn said worriedly.

'I can't think what it could be.'

'You'll have to find something, Tudor, we simply can't manage on what you earn.'

What began as a discussion turned into an argument; one they returned to time after time.

Karyn was no happier than Tudor. She soon found that she didn't like being a full-time mother. She loved Delia, but she didn't enjoy changing her, feeding her and being with her all the time. More and more she found herself becoming cross with the child and shouting at her when she wouldn't go to sleep or when she screamed for her bottle.

If Tudor was there when this happened, he took the baby from her, soothed her and had her gurgling happily in no time at all.

Reluctantly, Karyn had to admit that even

though he was dead lazy when it came to helping her in any other way Tudor certainly handled Delia much better than she did and this made her feel useless. If only he was as good at earning a living, she thought resentfully as she struggled to eke out the miserable pittance he handed over for housekeeping.

The idea that perhaps if Tudor wouldn't find a day job to supplement the meagre amount of money he managed to earn singing, then perhaps she should be the one to go out to work and let him look after Delia, lurked in the back of her mind. The money her mother had given her the day they'd left Pen-y-llyn had long gone.

She said nothing to him, but a couple of weeks later, when she went out shopping, she told Tudor that she was leaving Delia with him for an hour. Before he could protest she had picked up her shopping bag and gone.

Instead of shopping for food she went from shop to shop asking if there was a vacancy for an assistant. The two who did show some interest made it clear that she would have to work until half past seven each night, and nine o'clock on Fridays and Saturdays. Reluctantly, she turned them down. She didn't mind the long hours, but she knew that they wouldn't fit in with Tudor's singing arrangements, not unless Delia was left on her own and she didn't think that it was right to do that.

Tudor was furious when he heard what she'd

been up to. For a couple of days he wouldn't even speak to her and even turned his back on her in bed.

Like her, however, he knew they had to do something to obtain more money. The solution when it came to him was so obvious that he wondered why neither of them had thought of it before.

'What about you working downstairs at the pub now that you know the Parkers?' he suggested tentatively.

She looked at him in astonishment, 'Doing what?'

'Pulling pints, of course. What did you think I was suggesting?' he laughed.

'I don't know. I'm certainly not going to do any cleaning for them. I do enough of that trying to keep this place in order.'

'You'd be able to get all dressed up if you were working as a barmaid,' he said, grinning.

Karyn toyed with his suggestion and decided that she quite liked the idea.

'How long would I have to work each day?' she asked.

'Only from eleven in the morning until three in the afternoon. That would fit in pretty well, wouldn't it?'

She frowned. 'It means you'll have to look after Delia, and if I'm down there at midday you'll have to feed her and change her nappy.'

'Don't worry, cariad, I won't stick the safety-pin into her tummy and I'm quite capable of giving her a bottle,' he said with an easy smile.

'That's the point, though; there's more to it than that. I've started weaning her and giving her bits of solid food.'

'So what's so difficult about that? I can stuff a spoonful of mashed potato and gravy in her mouth every bit as well as you can. Probably better,' he added with a smirk. 'She doesn't grizzle half as much when I'm looking after her as she does when she's with you.'

'I suppose we could give it a try,' Karyn agreed dubiously.

Karyn quite enjoyed working behind the bar in the Voyager. The first few days she had found it difficult to master the pumps, but with Llew Parker's tuition she soon got the hang of it. His wife, Marged, was equally helpful and patient and gave her a lot of advice, including tips on how to handle the customers.

'You won't meet up with many awkward coves, not at midday,' she assured Karyn. 'It's the late-night drinkers who are inclined to be troublesome.'

'You mean they don't know when they've had enough?'

'That's more or less the problem. They drink themselves silly and then some of them get their dander up and it's fighting talk and a punch-up before you know what's happening. None of that sort of nonsense happens at midday though, cariad.'

88

Karyn expressed surprise at how many men did drop into the Voyager for a drink in the mornings.

'Well, some of them work night shift, see,' Marged explained. 'They get up, go for a stroll round and then drop in here before going back home for a bite to eat before starting work. Others are on the dole or the scrap heap. Lonely buggers most of them.'

'It's easy to pick them out, they sit nursing a half-pint for an hour or more,' Karyn agreed.

'You'll find them in here especially in the winter because it's a damned sight warmer than out on the streets. The men who are down on their luck often live in doss houses and you can't help feeling sorry for them, poor devils.'

'Don't they have any family, then?'

'Some of them don't. A lot of men who go to sea come back to find that their wife, or the woman they've been shacked up with, has got lonely and tired of waiting, see, and has upped sticks and gone. Some people can't do with being on their own. They need folks around them all the time. They even find rowing with someone is better than being on their own.'

Although she didn't tell Tudor so, Karyn found she enjoyed being in the pub more than looking after Delia. Getting dressed up, making sure her hair was brushed and shining and that she looked attractive as possible, made her feel good. When Llew Parker suggested that since they opened up again at six she might like to come down and do an hour in the evenings she was delighted and readily agreed.

Tudor was not so happy. 'That leaves me no time to get ready,' he protested.

'What do you mean by getting ready? You only have to put on a clean shirt and your best suit.'

'Not much point in doing that until the very last minute if I'm the one who has to bath Delia. She splashes like a little fish so she'd ruin my decent clothes.'

'The answer to that is simple enough,' Karyn laughed, 'don't give her a bath in the evening.'

'You've always said that she must have a bath at night, because it's part of her routine. A bath, a clean nappy and her bottle and then she knows it's time for bed.'

'She can have a bath in the morning just as well. Think of the extra money, Tudor. Heaven knows we need it.'

'All right, we'll give it a go. Make sure Llew lets you off prompt, mind, or else I'll be late.'

'So what does it matter if you are a few minutes late? He knows the reason and since it is his fault he's hardly likely to say anything to you about it now, is he?'

As Christmas approached the evening shifts gradually lengthened. Rarely did Karyn finish promptly at seven. It drifted to half past, then eight o'clock.

Tudor became more and more tetchy about this, but when he mentioned it to Llew Parker the landlord merely shrugged. 'The customers who come in before nine o'clock are usually only popping in for a quick drink before going home. They don't settle down for a session. After nine, now that's when we get busy and when they want a spot of entertainment. Not much point wasting your time singing to an empty pub, now is there, boyo!'

Tudor wanted to argue, but it seemed foolish to do so since he was still getting the same wage for singing whether he did so from seven o'clock or nine o'clock. What was more, Karyn was paid for the extra bar work she did in the evening which meant that she was now earning almost as much as he was.

Chapter Eight

Karyn sometimes felt as if she was dancing a jig on eggshells. She had to be so careful what she said about working as a barmaid for fear of putting Tudor's nose out of joint by implying that her work at the Voyager was more important than his. She missed her mother, but she had to be careful not to mention this to Tudor, or to say, or do, anything which would make him think she was criticising the way he looked after Delia.

As time passed it became more and more obvious that Tudor was spoiling Delia. She adored him and by the following spring, even though only a little more than eighteen months old, she could twist him round her tiny little finger.

Together the two of them led a charmed life. Tudor spent all his time keeping her amused and feeding her the sort of delicacies she asked for even though it was not the kind of food that was suitable for a toddler. Her favourite was a piece of bread, thickly spread with butter and then either coated with sweetened condensed milk or sugar sprinkled over it.

He took her out every day although he refused to push her in her pram and carried her everywhere. Where they went to, Karyn had no idea. The only thing she did know was that Delia demanded constant attention and Karyn found that when she arrived home from work, whether it was in the afternoon or evening, Delia was not prepared to do a thing that she wanted her to do. Tears and tantrums were the order of the day. In the afternoons, when Tudor was still at home, she ran to him with her little arms outstretched, tears trickling down her cheeks demanding that he pick her up.

'Me loves Dada, not you,' was her constant whine and although Karyn tried to smile and dismiss her fixation on Tudor as a childish whim, it cut her to the quick. Sometimes she found it was difficult to hold back her own tears.

She tried so hard, but more often than not she felt a failure. Only as a mother, though. The moment she took up her place behind the bar in the Voyager she was a different person. She was smiling and confident. She responded to the quips and repartee from the regulars with complete aplomb, enjoying every minute of it.

She loved the work. The smell of beer and the tobacco fumes no longer bothered her; she found the noisy, smoky atmosphere exhilarating. One thing she liked above all else was the variety; no two days were ever alike.

She sometimes wished she could be down there in the evening when Tudor was singing, but that was out of the question because one of them had to be with Delia. That was the only issue about which both Tudor and Karyn were in complete agreement.

She wished they hadn't become so estranged about most other things. She tried not to think about it too much, but whenever she did she realised that they both felt trapped. Tudor resented the fact that she earned more or less the same as him. She objected to the fact that most of the money she earned was spent on food and things for their home while he spent most of his on treats for Delia or on cigarettes.

In her job as barmaid she had to look smart because she didn't wear an overall like she'd done when working for Mrs Lewis at the corner shop.

In the beginning she'd worn her best dress, the one she'd got married in, but Marged had said it wasn't really suitable.

'You need blouses and a cotton skirt that washes easily,' she told her. 'No matter how careful you are you are bound to spill beer down the front of you when you are carrying it across to the tables.'

The only clothes Karyn had were so shabby that she had to buy new ones and even though she went to the cut-price stalls at the Hayes market they still cost quite a bit.

She couldn't understand how Tudor seemed to fritter his money away and have nothing to show for it. She'd tried to work out how much he spent on Delia and on cigarettes, and even though he smoked like a trooper, sometimes lighting a new one from the stub of the last one, it still meant he should have plenty left, yet he was always trying to cadge money off her.

It was weeks before she worked out that the reason why he was always broke might be because he had started betting on both the horses and the dogs.

Was that what also accounted for his moodiness, she wondered? Sometimes he was in excellent spirits, laughing and joking, tossing little Delia high in the air, and bringing in a bag of cakes, or some fish and chips, and insisting she shared them with him.

At other times it was a different picture. He was surly and sarcastic and grumbled about being tied to their home all day, and not free to come and go as he pleased.

When this happened Karyn always reminded him that if he didn't like the way they lived then the answer was in his hands.

'Find yourself a proper job, and I'll give up working in the pub, and we'll live like a normal family.'

This usually resulted in a full-scale row which sometimes lasted for days.

'You're putting me down because you earn as much as me, aren't you!' he complained.

'Not at all. Find yourself a different sort of job and you'll earn twice as much as I can.'

'I'm not going to work in a factory so don't think that I am, and I'm not cut out to be a shop assistant. I'm a professional singer, Karyn, and one of these days I'll be spotted by some talent scout and I'll be in the big time.'

'Then until that happens we'd better carry on as we are, hadn't we?' she would tell him resignedly.

The feelings between them were equally inconsistent. One minute he seemed to be head over heels in love with her and couldn't leave her alone for a minute, and then his mood would change, and it was almost as if he hated her and couldn't bear to touch her.

Tudor blamed his moods on his artistic temperament; Karyn worked out that it had more to do with how much money he had jingling in his pocket. Since she knew that Llew Parker paid him a set wage for his singing sessions in the pub, Karyn realised that he was getting money from some other source and she was sure it depended on whether his bets were successful or not.

She tried to talk to him about it, but he usually denied it and, more often than not, flew into a temper.

'Duw anwyl, how the hell can I be going to the race track when I have a young baby to look after every day? Do you think for one moment they'd let me go into a place like that if I arrived carrying Delia in my arms?'

'No, I'm sure they wouldn't, but you don't

have to go to the racecourse, now do you!'

'How else can I place a bet? Are you accusing me of breaking the law and using a bookie's runner?' he challenged her defiantly.

When she refused to argue with him about it he accused her of being jealous because he was clever enough to make money without having to work for it like she did.

She usually tried to dismiss his jibes with a smile, before it could develop into a full-scale row.

She knew he didn't like it if she came back from the pub in a light-hearted mood. He resented the idea that she had been enjoying the company of other men.

'I know the sort of buggers who drink down in the bar, remember. You can't expect me to like you being chatted up by that randy bunch, can you?'

'I've told you before that none of them ever try to chat me up,' she said exasperatedly.

'Most of them talk to you,' he argued, 'so don't try and tell me they don't.'

She laughed lightly. 'Of course they talk to me.'

'What about?'

She shrugged. I don't know. 'The weather, their work, their kids, their problems, sometimes.'

'And they tell you how nice you look?'

Karyn's eyebrows went up. 'Yes, occasionally one of them will make a comment. Not very often, though.'

97

'Often enough,' Tudor scowled. 'And I don't like it. You're my wife and don't you ever forget it.'

This could either spark off a row or lead to a night of passionate lovemaking. So much depended not only on how she answered him, but also on the mood he was in.

It was like being on a seesaw. One minute they were in each other's arms and the next they were at daggers drawn.

Still, Karyn told herself, they'd managed to stay together, which was something their families had prophesied wouldn't happen when they'd insisted on getting married.

When Tudor suggested going to see her parents on Delia's second birthday in September 1924, she wondered if he had changed his mind about leaving Pen-y-llyn. She sometimes felt that he missed his family although he assured her he didn't and refused to visit his mother on her fiftieth birthday, even though Olwyn had written and asked him to come.

The idea of all three of them going on a visit to Pen-y-llyn was quite an undertaking, one they had to plan well ahead.

'Shall I write and ask my mam if we can stay overnight?'

'I thought it would be more of a surprise if we simply turned up out of the blue,' he told her. 'That way, if there is any last-minute hitch and we can't go then no one will be disappointed.'

'I was thinking about sleeping arrangements,' she explained.

'Your bed is probably still there,' he laughed. 'You and Delia could share that and I could shake down on a sofa, or in a chair, or something. It will only be for the one night.'

Although it worried her a little because she felt it was rather inconsiderate on their part, Karyn agreed to his plans. She was sure her parents would be overjoyed to see Delia and between them they would soon organise somewhere for them all to sleep.

Enid and Owen Pryce were delighted to see their unexpected visitors.

Delia was immediately the centre of attention. Enid was enthusiastic about the way she had grown, and how well she looked, and was eager to cuddle her. The euphoria quickly turned to disappointment, however, when she realised that Delia had forgotten her.

'Come on, you remember your nanny, my little beauty, now don't you?' she persisted over and over again as she tried to take Delia into her arms.

Delia looked at her wide eyed, then opened her mouth and bawled with fright. Karyn tried to talk to her, to stop her crying, but to no avail. Delia cried all the louder, holding out her arms to Tudor. The moment he picked her up her sobbing ceased at once, and flinging her arms round his neck, she clung on to him tightly.

'Well, I must say, he certainly seems to have a way with her,' Enid admitted grudgingly. 'He handles her a lot better than you do, Karyn, and no mistake.'

'Yes, Tudor is a wonderful dad,' Karyn admitted. 'Delia is never happier than when she is with him.'

It wasn't the only cause for dissension between them all. Both her parents were shocked when they heard that Karyn had become a barmaid.

'Whoever looks after little Delia while you are out working, then?' her mother asked in a bewildered tone.

'Tudor does, of course.'

Her mother was full of righteous concern. 'I can't believe it,' she gasped, 'my daughter working in a pub! I'd never have let you go to Cardiff if I'd known you were going to end up doing something like that. What on earth made you decide to work there?'

Karyn did her best to explain how their accommodation was tied to the pub, but her mother refused to accept this as an excuse.

'You told me before that you were living there because Tudor was singing in the pub and had to live on the premises.'

'Well, that is right.'

'Then if Tudor is singing in the pub, why on earth do you have to work there as well?'

'It means more money . . .'

'Money, money, I might have known it,' her

mother exclaimed triumphantly. 'You've got to work because Tudor doesn't earn enough from this singing lark.'

Owen Pryce said nothing, but from the way he nodded his head in agreement Karyn knew he thought much the same as her mother did and that he didn't approve either.

'Even so, it strikes me as a bit strange that you can bring yourself to leave Tudor to look after her such a lot of the time,' her mother sniffed disapprovingly.

'How else would I be able to go to work?' Karyn asked. She felt annoyed that her mother was making such an issue of the matter. Surely it was enough that they were able to manage and had a place of their own and didn't have to ask anyone for help.

Bronwen Morgan was equally critical. 'Our Tudor having to look after the baby while you go to work,' she exclaimed in amazement. 'Never in my wildest dreams would I have ever thought he'd have to do something like that. Not a man's work, is it! I mean, a man should be the wage earner . . .'

'Tudor is a wage earner. He sings at the pub every night. Then he looks after Delia while I work down there in the mornings, so what is wrong with that?' Karyn defended.

'Nothing, I suppose, if that's the way you want to live,' Bronwen said huffily. 'I don't know what his da would have to say if he was still alive, mind you. Shocked, he would have been by such an arrangement, I can tell you.'

'Well, no one in Cardiff thinks that there's anything odd about it,' Karyn said with some exasperation. 'It works very well for us so can we stop going on about it.'

'They may as well have their say now as to do it behind our backs after we've gone home,' Tudor said sourly. 'I'm beginning to wish we hadn't taken the trouble to come here after all.'

'So why did you bother coming, then?' His mother asked somewhat irritated. 'You've been gone from Pen-y-llyn for well over a year now and not once have you come back to see how we are all getting on.'

'We thought you'd want to see how big your little granddaughter is growing, that's why we're here.'

'Oh yes! Not to show off your fancy new clothes, then?'

'It's Delia's birthday and she's two years old; we thought you'd be pleased to see her,' Tudor repeated stubbornly.

'Not come to see if I was all right or in need of anything, though,' his mother ranted. 'Left a widow and I have to fend for myself while my son lives it up down in Cardiff. Very nice, that is! If it wasn't for our Olwyn I'd probably starve to death for all you care.'

'You know that's not true, Mam,' Tudor protested. 'Griff agreed that he'd keep an eye on you in return for having the chance of them living here. He looks after you, doesn't he?'

'Yes, but why should he when he's only my son-in-law. It should be my own son who's taking care of me. If you'd got yourself a job down the mine, then you could have been living here and I wouldn't have to accept their charity.'

'Charity! What the hell are you on about, Mam?'

'Having to rely on Olwyn and Griff to pay for the food I eat is charity, isn't it?'

'Duw anwyl! You're providing a house for Griff and Olwyn and their kids to live in, aren't you? He's contributing by paying for the food and anything else needed in the house. That's not charity, that's sharing and he's doing his bit for you out of gratitude. Without you they'd still be cooped up in two rooms and they know it.'

'Yes, well, that's as maybe,' Bronwen said huffily, 'but I still think it should be my own son looking after me.'

With one thing and another Tudor decided he'd had enough and cut their visit short.

'I don't intend coming back here again a hurry, I can tell you, so don't ever ask me to do so, understand?' he muttered as they headed for the train to take them back to Cardiff.

'Do you think it was any better for me having to listen to all the criticism, about me working and leaving you to look after Delia?' Karyn scowled.

'That's it, then,' he stormed, 'it's been a waste of bloody money and upsetting for Delia, so

from now on we'll keep ourselves to ourselves.
If they want to see us, then they can come down
to Cardiff to do so.'

Chapter Nine

Although Karyn felt unhappy that they had fallen out with her parents and with Tudor's mother she realised it was better not to say anything more about it to Tudor when they got home, knowing how angry he was.

She hoped that in a few weeks time it would all be forgotten because she'd planned on going back again for Christmas. When she suggested the idea early in December, however, Tudor pointed out that it would be impossible because they would be far too busy at the pub over Christmas.

New Year's Eve was so hectic that Tudor had fed Delia, and popped her into her cot and was already down in the bar singing before Karyn managed to get free.

When she eventually got upstairs she found that Delia was sound asleep, so she made herself something to eat and then dozed off in the armchair. When she woke up the fire was almost out and she was startled to see that it was almost midnight.

She banked up the fire and prepared a meal for Tudor to have before he came to bed. Delia was still sleeping soundly, so she tucked the blankets in around her and went back downstairs to the pub to see what was going on.

Tudor was standing by the piano, his deep voice soaring above the general babble in the bar. He looked so handsome, his head held high, his dark eyes shining in his lean, intelligent face as he gave a heart-rending performance. Her deep love for him brought a lump to her throat, and as she listened, she thought with pride what a splendid singer he was.

At midnight, as the ships sounded their klaxons and sirens, and many of the nearby factory hooters joined in, everyone in the bar linked arms and started singing along with Tudor. It brought tears to Karyn's eyes and a fervent wish that 1925 would be the year when Tudor was able to make a real career for himself. From the rapturous applause he received there was no doubt that he deserved to perform somewhere other than a pub bar.

Tudor was too exhausted to bother with eating anything when he finally came upstairs around two in the morning. Karyn had already undressed, ready for bed. She was undecided whether or not to tell him she had been in the bar at midnight, and waited to see if he mentioned it. When he didn't, she assumed he hadn't seen her there, so she said nothing.

Neither of them mentioned anything about visiting Pen-y-llyn. As the New Year began they simply picked up the threads of their normal routine and gradually consolidated the new life they had built for themselves.

Tudor seemed to make friends easily. Sometimes she thought that his drinking was excessive, but after she had tentatively remarked on this he had been so incensed that she'd said nothing since. A lot of the men who came into the Voyager bought him drinks when he was singing and he claimed that it would rile the Parkers if he refused since it would be turning trade away.

When she'd suggested that he came to some arrangement with them where they simply kept his glass topped up, and gave him some extra money instead of so many extra pints, he'd merely scowled and told her to 'mind her own business'.

A few weeks later, though, she'd noticed that he was not only much more sober when he came up at night, but that he seemed to have more money in his pocket.

What Tudor did with the extra money she had no idea, but she rather thought that most of it went on bets because of the same old mood pattern. He was back-slappingly happy when he won, but dour and unresponsive when he lost.

One thing she was thankful for was that no matter what his mood towards her might be he was never anything but loving and caring with Delia. He was always buying her new clothes and toys. He liked to see her in dainty dresses and matching pretty bonnets and he still let her rule his life. Wonderful though this was it made Karyn unhappy to see what a precocious child Delia was becoming.

Even Marged Parker had started to notice. 'Quite a temper on her, your little Delia has, when she can't have her own way,' she commented critically after witnessing one of Delia's tantrums when Karyn had refused her something. 'Llew's commented on it several times lately because we can hear her carrying on down in our place.'

'It's all a flash in the pan,' Karyn told her quickly. 'She doesn't like being told what to do, not unless it is something she wants to do herself,' she laughed.

'I can see that! Now I wonder who she takes after,' Marged said dryly. 'I think I know someone else who doesn't like to be told anything. In fact, I'd go so far as to say she's the spitting image of her dad, in her manner as well as her looks. No wonder they get on so well.'

'Yes, he's a great dad and they certainly are happy when they're together, there is no doubt about that and it is something I'm thankful for, I can tell you,' Karyn agreed.

If Tudor was at home when Karyn finished down in the pub in the afternoon, they sat down for half an hour and had a cup of tea together and played with Delia. After that she usually

108

tackled all the domestic chores and started preparing their main meal. Tudor liked them to sit down to eat well before six so that he had plenty of time to get ready for his evening session in the pub.

This meant that Delia was usually in bed at almost the same time as Tudor started work, and Karyn was faced with a long evening on her own.

Sometimes she waited up for Tudor, but since he often stayed late down in the pub, drinking with cronies of the Parkers, more and more often she went to bed around nine o'clock.

Most nights Delia slept the whole night through, and if Tudor didn't wake her up when he came to bed then Karyn found she was up very early the next morning.

As spring advanced and it became lighter in the mornings, and the weather improved, Karyn would dress Delia as soon as she was awake, then give her some breakfast and take her for a walk.

Usually there was some shopping to be done in St James's Street, but after that she walked along the Esplanade, enjoying the sun and stopping to chat to people who became more and more familiar as they met each day. Mothers with young children would pause, peep into each other's prams and comment on how their babies were growing, or chat about their minor problems.

Most of them recognised Karyn because she

worked at the Voyager, but it took her rather longer to get to know their names. She enjoyed the challenge and companionship, however, and looked forward to seeing them each morning before she started her shift at the pub.

As the days lengthened, and Delia became more reluctant to settle to sleep at night, Karyn waited until Tudor had gone to work, then popped Delia into her pram and went out for a stroll.

It was all so different from the mornings. On a nice evening there were couples of all ages strolling along the Esplanade or even sitting on the low wall that bordered the canal.

Other young mums began to join her for an evening stroll, pushing their prams side by side until the little ones were sleeping and it was time to take them home. Occasionally, Karyn found herself being invited into their homes for a cuppa and a gossip and she readily accepted.

Tudor neither approved nor disapproved. As long as his meal was on the table, and his clean shirt was laid out ready when it was time for him to get washed, shaved and dolled up, he shrugged his shoulders about what Karyn did the rest of the time.

He did very little in the home, and he hated shopping, but he never tired of looking after Delia. She still adored him and was never happier than when they were together.

As she grew older and more aware of what

was happening around her she could never understand why he had to leave her to go to work and would dissolve into a storm of tears. This became one of the reasons why Karyn took her out in her pram for an hour or so most evenings.

Karyn found that her life had changed in other ways. With both of them earning regular money it had meant that she could afford to buy things for herself and she had more clothes than she'd ever had in her life before.

She let Tudor think that she was clever at managing the housekeeping money he gave her; what she didn't tell him was that she also earned tips. They weren't big amounts, sometimes only a few coppers, but she secreted them away and then, when she'd managed to save up enough for a new blouse or skirt or dress, she indulged in a shopping trip.

She'd discovered there were bargains to be found at the stalls on the Hayes and she enjoyed hunting for them. From time to time she even found things in the pawnbrokers; smart dresses and shoes that had obviously been bought for some special occasion and later had been pawned when the owner fell on hard times and had been unable to redeem them again.

Frequently, she felt guilty about taking advantage of other people's hardships in this way, but she'd come to realise that life was like that. Some people had it all, others nothing; sometimes you were on top of things and then, for no fault of your own, you were the underdog.

Given the chance to start all over again she wondered if she would have rushed into marriage at quite such a young age as she had done. As it was, with Delia on the way she'd had no option, she kept telling herself.

She often wondered what Tudor felt about their current circumstances. The closeness that had existed between them when they were growing up and they had told each other absolutely everything, even their innermost thoughts, seemed to have gradually gone.

She sometimes pondered over whether he still loved her or not; he certainly wanted her and needed her. He left her in no doubt about that, but their lovemaking had a different feel about it. These days they were no longer ardent young lovers, anxious to please each other. Sometimes she felt that all he was interested in was satisfying his own needs. The sweet talk and tenderness had gone out of their lovemaking. When she'd tried to talk to him about the lack of romance he laughed cynically.

'You're a married woman now, it's time you grew up and forgot all about that sort of flowery talk and girlish moonshine. We're not still courting, you know.'

'I know that, but I don't like being taken for granted,' she protested.

'Damnio di, Karyn! All that soppy stuff was

all right when we were still at school, but you can't expect it to go on for ever,' he told her scathingly.

'How do I know you still love me, if you never tell me so?' she protested.

'I live with you, look after you and take care of Delia, don't I? I never say a word about all the fripperies you buy yourself. I give you and Delia the odd present out of my winnings from time to time. What more do you want from me?'

He made her feel so ungrateful that she found it difficult to answer. She always felt so near to tears whenever she tried to discuss the state of their relationship that she found it impossible to reason properly.

In the old days, when they were still in Pen-y-llyn, his constant desire was for them to be together, for her to be his and his alone. Perhaps if she'd held out more, not given in to him quite so readily as she did, then he would still be striving to win her love, she thought despondently. Now his sole ambition was to become a professional singer, and his mind seemed to be centred entirely on his longing to be discovered.

Leaving Pen-y-llyn had hardened him, made him insensitive as well as impatient and stubborn. The only tenderness he seemed to show was towards Delia. He was never happier than when she was in his care. Because he worked so late at night it was usually mid-morning

113

before he got up. The first thing he did was to make straight for Delia, toss her high in the air and give her some little treat or the other, like a sweet or a biscuit.

If Karyn grumbled that he shouldn't do it so near to her meal time because it would spoil her appetite, he'd scowl and take no notice.

For Delia's third birthday in September 1925, he bought her a soft-bodied cuddly doll that was almost as big as she was and each morning after that he would sweep them both up in his arms and call them 'his girls'.

Delia laughed uproariously at this and would point a finger at herself and say 'Delia' and at the doll and say 'Dolly' as if trying to explain to him that she was real but that the doll wasn't.

Very soon, though, she was turning her father's little joke very much to her own advantage. She was never naughty, never spilled anything, never made crumbs. It was always 'Dolly' who did all these things.

When Karyn wanted her to do something that she didn't want to do, she always said that 'Dolly' was the naughty one who didn't want to do it.

'I don't know what your nana is going to say when you tell her things like that when we go to see her at Christmas,' Karyn said.

'We won't be going to see her at Christmas,' Tudor said firmly. 'I had a bellyful the last time we went to Pen-y-llyn so I'm not going

114

to drag her all the way up there in the cold again.'

'They'll be expecting us,' Karyn protested. 'We didn't go last year and we didn't even take Delia to see them on her birthday.'

'No, and we won't be taking her there this Christmas either so I don't want to hear any more about it.'

Once again Christmas was so busy in the pub that in some ways Karyn was pleased they weren't going to have to make the journey. She tried to explain about their heavy workload and the wintry weather in a letter to her own mother and promised they'd come at Easter when it was warmer and the days were longer. She left Tudor to explain things to his own mother.

1926 looked as though it was going to be a repeat of the previous year. After a hectic New Year's Eve they settled back into their old routine of Karyn working as a barmaid from eleven in the morning and Tudor singing down in the bar every evening.

Neither of them was altogether happy about this arrangement. Delia was now three years old and although adorable to look at with her dark hair, big, dark eyes and captivating smile, she was becoming ever more precocious.

Her habit of playing Tudor off against Karyn was also becoming more pronounced and although Tudor merely laughed and gave in to her wiles Karyn thought it was high time she was disciplined. 'If one of us tells her to do something, or not to do something, then it should mean that we are both agreed about it,' she insisted.

'Duw anwyl, what are you trying to do? She's only three years old, she doesn't understand.'

'She understands far more than you give her credit for,' Karyn told him. 'It's time she learned right from wrong. Another eighteen months and she will be going to school and she'll have to behave herself then.'

'Eighteen months! That's for ever to someone of her age. Let her enjoy life. She'll have to conform to rules soon enough and once that happens it will last for the rest of her life,' he said gloomily.

Karyn bit back the retort that was on her lips. She realised that Tudor was far more quick tempered these days and with one wrong word she could easily find herself caught up in a full-scale row.

She rightly surmised that it was because Tudor was no nearer being discovered, despite the fact that he'd been singing his lungs out every night at the Voyager. His career as a fully fledged singer was still as far away as it had ever been.

He made no bones of the fact that he was tired of singing in the Voyager. A couple of times he had pretended to have a cold and explained that he couldn't sing because he had a sore throat. Karyn knew different, and when she'd said that if he wasn't well enough to work at the Voyager then he shouldn't be going out for the evening, he had rather aggressively told her to mind her own business.

'I'm not going to get better shut in here listening to you griping and fussing over me as if I was Delia's age,' he told her. 'Half an hour looking around town will do me a damn sight more good.'

She knew it was useless arguing, but when he demanded a clean shirt and dressed up in his best suit she knew he was up to something, and for one heart-stopping moment she wondered if he was seeing another woman.

Was he tired of their marriage? she asked herself. Did he still love her as much as he had done when they'd lived in Pen-y-llyn? Their life here had become so routine and so had their lovemaking. It was as if all the zip had gone out of it. If it wasn't for working in the bar, and enjoying all the laughs and repartee with the regulars, she would have suggested that they change their whole way of living in some way or the other.

If only there was someone she could talk things over with, she thought disconsolately, especially now that she knew she was pregnant again. She missed having her mother to turn to when she needed advice. She hadn't realised how understanding and helpful she had always been, not until they'd moved away.

It was so long since she'd seen her that she felt they were growing ever more apart. Letters weren't the same and she knew her mam must be feeling hurt at not seeing little Delia more often.

When she suggested to Tudor that it was high time they took Delia to Pen-y-llyn to see her grandparents he turned the idea down flat.

'The last time we went we got the cold shoulder so why the hell should we go to the expense of going all that way. All I'll get is a load of smirks when they find out that I'm still singing in a pub and a telling off because you are still working as a barmaid. How do you think that makes me feel?'

'That was over two years ago and they weren't really criticising you, Tudor, only commenting on things. It is just a different sort of life to what they are used to.'

'Yes, and my mam will still be going on about how I should be looking after her or else about the fact that she has to accept charity from our Olwyn's Griff.'

'It's only her silly old way, Tudor. She doesn't mean any harm by it. Anyway, surely you can laugh it off. She must be longing to see little Delia.'

'Why? She's got a houseful of bloody grandchildren living with her, hasn't she, so what's one more matter?'

'Well, my mam and dad are dying to see Delia again. Mam's always saying in her letters how much she must have grown and what a big girl she must be by now.'

'Then why doesn't she bloody well make the effort to come here to Cardiff and see her?'

Chapter Ten

Karyn had made up her mind. Whether Tudor wanted to do so or not she was determined to make a trip to Pen-y-llyn and visit her mam and dad and see his mother.

Now that she was turned three Delia no longer needed her pushchair and it would be simple enough to catch the tram to Wood Street Station and to get to Pen-y-llyn by bus when she left the train at Pontypridd. She could manage on her own so if Tudor didn't want to come then he could stay home and fend for himself for a few days.

They weren't so mad busy at the Voyager now that Christmas and New Year celebrations were over, so if she explained her reasons to the Parkers she was sure that they would understand why she felt it was necessary to take the time off.

For weeks she planned and schemed. She'd leave plenty of food in the larder for Tudor – things that he could eat cold if he didn't want to go to the trouble of cooking.

She decided what clothes she'd need to take with her and even what she and Delia would wear to travel in. She put away the money for their fares and a bit extra in case of any emergencies. She even bought presents for both her mum and dad and then, as an afterthought, she bought one for Bronwen Morgan as well. She'd say it was from Tudor and that would help to smooth matters over if he decided not to come.

She didn't say anything at all about her plans to Tudor until the very last minute and then, much to her surprise, he said he'd come along as well.

'I know why you're going,' he told her.

'I'm going because I think it is high time Delia saw a little bit more of her grandparents.'

'Is that the only reason?'

'I want to see my mam and dad as well, it's ages since I did!'

Tudor scowled. 'Whose fault is that? I told you we couldn't afford to keep running backwards and forwards to Pen-y-llyn and they've never come here to Cardiff to visit us and find out how we are getting on.'

'You know my mam wouldn't dare to travel all this way on her own . . .'

'And your dad can't be bothered to make the effort to come with her?'

'Well, you know what he's like.'

'You mean he's shit scared to put a foot outside Pen-y-llyn,' Tudor commented cynically.

'Your mam's as bad! She doesn't even bother to write! At least my mam answers my letters.'

'So why can't you tell her that you're going to have another baby in a letter, then?'

Karyn bit her lower lip and looked uncomfortable. 'I think she deserves to hear it from my own lips,' she said defensively.

Tudor shrugged. 'Bit early to be telling anyone, I would have thought.'

'No it's not. It will help to prove to them all that we are happy and settled in our new life.'

He gave a short, sharp laugh. 'You might be, cariad, but I'm not! What have I achieved since coming to Cardiff?'

'You've made a living as a singer, which was what you said you wanted to do.'

'Yes, singing as a proper career, not warbling in a bloody pub. I thought I'd be discovered . . .'

'And you will be if you give it time, cariad,' she assured him quickly. Crossing the room she reached up and slipped a hand around his neck and pulled his face down so that she could kiss him. 'You'll make it yet.'

He laughed again. 'So you've still got faith in me, have you?' he asked ruefully.

'Of course I have. I've always had faith in you,' she insisted huskily.

Tudor shook his head but said nothing. He felt too bitter about the way things had worked out to be able to discuss the matter rationally.

Delia's dark eyes widened excitedly when they told her she was going to Pen-y-llyn and would be able to see both her granny and her nanny.

'How do I know which one is Granny and which one is Nanny?' she asked, looking puzzled. 'I don't remember them, not even their faces.'

'That's because you were only a baby the last time we took you to see them.'

After that she was full of questions. Karyn told her endless stories about her granny, who was her daddy's mother, and her nanny, who was her mother's mother, and how they had always lived next door to each other.

'And you and daddy also lived next door to each other when you were little like me?'

'Yes, and when we grew up we married each other.'

This information fascinated Delia. 'Why can't I have a friend living next door and then when we are both grown up I can marry him?' she questioned.

'Perhaps you will someday.' Karyn smiled.

'When?' Delia pouted. 'I want him to live there now, and have someone to play with every day.'

'I wonder what she is going to say when we tell her about the baby,' Karyn said in a whisper to Tudor.

By the time they reached Pen-y-llyn, Delia was so excited by riding in a train, and by everything they saw out of the carriage window, that they had difficulty controlling her. Yet the moment Enid Pryce opened her front door to them, Delia became shy and timid, clinging on to Tudor and hiding her face from everyone.

'Still the same, I see,' Enid Pryce commented. 'I remember the last time she was here she was so shy that she kept hiding her face all the time.'

'She was only a little baby then,' Karyn said defensively. 'She'll be all right in a minute or so. Take no notice, leave her to get used to everyone.'

'She's been talking about you for days, ever since we said we were coming here, but it's been such a long time since she saw you that you're like strangers to her,' Tudor pointed out.

'The same as you are to us, boyo!' Owen Pryce commented. 'It's two years, perhaps more, since we last saw you, how do you think we feel about that?'

'Nothing to stop you coming down to Cardiff to see us, now is there?' Tudor said huffily.

'We're here now and that's all that matters,' Karyn said in a conciliatory tone. 'Let's have a cuppa and see if we can catch up with each other's news and then Tudor will want to go next door to see his own mam.'

'I'll go now, so don't bother making any tea for me,' Tudor said curtly.

Delia clung to him like a limpet as he moved towards the door. Enid tried to coax her back, and so did Owen, but she still hung on to Tudor.

'Let her go with Tudor,' Karyn sighed. 'She'll be sleeping here tonight so you'll have a chance to get to know her then once she's stopped being so shy.'

Bridging the gap was nowhere as easy as Karyn had hoped. Enid and Owen still seemed to think that Karyn and Tudor should have stayed in Pen-y-llyn and made their home there.

'We'd never have been able to hold our heads up, there'd have been too much gossip,' Karyn pointed out. 'It was the only way, Mam; we needed our independence.'

'Yes, that's all very well, my girl, but look where it has landed you!' her father exploded.

'We don't like the idea of you working as a barmaid, or that Tudor is still having to make a living by singing at night in a pub,' Enid Pryce sighed.

'Or the fact that you are living in rooms over a pub,' added her father. 'That's not the right sort of place for young Delia, not now that she's able to run around. She needs to be somewhere with a bit of garden where she can play out in the fresh air.'

They were both so concerned about Delia's welfare that Karyn dreaded what they would say when she told them that she was expecting another baby.

Bronwen Morgan was equally critical. She vented her frustration on Tudor, accusing him of staying away from Pen-y-llyn because he didn't want to see her. She grumbled about the deprivations she had to put up with and the strain she was under because she had to share her home with Olwyn and Griff and their children. She criticised the way Delia behaved, and expressed the opinion that she was spoiled.

Karyn had intended that they would be staying in Pen-y-llyn for three days and was startled when after one night there Tudor said they were going back to Cardiff.

'Stay another night,' she begged, but he staunchly refused.

'You stay if you want to, but I can't stand any more of this nagging and belly-aching.'

Delia created a scene when Tudor prepared to leave. She sobbed for almost an hour after he'd left and Karyn was almost on the point of following on after him.

'Nonsense, cariad,' Owen Pryce said severely. 'You can't let a three-year-old dominate your life. She'll calm down.'

Delia did of course. An hour later and she was all dimples and smiles as she tried her hardest to win favour with Granddad Pryce. Although there was certainly a warm rapport between them, and he was enraptured by her pretty little ways, he was not nearly so easily won over as Tudor.

Once Tudor had left there seemed to be a more relaxed atmosphere between Karyn and her parents. There was so much to say, so many confidences to be exchanged and news to catch up on.

Karyn was distressed to hear that the row

that had flared up between her mother and Bronwen Morgan when she and Tudor had said they were getting married was still causing friction.

'Surely not; not after all this time. It's well over two years since we moved to Cardiff,' Karyn said.

'Yes, and never a day goes by when Bronny doesn't remind me of the fact,' her mother replied.

Karyn put her arms around her mother's shoulders and hugged her close. 'I'm sorry, Mam; the pair of you used to be such good friends. I'm sure it will come right between you eventually.'

'Poor Bronny, she's not happy at having Olwyn and her crowd living with her,' Enid sighed.

'You mean she thinks it should be me and Tudor making our home there?'

Enid nodded grimly. 'I'm afraid so, cariad. I imagine that's what she's been saying to Tudor which is probably why he's cleared off back to Cardiff.'

'Fed up with her belly-aching! Either that or else he's gone off with a flea in his ear,' Owen chuckled.

'I'll pop in later on and see if I can talk her round,' Karyn murmured.

'Leave well alone if you've got any sense, girl,' Owen warned. 'You'll find Bronwen is as sour as a dried-up lemon these days.'

'Then I owe it to Tudor to try and explain things to her and to cheer her up. I'll take Delia in to see her; she won't be able to resist one of her little smiles.'

'I'm not so sure,' Enid warned. 'Bronny's fed up to the back teeth with having kids underfoot. Go round on your own first and see if you can have a heart-to-heart with her, cariad. If she will talk to you and get all this resentment she is feeling off her chest, it will be like a tonic and do her the world of good.'

'All right, if that's what you think is best,' Mam,' Karyn agreed dubiously.

'I'll try and persuade Olwyn to take her lot out for a walk and then you can go and see Bronwen when she's on her own,' Enid suggested. 'More cosy like, see.'

'You don't think I should take Delia with me?' Karyn frowned.

'No! You go and have a quiet cuppa with Bronwen and let her be the one to ask for Delia to come round to see her.'

Karyn was shocked at the difference in Bronwen. Her own mam looked older, but then that's what happened when you didn't see each other for a couple of years. They probably thought she looked older and certainly more grown up, Karyn reflected.

Bronwen, however, looked like a completely different person. She'd always been so brawny and full of life; now she seemed to have shrunk, and she looked so defeated and weary that it made her look old. Even her shiny black hair, drawn back into a bun, was streaked with grey.

'I thought I'd better come and let you know that Tudor has gone back to Cardiff,' she said hesitantly. 'Work, see,' she added lamely by way of explanation.

'Work! Spare me the excuses, my lovely. I know him too well to be taken in. Fed up with me telling him a few home truths more likely!'

Bronwen continued to be rather huffy at first, but remembering her mother's advice, Karyn tried to be as patient and understanding as possible. As they drank their tea she began telling her all she could about their new life in Cardiff.

'He's not made a success of his singing, though, has he?' Bronwen said wearily. 'Singing in a pub, that's not good enough for my Tudor, it's not what he left Pen-y-llyn for, now is it.'

'He'll be discovered and get to the top, these things take time,' Karyn said confidently.

'It's no good you boasting like that, Karyn, you can't pull the wool over my eyes. Ruined that boy, I did. I should have listened to his dad. My Madoc wanted to make him go down the pit when he left school. All the Morgans have been miners going back generations. Proud of the fact, see. He's the only one who's failed us.'

'He's not failed; he'll succeed in what he wants to do if you give him time.'

'I lashed out at him yesterday. I shouldn't

have done that, but I'm disappointed in him, see. Fed up I am with everything,' she confessed, refilling their cups. 'Olwyn and her lot get on my nerves bawling at each other night and day. Bit of peace is what I want.'

'I'm sure Tudor understood,' Karyn said awkwardly.

'Griff's a good man, mind, and I suppose our Olwyn does her best,' Bronwen went on. 'I miss my Madoc, though,' she said sadly, wiping tears from her eyes with the corner of her pinny. 'Even though the house is bursting at the seams and there's a big noisy family all around me, I feel so lonely.'

'You could always go in next door and have a quiet half-hour with my mam,' Karyn pointed out.

Bronwen shook her head. 'Pair of love birds those two, feel like an interloper every time I go in there, if your dad is at home.'

'You and my mam have been best friends all your lives. She's feeling lonely without you,' Karyn persisted. 'Anyway,' she added almost shyly, 'I like to feel that you and Mam are keeping an eye on each other.' She walked over and put an arm round Bronwen's shoulders and kissed her on the cheek. 'Being so far away from both of you it would set my mind at rest, see.'

Bronwen nodded and gave her a watery smile. 'You're a good girl, Karyn; my Tudor's a lucky boyo having you standing by him like you do and no mistake.'

'I do my best,' Karyn assured her, 'and we've got little Delia, of course. Tudor absolutely dotes on her.'

'Yes, I can see that.' Bronwen's mouth tightened. 'He'll spoil her if you're not careful. How is she ever going to face up to things if you have another baby? That would put her little nose out of joint and no mistake.'

'We'll know all about that soon enough.' Karyn smiled. 'One of the reasons we came on a visit was because we wanted to tell you that I'm expecting again.'

'Tudor never said!'

'Well, it's very early days yet. The baby's not due until the summer.'

'So how will you manage? You won't be able to work when you've got another babba.'

'Tudor will look after the baby and Delia while I do my midday stint, the same as he has always done. He's looked after Delia from the time she was a couple of months old,' Karyn said.

Bronwen shook her head. 'It's all wrong, Karyn. You shouldn't need to work. Tudor should be doing a job that brings in enough for you all to live on. Why do you have to be the one to serve in the pub in the middle of the day, why can't he?'

'I enjoy it, honestly I do.' She gave a short laugh. 'I'll let you into a secret, Tudor is better at looking after Delia than I am.'

*   *   *

Enid and Owen showed a mixture of pleasure and concern when Karyn told them that she was pregnant.

'You'll have your hands full, my lovely,' Enid warned her. Delia will need a lot of attention or she'll be jealous of the little newcomer. You haven't told her yet, of course?'

'Oh no! It's far too early to do that. I'll leave it until about a month or so before the baby is due, just long enough to get her used to the idea. After that I'll let her help me to get things ready for it.'

'If you say so, cariad. She'll be almost four by the time it is born and remember, she's been your little star all this time. She's not going to like having to play second fiddle.'

'She won't be expected to, Mam. We'll both make sure of that. It's going to be her baby as well as ours. She'll love it and enjoy helping to look after it, you'll see.'

'Don't leave it so long before you come to see us again,' Enid Pryce begged when Karyn took her leave.

'I promise I'll come again soon but it may not be for quite a while and you know why.' She smiled, placing a finger to her lips and nodding towards Delia.

Chapter Eleven

During the early months of 1926, Karyn's pregnancy went so smoothly and she felt so fit and
healthy that sometimes she wondered if it was
all a dream.

She felt that her short visit to Pen-y-llyn and
the opportunity to talk to her mother had
cleared up any misunderstandings caused by
their estrangement.

'I understand you can't visit us as often as
you'd like,' her mother had agreed. 'You're a
married woman now with a life of your own,
but to me you are still my little girl. You always
will be, I suppose, that's the way of things.'

'I'll try and write to you more often,' Karyn
promised. 'I have missed you, and Dad, so
much.'

'We're always here for you,' her mother told
her. 'Never be afraid to ask for our help if you
need it.'

She'd made her peace with Tudor's mam as
well and she liked to think that it had helped
to restore the old friendship between her own
mother and Bronwen and that they would be
seeing much more of each other in the future.

She would have felt completely content if it

had not been that Tudor seemed to be increasingly restless. She wondered if it was because of the berating he'd received from his mother and her disappointment that he had still not attained the success he had hoped to achieve. Or was he tired of having to take care of Delia while she did her morning and early evening stints each day down in pub?

As far as she was concerned, as long as they had enough money to get by on, and he enjoyed what he was doing, then they had nothing to worry about. She was far happier knowing that he was safe and sound than that he was earning more money working underground as a miner as his mother felt he should be.

Far too many of the people she had known in Pen-y-llyn had been killed or seriously injured because they'd been caught up in an explosion or a cave-in, or some other sort of pit accident. Her own dad had been one of the lucky ones, but he'd lost a good many friends as well as his only brother in mining accidents. Like her mother, she would be glad when he was old enough to retire. She knew her mam was always pleading with him to apply for a surface job of some kind, but pride wouldn't let him do that.

'I'm a miner, born and bred, and I'll go on being a miner for as long as I'm fit enough to be one,' he would state emphatically.

'You could still work at the pit,' Enid always protested, 'as a time-keeper, or one of the other jobs where you wouldn't have to go down into the bowels of the earth like you do now.'

She might as well have saved her breath, Karyn reflected. Her dad would never capitulate. He was as stubborn as Tudor. Tudor wanted to be a singer and he'd never rest until his talent was discovered and his name was up on the billboards outside the theatres and music halls.

The chances of that happening seemed pretty remote as far as she could see. Talent scouts simply didn't come to the Voyager for a night out.

There was one other small cloud on the horizon. Although she felt so well, and couldn't imagine that there would be any complications during the rest of her pregnancy, Karyn was also practical enough to realise that the Parkers weren't going to want her serving in the bar now that her pregnancy was becoming obvious.

The baby was due in July, so she would probably have to stop working around Easter time. The money she earned was so important to them that she hoped she could persuade Tudor to work in the bar from then until after she'd had the baby to make sure that they kept her job for her.

Several times she tentatively tried to discuss the matter with him and to persuade him to think about it, but he wouldn't listen to her.

'I've told you before, girl, that I'll never stoop to that,' he said scornfully. 'Let the Parkers get someone else in if they can't manage on their own.'

'If they do that then they might decide to keep her,' Karyn said worriedly. 'I don't want to lose my job, Tudor. We'll need the money more than ever when we have another baby to bring up.'

'Not for a long time. You'll be feeding it yourself so it won't cost us a penny piece.'

'There're all sorts of other things we'll be needing, though,' she persisted.

'We still have all Delia's stuff.'

'Yes, we have her pram and cot, but what if this one is a boy. We'll have to buy all new clothes for him.'

'Not at first, we won't. Wrapped up in a pram it doesn't much matter what they've got on.'

'You'd put a little boy in a pink dress and a sun bonnet, would you?' she said witheringly.

Tudor scowled. 'That would be taking it a bit far, but there are plenty of other things the baby will be able to wear that are all right whether it is a boy or a girl. By the time you need to dress it any differently I'll be earning more money.'

'Oh yes, and how are you going to do that?'

Tudor frowned darkly. 'You ask too many bloody questions. It's been the same ever since we went to Pen-y-llyn. I don't know what my mam said to you but you've been like a broody old hen ever since we came home. I'm fed up with you fussing about how much money we

136

have and checking up to see if we have all the right things and—'

'I'm expecting a baby so is it any wonder that I'm concerned about how we are going to provide for it?' Karyn interrupted.

'We managed before when Delia arrived and we'll do so again,' he said dismissively.

Karyn knew it was pointless arguing with Tudor once he'd dug his heels in. From then on each week she squirrelled away every penny she could as a safeguard against when she wouldn't be able to earn anything. She no longer bought clothes for herself and she even cut back on Delia's little treats.

Tudor seemed to have blithely banished the problem from his mind. Karyn didn't know where he was getting extra money from, but he certainly seemed to have plenty to spend. Over and over again she reminded him that he shouldn't be buying so many new things for Delia, especially toys. His only response was to jingle the small change in his pocket in a tantalising manner and then go out and buy her something else.

She felt utterly confused. Although he wouldn't agree with her idea that he should do her job in the bar, he didn't seem to be in the least troubled at the thought of her not earning any money for several months. In fact, he seemed to be in such an affable mood that nothing she said seemed to upset him.

There were times when she felt left out

because he and Delia were so close. She was
forever clambering up on to his knee, winding
her arms round his neck and kissing his cheek
and trying to wheedle him into taking her out.

Every time he did so she seemed to come
back with something new. When the weather
turned exceptionally cold at the end of March,
he bought her a little white fur muff. She looked
so cute when she was carrying it that the next
time he took her out she came home wearing
a little cloche hat that was also trimmed with
white fur.

'Tudor's turning your little Delia into a right
little fashion plate, if you ask me,' Marged
Parker observed. 'Never in my life have I seen
a dad so besotted with his child. If you have
another child, I only hope he'll feel the same
way about it.'

'I'm sure he would,' Karyn said confidently.
'Tudor loves children and he's so good with
them. He's planning to buy Delia a little
umbrella when they go out today. She's been
on about having one for weeks, ever since she
saw my mother using one when we were at
Pen-y-llyn.'

'Give it a few weeks and he could have made
it a little parasol to keep the sun off her.'

'I said that, too,' Karyn laughed, 'but Tudor
she said she wanted it now. He said they'd seen
one on a stall up at the Hayes and they were
going up there today to buy it.'

The two of them still hadn't returned by the

time she'd finished work so, as the sun was shining, Karyn decided to walk as far as Clarence Road Bridge to meet them.

'Wasting your time hanging around here waiting for your Tudor, my lovely,' a workman told her. 'I saw him getting off a tram with the little one about twenty minutes ago.'

'Then I'd better get home and see if he's bought Delia the umbrella they were going to the Hayes to buy.'

'Don't worry, he has. She had it up even though it's not raining.'

'Oh she would!' Karyn laughed. 'She'll probably want to take it to bed with her tonight!'

'Well, they were setting out along the canal embankment the last time I saw them.'

'Really?' Karyn frowned. 'I'll walk along that way and probably overtake them, then.'

There was no sign of them and she felt puzzled about where they might be. Tudor knew she would be finishing her midday stint about half past two and usually he made a point of being home and having the kettle on, knowing the first thing she liked was a cup of tea.

She passed several of the Voyager's regulars who were unloading the barges that were moored in the Glamorganshire Canal and they confirmed that they'd spotted Tudor and Delia walking along by the side of the canal about ten minutes ago and that they'd been going in the direction of Margaret Street.

She couldn't think what Tudor was doing there, not unless he was going to the Torbay pub, but why would he want to do that, she asked herself as she hurried along the canal embankment.

The water was dark and oily and flotsam floated on the surface. She shivered and pulled her coat closer as protection against the cold wind. She shuddered at the sight of a lump of white fur floating in mid-stream. Someone's poor cat had met its fate, she thought sadly, then her heart began to pound as she looked more closely and realised that it wasn't a cat at all.

At the same time she heard voices shouting as people raced from one of the side streets, calling out something she couldn't hear properly. Almost simultaneously she saw something else floating on the greasy water – a small umbrella in a brilliant shade of blue.

For a moment she thought her heart would stop as her startled brain registered what the white fur was – it certainly wasn't a dead cat!

The current was carrying both the white fur and the umbrella downstream, with increasing speed towards the mouth of the canal where it emptied out into the Bristol Channel.

She hesitated for one brief moment because she knew she couldn't swim then, taking a deep breath, she jumped, threshing her way through the freezing water towards the bedraggled mass of fur and the little body it was attached to.

She felt herself sinking like a lead weight, deep into the foul water, but she was determined not to give up. Kicking with her legs and thrashing at the water with her arms she not only managed to keep afloat, but she knew that the distance between her and the floating bundle was lessening.

With a superhuman effort, although her lungs were bursting and the filthy water filled her ears and nostrils, she reached out and grasped at Delia and, struggling desperately, managed to hold the tiny body of her little daughter clear of the foul water.

Then the icy water lapped over her own head, but even as it did she realised that someone else was in the water alongside her. She was aware that Delia had been lifted from her hands and that someone had grasped her own arms and was dragging her through the flotsam. She was no longer being swept towards the sea, but being hauled towards the embankment.

As more hands clutched at her, she heard a medley of voices and then everything went black.

Karyn had no idea where she was when she eventually opened her eyes. She was in bed, in a strange room, with dark green curtains surrounding the sides of the bed and a woman in a blue dress and white apron was leaning over her.

She closed her eyes again. She felt ill. Every

bone in her body ached, her mouth felt parched and her eyelids heavy.

She tried to ask for a drink, but no sound came. Then she sensed the woman was supporting her head and holding a glass to her lips. She tried to drink, but it was as if her lips had no feeling in them and the liquid dribbled down her chin. She tried to sip again and this time the water slid over her parched tongue and down her throat, making her choke.

She lay back exhausted and slept again.

For the whole of the day Karyn floated in limbo, then gradually the mists cleared, she realised where she was, and recalled what had happened.

Reaching out she clutched at the nurse's hand. 'Delia ... my little girl ... is she ... is she ... ?'

'Hush, try and rest. Your little girl is quite safe. She is in hospital here. Someone will bring her along as soon as you feel fit enough to see her.'

'Now! Bring her now, please,' Karyn begged. 'I need to see her, to make sure she is all right.'

'For a couple of minutes, then, but you must promise not to alarm her. She has recovered from her ordeal much more quickly than you have, Mrs Morgan, but she is still a very sick little girl.'

'Why? What is the matter with her?'

'Nothing too serious,' the nurse told her soothingly. 'A chill, that's all. She has been in good hands and her father has been with her most of the time since she has been in here.'

Karyn felt distraught when Tudor came to her bedside cradling Delia in his arms. She seemed so fragile, and her eyes looked huge in her chalk-white face. She was wrapped in a blanket and they were accompanied by a nurse.

When he laid Delia on the bed beside Karyn so that she could cuddle her, Delia whimpered and held out a hand to him, insisting that he held one of her hands.

The nurse would only allow her to stay for a few minutes, but it was enough to set Karyn's mind at rest that she was safe.

'Safe and sound and she'll be well enough to go home in a few days,' the nurse caring for Delia assured her.

'And so will you,' the nurse added with a smile. 'You'll probably both be able to go home together. There's lucky you've both been. Not only the cold but the filthy water in that old canal could have made you both very ill indeed.'

Karyn smiled weakly. Seeing Delia and knowing she was all right had made her feel so much better. The events leading up to it all came back to her and she tried to puzzle out how Delia had fallen into the canal. Where had Tudor been? He was usually so careful and looked after her so well.

She worried so much about the accident and how it had all happened that finally one of the nurses asked Tudor to come and explain everything to her.

'What on earth were you both doing down by the canal in the first place?'

'It was all a dreadful accident. She wandered off, see, while I was doing a bit of business, cariad,' he blustered. 'She was playing with the umbrella I'd bought her and the wind must have caught at it, whisked it out of her hand and into the water. I suppose she tried to reach out and save it and then toppled over and fell in. Seconds later you must have been coming along the side of the canal and spotted her.

'At first I thought it was a dead cat floating there, but it was her little white muff.' Karyn shivered. 'The moment I realised that, I didn't stop to think, I just jumped in.'

'I never knew you could swim,' he said in surprise.

'I can't! Heaven alone knows how I managed to stay afloat. It was some sort of miracle, now I come to think of it,' she added with a little deprecating laugh.

'Well it was very brave of you, cariad. She owes her life to you. It's a terrible shame about the baby . . .'

'Baby? What baby?' Karyn looked at him puzzled. 'What are you talking about?'

'The baby you were expecting in a few months' time.' He looked at her, thunderstruck. 'Haven't they told you? You've lost the baby, my lovely.'

144

'My baby's gone.' Her mouth quivered and she shook her head in disbelief.

'You've had a miscarriage, cariad,' he said gently.

'Is that why they're keeping me in hospital?'

'Yes, but it will only be for a day or two, just to make sure that you are all right, see.'

He watched as her hands went beneath the bedclothes and moved over her stomach in disbelief. The look of distress in her eyes as she looked up at him and the realisation of what he had told her hit him so hard that he had to look away.

As her face crumpled and her eyes filled with tears he leaned down and kissed her very tenderly, holding her hands tightly in his. 'Try not to worry about it, cariad,' he said awkwardly, 'I know it's tragic, but there will be a next time.'

Chapter Twelve

It was a week before Karyn was discharged from hospital and even then she was far from well. Weak, and suffering from depression, she was tearful and touchy. It was obvious, even to Tudor, that she was in no fit state to carry out her duties as a barmaid.

The Parkers were very understanding, but also very surprised that Karyn hadn't told them that she was pregnant. They were also concerned about how long it was likely to be before she was well enough to return to work.

'Give her a week or two,' Tudor told them. 'Now she's back at home she'll recover in next to no time.'

Tudor was wrong, however. At the beginning of April, Karyn decided that she and Delia would spend Easter at Pen-y-llyn. She was hoping that the familiar surroundings, and her mother's company, would help her to feel better. She knew she needed to talk to someone and expunge the misery she still felt over losing the baby.

Back in her own room in Clydach Street, she enjoyed her mother's cosseting for ten days. She would have stayed longer but Delia was pining for Tudor.

She could see that the child's constant crying and wingeing distressed both her mam and dad and she felt that it was unfair to impose on her mother's hospitality any longer because she knew her parents had another major problem to face.

Owen was concerned about what was happening at the mine where he worked. There was a lot of discontent and even talk of a strike in the offing. Both Bronwen and Enid had lived through strikes before and knew the hardship they could cause. When there was no money coming in, every penny counted. Karyn knew that her mother wouldn't ask her to leave, but if there was a strike, and it lasted for any length of time, it would put a strain on their meagre savings if she had to feed her and Delia.

She had hoped Tudor would have sent her some money, but there hadn't been a penny piece from him the whole time she'd been staying at Clydach Street. She'd given her mother almost every penny she had saved up to buy things for the new baby towards her and Delia's keep. Now, all she had left was only enough for their fare back to Cardiff so she decided that it was time to leave.

Her mother made no protest when she told her she was going home. In fact, Karyn suspected she was relieved.

Tudor seemed surprised to see her. 'If you'd let me know you were coming back, then I'd have come to Cardiff Central to meet you,' he told her.

'I only made up my mind yesterday.'

'Why? Have you fallen out with everyone in Pen-y-llyn or something?'

'No, nothing of the sort. My mam and dad are both worrying about the threat of a strike. Your mam as well, if it comes to that, so I thought I'd come home before it happened. Terrible burden for them to have to feed us as well as themselves, see.'

'Are you hinting that I should have sent you some money?' he asked querulously.

'No, not really. It would have been nice if you had, mind. I'll send them a few bob from my wages next week, that'll help.'

Delia was wildly excited at seeing her dad again. She clung round his neck like a little leech, refusing to be parted from him. Even when he protested that she was such a big girl now that it was breaking his back to have to carry her round with him she took no notice. She continued to hug and kiss him and tell him how much she had missed him.

'While you two enjoy each other's company I'll nip down and let the Parkers know that I'm back and that I can start work tomorrow,' Karyn told him as soon as she'd drunk the cup of tea she'd made the moment she got in.

'Go on, then, and I'll pop out to the shops with Delia for some fish and chips. I'm starving and by the time we've eaten that it will be time for me to get changed and ready for work tonight.'

Karyn was sitting at the table with tears streaming down her face when Tudor and Delia returned with the fish and chips.

Tudor stared at her in alarm. Dumping the package he was carrying on to the table, he pulled her into his arms, stroking her hair back from her face and asking her what was the matter.

There was genuine concern in his voice. 'You seemed fine when you arrived back, cariad, what's happened to upset you like this?'

Karyn tried to tell him, but the words were choked by her sobs. Frightened because she couldn't understand what was going on, Delia also started to cry, but for once Tudor ignored her and gave all his attention to Karyn.

'Was it something Llew Parker said?'

Karyn nodded, her sobs growing louder.

Tudor looked bewildered. 'Why? What on earth did he say to upset you so much?'

With an effort Karyn controlled herself long enough to gulp out, 'They don't want me . . . my job's gone.'

'Gone?' Tudor looked puzzled. 'It can't be! They haven't taken on anyone else.'

'They're not going to, they say they can't afford a barmaid any more.'

The colour drained from Tudor's face. 'Duw anwyl! They never breathed a word of this to me.'

Karyn raised a tear-stained face to his. 'Whatever are we going to do?' she whispered.

Tudor pursed his mouth into a silent whistle. 'We'll manage,' he assured her. 'Don't worry about it, cariad. Let's sit down and eat these fish and chips and then see if we can work something out. Come on, they cost money, so we can't afford to waste them,' he added with a forced laugh as he lifted Delia on to a chair and began sharing out the food between the three of them.

They ate in silence and the moment Tudor finished he dashed off to get ready for his evening stint. 'Wouldn't do to be late,' he said, grimacing as he gave Karyn a hasty kiss and ruffled Delia's hair. 'I don't want to give them any reason for sacking me, now do I?' He smiled as he made for the door.

Karyn sat for a long time after he'd left, turning things over in her own mind about what they should do. The only solution she could see was to try and find another job as a barmaid or some other kind of work that she could do during the day while Tudor looked after Delia.

I can probably get something that pays much better than the money the Parkers have paid me, she told herself hopefully as she cleared the table and washed up.

Delia was enjoying herself playing with all the toys she had missed while she'd been in Pen-y-llyn and didn't want to go to bed, but Karyn was insistent.

'I'm tired even if you're not, and I have to be up early tomorrow morning,' she said firmly.

Finding another job proved impossible for Karyn. Business was not brisk and shopkeepers and publicans alike were more interested in cutting back, not taking on any new staff. Even Currans, one of the largest factories in the area, had no vacancies at all.

'We'll be able to manage, so stop worrying,' Tudor told her confidently.

Karyn wasn't so sure. If the Parkers were cutting back then Tudor might well be next on their list.

When she told him this he laughed. 'No, I bring in the customers,' he boasted, 'they wouldn't dare sack me.'

'I hope you're right, but I'm still not certain that can we manage without my money.'

'I've already told you we can. We'll pull in our horns a bit. I'll give up ciggies for a start.'

After that the pattern of their lives seemed to be back to normal except that Karyn had all the time in the world to do her cleaning, shopping and caring for their home. They'd worked hard to make it comfortable and now she took pleasure in making some new curtains and matching cushions for the living room.

In spite of Karyn's protests that she would rather Delia was safely at home with her, Tudor still insisted on taking Delia out every day just as he had always done.

'I can't help worrying after what happened

down at the canal in case anything like that happens again.'

'Of course it won't,' Tudor blustered. 'I've been taking her out ever since she was a tiny baby.'

'Yes, I know what a good father you've always been, but Delia could have died!'

'You can't change everything because of one accident,' he protested. 'Going out with me is a way of life for her. She enjoys it.'

Delia added her own pleading, but when Karyn offered to come along with them she became sulky, stamping her foot and saying that she wanted her daddy to herself.

Tudor took her side over this and told Karyn to dress her up and make her look special in one of the pretty little dresses he'd bought for her the summer before.

'She can't wear those,' Karyn protested, 'they're too short for her now. She's grown since last year . . .'

'Well, that's too bad because we can't afford to lash out on any new ones, not at the moment, anyway, so they'll have to do,' he told her abruptly.

'I like my pretty dresses,' Delia giggled excitedly and ran to fetch them. When Karyn held them up against her to see how short they were, and tried to persuade her to keep on the dress she was wearing, Delia pouted and stamped her foot. She created such a scene that Tudor intervened.

'Duw anwyl, what's the matter with you, woman?' he railed at Karyn. 'She looks lovely in her little frilly dresses, so put one of them on her. I'm the one taking her out and if I like to see her in then, what the hell does it matter what other people think?'

Karyn felt too defeated to argue. She felt almost jealous as the pair of them set off so happily hand-in-hand out into the bright May sunshine.

Nothing had gone right for her since the accident when Delia had fallen into the canal, she reflected as she tidied up. She wished she could have stayed on with her mam and dad, but they had their own problems. As they had feared the miner's strike had happened and no one seemed to know how long it was going to last. It wasn't simply the miners who'd come out, other unions had offered their support and now it was classified as a General Strike. It was already affecting the shipping in Cardiff as well as in most of the other ports throughout the country.

'The dockers are being stood off as well as the miners so they haven't the money in their pockets to spend on beer,' had been Marged Parker's excuse for sacking her. 'That's why we had to take steps to reduce our overheads and why we decided that you were the one we could best manage without,' she'd explained.

Karyn felt so depressed that she decided she had to do something to cheer herself up because she knew she was making life hell for both Tudor and Delia with her moods.

She paced the room restlessly. If only they would let her go out with them occasionally. Delia always seemed so tired when they came home that she was sure Tudor must be walking her too far for her little legs. These days, she noticed that in the evenings, after Tudor had gone to work, when she offered to take Delia to the park in Loudon Square or to Grange Gardens, she always said no. Karyn wondered if it was because of the accident and remembering them being in the water together, and because she was afraid it might happen again.

I'm going mental thinking silly things like that, she thought agitatedly. She leaned on the window sill, looking out at the sunny world outside, and felt like a prisoner shut up in their attic rooms.

'Why don't I go out? Anything is better than being cooped up here when the sun is shining,' she told herself out loud.

She decided to go up to the Hayes. She had no money to spend, but you didn't need money to look around. She might even walk along St Mary's Street where all the posh shops were and pretend she could buy anything she liked if she wanted to.

Whipping off her apron, she combed her hair and put on her best straw hat and light blue summer coat before she had a chance to change her mind.

A tram was just pulling away from Clarence Road and in a matter of minutes she was on it and they were rattling their way towards the city centre.

As she wandered along St Mary's Street, idly looking in the windows of James Howell's at the lovely summer outfits on display, she felt a great deal more optimistic even though the news-vendors' placards carried headlines about the miner's strike.

A crowd was gathered at the entrance of Morgan's Arcade and her heart pounded as she heard a man singing, a strong powerful baritone voice as rich as dark treacle; a voice she knew so well that it felt like a part of her.

Unable to believe her ears, she elbowed her way through the crowd then gasped out loud. It was Tudor! He was singing his heart out, but what startled her even more was seeing Delia there. She had a piece of card round her neck and written on it were the words: *Please help my daddy; he's an out-of-work miner.*

Delia was walking around holding Tudor's trilby in her two little hands and people were tossing coins into it.

With Tudor's rich baritone voice still ringing in her ears, Karyn drew back into the shelter of a shop doorway, covering her face with her hands and praying that neither of them had spotted her. She didn't think they had, they were both too intent on what they were doing.

She didn't know what to think, her mind was

in such a whirl. All she knew was that it was like a bad dream and she wanted to get away from the Arcade and to try and forget what she had seen.

She walked so fast that she was breathless by the time she reached the Hayes. There was no sign of a tram so she went on walking, down Wood Street into Penarth Road, and then along the Taff Embankment. She had reached Clarence Road Bridge before she realised that she had walked all the way home.

Back in the safety of their rooms she paced backwards and forwards trying to come to terms with what she had witnessed. After half an hour she was still no nearer to working out what she should do, or say, when Tudor and Delia returned home.

The problem was beyond her. To pose as a miner! She couldn't believe it. His dad would have felt so humiliated. Involving Delia in his misrepresentation was unforgivable. She felt mortified, it was little better than begging.

She made herself a cup of tea. Strong, sweet tea was good for shock, she told herself.

She sat with both hands clasped round the cup, trying to decide what to do. The sensible thing, she reasoned, was to let Tudor tell her himself, when he was good and ready. Until then, perhaps it was best if she said nothing. She didn't like what he was doing, but since she'd lost her job it was probably his way of trying to make some extra money. She shuddered; if only he hadn't involved Delia and hung that awful card around her little neck. Yet without her it was unlikely that he'd collect very much, she reflected ruefully.

Tudor Morgan finished his repertoire and bowed to the crowd. Then he took his trilby from Delia and transferred the contents to his pocket before taking her hand and walking away.

He went into a café halfway along the Arcade and ordered a cup of tea for himself and a milk shake for Delia before setting off for their second session of the day.

It was a brilliant way of earning money, he reflected. Delia had taken to the idea of going round with his hat like the little trooper she was. They could earn more money in one day than Karyn had earned in a week as a barmaid, only he couldn't tell her that. He was pretty sure that she would be furious if she got an inkling of what he was doing.

He'd wait for Delia to finish her drink, then he'd move on for another half-hour's singing before going home. Going to a different venue was a precaution just in case anyone reported him to the authorities for what he was doing.

It also meant that since it was an entirely different crowd of people who would gather he could repeat the songs he had already been singing.

Delia was not always too happy with the

arrangement. She seemed to enjoy their first session, but after that she often complained that she was tired, but the promise of a little treat soon won her round.

'Come on, cariad,' he said, holding out his hand. 'Your milkshake is all gone. Half an hour singing and then we'll go home.'

Tudor was in full stretch, delighting the crowd with his rendering of 'Look for the Silver Lining', one of the most popular songs of the day, when a heavy hand rested firmly on his shoulder and a voice almost as dark as his own said, 'I'm arresting you.'

He tried to protest, saying that he was only entertaining the crowd for a bit of fun. He even thought he was getting away with it and reflected that he probably would have done, but at that moment Delia came running up to him with his trilby half full of the coins that she had been collecting.

Frowning, the policeman reached out and took hold of the card hanging round her neck and read the inscription aloud, his eyebrows rising as he did so.

After that Tudor knew that there was no point in making any more excuses so he went with them quietly, carrying Delia in his arms and trying to explain to her why they couldn't go home yet.

Karyn felt apprehensive when Tudor and Delia failed to come home at their usual time. She'd laid the table ready for their meal and as the time went by she became increasingly worried because it meant that Tudor was going to be late going down into the Voyager.

By six o'clock, she was convinced that there was something drastically wrong and when there was a sharp rap at the door and she heard Marged Parker's voice calling out to her, waves of panic swept over her.

She was shaking as she opened the door, trying desperately to think what to say to account for Tudor's absence. Marged spoke before she could utter a word.

Waving a copy of the *South Wales Echo* she advanced menacingly into the room. She was extremely angry and was talking so loud and so fast that Karyn couldn't understand what she was saying. As Marged thrust the newspaper at her Karyn saw the glaring headline and her heart almost stopped:

MAN POSING AS OUT-OF-WORK
MINER ARRESTED IN MORGAN'S
ARCADE FOR BEGGING

The printed words underneath danced like a mist before her eyes but it was the picture of Delia holding out Tudor's trilby and someone dropping a coin into it that seared into her brain.

'That's it!' Marged shrilled. 'He's finished here. We don't employ beggars. The nerve of the man! Damnio di! How could you let him involve that poor little mite in something so degrading? A fine mother you are!'

Karyn stared at her blankly. She had no explanation. To say that she knew nothing about what Tudor was up to seemed to be too feeble an excuse to even voice aloud; she could only shake her head in utter despair.

Chapter Thirteen

It was well after nine o' clock before Tudor arrived home tired and dishevelled. He was carrying Delia in his arms and her little white face was streaked with tears.

As they came into the room Delia held out her arms to her mother and when Karyn took her from Tudor and held her close Delia buried her face in Karyn's neck and started sobbing.

The newspaper that Marged Parker had brought upstairs earlier in the evening was on the table and Karyn saw Tudor stiffen as he spotted the glaring headlines.

'So you know what happened, do you?'

'Marged Parker brought the paper up, but . . .'

He waved her to silence before she could tell him that she had been in the city centre earlier in the day and had witnessed for herself what he had been doing.

'You don't want to believe that rubbish. Newspaper talk, that's all it is.' He gave a sharp laugh. 'You know how they like to make things as sensational as they can. It's what sells their papers.'

'Maybe, but I . . .'

Again Karyn tried to tell him that she had

been in Morgan's Arcade that afternoon and had seen what he was up to with her own eyes, but before she could do so there was a rap on the door.

'Who the hell's that!' Tudor muttered irritably as he strode across the room. His scowl changed to a polite smile when he opened the door and saw that it was Marged Parker.

'Looking for me are you?' he exclaimed jovially. 'Sorry if I'm a bit late, a family problem to sort out, but I'll be down in two seconds.'

'You needn't bother!' She pointed at the newspaper. 'I suppose that was the family business, was it?' she said coldly.

'You don't believe everything you read in the papers, surely,' Tudor blustered.

'One of our customers saw you ... and it wasn't the first time. He said he'd seen you singing there more than once. Using that poor innocent little child in such a despicable way, you ought to be thoroughly ashamed of yourself.'

Tudor spread his hands helplessly. 'I needed the money, see, Marged. After all,' he added slyly, 'you did sack Karyn so how did you expect us to manage on the pittance you pay me for entertaining your customers every night?'

Karyn saw Marged's face flush furiously and placed a restraining hand on Tudor's arm to try and stop him from saying anything more, but he shook her off angrily.

'What we pay you is far more than you are worth,' Marged told him cuttingly. 'What is more,' she went on relentlessly, 'we don't want the Voyager to be linked with criminal activities.'

'Don't worry, it hasn't been. If you'd read that report right through,' he went on, picking up the paper and waving it in front of her face, 'you would have seen that I gave my home address as Clydach Road, Pen-y-llyn, not this place.'

'You did what!' Karyn's voice quavered with fury. 'You told the police that you lived in Pen-y-llyn?'

Tudor looked uncomfortable. 'Well, I could hardly convince them that I was an out-of-work miner if I was living in a pub in Tiger Bay, now could I?' he blustered.

'Your mam, though, Tudor! She'll be so ashamed and humiliated that you could do such a thing.'

'She'll probably never even see the paper!'

'Of course she will! Someone in Clydach Street is bound to show it to her.'

'Yes, your mam and dad, no doubt,' he sneered.

'Tudor! That's a despicable thing to say.'

'Can you two stop bickering until after I've said my piece?' Marged Parker interrupted.

'Get off my back both of you,' Tudor said wearily. 'I've already told you, Marged, that I'll be down in a couple of minutes.'

'We don't need you, Tudor. We don't want you singing in the bar any more and we don't want you living here any longer either, so pack your things, the pair of you, and get out,' she added coldly as she backed towards the door.

'Hold on, you can't do this!' Tudor roared. 'Where the hell can we go?'

Marged shrugged. 'You could go back to the address in Pen-y-llyn that you gave to the police,' she said waspishly. 'Anyway, that's your problem, but we want you out of here before midnight so you'd better get a move on.'

'Do you think she really means it?' Karyn panicked as the door slammed behind Marged.

'No, of course she doesn't. She's just trying to frighten us. A bit annoyed because I'm late. People have probably been pestering her, wondering where I am. Quiet in the bar without me singing, see. I'd better get down there right away. You can manage to put Delia to bed, can't you? Whacked, she is, after such an adventurous day.'

Before Karyn could protest he dropped a fleeting kiss on the top of her head and was gone.

'Come on, my precious,' she said softly as Delia stirred uneasily in her arms, 'let's get you off to bed, then.'

As she lowered the sleeping child into her cot she heard the living room door slam open and then crash shut.

With her heart in her mouth, she rushed to

see what was happening. Tudor stood there, slamming a fist into the palm of his other hand over and over again. His face was almost as white as Delia's had been when they'd arrived home.

'What's happened now, what's the matter?'

'She meant it! They want us out. Now! Tonight!'

'We can't go tonight,' Karyn protested. 'I've just settled Delia to sleep.'

'They mean it, Karyn, they want us out before midnight,' he repeated exasperatedly.

'I'll go and talk to them, I'll tell them we'll go first thing in the morning. I'm sure they'll agree to that if I ask them nicely.'

'You mean you intend to go and plead with those two buggers,' he sneered.

She shrugged. 'What else can we do? We can't walk the streets. If they let us stay here tonight, then tomorrow, bright and early, you can go and find us a room somewhere.'

'You think we'd better stay here in Cardiff?'

'We haven't any option, boyo,' Karyn said bitterly. 'They certainly won't welcome us back in Pen-y-llyn.'

Finding somewhere else to live was not easy. News about what Tudor had been caught doing had spread through Tiger Bay and even the most notorious villains were disgusted by him pretending to be an out-of-work miner.

Llew Parker had given them until midday to

165

be clear of the Voyager. 'If you're not out by then I shall dump your belongings on the pavement,' he warned. 'You may have pulled the wool over the eyes of the police and managed to get let off with a caution, but nothing you say will have any effect on me.'

'Everything is packed,' Karyn told him, 'Tudor is out scouting around now trying to find us a place.'

'Midday! That's my last word,' Llew Parker said grimly.

Karyn was so on edge that the address barely registered when Tudor finally returned and said that there was a man with a handcart outside waiting to move their belongings to a room at a house in Mount Stuart Square. Strapping Delia into her pushchair she followed blindly behind Tudor and the man with the cart.

When they reached Clarence Road Bridge and took a path that led along one of the banks of the Glamorgan canal she shivered at the memory of what had happened there only a few months earlier. Surely they could have found another route, she thought bitterly, not one that stirred up such frightening memories for her and Delia.

She breathed a sigh of relief when they left the canal path and turned into Mount Stuart Square, then her fear mounted again as they turned down a grimy alley that led to the back of a tall office building.

When they stopped, Tudor indicated some

broken steps leading down to what looked like a cellar. As they went down into a dank, basement room she clamped her hand over her mouth to stop herself from protesting out loud as something dark and furry scampered over her feet. She looked round her in disbelief: there was mould on the walls, and there were spiders' webs in the corners and mice droppings on the floor. The smell of cockroaches filled the musty air. There was one small window which was on a level with the pavement outside, and the glass in it was badly cracked.

A sagging double bed occupied one side of the room; a rickety table, two wooden chairs and a battered couch were on the other side. Grey ash spewed from the small iron grate, and on the mantelpiece was an oil lamp with a smoke-stained glass chimney.

'We can't move our things in here,' Karyn protested as Tudor and the man helping him began to unpack the handcart. 'Look at it; the place is absolutely filthy!'

The man paused, pushed back his greasy cap and looked questioningly at Tudor.

'Take no notice. Get on with it, mun, and get our things inside,' Tudor told him curtly, shoving Karyn to one side.

'For heaven's sake stop Delia crying,' he said turning back to Karyn. 'Take her for a walk or do something to keep her out of the way. We're paying this chap for his time so I want to get done here as fast as I can. Once he's gone I'll

167

clean the place up a bit and then you can get things straight.'

Without a word Karyn turned the pushchair round and made her way back into the front of Mount Stuart Square where the imposing Georgian houses and offices, with their polished name plates on the door, bore no resemblance at all to the cellar they were now going to call home. She stared in awe at the mighty Coal Exchange building and the officious-looking men in dark suits, bowler hats and smart spats as they dashed from there to the Cambrian Buildings, or to one of the several banks. She felt so out of place. A few of them looked at her, as if wondering what a shabby-looking woman wearing a cotton summer dress and a straw hat, with a small child in a push chair, was doing in their business environment.

Most of them, though, took not the slightest notice of her and she found herself wondering where they lived. It was certainly not in one the cellars beneath their grand buildings. They probably don't even know such places exist, she thought bitterly as she passed by the gleaming stone steps with their shiny handrails leading up to plate-glass doors.

Even though there was a full-scale miners' strike in progress the immense Coal Board Offices had a pristine splendour. Their appearance was so very different from the coal-grimed pitheads or the terraces of miners' houses around Pen-y-llyn.

168

Thoughts of her home brought tears to her eyes and she wished with all her being that she was back there. Her life had been so carefree while she'd been growing up, but those days had gone for ever.

Then she remembered that her own dad would be on strike and her mam would be struggling to manage on what little savings they had. Tudor's mam would be in a similar fix. Griff would be out of work and Olwyn would be pinching and scraping to make every penny do the work of five to make ends meet and keep their three growing children from starving.

The cellar was not only dreary, but so damp and cramped that after their very first night Karyn vowed that she didn't intend to live there a moment longer than they had to.

Once they had put up Delia's cot there was so little space left that they could barely move around and what was even more unsettling was that there was no space for Delia to play with any of her toys.

The situation became worse, not better, over the next few days. Tudor no longer took Delia out each day as he had done when they'd lived over the Voyager. He insisted on going out on his own because, he said, he needed to try and find work and he could hardly do that if he had a small child in tow.

When he came back with a pocketful of small

change Karyn was afraid that he'd been singing in the arcades again but he always insisted that he hadn't.

'Duw anwyl, do you think I'm mad, girl? If I show my face back there the bobbies will be on me like a ton of bricks. Next time it won't be a caution, next time I'll go down. Three months at least! They told me that when they had me at the station that first time.'

'So how are you earning money, then?' she asked suspiciously.

'Singing, of course! It's my life, the only thing I'm good at; the only thing I want to do. Pubs, clubs, anywhere they'll let me, but not out in the street.'

Karyn sighed. 'One day you'll be discovered and your name will be up in lights,' she promised.

He took her into his arms and buried his face in her hair. 'I'm not happy about living in this hell hole any more than you are. It's not what I want for you and little Delia. Look, cariad, why don't the two of you go back to Pen-y-llyn. Your mam'll have you; she'll welcome you with open arms.'

Karyn shook her head, 'I'm not sure she will. With this strike on my dad will be out of work, remember.'

He nodded. 'I've thought of that, but you'd be better off with them than you are here with me. I thought that perhaps you could get some sort of a job? Temporary like, I mean.'

'It would be much easier to get a job down here in Cardiff than back there,' she said thoughtfully. 'You could look after Delia, like you did when we were at the Voyager.'

'And what about my singing?'

'Let me find a job and then see how the hours work out. If I can work in the daytime, and you can go out round the clubs and pubs singing in the evenings, then we'll soon be able to move out of here to something better.'

Even though she was now free to do whatever hours were asked of her Karyn still found it was impossible to get a job. The strike was becoming ever more widespread and was affecting trade. Shops were closing, factories cutting back and those who had a job of any sort were hanging on to it.

She tried all the local shops and factories and then began to look further afield. She knew she would never get taken on as a shop assistant in any of the big shops, but there were other jobs like cleaning or even washing up that she was prepared to do.

She was determined not to give up, but the day she saw the miners from the valleys carrying their banners and marching through St Mary Street tears of despair misted her eyes. As she stood on the edge of the pavement watching them pass by, she felt her courage waning. It seemed to her as though the entire world was plunged into misery and despair.

A voice from the marching men, someone

calling out to her by name, caught her attention.

'Griff! Griff Baker, what are you doing here!' she gasped.

He detached himself from the rest of the column and came over to her. 'Thank God I've spotted you, Karyn. Your mam asked me to keep an eye out for you. It's your dad, see. Not well at all, he isn't. Your mam's beside herself, worried out of her mind.'

'Then why didn't she write and tell me?'

'She did, but when you didn't answer she thought you had enough troubles of your own. We'd seen in the newspaper about Tudor. Not got himself locked up, has he?'

'No, no. It was nothing as bad as that. They let him off with a caution.'

'So didn't you get your mam's letter?'

Karyn shook her head. 'We've had to move. They didn't want us at the Voyager after what happened. Mam's letter must have gone there, see.'

Griff nodded understandingly. 'I must go, girl. Do you want me to tell your mam that you'll be in touch?'

Karyn hesitated. 'No, say nothing. Don't raise her hopes. I will do my best to come home,' she promised. 'I'll have to wait and see what Tudor says, though.'

Griff nodded understandingly. 'I must go, cariad.'

'Thanks, anyway, Griff,' she called after him

as he broke into a loping run in an attempt to catch up with the tail end of the marchers.

All the way back to Mount Stuart Square she went over and over in her mind what Griff had told her. The thought of her father being ill and her mother needing her made her long to be with them and do what she could to help. She wished Griff had been able to stop and talk and tell her more, but she understood that he needed to get back with the rest of the marching miners.

Tudor had suggested that she should go home for a while when they had first moved into Mount Stuart Square, she reminded herself, so why not do so? Delia was not only very unhappy in their new living quarters, but she'd had a chesty cold ever since they'd been living in such squalid conditions because it was so damp.

'Looking for you, was he?' Tudor scowled when she arrived home and told him about seeing Griff.

'Yes, as a matter of fact he was. It seems my dad's not well. My mam wrote to tell me, but the letter must have gone to the Voyager. Griff seemed to think she needed me.'

'So what are you going to do?'

'We could go back to Pen-y-llyn,' she said tentatively.

Tudor shook his head doubtfully. 'Now that they've heard what happened and know that I was picked up by the police, my mam won't even give me the time of day.'

173

'Griff said that they had seen the newspapers and they know all about it,' she confirmed.

'Well, there you are, then, no point in showing our noses back there then, is there!'

'My dad's ill and my mam needs me . . .'

'Then go,' Tudor urged, 'and take Delia with you. I told you when we first moved in here to go back home to your mam, so why don't you do so?'

'What about you? I'd feel better about things if you were coming with me. I can't bear to think of you staying here on your own; not in this hovel.'

Tudor shrugged. 'Don't worry about me, cariad, this will do me for the moment.'

'I really don't like the idea of leaving you behind,' Karyn protested, a worried look on her face.

He took her into his arms, stroking her hair tenderly. 'I'll be all right, cariad,' he said confidently. 'It's somewhere to put my head down at night and that's all I need. I'll be out most of the time singing. It will be a load off my mind to know that you and little Delia are somewhere safe and comfortable. I'll try and send some money.' He reached into his trouser pocket and brought out a handful of silver coins and handed them to her. 'There's enough here for your train fare and for you to give your mam something towards your keep.'

Chapter Fourteen

Karyn was shocked at how washed-out and unwell her mother looked. She had always been a small, neat person, but she seemed to have shrunk to half her normal size. Her face was deeply lined and there were dark rings under her eyes.

'Mam, I've only just heard that Da has been ill, but what about you? You look ill, too,' she exclaimed as they hugged and kissed each other.

'I'm all right, cariad. Worn out looking after your dad, that's all, and worrying when you didn't answer my letter.'

Karyn bit her lip. 'I'm afraid I never received it. We've moved, see!' she said hesitantly.

'Yes.' Her mother nodded. 'Griff told me. Turned you out of that pub place, did they? I thought that might happen,' she added. 'As soon as I saw that account in the paper about what Tudor had been up to I guessed it would spell trouble. Come on, the kettle's boiling so you can tell me all about it over a cup of tea.'

'I think I ought to see my dad first,' Karyn said gently.

'Go on up and see him, then. Leave Delia

here with me, I'll find her a biscuit,' she added, taking the child by the hand and moving towards the kitchen.

Karyn was upset to discover that her father looked even worse than her mother did. He'd not only lost weight, but he also seemed to be so frail that it frightened her.

As she bent down and kissed him he grabbed hold of her hand and held it tightly between both of his own. 'Stay with us for a while, Karyn,' he wheezed hoarsely. 'Your mam needs you.'

'I will. I'll be staying to help her all I can until you are better,' she assured him.

'I'm pleased to hear that because she's utterly worn out.' He sighed exhaustedly as he lay back against the pillows and closed his eyes.

Karyn tiptoed out of the room and went back downstairs. Her mother had brewed the tea and Delia was munching a biscuit and chattering away happily.

'Delia has been telling me about your new home,' Enid said, raising her eyebrows.

'It's only a temporary arrangement,' Karyn said non-committally.

'Things are pretty bad, are they?'

Karyn shook her head and frowned in Delia's direction. 'Perhaps it would be a good idea if I took Delia next door to see her other nanny,' she said brightly.

'Daddy's mammy is my granny, I'm with my nanny now,' Delia interrupted.

'Yes, you're quite right, it is your granny who

lives next door,' Karyn agreed. She looked at her mother. 'I'll be back in a jiffy and then we'll have a chat.'

'So you've come home to help your mam, have you?' Bronwen greeted her. 'Our Griff said he'd seen you when he went down to Cardiff on that march they had, and that he'd managed to have a word with you. He said you'd moved out from the pub. You're still staying in Cardiff, though?'

'Yes, that's right. I'll be back later and will tell you all about it. Delia wanted to see you on her own. I'll leave her with you for half an hour, shall I?'

'You mean you want her out of the way so that you can explain to your mam what's been going on,' Bronwen sniffed critically. 'Come on, cariad.' She held a hand out to Delia. 'Come on, my lovely; let's see what special treat Granny can find for you.'

Enid Pryce listened in silence, but shook her head from time to time at her daughter's account of what had happened since the police had arrested Tudor for busking in Cardiff.

'It's a wonder he managed to get away with it,' she commented when Karyn paused to drink her tea.

'Well, he didn't really, did he! They took both him and little Delia to the police station . . .'

'They didn't lock him away, though!' Enid declared, dunking a biscuit in her tea.

'No, but they gave him a caution before they let him go. I was out of my mind when he didn't come home until after nine o'clock that night, I can tell you.'

'We never did like the idea of you living over a pub anyway,' her mother told her.

'It was a much better place than where we are now.' Karyn shuddered. 'It's a room down in a cellar, mam. There are mice, rats and every sort of bugs imaginable.'

'You're here now, my lovely, so put it all out of your head and see if you can forget about it,' her mother murmured, pushing the plate of biscuits towards Karyn.

'Yes, I'll try,' Karyn agreed. 'I'm more worried about you two at the moment than anything else.'

'Well,' Enid sighed, 'it's your dad's chest that is so bad. The doctor thinks it is silicosis. He should have done as I wanted him to do years ago and asked them to give him a job up on the surface, as far from the old coal dust as he could get.'

'Being a miner is his life, Mam.'

'I know that. And, given time, it will be his death and he'll be six foot under, the same as poor Madoc Morgan.'

'That's different altogether, Mam. Tudor's dad was killed in an explosion.'

'Explosion, silicosis, what's the difference? The mine claims them all sooner or later. Sometimes I think it's better to go in an explosion. It's all over in a flash. There's no lingering illness, no watching death creeping up on you.'

'What about those who survive and are so badly injured that they can't work again?'

Enid Price shook her head, rocking backwards and forwards in her chair, her thin arms wrapped round her own body as though trying to hold in her unhappiness.

'Mam! It's not like you to talk like this,' Karyn said in a startled voice. 'Da's illness has got to you. He's on the mend now, though. Give it a week or two and he'll be back on his feet, you'll see.'

'Yes, he'll be fine until he has another attack,' she agreed gloomily.

'It's you who needs looking after,' Karyn told her warmly. 'You're feeling depressed because you're worn out with taking care of him, but I'm here now so you can take things easy.'

Enid smiled wanly and patted Karyn's arm. 'I'll brighten up now with little Delia here to amuse me with her chatter. Right little tonic she'll be.'

'Yes, and you must go out for a walk in the sunshine with her each day, remember, because I'll be here to keep an eye on my da,' Karyn insisted.

'Simply knowing you are both here safe and sound has made me feel better already,' her mother assured her. 'Now you go and collect young Delia from Bronwen's place while I see what I can rustle up for us all to eat.'

'Would it be all right if I sent Delia back on her own and stayed and had a chat with Tudor's mam? I think she must be worried about how he is after what she read in the newspaper, the same as you were about me.'

'Yes, do that. Better to clear the air now, right at the start of your visit,' Enid agreed.

Karyn found that Bronwen was not as easily placated as her own mother had been.

'So that son of mine is afraid to come and face me himself,' she said harshly. 'Impersonating a miner and saying he was on strike! I'd strike *him* if he was within reach, I can tell you. Enough to make my Madoc turn in his grave. Insult to the miners, saying that he was one of them! He's never been down the pit in his life! I sometimes wonder if he isn't a great coward and afraid of the dark as well as hard work.'

'That's rubbish! He saw what happened to all the men around here who went to work down the pit and that's why he didn't want to go down the pit,' Karyn defended.

'Duw anwyl! Talk sense, cariad. It's the way of life for the menfolk around here.'

'Yes, and look what it does to them. You've lost your husband and my mam has my dad sick in bed and all because of the old mine,' Karyn pointed out furiously.

Their argument became so heated that Karyn was almost in tears. Bronwen refused to accept that Tudor would ever make a decent living singing and kept repeating how ashamed she'd been to read in the paper that he had been picked up by the police for fraud because he'd been impersonating a miner.

'That's not the worst of it though, is it?' Bronwen said, her face red with anger. 'Taking that poor little child with him and getting her to go round with his hat. I still can't believe that he would stoop so low. Come to that,' she stormed, staring angrily at Karyn, 'where were you in all this? Why weren't you looking after Delia? Why did you let him take her along with him in the first place?'

'Tudor always took her out every day, it started when I was working in the pub as a barmaid,' Karyn reminded her.

'So what was all that gab about him earning a living singing when the pair of you came here before?'

'Tudor was singing, in the pub at night and I worked in the bar at midday and again for a couple of hours in the early evening while Tudor looked after Delia.'

'Singing!' Bronwen Morgan exclaimed scornfully. 'That's no way for a man to earn a living.'

'You won't say that when you see his name up in lights outside a theatre.'

'Up in lights outside the jail, more likely!' Bronwen chortled. 'What's he doing now, then? Griff said something about you being kicked out of the pub when he got into trouble and that there was all that scandal.'

Karyn hesitated for a moment. 'Yes we were,' she admitted, 'and out of the rooms where we were living.'

Bronwen's jowls trembled. 'So what happened after that?'

'We . . . we moved into a room in a cellar in Mount Stuart Square. It was all we could get.'

'Or afford!' Bronwen Morgan added tartly.

'Yes, you're quite right. It's only temporary, though. We will find somewhere else, give us time.'

'I was right you know, cariad.' Bronwen sighed. 'The two of you should never have married when you did. My Tudor was only a boy, no idea about what it cost to keep a family, or the responsibility he was taking on.'

'That'll do!' Karyn's face flamed. 'Tudor is a wonderful dad, he adores little Delia and he looks after her better than I do,' she added vehemently.

'That's as maybe, and so he should when you are the only one who panders to this whim of his about being a singer.'

'So you're blaming me for all this, are you?'

'No, my lovely, of course I'm not. Little brick you've been and no mistake. I'm glad you are here now with your mam, though. She's hit a rough patch and she needs you. Do her and your dad a power of good having you home for a bit. Do Tudor good and all to have to fend for himself for a while,' she added tersely.

* * *

Being back home in Clydach Street was doing her good too, Karyn realised at the end of a fortnight. Her father was up and about again and her mother had lost her weary, drawn look and was much more like the lively, happy person she'd always been.

The weather was warm and sunny, so most days the three of them took Delia to the park so that she could play on the swings there.

Her father was still concerned about what was happening in the country. Apart from the miners, the rest of the men involved in the General Strike were back at work and slowly things were returning to normal.

On the one hand Enid Pryce welcomed this news, but because the local pit was still at a standstill she knew Owen was fretting about being out of work because they both knew that they couldn't manage much longer without any money coming in.

Bronwen was already in dire straits and very often they heard Olwyn's children crying long after they'd been put to bed because they were hungry. Most days Griff went up to the pit face, along with many of the other out-of-work miners in Pen-y-llyn. There they would rake over the slag heaps to try and find enough nuggets of coal to keep their fires alive long enough to boil a kettle and simmer a pot of cawl made mostly out of vegetables. At the weekends they scrounged scrag ends of meat from the butcher which they vowed they would pay for as soon as they were back at work.

Karyn felt guilty because she was not able to offer either her mother or her mother-in-law any money to help them out. She was young and fit and she felt it was her duty to do so.

Finally, she took her courage in both hands and asked her mother if she could leave Delia with her so that she could go back to Cardiff to see if she could find work.

Enid hesitated, but, knowing that her own savings were now all gone, she reluctantly agreed.

'I'll write and tell Tudor and see what he says, then,' Karyn told her.

After a week had passed and there was still no reply from him, she felt both annoyed and puzzled. In the end she took matters into her own hands and decided she would go anyway.

The steps leading down to the cellar in Mount Pleasant Square were piled up with rubbish and old newspapers which had blown in there while she'd been gone and Tudor hadn't bothered to clear away. As she pushed open the door an angry voice called out asking her what the hell she wanted.

'Who are you?' she demanded, her heart thundering as an elderly unshaven man, dirty and dressed in rags, a whisky bottle in his hand, tottered across the room towards her.

'Who are you? she repeated. 'What are you

doing in my home? Where's my husband, where's Tudor Morgan?'

'How the hell should I know that?' he muttered. He lifted the bottle to his lips and took a deep swig. 'He comes and goes, I never know when the bugger is going to be here or where he goes or what he does the rest of the time.'

'When did you last see him?'

The old man tightened the piece of string that was holding his ragged coat together. 'I'm not answering any more of your bloody questions, missus,' he said, pushing past her and stumbling up the steps.

Left on her own, Karyn sat down on one of the wooden chairs and burst into tears. Her head buzzed with questions. How could she possibly stay here in this dirty dank room that reeked of alcohol and heaven knows what else? How could Tudor have tolerated such conditions all this time, and who was the disgusting old man who'd just left and why was he here anyway?

She knew she ought to do something to restore some sort of order to the room and to try and get rid of the filth that had accumulated everywhere. She looked at the stack of dirty dishes and shuddered. She felt it was all so hopeless that she couldn't bring herself to even try to do anything about it.

She was still feeling hopeless when Tudor returned. He was startled to see her there.

'Why didn't you say you were coming back?' he blustered. 'I'd have cleaned the place up, if I'd known.'

'And would you have told that disgusting old man I found in here to get out?'

'Old man?'

'Horrible old fellow, dressed in rags and drinking from a bottle . . .'

'Duw anwyl! You disturbed old Dai while he was dossing down in here, did you?'

'I don't know, you tell me! If that's his name, then he was certainly here when I walked in. He didn't seem to know much about where you were or what time you were coming back.'

'Old liar. Watches this place like a bloody hawk. The minute I go out he comes in and gets his head down. Makes himself scarce though, as soon as I get back.'

'Why don't you put a lock on the door and keep him out? That would stop him coming here!'

He shrugged. 'Don't be twp! How the hell can I? It's his place.'

Karyn stared at him in wide-eyed disbelief. 'Are you saying that even when Delia and me were living here it was really his home?'

Tudor nodded.

'So where was he? I never saw him before today.'

'Inside, doing a stretch. I was only borrowing the room, taking care of it for him, see.' Tudor grinned. 'How the hell did you think I'd managed to find somewhere for us to move into so quickly?'

'So what happens now that I'm back?' Karyn asked in alarm. I'm not living here with him, so don't think I am.'

'Then you'd better go home to Pen-y-llyn again and stay with your mother,' Tudor said balefully.

'I've come back to find work, to earn some money. My da's been ill and they've spent every penny of their savings. They can't afford to keep me and Delia any longer.'

'So it's money you're after, and I thought you'd come back because you couldn't live without me,' Tudor said sarcastically.

'I do want to be with you, Tudor,' she defended. 'Being parted from you has been terrible, so please, don't let us quarrel. Tell me what we are going to do.'

'Ask old Dai if we can stay on here, I suppose,' Tudor muttered, running a hand through his hair.

'No, I'm not living here with him,' Karyn protested. 'Tell him to go and find somewhere else.'

'I've already told you it's his place, so you'll just have to make the best of it.'

'I can't bring Delia back here, not with him living here as well! It's not healthy. He's filthy.'

'Then leave her where she is. You and me can manage. Think of old Dai as a lodger.'

'But there's only one room . . .'

'He'll sleep in the armchair, that's where he always dosses down.'

Karyn drew back in horror. 'Surely you don't expect me to sleep in the same room as him!'

Tudor pulled her towards him, burying his face in her hair and pulling her dress away from her shoulders. 'Come on, my lovely, he's not here now and I've been missing you so much,' he groaned as he pushed her backwards on to the bed, loosening his own clothes as he did so.

'No . . . no . . . leave me alone! Stop it, Tudor!' She panicked. 'He might walk back in here at any minute,' she gasped, fighting him away with both hands.

'Give over, remember you're my wife!' Savagely he grabbed hold of her again, forcing her back on to the bed. 'You've cleared off and left me here on my own for nearly a month so don't try holding out on me, I'm desperate.'

As she looked into his glittering eyes Karyn felt so scared that all the fight went out of her. She felt completely numb as she lay there on the filthy bedcovers, unable to protest any more as Tudor took possession of her.

Her mind felt like cotton wool. This unbelievably savage assault wasn't the sort of loving she and Tudor enjoyed together. She felt degraded, as if she was being abused by a stranger.

Chapter Fifteen

Enid Pryce couldn't believe her eyes when she opened her front door later that same evening and found Karyn standing on the doorstep.

'Duw anwyl! What's happened, girl? What are you doing back here again?' She peered outside. 'Is Tudor with you?'

'Mam! Stop asking so many questions and let me in,' Karyn protested.

'Yes, cariad. Of course! Startled me out of my wits, see. I never dreamed of seeing you again so soon. I'd better go and put the kettle on, hadn't I?'

Over a cup of tea Karyn explained to her mother what had happened when she'd got back to Cardiff. The only thing she didn't tell her about was what had taken place between her and Tudor while she had been at Mount Stuart Square.

It had haunted her all the way back and she'd kept asking herself if it had really happened or if she'd imagined it to be far worse than it was. A shudder went through her; it had all happened so quickly.

Each time she thought about it she felt more and more confused. There'd been no tenderness of any kind between them and, in such terrible surroundings, she'd felt terrified.

Afterwards, she wanted to believe Tudor when he'd tried to tell her that he'd got carried away because he wanted her so desperately and they'd been apart for so long, but it wasn't easy. He'd bridged the thin brief line between love and hate and on the train coming back to Pen-y-llyn for one desperate moment she had even thought about leaving him for good. For Delia's sake she knew that must never happen, so she was determined to try and put the whole episode out of her mind.

What she'd done afterwards also disgusted her so much that she felt her cheeks burning with shame every time she thought about it. She'd waited until Tudor had fallen asleep, then she'd turned out his pockets and taken every penny he possessed. She tried to justify her despicable action by telling herself that he owed it to her. She needed money to pay for her train fare back to Pen-y-llyn, and knowing how desperately hard up her mother was, she was also anxious to pay something towards her keep.

She considered every possibility for their future over and over in her mind long after she was in bed that night. She knew that, despite everything, she still loved Tudor as deeply and desperately as she had always done. She wished he was there beside her. What had happened in Mount Stuart Square, she decided, had been regrettable, but forgivable. Theirs hadn't been merely a childhood romance, it was a lifetime commitment. No matter what happened, the love she felt for him was deep and would last for ever.

Before she fell asleep she resolved that first thing next morning she would write to Tudor to tell him so, and also to explain why she had taken all his money. One thing she was quite determined about, however, was that she would never take Delia back to that awful room in Mount Stuart Square.

He replied a few days later to tell her that Dai had thrown him out and he had moved into a doss house in Bute Street. There were no recriminations about the money she had taken. In fact, he wrote that he would try and send her a few bob each week towards her keep if she wanted to stay on at Pen-y-llyn. His letter ended with a plea that she wouldn't stay away too long because he missed her and Delia so much.

It was Delia who eventually forced Karyn to make a decision. Much as she loved being with her grandparents she kept pestering all of them that she wanted to go to Cardiff to see her daddy until Owen could stand it no longer.

Although he was up and about again and looking quite well, his illness had left him more irritable than they had ever known him to be. He wanted peace and quiet, not a three-year-old moithering him all the time and constantly whining that she wanted her dad.

'I thought you were talking about going home weeks ago?' he remarked to Karyn. 'Young Delia wants to be with her dad and Tudor must also be thinking that it was time you were all together again as a family.'

Realising that her mother had remained silent Karyn accepted that they both thought that it was time for her to go back to Cardiff so she had no option but to write to Tudor and lay it on the line that she couldn't stay at Clydach Street any longer and that he must get them somewhere decent to live.

A week passed before there was a letter back from Tudor to say he'd found a place for them in Adeline Street and that this time it was two rooms and that they were very clean and tidy.

'Well, that's settled, then,' Enid Pryce said with such evident relief that although it was on the tip of Karyn's tongue to say she wanted to go and have a look at the place before she took Delia there she found herself smiling in agreement with her mother.

'There you are, girl, he's doing his best for you,' her mother said encouragingly. 'Adeline Street sounds nice enough. Must be better than that old Square where you were living. That sounded a right dump from what you told me.'

'The room was, Mam, but not Mount Stuart Square. That's where the Coal Board have their offices and the building they're in is really magnificent.'

Enid looked puzzled. 'I thought you said it was dirty and squalid.' she frowned.

'The room we were living in was, but then it was a cellar at the back of a block of offices.' She looked again at Tudor's letter. 'I've never heard of Adeline Street, so I don't even know where it is or how to get there.'

'Then you'd better find out the time of your train and write and ask Tudor to meet you at the station.'

Adeline Street, she discovered, was in Splott, a dockland area that she knew had a reputation almost as bad as Tiger Bay, but Tudor seemed to be so pleased to see her that she said nothing.

The red-brick terraced house looked plain and solid from the outside and the street seemed to be clean and respectable. There was no one about; except for a black and white terrier running from one lamp post to the next, it was deserted.

'We've got the middle room downstairs and the middle bedroom upstairs. We share the scullery with the people living downstairs and there's a lavatory in the yard outside. There's a single bed in the bedroom as well as a double one,' he added as he used a door key to open the front door.

'What's that strange smell?' she wrinkled her nose as they walked down the hall.

'I don't know, something they're cooking, probably. Don't start finding fault before you've even seen the place,' Tudor warned as he led the way into the middle room of the house.

Karyn looked around with interest. It was a fairly large room and at the far end was a glass-panelled door leading into a paved yard. This was the only means of light and Karyn noted that a large mirror in a gilt frame had been hung on the wall facing the door to reflect more light into the room.

'Well, what do you think?' Tudor smiled at her expectantly.

Karyn nodded cautiously.

'Solid table, four chairs, couple of armchairs, a sideboard and a decent-sized firegrate, so what more do you want? There's even a rug on the floor.'

'What about the bedroom, what's that like?'

'Come on upstairs and I'll show you.'

Delia scampered ahead of them up the narrow staircase and then stood at the top looking round, uncertain as to which of the three doors to open.

'That one,' Tudor told her, pointing to the one nearest to them.

The bedroom was immediately over the middle room downstairs and was the same long narrow shape with a window at one end.

Karyn walked over to the double bed and folded back the white honeycomb bedspread. There was a thick blue blanket and a thread-bare green one under it, but she was pleasantly surprised at how clean the white cotton sheet and white slips on the pillows and bolster were. The sheets and covers on the smaller iron bedspread were also very clean and acceptable.

'Satisfied?'

'Yes, it certainly seems a great deal better than the last place.' Karyn smiled appreciatively.

'It should be a lot better, it's costing me a pretty penny in rent, I can tell you. Come on.' He shooed them out of the bedroom and back down the stairs. 'You'd better take a look at the scullery. You'll have to go across the yard to get to it, mind. It's at the back of the kitchen and the people we're renting this place from use it as their main living room.'

'Oh, I see.' Karyn frowned. 'Do the people who own the house also use the scullery as well to do their cooking?'

'Of course they do! Come on, don't turn your nose up like that until you've seen the place. Clean as whistle it is and there's a separate cupboard in there for all our things, and no one else will be using them. Mind you, it would probably be best if you come to some arrangement about when you use the kitchen so that you and Sophia Earl don't get in each other's way.'

Karyn's lips tightened, but she said nothing. As they crossed the yard Tudor started to say something, then stopped abruptly. She saw him shrug his shoulders, almost as if he had asked himself a question and then provided the answer.

When they reached the scullery door, Karyn could see that there was someone already in there. Then she caught her breath as Tudor opened the door and she came face to face with a man and woman who were as black as miners when they first came up to the surface at the end of a shift. The only difference was, she thought in alarm, that the black wouldn't wash off these two.

They weren't the first black people she had seen since she'd been living in Cardiff, but she had never had very much to do with those who came into the Voyager or the ones who were shopkeepers in St James's Street. She had certainly never lived in the same house as any of them before and she felt apprehensive wondering if their ways were very different.

'Karyn, this is Josiah and Sophia Earl,' Tudor introduced them.

The tall, lean man with black goatee beard and big white teeth extended his hand politely. The plump, smiling woman had a shock of black frizzy hair. She threw her arms around Karyn, kissed her on the cheek, and welcomed her with a warm hug.

'And this is our little girl,' Tudor added, propelling Delia towards them.

Ten minutes later and they were all chattering away like old friends and Karyn no longer felt apprehensive. Sophia was enchanted by Delia and kept patting her on the head and making a tremendous fuss of her.

Karyn had to admit that their new home was a tremendous improvement. If only Tudor had a regular job, she thought wistfully, then possibly they could be happy there. As it was they seemed to live a hand-to-mouth existence. He was still determined to have a singing career and he still spent most evenings singing in different clubs and pubs in Tiger Bay. She never knew exactly where he was, but she knew it was no good expecting him home until nearly midnight.

She had grown accustomed to this. What worried her far more was where he spent the rest of the day. He never told her and he no longer took Delia out with him. Instead, he disappeared mid-morning and didn't come back again until four o'clock or even later.

Sometimes when he came home he was in the best of moods and handed her a fistful of money. On other days he was scowling and miserable and snapped at her if she passed any comment or asked where he'd been or what was wrong. He would even push Delia away when she tried to climb on his lap.

Sophia Earl was quick to pick up on this and was always ready with an encouraging word or a reassuring smile.

'Bit of a devil, your Tudor, isn't he?' she commented from time to time, giving Karyn a knowing wink.

Karyn didn't understand what she meant, not until the day the police arrived at the house looking for Tudor.

She listened apprehensively as she heard Sophia telling them that she had no idea where he was or when he would be back.

Once they'd gone Sophia came hurrying in to warn Karyn that they'd be back. 'They've got a warrant for Tudor's arrest so they won't be happy until they find him and take him in.'

'I don't understand . . . what has he done?' Karyn asked.

Sophia ignored her question. 'Try not to worry. I'll send Josiah out to see if he can track Tudor down and warn him that the police have been here,' she promised.

'Yes, but what did they want? What has Tudor done? Why are they after him?'

'You mean you really don't know!' Sophia exclaimed, a look of surprise on her shiny black face. 'He's been gambling again, and if I know anything about it he's been cheating. Well known for it, he is. It's a wonder to me that someone hasn't informed the cops about him long before this.'

Karyn was on tenterhooks for the rest of the day, jumping at every sound. Even Delia sensed that there was something wrong and was unusually quiet.

It was late in the evening before Tudor came home. Having been warned by Josiah Earl that the police were out looking for him he had taken a devious route and found a way through a maze of back alleyways.

'I've got to get away. The police are bound

to come back and if they find me here, they'll take me in,' he told Karyn.

'Sophia says you've been gambling and cheating people out of their money, is that right?'

He shrugged. 'Amongst other things.'

'So why did you come back here, why didn't you hide out somewhere else?'

'I wanted to make sure that you had this,' he told her and, delving down the back of one of the armchairs, he rummaged around, bringing out a grubby leather pouch. 'Here, look after it,' he said, thrusting it towards her.

'What is it?'

'Hush,' he held up a warning hand. 'That sounds like someone coming now,' he said jumpily. 'Stuff it down your blouse out of sight and say nothing.'

She barely had a chance to do so before the door burst open and two uniformed officers stood there.

Tudor didn't even try to escape. With a resigned shrug he picked Delia up and kissed and hugged her.

'Be a good girl for me, cariad,' he told her. 'I've got to go away for a while and I want you to look after your mam until I get back. Understand?'

Setting Delia down on the floor again he took Karyn in his arms.

'Look after yourself and take care of Delia. The Earls have promised to keep an eye on you both,' he murmured as he kissed her on the brow.

As the two policemen began to walk him towards the door, one on each side of him, Delia screamed that she didn't want him to go away, but they were impervious to her protests.

Karyn waited until Josiah and Sophia had gone back to their own part of the house before she retrieved the leather pouch from inside her blouse. Timorously she opened it up, and then gasped as she saw the wad of notes inside it.

She waited until she'd tucked a tearful Delia up in bed before she sat down to count the money Tudor had given her. She did it three times before she could convince herself that there was so much there. She couldn't believe he had never mentioned a word about it to her before.

At first she felt elated at having so much money and being able to afford the odd treat for herself and Delia. Doing so helped to banish the loneliness they both felt because Tudor wasn't with them. Delia still cried for him most nights when she went to bed, but during the daytime, she seemed to be happy enough and, as the days passed, she seemed to miss him less and less.

When Tudor's case came to court and Karyn heard all the evidence linking him to gambling and drugs she was shocked. It came as no real surprise at all when he was given a six-month sentence. Afterwards, though, when she realised she was now completely on her own, all her worries surfaced anew. She wasn't sure what to do.

She counted out what was left of the money Tudor had given her, wishing she hadn't frittered so much of it away. With paper and pencil she tried to work out how long it would last her. If she stayed where she was at Adeline Street, then would she be able to pay rent to the Earls and have enough for food for her and Delia until Tudor came out of prison again?

Although the stash of money had seemed enormous she soon realised that at the rate she was spending it she would have to find a job of some kind to help eke it out. How on earth was she going to manage to do that and look after Delia at the same time? she asked herself.

She wondered if Sophia Earl would care for Delia, but she thought it unlikely. Sophia seemed to have a busy life and she wouldn't want to have to look after a young child, or to take her along when she went to visit her friends.

She went to bed still puzzling out what she must do and how she was going to manage. She hated the thought that once again she would have to go back to Pen-y-llyn and ask her mother if she could live with them.

Halfway through the night she woke up with what seemed to be the perfect answer. She'd ask Tudor's mother, Bronwen Morgan, if she would come and stay with them here in Cardiff until Tudor came out of prison.

If Bronwen agreed, then it would give her the chance to find a job and it would also give Bronwen a break from having Olwyn's three children always underfoot. Bronwen had never been to Cardiff in her life so it would be a like a holiday for her.

There was only one problem, it would mean telling Bronwen about what had happened to Tudor.

She's probably already read about it in the newspaper, she decided the next day, when she saw that details of his crime and conviction had been splashed all across the *South Wales Echo*.

There was even a picture of Tudor in his best suit and wearing his trilby at a jaunty angle and looking like a really sharp villain. He's always wanted to hit the headlines, she thought wryly, it's a pity they didn't mention that he was a singer.

Chapter Sixteen

Karyn found that it was a harrowing ordeal explaining to her mother and father all the details about how Tudor came to be in prison.

'Bronny saw a piece about it in the newspaper and she's terribly upset,' her mother told her. 'It seems as though Tudor has gone from bad to worse since he's been down in Cardiff. Bitter about it, she is. You'd better go and tell her what you've told us, but don't be surprised if you get an earful from her.'

'I'll go and see her in a minute,' Karyn agreed. 'I wanted you both to know all about it first.'

Her mother nodded resignedly. 'You'd better come back here and stay with us until he gets out, I suppose,' her mother invited. 'You can't stay down there in Cardiff all on your own.'

'That's kind of you, Mam, but I don't want to impose on you again.'

'Impose! What sort of talk is that? You're our daughter, this is your home still, so where else would you go when you are in a spot of trouble?' Enid hugged Karyn close. 'I've told you before, never be afraid to ask us for help, cariad.'

'Thanks, Mam, but this time I'm going to try

and work it out on my own.' She hesitated, and then said in a rush, 'I thought of asking Tudor's mam to come and stay with me while he is in prison. If she would keep an eye on Delia, then I could get a job. What do you think of that for an idea, Mam?'

Enid Pryce looked startled. 'I don't think Bronny has ever been to Cardiff in her life.'

'I don't suppose she has, so I thought she'd like to come because it would be like a holiday for her.'

Enid looked thoughtful. 'It certainly might perk her up a bit. She's been very much down in the dumps for ages. She and Olwyn always seem to be at loggerheads with each other over something or other these days.'

'Well, there you are, then. It would be a break for both of them to be apart from each other for a couple of months.'

'Is that how long your Tudor's got?'

'No.' Karyn shook her head. 'They've given him six months but because he's been detained inside waiting for his trial there're only about four months left for him to do. His mam might not want to stay that long, though.'

Her mother nodded again. 'You mightn't want her to stay that long either. See how things go.' She gave a little sigh. 'I wouldn't mind coming and staying with you for a couple of weeks if she gets fed up.'

'What about Dad? Do you think he would be all right left on his own?'

'I'm sure he could manage for a week or two. Not for four months, though. That's a bit of a long stretch they've given Tudor just for diddling some idiots out of their spare cash isn't it?' She frowned. 'Bigger fools them for parting with it, I'd say.'

'Mam!' Karyn tried to look shocked, but her smile was as wide as the one Enid was trying to hide.

Bronwen appeared very uncertain about going back with her when Karyn told her why she was there. First, she insisted that Karyn told her everything she knew about what Tudor had been doing wrong to be given a sentence of six months in prison.

'Silly young fool getting mixed up with people of that sort,' she said angrily when Karyn ended her account. 'He hasn't got the sense he was born with! He should have gone down the pit like his dad wanted him to do and then he'd never have ended up in prison.'

'No, he would probably have ended up dead like Dad did,' Olwyn interrupted. 'Anyway,' she added sourly, 'what's the good of raking over the past? You do it all the time, Mam. If only this, if only that. Why can't you wake up to the fact that you can't change things, and that you've got to accept whatever life throws at you?'

'What's all that claptrap supposed to mean?' Bronwen asked querulously. She turned back to Karyn, 'And you, are you out of our mind girl! I can't just drop everything like you want me to do. Things will simply go to pot if I'm not here; my Olwyn can't manage on her own.'

'Oh yes I can, Mam!'

'If you are hinting that I should to down to Cardiff and keep an eye on little Delia while Karyn gets a job, then say so and stop beating about the bush.'

'All right, I will have my say, then,' Olwyn blustered. 'It will be like a holiday for me to have the house to myself for a bit. I'm fed up with you finding fault with all I do and with everything my kiddies do and even bickering with Griff. Half the time you treat him like an odd-job man with your "do this" and "do that", even though he does everything possible to help you.'

For one wild moment Karyn wished she could withdraw her invitation. She had forgotten what a tartar Bronwen could be. It was too late now, but she hoped that Bronwen would insist that she couldn't go back with her. Instead, Bronwen gave a huge, resigned sigh. 'Well, if you need me, Karyn, then I suppose I'll have to do my duty, but I can't come until next week.'

Karyn spotted Bronwen the moment the train drew into Cardiff General. Bronwen had dressed up in her best clothes for the occasion and in her navy blue coat and a matching blue hat with a bright green feather in it she was such a dominating figure that she stood out from the other passengers as she dragged her suitcases off the train and stood looking about her.

Holding Delia by the hand Karyn hurried along the platform to greet her. 'Have you had a good journey?' she asked, kissing Bronwen on the cheek.

'No I most certainly did not. We were packed into the carriage like sardines. I'm glad to get it over with and now all I want is a nice cup of tea.'

'We can have one here in the station buffet, if you like. Delia would love that,' Karyn suggested.

'Here! At the station! Duw anwyl, girl, what are you thinking about! I want a comfortable chair and a chance to get my shoes off and rest my feet, my corns are killing me.'

'Come on, then.' Karyn bent down and picked up the larger of the two suitcases. 'We'd better make our way home.'

She'd intended to warn Bronwen about the Earls being black before they reached Adeline Street, but Delia was chattering away to Bronwen so she decided that this probably wasn't the right moment to do so. Both Josiah and Sophia had been out when she'd left and so there was just a faint chance that perhaps she would be able to get Bronwen indoors and settled before they came home.

Bronwen didn't enjoy the ride on the tram

from Wood Street. 'Nasty noisy things; they shake every bone in your body,' she grumbled as they rattled their way towards Splott.

Once they were off the tram, and the three of them began walking towards Adeline Street, Karyn felt more and more worried knowing that it was now too late to explain to Bronwen about the Earls.

'This is the first time you've been to Cardiff, isn't it,' she said conversationally. 'Things are ever so different here than they are back home in Pen-y-llyn.'

Bronwen frowned. 'I'm not completely twp, girl, I'm well aware of that. I may not have been to Cardiff before, but I've been to Pontypridd and Merthyr, so I do know what towns are like.'

'I know you're not stupid,' Karyn said quickly. 'I was only remarking that things are not the same in a big city as they are in Pen-y-llyn; even the sort of people who live here are different.'

'Where did you get that silly idea from? Folks are folks, there're good and bad ones wherever you go.'

'There are all sorts of foreign people living in Cardiff and their ways sometimes seem a bit strange compared to ours,' Karyn pointed out.

'I don't think that's likely to bother me very much, cariad,' Bronwen sniffed. 'I keep myself to myself most of the time and you should do the same.'

As they turned into Adeline Street Karyn made one last desperate attempt to warn her that Josiah and Sophia were black, but it was impossible. Delia had already taken hold of her grandmother's hand and was pulling her towards their house, pointing out excitedly that it was where they lived.

When she saw Sophia was standing on the doorstep waiting to welcome them, Karyn repressed an inward shiver. It was certainly too late to do anything now, she thought uncomfortably.

'Sophia, Sophia, this is my granny,' Delia shouted.

Karyn saw the startled look on Bronwen's face and waited for an outburst. To her great relief, her mother-in-law took a deep breath, squared her huge shoulders, and then acknowledged Sophia with a pleasant nod.

'Come along in then, Mrs Morgan,' Sophia greeted her with a beaming smile before she turned and bustled back indoors. 'Karyn, I've got the kettle boiling and I'll bring you in some tea the minute you've got your coats off and then we can all get to know each other,' she said over her shoulder.

Sophia didn't stay talking to them for very long because she had to get a meal ready for Josiah. After she left there was a deadly silence and Karyn waited uneasily for Bronwen's reaction.

'Duw anwyl! Are there any other surprises

in store for me?' Bronwen demanded, an indignant tone in her voice.

'I did try to warn you on the way home. I told you things and people were different here in Cardiff,' Karyn said defensively. 'We get on very well,' she added lamely. 'Her husband Josiah is as friendly as she is. It's their house, we rent two rooms from them,' Karyn went on quickly, hoping it would give her mother-in-law a realisation of how indebted they were to the Earls.

'Oh, I'd managed to work all that out for myself,' Bronwen told her tartly as she looked around the room critically. 'So where's your kitchen, then?'

'Across the yard . . . we share it with the Earls. There's one other thing you should know,' Karyn went on quickly, deciding to get all the shocks over at once. 'You're going to have to share a bed.'

'Not with one of them!' The look of horror on Bronwen's face made Karyn want to burst out laughing. 'No,' she said, as solemnly as she could, 'either with Delia or with me. We've got one double bed and one single bed. At the moment Delia sleeps in the single bed, but if you wish, you can have that and she can sleep with me; or you can sleep with me in the big bed.'

'I'll take the single bed,' Bronwen told her sharply. 'If I find that's not comfortable, then I'll try the big bed and Delia can sleep in it with me.'

For the first few days there was a strained atmosphere between Bronwen and the Earls and Karyn wondered if she had made a big mistake in asking her mother-in-law to come and stay. How could she go out and leave Bronwen to look after Delia if she was averse to using the kitchen in case she bumped into the Earls if she did?

Bronwen herself brought the problem to a head. 'I came here so that you would get yourself a job. Are you going to do that or shall I pack my bags and get back home to Clydach Street?'

'I was just giving you a chance to settle in,' Karyn told her. 'I'll start looking tomorrow, if that's all right with you.'

'So what sort of job are you thinking about, then?' Bronwen questioned.

Karyn looked doubtful. 'I don't really know. The only thing I've done since I've been in Cardiff is work as barmaid.'

Bronwen shook her head. 'I don't think you ought to do that sort of job. Can't you find something else? I would have thought that shop work, or something like that, would be far more suitable.'

Karyn was lucky. Two day later she'd found herself a job as a waitress in a fish and chip parlour only a few streets away from where they lived.

At first the smell of hot oil and vinegar turned her stomach, but in a surprisingly short time she adjusted to it. There was the added bonus that occasionally she was able to bring home leftover pieces of fried fish for their evening meal. If there were chips to bring home as well, then that was an added perk; when there wasn't, then they ate the fish with bread and butter.

It was only a part-time job, from eleven in the morning until four in the afternoon, but with the wages she received, together with what was left of the money Tudor had given her, she was able to make ends meet. Bronwen had not only learned to be frugal over the years, but she was also a careful shopper and had a good eye for a bargain.

The four months passed so quickly that Karyn felt quite sad when it was time for Bronwen to go home. She quickly realised that her mother-in-law had a heart of gold behind her rather aggressive manner. She was kind but firm with Delia and once the little girl understood that her granny wouldn't stand for any nonsense, and that pouting or stamping her foot brought no results, she became far more obedient and cooperative.

'I've enjoyed it here and no mistake,' Bronwen told Karyn, 'I'll be quite sorry to go home.'

'I'm sure Olwyn will be glad to have you back, but I'm going to miss you,' Karyn told her warmly. 'It's worked out better than I ever hoped it would.'

'You've got that Sophia to thank for that,' Bronwen told her. 'She's taken me out and about quite a bit, see. Showed me things I'd never heard about before. That religion of hers with all its singing and dancing and clapping hands is like opening up a new world.'

Karyn looked bemused. 'You've never mentioned any of this before, I thought you simply went shopping or for walks in the park with Delia.'

'Oh, no! Some afternoons we've gone with Sophia to one of her get-togethers. None of your po-faced preachers full of doom and gloom amongst her lot, I can tell you. A happy bunch, they are, and I enjoyed going with her.'

As Karyn listened to her she couldn't believe how such a strong friendship had developed so quickly between Bronwen and Sophia. Her mother-in-law, she reflected with some amusement, knew far more about the Earls than she did.

'Nice voice that Sophia has, and you should hear Josiah play the accordion. They belong to a revivalist church and they took Delia and me there to some special occasion they were having, Lovely it was, and there were plenty of little children for Delia to play with and she thoroughly enjoyed herself. I'm surprised she didn't tell you all about it herself.'

'So am I,' Karyn mused. 'She never mentioned a word.'

'Likes having her little secrets with her

granny, I expect,' Bronwen observed thoughtfully. 'I'm going to miss all her chatter.'

'You'll stay on for a couple of days and see Tudor when he comes home?' Karyn invited.

'Oh, I don't know about that, cariad,' Bronwen said dubiously. 'I might say something he wouldn't want to hear. Young scoundrel! I never brought him up to be a criminal as you very well know. Damn well ashamed of him, I am.'

'He'll want to see you, though,' Karyn persisted. 'He'll want to thank you for helping me out.'

'No, he won't,' Bronwen interrupted. 'Much better if I'm not here. Anyway, I want to be back home in my own place for Christmas. Wait until he's settled back in, and found himself a decent job, and then bring him up to Pen-y-llyn to see us all and we'll let bygones be bygones.'

'You will come again to stay with us? For a proper holiday next time, I mean? Delia will be starting school soon and then the two of us can go out and about together.'

'You make sure you give up that waitressing job as soon as Tudor comes home. He's the one who should be the breadwinner and don't you let him forget it,' Bronwen advised her sharply. 'Try and talk him out of this silly business of singing, girl. I've said it before and I'll say it again, he'll never make a living out of it. You must know as well as I do that's it's all a fantasy.

He's got a nice voice, I'll give you that, but he'll never make a living singing.'

'It's his life, though; it's all he wants to do.'

'Then tell him to go with Sophia and Josiah to one of their religious meetings, or join the Salvation Army. He can sing his heart out there and do no harm to anyone. Make sure that if he ever goes singing in the streets again that he doesn't take little Delia along with him because next time he won't get away with it like he did before. Remember he's got a prison record now and they'll come down hard on him and you might end up having her taken away from you and put in a home of some kind.'

Chapter Seventeen

Tudor was released from Cardiff prison on Wednesday, 15 December 1926, a cold, bleak day with a threat of snow in the air. His breath formed a plume before him as he strode to freedom.

The four months of his incarceration had not been wasted as far as he was concerned. He'd made a number of new acquaintances and he'd learned a great deal about how to avoid being caught in the future. He'd also lost weight, he felt fit and sharp, and he had a head full of ideas of what he was going to do in the future.

He hadn't told Karyn the exact date of his release the last time she had visited him even though he'd known when it would be. He wanted some time to himself, to appreciate regaining his freedom. He had one or two contacts to make and he intended to find out how the land lay with one or two deals he'd negotiated while inside before he knuckled down to being a husband and father again.

What Karyn didn't know she couldn't do anything about, he reasoned. He'd checked up each time she'd come in to see him that she was still living in Adeline Street and tried to find out when his mother would be going back to Pen-y-llyn. One thing he could do without was a face-to-face confrontation with her.

Karyn had told him that his mam said she was too ashamed of what he had done, and where he had ended up, to come and visit him. Well, that had suited him fine. He didn't give a tinker's cuss whether she did or not, but he wanted to make sure that she was safely back in her own home before he went back to Adeline Street.

His first port of call was going to be the Voyager. He'd drop by for a pint and test the water. He wanted to try and renew all his singing spots. If Llew Parker was interested in hiring him again, it would be a good test about how his sort felt about him after he'd served a prison sentence.

He found Marged Parker was a mite frosty, but Llew Parker, being a man of the world, greeted him reasonably enough. He'd hoped they would offer him a drink on the house, but when it wasn't forthcoming he not only dibbed up for it, but invited Llew to have a pint as well.

While he'd been inside he'd managed to make almost as much money as he'd been earning when singing, he thought happily as he jingled the coins in his pocket.

Most of the other inmates had enjoyed having a bet and when it came to cards there weren't many sharper than him, he recalled with satisfaction.

He decided to spend his first night in the doss house he'd used before he'd moved into Adeline Street. He'd probably meet up with some old mates there and find out what had been going on while he'd been inside.

What was more he had some new skills that he'd acquired while he'd been in jail and he wanted the opportunity to put them into practice.

Poker, blackjack, cribbage . . . he had enough knowledge to open his own casino if he could find the premises and a backer.

He'd get there one day. The only singing casino owner in the country. He still intended to make a name for himself as a singer, but he'd even learned a thing or two about how to go about doing that while he'd been inside and it certainly wasn't the way he'd been trying to do it in the past.

They'd been a mixed crowd inside, but by keeping his mouth shut and his ears open for most of the time he'd learned a lot from some of the old lags and now he intended to make use of it.

Even though she'd enjoyed having Bronwen to stay, Karyn decided that having her home back to herself and being able to do exactly what she wanted when she felt like doing it was like being on holiday.

There was the added advantage that she had given up her job at the fish parlour so she intended to make the most of the few days left before Tudor came home.

He hadn't given her the exact date of his release but he'd said he'd be home in good time for Christmas and she was determined that it was going to be the best one they'd ever had.

Each week while she'd been working she'd not only squirrelled away a few shillings, but she'd also kept her eye open for little treats to make Christmas special. Delia was now old enough to really enjoy the fun of a stocking on the end of her bed and opening presents on Christmas Day.

Bronwen had also bought one or two little things and these had also been secreted away from Delia's prying eyes.

'No point in my taking them back to Pen-y-llyn and then having to spend money posting them back to you,' Bronwen had said as she'd handed them over before she left. 'I haven't bought you or Tudor anything because I think Christmas is a time for spending money on the little ones. I've one or two nice things for Olwyn's three so it should be a good time for all of us.'

Karyn would have liked to send presents for her own mam and dad, but that would have meant giving Bronwen a present as well and probably sending back something for Olwyn and all her children and she wasn't sure she wanted to be quite so reckless with her money. Tudor might be coming home any day, but he had no work and it might be a long time before he was earning money again. In fact, she might have to be the one who went out to work and left Tudor to look after Delia again.

She had explained all this to Rickie Jenkins who owned the Fish Parlour and asked whether, if she could find someone to look after Delia, she could have her job back after the Christmas Holidays were over. He felt she was letting him down by not working right up to Christmas so he wouldn't make any promises.

For the first couple of days after Bronwen went home Delia was also happy for the two of them to spend their time together and have their home to themselves. Then she began to fret about when her dad would be coming home.

'Before Christmas,' Karyn assured her. 'Let's find a piece of paper and mark down the days from now until Christmas Day and you can cross them off each morning.'

When it came to Sunday, 19 December, and there was still no word from Tudor, Karyn herself became apprehensive. Was he still coming home as he'd said, she wondered? The only thing that could possibly delay his release was if he had broken some of the rules and done something for which they were punishing him. As he seemed to have been on his best behaviour ever since the first day he went in there, it was highly unlikely that he would spoil things for himself at this late stage.

When there was still no sign of him on the Sunday, Karyn made up her mind that she was going to go along to the prison and make enquiries. It was visiting day and she would be allowed to see him for an hour in the afternoon, so it was the best way of finding out what had happened.

She said nothing to Delia, deciding to leave it until the very last minute to tell her where she was going. She couldn't take her with her, of course, but she was pretty sure that Sophia would keep an eye on her for an hour. Usually Sophia and Josiah went to one of their religious meetings in the morning but they always spent Sunday afternoons playing records on their gramophone and Delia would enjoy that.

They had just finished eating their meal and as she collected up their dishes Karyn was about to tell Delia what she had arranged when Tudor walked in, startling them both.

Delia rushed at him, flinging herself into his arms, hugging and kissing him, demanding to know where he'd been for such a long time.

'Funny day for them to let you come home,' Karyn said quietly as he freed himself from Delia's clutches and took her in his arms and kissed her.

Before he could answer Delia had pushed her way between them, demanding attention and trying to tell him all about what she had done when her granny had come to stay with them.

Karyn felt at a disadvantage. It was as if he

had never been away, she thought in amazement, He even looked fit and well.

'Are you hungry?' she asked. 'We've had our meal, but I can soon cook you something.'

Tudor shook his head. 'Not really. A cup of tea would be nice though.'

Karyn carried their dirty dishes out to the scullery and washed them up while she waited for the kettle to boil. She suspected that Tudor had been let out several days ago, so where had he been until now? Wherever it was, it was obvious he had no intention of telling her, at least not in front of Delia.

The suspense made her uneasy and rather abrupt with him when she took their tea back in. What had he been up to? Surely he wasn't going to land himself in any fresh trouble. He must know that the police would be watching him and that if they caught him doing anything at all wrong they'd come down hard on him.

For the rest of the afternoon she tried to be as cheerful and cooperative as possible, but what she really wanted was for it to be time to put Delia to bed so that they could be on their own and have a real heart-to-heart talk.

Tudor didn't seem to notice how stressed she was. He kept telling her how nice she looked, and that he liked her new shorter hairstyle. He asked both her and Delia about what they'd done while Granny had been there visiting them and once more Delia took centre stage, regaling him with even more stories of the outings she'd had with Bronwen.

'Didn't your mam go with you as well?' he asked in surprise, looking across at Karyn questioningly.

'No, she was working,' Delia told him. 'Serving fish and chips in a café. If there was any left over at the end of the day she brought them home and we had them before I went to bed,' she giggled.

'So you've got a job, have you? Well, that's good news.' He grinned.

'I had a job,' Karyn told him quietly. 'I gave it up when your mam went home.'

'Why did you have to go and do a daft thing like that, cariad?' he frowned.

'How could I go out to work? I couldn't leave Delia on her own, now could I?'

'What was wrong with taking her with you? You could have sat her in a corner with a book to scribble in and kept an eye on her while you were serving.'

Karyn gave him a disgusted look. 'Can you see the owner of the place letting me do that?'

Tudor shrugged. 'If you'd told him it was only for a few days he probably wouldn't have minded.'

'I couldn't be sure about that though, could I? You never said when you were coming out . . . or when you would be coming home when you did,' she added waspishly.

'Don't start!' Tudor held his hands up in front

of him. 'There were one or two things that I'd promised some of the boyos who are still inside that I'd do for them so I thought I'd better get those done and dusted and out of the way before Christmas.'

'What sort of things? Couldn't you have come home and seen us first and then done them?' Karyn fumed indignantly.

Tudor shook his head. 'Not a good thing to mix business with pleasure,' he said disarmingly. 'I'm home now, and I'm all yours and I hope we can enjoy Christmas.'

'Mam says that it's going to be the best Christmas ever and that because I've been so good Father Christmas is going to bring me a really special present,' Delia told him excitedly.

'I'm sure he will,' Tudor agreed, swinging her up in his arms and kissing her. 'Now if you toddle off upstairs to bed, then tomorrow I'll take you up to town. We'll see if we can find Father Christmas so that you can tell him yourself where you live and make sure he doesn't forget to bring that special present.'

'Why did you tell her a cock-and-bull yarn like that?' Karyn asked furiously the moment Delia was tucked up in bed.

'What do you mean? Why not take her to Morgan's or Howell's to see Father Christmas?'

'Because it's a waste of money to do things like that and you haven't got a job and I've just given up mine,' Karyn reminded him, her eyes flashing angrily.

'I've got money!' He jingled the coins in his trouser pockets. 'I've enough to make sure we have everything we want for Christmas. I might even ask Father Christmas to buy you something,' he added teasingly.

'How can you have any money?' she asked in disbelief.

'Aah, wouldn't you like to know.' He grinned. 'There're ways and means of getting hold of money even when you are inside, if you know the ropes.'

'Has this got something to do with those so-called messages you have been delivering?' she asked suspiciously.

'Don't you worry your pretty head about any of that,' he said in a patronising tone. 'I'll see you have enough money to put a decent spread on the table on Christmas Day. I'll make sure you can keep your promise to make it a very special day for Delia.'

'What about afterwards? How are we going to get by then? Please, Tudor,' she laid a hand on his arm pleadingly, 'don't break the law again. Next time they'll give you such a long stretch that by the time you come out Delia will have forgotten what you look like or who you are.'

'I think it is about time that I reminded you who I am,' he said softly. 'Being on your own all these months has hardened you and made you suspicious. Where's the loving girl from Pen-y-llyn that I married?'

'These days she's slightly disillusioned with life,' Karyn told him tartly.

'And does she blame me?' he asked softly. He drew her into his arms, holding her so close that she could feel the heat of his body. 'You've every right to do so, cariad. I've made a mess of things up until now, but from now on I'm determined to make things so much better for all of us. That's a promise I'm determined to keep.'

'That means no more taking Delia out busking or begging? You promise.'

'That was twp! Utterly stupid. I'll never forgive myself for doing a daft thing like that. Has she ever said anything to you about it?'

Karyn shook her head. 'No, I'm not sure if she even remembers what happened.'

'Then let's put it behind us and never mention it again. No more regrets, cariad. 1927 is going to be a new start for me and a new way of life for all of us.'

'Only if you are able to get a job,' Karyn sighed.

'That's all taken care of. I'm taking over a business belonging to one of the boyos I met up with inside. That's why I didn't come straight home, see. I had to go and finalise the arrangements. He set it all up for me, but I had to go along myself to see the chap who has been looking after everything for him and to fix up when I would be starting work.'

'Tudor, that's absolutely wonderful,' she

enthused. 'What sort of job is it? When do you start work?'

'Steady on, cariad, don't get carried away now. I start as soon as I like after Christmas. I've taken over this handyman business. Good money, so he tells me, but I shall be able to find out for myself in a week or so.'

Karyn's enthusiasm dimmed. 'What happens when he comes out of prison? Won't he want it back again?' she asked cautiously.

'There's plenty enough time to sort all that out because he still has another three or four years to do.'

Karyn looked shocked. 'What on earth did he do to get such a long sentence?'

Tudor laughed. 'Nothing that you need worry about. Now, as I said before, I think it is time we both got to know each other again, don't you? Come on upstairs to bed, or else I shall think that you've forgotten how much you love me.'

Long after they'd made love and Tudor was deep in sleep, Karyn lay awake thinking over the day's events.

Tudor had changed in so many ways, but he was still as passionate as he had ever been. It had been wonderful to lie in his arms and to discover that his touch could still send ripples of longing through her.

He had been so eager to make love, bursting with pent-up passion, which proved that he had missed her as much as she had missed him over the past months. His urgent arousal had been reassuring. She had been so afraid that after such a long absence they might be like strangers.

He seemed to be more patient and considerate in other ways, too, more like the handsome ambitious young man she had married. He had been so reassuring with his promises and plans for the future that she felt that all her pent-up tension start to vanish. This time Tudor seemed to be trying really hard and she was sure she could trust him not to get into any more trouble.

He was right, she reflected, this was going to be the most wonderful Christmas they had ever known. She would make sure that they celebrated in style and that nothing clouded the day; for his sake as well as Delia's.

She wasn't sure how much Delia understood about Tudor's absence or what she ought to tell her. Perhaps the best thing would be to do as Tudor suggested and to put it all behind them, forgetting all about the past and not mentioning it again.

Curled into the warmth of Tudor's back she relaxed and tried to sleep, but there was a niggling doubt at the back of her mind that simply wouldn't go away. What exactly had Tudor meant when he spoke of taking over a handyman business for a chap who was still inside?

Who on earth would give up a business like that if it was any good? And why was the man inside in the first place? Was it something to do with the business? Why was Tudor prepared to do that sort of work when he had always said that he would never do anything except sing? Had prison changed him so much, or was there some other underlying reason?

The last thing on Karyn's mind as she slowly drifted into sleep was that she must question Tudor more about it the next day. But how would she know if he was telling her the truth?

She hated herself for being so critical, so suspicious, but there had been so many reasons in the past for not taking everything Tudor told her at face value. As far as she knew he didn't have any skills when it came to painting and decorating or even repairing and mending things.

Chapter Eighteen

Christmas was every bit as good as Karyn had hoped. Tudor played his part to perfection, giving her a hand around the house, putting up paper chains and sprigs of holly and, after Delia had gone to bed on Christmas Eve, helping her to fill her stocking then creeping in to lay it at the foot of her bed.

The happy atmosphere lasted all week and 1927 started off so well, that Karyn had to admit that Tudor was certainly keeping his promise and putting his heart and soul into his new way of life.

Although it was cold and frosty, which meant that when he was working out of doors he often came home absolutely frozen, he seemed to be so enthusiastic about what he was doing that she could hardly believe it.

Each day she waited for him to say that he'd had enough and that he was giving up. She'd already resolved that if he did decide to do that then she would suggest that he looked after Delia and she'd go out to work.

Delia was looking forward to the summer and her next birthday because it meant that she would then be five and be able to go to school.

Since the new term would begin a couple of weeks before Delia's fifth birthday, Karyn had promised that she would make enquiries to see if she would be able to start school then, even though it was a few weeks early.

'Will we still be living here in Adeline Street next September?' she asked Tudor.

'Of course, cariad. Why ever not?'

'I wasn't sure. Since most of your work seems to be in the Roath area I wondered whether perhaps we should move that way so that you wouldn't have so far to travel each day.'

Tudor laughed. 'We couldn't afford to rent a coal shed in one of those sorts of houses! You want to see them, cariad. The ones in Wyvern Road are so big that we could drop the whole of this place into their hallway.'

'I didn't mean to live anywhere like that. I thought perhaps somewhere in Cathays, though. There're plenty of streets of small houses round there.'

'Why do you suddenly want to move, cariad?' he asked, looking puzzled.

'I don't. I simply want to start making arrangements for Delia to go to school.'

'Then find her a school around here.'

'I will, if you are quite sure you don't want to live a bit nearer to Roath.'

'No.' He shook his head. 'I think it is better to live well away from where you work. The journey home gives me a chance to unwind and put the working day behind me.'

Karyn didn't argue, but she still wondered why he felt this way. She was also concerned about the erratic way Tudor provided her with money. It was not that he kept her short – on the contrary, he was, if anything, often over-generous. She had only to mention that she needed something, or that the housekeeping money was getting low, and he'd dig into his pocket and thrust a handful of money at her without even counting it.

When she commented on this he merely laughed.

'You should count it, Tudor.' she said worriedly. 'How can you keep your books straight if you don't know how much you've handed over to me?'

'Books!' Tudor threw back his head and laughed. 'I don't keep any accounts!'

'Don't you have to let this chap who is still in jail know how much you are earning, seeing it's his business?'

'Of course not! It's not like that. What I do and how I run it is up to me.'

Karyn accepted what he said but it still sounded odd to her. If she were to have a business, and to entrust the running of it to someone else, then she would want to know how it was doing and also to make sure that they were running it properly.

As spring turned into summer Karyn began to take Delia out most days. A trip to Victoria Park to see Sammy the Seal was always a strong attraction. Karyn always made a point of walking around some of the surrounding streets to see if they could catch a glimpse of Tudor at work, but they never did.

For all that he seemed to be working hard. He set off promptly at eight o'clock every morning and didn't arrive back home until around five o'clock each evening. Even though he had presumably been tackling all sorts of maintenance jobs it puzzled her that he never seemed to be in the least bit dirty or tired. To her surprise he didn't seem to be at all worried that he was no longer going out singing.

'I do sing,' he told her. 'I warble away while I'm working. If I'm outside, the birds seem to like it, but I'm not sure about what my customers think when they hear me.'

'They must like listening to you, perhaps that's why they give you so many presents?' She smiled.

Tudor shrugged. 'It's usually only vases or stuff that they are fed up with and they're going to throw out anyway. When they say, "Take it with you, if you like it", then I don't like to offend them by refusing it.'

'We have at least a dozen vases now, so what are we going to do with them all?' Karyn asked bewildered.

'Don't worry, I'll find a way to get rid of them.'

'Should you, if they were presents, I mean?'

He shrugged. 'Who is going to know? They're

hardly likely to come here to visit us, are they? Why don't you take them along to Old Sol in Bute Road and pawn them if they are in your way? You might get a few bob for them and you can have it and get yourself something you'd like . . . or something for Delia.'

'I don't fancy doing that,' she protested.

'Why not? All you have to do is to take the stuff in and ask him how much he'll lend you on it. Old Sol makes you an offer and takes whatever you have brought in and then hands you the money and a ticket. The ticket is so that you can redeem the item later on; that's if you want to, of course. If you haven't claimed it after about six months then he can sell it. It says on the ticket how long you've got in which to buy it back.'

'Yes, I know all that, but as I've just said it doesn't seem right to pawn things that have been given to you as presents.'

She remembered the first time this had happened. Now there was a collection of almost twenty tickets in the dressing-table drawer. They weren't just for vases. Over the months Tudor had brought home all sorts of other things that the people he did jobs for didn't have any use for and so she'd visited Old Sol quite regularly.

She didn't really like going there, but as Tudor pointed out, it was better to go back to Tiger Bay to pawn things rather than to a pawn-broker in Splott because they didn't want the

Earls, or any of their neighbours, knowing all their business.

'No, you're right,' Karyn agreed. 'We don't want Sophia telling your mam about it when she comes to stay for a few days. In her last letter she says she's looking forward to seeing how you're getting on now that you are out of prison and doing so well.'

'Can't you put her off?' Tudor protested. 'Where is she going to sleep?'

'I hadn't thought about that, but I suppose she can have Delia's bed, like she did when she stayed here before, and Delia can sleep with me.'

'Oh, no! I don't want Delia in our bed along with us!' Tudor grumbled.

'Well, you would be sleeping down here in the armchair,' Karyn explained sweetly.

'Happy families! I'm the one who gets turned out of his bed. Don't forget that I have to go to work next day.'

'It would only be for two or three nights. She says in her letter that since Delia will be starting school in September she thought she'd come for a few days in August.'

Tudor still didn't like the idea but as Karyn pointed out they owed it to her. 'She was good enough to come and stay while you were in prison so that I could go out to work,' she reminded him.

They argued about it so much that in the end it was only Delia who was looking forward to

Bronwen's visit. Several times Karyn thought about writing and telling her that they weren't well and that it would be better if she didn't come. The thought that if she did that then it might make Bronwen all the more determined because she would feel they needed her help, stopped her. It would be terrible if she turned up and found all three of them fit and healthy and realised they'd been lying because they hadn't wanted to see her.

It was a warm sunny August and Karyn and Delia were able to take Bronwen out every day to all their favourite places. They went to Victoria Park to see Sammy the Seal and to Roath Park to show her the boating lake. They wanted to take her to Cardiff Castle, but she declared that she would much rather be out of doors, not shut up in some dingy old place like that so they agreed they'd leave that until last, or they could go there if the weather changed.

Bronwen seemed to be very pleased when they pointed out the area where Tudor was working as a handyman, doing painting and repairs.

'Seen some sense at last have you, boyo?' she commented, when they were having their meal that night. 'Taken you long enough.'

'All right, Mam, there's no need to go on about it.'

'Have you given up that singing lark completely, then?' she persisted.

'No, I'll be a singer one day. This business is just to get me back on my feet, see.'

'He's running it for a friend,' Karyn put in quickly. 'He'll have to give it back in a year or two's time.'

'Give it back? What sort of an arrangement is that, then? Sounds twp to me.'

'It's not daft, Mam,' Tudor said huffily. 'It's a perfectly good arrangement. It gives me breathing space to make enquiries about how I should go about being discovered.'

'Being discovered!' Bronwen's voice was shrill with contempt. 'You've been discovered once, boyo. The police discovered you and put you inside, or have you forgotten!'

'I'm hardly likely to do so while you keep on reminding me about it, now am I?' he retorted, helping himself to a slice of cake.

'Well, you want to watch your step, boyo, and make sure you keep your nose clean,' she added ominously.

'Tudor's working very hard, Mam,' Karyn assured her as she poured out tea for them all. 'He must be pleasing his customers because they are always giving him nice things to bring home.'

'What sort of nice things?' Once again Bronwen was alert and wanting to know more.

'It's nothing, Mam,' Tudor laughed and at the same time shot a warning glance at Karyn, but it was too late. Karyn had already passed her the pair of candlesticks that he had brought home a few days before and which she hadn't yet taken along to the pawnbrokers.

His mother almost snatched them out of Karyn's hand. Turning one of them upside down she screwed up her eyes and held the base up to the light as she studied the markings on the bottom.

'These are real silver!' she exclaimed in a startled voice. 'Who on earth would throw these out?'

'They weren't thrown out, Mam, they were given to Tudor as a present by one of his customers.'

As she spoke Karyn looked at Tudor for confirmation, but he avoided her eyes. A niggling worm of suspicion wriggled inside her head. Had Tudor been telling her the truth or had he come by them in some other way?

Bronwen seemed to have similar misgivings. Squaring her shoulders she glared at her son across the table and stated in a voice that held no doubt in it at all, 'You stole these, boyo, didn't you!'

'Mam! How can you say such a thing!' he blustered, but his voice quavered as he met her hard stare.

Karyn was aghast as she saw the colour creep upwards from his neck and flood his cheeks with guilt. All she could think about at that moment was the drawer in the dressing table where she had stowed away all the pawnbroker's tickets. What on earth would Bronwen say if she caught sight of those! At the last count there had been over thirty of them.

Her mind in turmoil, Karyn began to remember the assortment of items Tudor had brought home. At first it had been pretty vases or trinket holders, then more expensive things. She remembered a man's silver watch, a gold necklace that she'd wanted to keep for herself, but Tudor had told her it was being thrown away because it was only brass and would discolour her clothes.

Old Sol hadn't realised that, though; he had advanced her three pounds on it. At the time she wondered if she ought to tell him, but she'd been hard pressed for money so she had resolved to take what he was offering and then to buy the necklace back later so that he never discovered his mistake.

Through the mish-mash of her thoughts Karyn could hear Bronwen's voice rising higher and higher as she accused Tudor of thieving.

'Handyman business indeed, that's nothing but a cover-up! You're a bloody thief! I can't believe that my own son would stoop so low. Duw anwyl, your dad must be turning in his grave. Starve, he would, rather than take a penny piece that didn't belong to him.'

The more Tudor tried to quieten her down the more incensed Bronwen became. Tears were streaming down her podgy face, making wet rivulets in the creases and her voice was becoming hoarse with shouting at him.

'Mam, for God's sake put a sock in it, before the Earls and the rest of the street hear you.'

'Yes, it wouldn't do for that to happen. They'd all be afraid to sleep in their beds at night in case you broke into their homes and stole things from them.'

'It's not like that, Mam. You don't understand.'

'Damnio di! I understand all right. Big posh houses are they, where you're doing these odd jobs? At this time of the year folks leave their windows wide open so that when no one is about you've been pinching whatever you can manage to reach, haven't you?'

'Give it a rest, Mam, you're out of your mind,' Tudor blustered.

'Am I indeed!' Bronwen retaliated, her face flushed with anger. 'Those candlesticks came from someone's dining room. You think that because they've got plenty they won't miss them. If they do, then you trust to luck that it will be the daily charwoman, or the washerwoman, or one of the maids who live in who will get the blame. No wonder you are singing as you work! Well you might be, boyo, though how you can live with your guilty conscience afterwards I'll never know.'

'That will do, you're only guessing at all this,' Karyn interrupted. 'Tudor's right, you're getting yourself worked up into a right state and you're frightening Delia. I'll make us all a fresh pot of tea . . .'

'Karyn, you needn't try to pull the wool over my eyes either. As I've told you before I'm not twp. If you've been accepting these things he steals, instead of making him take them back, then you're as guilty as he is and you're an accomplice.'

'That will do, Mam. Karyn hadn't any idea about what I was doing, not until this moment.' His eyes glittered and his mouth twisted into a sneer as he added, 'She wouldn't know now if you hadn't opened your big gob.'

Bronwen's fighting spirit suddenly evaporated. She collapsed like a pricked balloon and the tears rolling down her cheeks became great body-shaking sobs.

Karyn rushed to her side and put her arms around her to try and comfort her, but Bronwen pushed her away, gasping for air. Her breathing became even more strained and as the colour drained from her face she slumped backwards.

'Tudor, do something! I think she's fainted.'

'Duw anwyl! I don't know what to do,' he exclaimed. 'Shall I go for a doctor?'

'You can't leave me here on my own with her like this. Help me to get her into the armchair.'

They tried to lift Bronwen, but she was far too heavy.

'If you can hold her steady so that she doesn't slip off the chair, then I'll go and see if Josiah will come and give me a hand,' Tudor told her.

'She's much too heavy for me to hold on my own,' Karyn exclaimed.

'Shall I go and fetch them for you?' Delia asked in a frightened little voice.

Both Josiah and Sophia were anxious to help. 'If you help me to lie her down on the floor then I'll cover her over with a blanket to keep her warm and Tudor will go for a doctor,' Karyn told them.

As Josiah and Tudor tried to lift Bronwen, Sophia held up a hand to stop them. She pressed two fingers to the underside of Bronwen's chin, and then shook her head.

'What is it? Why did you do that? What's the matter with her?' Karyn asked anxiously.

'It's too late for a doctor to be of any help, cariad,' Sophia said gently. 'Bronwen's either had a massive stroke or a heart attack . . . she's dead.'

Chapter Nineteen

Bronwen's sudden death was terribly upsetting for all of them. Karyn had never been faced with such a situation before and she had no idea what to do next.

The sight of Bronwen slumped in her chair, not breathing, and blue around the lips, was etched so deeply on her mind that she was quite sure she would never be able to forget it.

She insisted that Tudor went for a doctor, even though they were pretty sure that Sophia was right and that there would be nothing either he, or anyone else, could do.

The waiting for the doctor to come seemed interminable. He was a short dapper man, a complete stranger, and very brusque. His examination was brief and impersonal.

The days that followed were also a nightmare. Delia was heartbroken and no sooner had they calmed her down from one outburst of crying than she started again.

Sophia and Josiah were both very upset. Even though they did all they could to help; they kept asking endless questions about how it had happened, which irritated Tudor and distressed Karyn.

'She was so happy to be here again, Karyn, and kept telling us about all the places you'd taken her to see,' Sophia said over and over again. 'She couldn't get over the seal in Victoria Park. She said she'd never seen anything like it in her life before and how much her daughter's children would love to come and see it.'

Sophia offered to take Delia out or have her in her room while Tudor and Karyn discussed details for Bronwen's funeral, but Delia refused to go with them. Tears streaming down her little face, she clung on to Tudor so tightly that he couldn't move and had no alternative but to sit and cuddle her.

'We've got to let your Olwyn and Griff know what's happened,' Karyn told him worriedly.

'Yes, I know, but I can't simply write and tell them in a letter, now can I? How on earth would I word it? They'd be shocked out of their minds. They think that she's here having a good holiday. She's never really had a day's illness in her life as far as I know.'

'We could write and tell my mam and dad and ask them to go round and tell Olwyn and Griff,' Karyn suggested.

'No, they deserve better than that. She's Olwyn's mam as well as mine, remember. What's more, they've been living with her for the past few years so it's going to come as a terrible blow!'

'I know that, but whatever else can we do?'

244

'I think I ought to go to Pen-y-llyn and tell them myself,' Tudor sighed.

'That means leaving me and Delia here all on our own,' Karyn protested.

Tudor ran a hand over his chin, shaking his head and looking completely overwhelmed. 'I know, but it's my duty, surely you can see that.' He grimaced.

'Yes, I suppose you're right,' Karyn agreed reluctantly. 'There's the question of the funeral to be arranged and no doubt they'll want to have a say about that,' she pointed out. 'Olwyn will probably want it to be from Clydach Street.'

'Duw anwyl, we can't afford that!' Tudor exclaimed. 'Think about it, my lovely! It would cost a small fortune to get her body all the way from here to Pen-y-llyn.'

'It's only natural that she should end up in her own home, though, Tudor.'

'What's wrong with her being buried here in Cardiff?' he argued stubbornly.

'Your family won't like it. They'll expect her to lie next to your dad.'

'It's out of the question,' he muttered obstinately.

'There's a grave there waiting for her,' Karyn persisted. 'It's probably what she'd want as well.'

Tudor shook his head. 'If she'd died at home in Clydach Street then that would have been possible, but since it's happened down here then this is where she'll have to be buried.'

Karyn looked at him in disbelief. 'This is all to do with money, isn't it?'

Tudor shrugged. 'Her funeral is going to cost a packet as it is and I don't suppose our Olwyn will be able to come up with anything to help towards it.'

'It's your mam, though, that we have to think about, Tudor. For her it will almost be like being banished to a foreign country,' Karyn protested.

'Don't talk so daft, girl! Sometimes you are as stupid as she was. She's dead, so what does it matter what happens to her body? Whether she's buried down here or back in Pen-y-llyn she's still going to be put in a box and stuck in the ground and that's that.'

'She'll know no one and I don't even know where the cemetery is,' Karyn shuddered

'It's a huge place at Cathays. I often pass by it when I'm working up that way.'

'I don't think that's where she would want to be,' Karyn insisted.

'Well, we'll have to see what our Olwyn says, I suppose,' Tudor admitted. 'I shouldn't think Griff will care one way or the other as long as he doesn't have to put his hand in his pocket to pay for any of it.'

'Sometimes you can be quite pitiless,' Karyn told him with a tremor in her voice.

'We can't wait until we talk to them about where it is to be, we'll have to make a decision ourselves about what we are going to do. We've got to get in touch with an undertaker right away so that they can collect my mam's body.'

'Do you mean they'll take her away before the funeral?' Karyn asked hesitantly.

'Yes, of course! The sooner we arrange it the better; we don't want her body here any longer than is absolutely necessary because it's upsetting Delia.'

Tears glistened in Karyn's eyes. 'What we're doing seems so heartless,' she sniffed. 'Perhaps I could ask Sophia if she would let Delia stay with her.'

'No, no. Delia needs to be with us,' Tudor stated firmly. 'She's too upset to stay with strangers.'

'What are you talking about? The Earls aren't strangers!'

'They are as far as I am concerned. They'll get her gabbing to them and the next thing you know Delia will be telling them about the row I was having with my mam when she collapsed and before we know it I'll be getting blamed for her death.'

'Well, I suppose in some ways you are responsible,' Karyn mused. 'She was out of her mind when she found out that you were pinching stuff from the houses where you were working. It was the idea that you had become a thief that caused her to have a heart attack or whatever it was.'

'You didn't believe all that twaddle she was spouting did you?' he blustered.

'It doesn't matter now,' she sighed dismissively. 'Let's get on with arranging your mother's funeral and then we can talk about all that afterwards,' she added as she turned away.

Bronwen's funeral was a very quiet affair. They timed it to take place at half past two on the last Thursday in August.

Olwyn and Griff had left their three children with their next-door neighbour and made the journey to Cardiff along with Owen and Enid Pryce. No one else from Clydach Street came, but many of the neighbours had clubbed together to send a magnificent wreath.

Tudor went to Cardiff Central station to meet them. Apart from Griff, they were all so overcome by the journey that they had very little to say as they caught a tram back to Adeline Street.

Karyn was waiting for them with the kettle boiling and a cold meal ready on the table to have before they went to the cemetery, but they hardly touched the food or even seemed interested in Tudor and Karyn's home.

Dressed in black they were all like strangers with each other. Karyn thought that her mother looked thinner than ever, almost frail, as she perched on the edge of a chair while they waited for the hearse to arrive.

'It's going to be a bit of a squash with all of us in one car,' Tudor explained, 'so Sophia and

Josiah have taken Delia and gone on ahead on the tram; they'll meet us at the cemetery.'

'If you'd mentioned it earlier, then we could have gone on the tram as well,' Owen Pryce commented. 'It would have given us a chance to see a bit of Cardiff at the same time.'

'Really, Owen! We're down here for Bronny's funeral, not for a sightseeing trip,' Karyn's mother said in a disapproving tone.

'We'll be coming back afterwards on the tram so you will be able to see some of the city, Owen,' Tudor promised.

'Well, Olwyn and me will want to go straight to the railway station, we're going home right after the interment,' Griff reminded him.

'Yes, we have to do so,' Olwyn agreed. 'We can't leave our three next door for too long, they're little terrors! They'll wreck the place if we are away from them for any length of time.'

'You don't have to go straight back, do you, Mam?' Karyn asked looking at her mother hopefully.

'Well, cariad, maybe it's best if we do. I'll feel safer if we all travel together, see. I've seen where you live, now,' she smiled, 'so I'll be a bit more settled in my mind than I was before. Sad about poor Bronny, though,' she added as she wiped the tears from her eyes. 'Miss her, I will. She was the best friend I ever had. We've known each other ever since we were Delia's age.'

Karyn gave her a hug, too full of grief herself

to know what to say to comfort her mother. This was one of the times when she wished they'd never left Pen-y-llyn.

'You're going to miss her dreadfully as well, Olwyn,' she said sadly.

Olwyn nodded glumly. 'Not sure how it is going to leave us,' she said worriedly. 'It was Mam's name in the rent book, see. They might turn us out.'

'I thought you fixed all that up after my dad died and you moved to our place?' Tudor frowned.

'No, all we did was ask if it was all right for us to live there with Mam,' Olwyn told him. 'It's a pit house, see, so they could have turned your mam out if they'd wanted to because she had no one working down the pit.'

'Yes, and that was the whole point of you and Griff moving in with her. It made sense since Griff was working at the pit because it meant that Mam could stay on in Clydach Street,' Tudor reminded his sister.

'Well, my Griff still does work down the pit, of course.' Olwyn frowned.

'There you are, then. Nothing to worry about, is there? They won't make any fuss about changing the name in the rent book; it's only a formality, boyo! Lucky you are and no maybe. The whole house to yourselves. What more could you possibly want!'

'I want my poor mam back, that's what I really want,' Olwyn gulped, her fat face creasing into fresh tears. 'Who is going to be there to help me now? It's all your fault, Tudor. I don't know what you said or did this time, but you were always upsetting her one way or another. It must have been something pretty awful to cause her to have a heart attack. It's your fault she's dead, just as if you'd killed her with your own hands.'

'Come on, Olwyn, don't take on so,' Enid said worriedly. 'We are all going to miss your mam, of course we are, so we must all do what we can for each other.'

To Karyn's relief the hearse arrived before Olwyn could launch into her tirade. She knew that to some extent she was right and she was determined to get to the bottom of things just as soon as she and Tudor were on their own again.

She wondered how she could have been so stupid as not to realise that people didn't give away vases and necklaces and all the other things Tudor had brought home since he'd started being a handyman. She wanted a straightforward explanation about the entire thing. The more she thought about it the more suspicious she became. She also wanted to know the truth about how he came to get hold of the business in the first place.

Tudor went back to work the day after his mother's funeral as if nothing at all had happened. Karyn couldn't understand it. As she set about washing up their breakfast dishes and tidying the house, Karyn wondered if she was the only one who felt sad about Bronwen's death.

She was desperate to have a serious talk with Tudor so that she could set matters right in her own mind. She kept going over what they had all been discussing before Bronwen had collapsed and wondering why Bronwen had become so terribly upset.

She kept trying to remember exactly what had been said because Bronwen had seemed so incensed that she couldn't help wondering if there had been something more than the fact that Tudor was a petty thief.

What else had Bronwen known or suspected that she still didn't know about? Until it was all clear to her she'd never be able to put it out of her mind.

She decided to wait until Delia was settled at school and then ask Tudor to take a day off so that they could be on their own and she could ask all the questions she wanted to. Whether she got truthful answers would be another matter, she realised.

She sincerely hoped that Tudor would be honest with her. There had been so many lies, so much deceit, that she felt she needed to have the slate wiped clean.

Now with Delia at school she hoped it would be possible for her to go out to work again. If they could arrange things so that Tudor could be the one who collected Delia from school each afternoon then she could take on a full-time job.

If they were both earning and they saved hard, she reasoned, then they might be able to move away from the rooms in Adeline Street and rent a small house in another part of Cardiff. She would never feel comfortable living there; the memory of Bronwen collapsing in front of her eyes would always haunt her.

Delia was so excited to be at last starting school that she seemed to quickly forget about her grandmother's death. All she could talk about was what her new life was going to be like and deciding which dress and hair ribbon she wanted to wear on her first day.

Delia had mixed so little with other children that Karyn was apprehensive about her starting school. She was afraid that even though she was so eager to do so she would find it frightening.

She'd made a point of walking past Eleanor Street School with her whenever possible so that she could become accustomed to the sight of all the children running about in the playground. If it was late in the afternoon, around four o'clock, then they would see them streaming out as they made their way home.

'There will be at least twenty other five-year-olds starting at the same time as she is,' Miss Sherman, the teacher at Eleanor Street, told her.

'Many of them will have no idea what it is all about either.'

'They'll probably know each other, though,' Karyn pointed out worriedly.

'She'll soon make friends with one or two of them so don't worry too much about it,' Miss Sherman assured her.

Tudor said much the same thing. 'She'll soon settle in,' he affirmed. 'Give her a week or two and she'll have found her place in the pecking order and be as happy as Larry.'

'Yes, as long as she doesn't find herself at the bottom of the pile. She's not used to other children, or having to share her books and toys, or even playing games if it comes to that.'

Tudor merely shrugged and set off for work whistling cheerfully as if he hadn't a care in the world; as if his mother's recent death was completely banished from his mind.

Chapter Twenty

Karyn Morgan felt tears welling up in her eyes as Delia, in a spotless blue cotton dress trimmed with a white Peter Pan collar, joined the group of other five-year-olds who were being shepherded into the classroom by their teacher.

She'd expected her to hang back, clutch hold of her hand, and not want to leave her. Instead, Delia had run across the playground, her new black patent leather shoes hardly touching the ground, without even a backward glance.

Still, Karyn consoled herself as she walked away down Singleton Road, it was probably better for it to be like that than for her to be crying.

She remembered her own first day at school in Pen-y-llyn. Her mam had thought she was crying at the thought of leaving her but it hadn't been that at all. She had been in floods of tears because she'd thought Tudor would be in the same class as her and of course, because he was two years older than she was, he wasn't.

He had waited for her after school, though, and from then on they'd always walked to and from school together until the day he'd left because he was old enough to start work.

After that, when he had refused to go down the mine like most of the other men in Pen-y-llyn, he had met her from school whenever he wasn't working. That had been a great deal of the time, she thought ruefully.

Singing and becoming famous, with his name on the playbills outside theatres and music halls, had been all Tudor had ever wanted.

She'd believed him and thought it an exciting prospect. She'd never laughed or scoffed like everyone else did because she was convinced that even though it was only a dream one day he would make it come true.

When he'd stood up to his father and everyone else and refused to work in the pit she'd admired him and thought it heroic. The fact that it meant that he only earned money by doing odd jobs such as deliveries for the butcher and greengrocer when they needed him, had an air of romance about it for her.

She'd loved Tudor ever since she could remember and she still did, even though his career as a singer was still an unfulfilled dream.

She smiled as she remembered the furore it had caused when they'd announced they were going to be married. Everyone in Pen-y-llyn had disapproved when they insisted on going ahead with their wedding after Tudor's dad had been killed.

Even though she'd been pregnant she had half expected Tudor to say that he'd have to put his mam first and call off their wedding plans. Or else tell her that he couldn't leave his mother on her own so they must live with her. He hadn't. He'd stuck by her and done his best to provide her and their baby with a home.

Things at the Voyager might have worked out if only he hadn't been caught begging. He insisted that he had only been singing to entertain the crowd, but it hadn't looked like that to the police. He might have got away with it if Delia hadn't been going around holding out his hat and wearing the placard he'd pinned on her.

She'd found it hard to believe that he could do a thing like that. If she'd known she would have tried to stop him. Would he have listened to her, though?

It was a question she'd asked herself over and over while he was in prison. He had changed a great deal since they'd moved to Cardiff. He looked more mature and even though he seemed to be enjoying his work these days, she was sure he resented the sort of life he was being forced to lead because he was still not recognised as a professional singer.

Sometimes, when their lovemaking lacked the deep tenderness of their early days together, she often wondered if perhaps deep down he thought he'd made a mistake in marrying so young. Yet he showed such deep affection towards Delia that she was sure he wouldn't want to be without her. Tudor's whole manner seemed to change when Delia was sitting on his knee, and he was listening to her prattling on about something.

She had pointed this out to his mother when she had brought the subject up and reminded her that he was still only in his early twenties. It hadn't appeased Bronwen, though. She'd still been determined to have what she called a good, straight talk with him, to tell him what was what and to try and talk some sense into him.

Whether she'd ever done so or not Karyn wasn't too sure, but there had been a lot of tension and bitterness in the air, to make Bronwen lose her temper as she had done.

The way she had become so incensed, rumbling like a volcano, had been frightening. There had been such violent emotion unleashed during the bitter argument that it had led to her collapse. It was almost as if the tremendous surge of anger had seemed to take her breath away and had choked her.

Karyn felt a shudder run through her as she remembered the way Bronwen had turned grey and slumped in her chair like a huge, deflated balloon before they could do anything to help her.

She still felt that it was important that she should know what had been the underlying cause of her anger, but only Tudor could tell her that and the right moment to discuss it with him never seemed to arise. It was almost as if

Tudor had deliberately put the entire incident out of his mind.

When she'd broached the subject that perhaps she should find a job again now that Delia was at school, Tudor had agreed without any fuss. Indeed, he had seemed almost eager that she should do so. When she had asked him if he thought they could arrange things so that she could work a full day, he'd been the one to suggest that he could pick Delia up after school each day.

She'd noticed, too, that he was leaving the house later and later in the morning. He still seemed to have plenty of money, though, and since he certainly wasn't working a full day that was another thing that worried her and which she wanted to talk to him about.

Tudor knew that he couldn't avoid explaining to Karyn what was going on for much longer because she was becoming more and more persistent.

He pondered over what he should tell her. He wasn't sure how she would react if he told her the complete truth. Yet if he didn't and it came out at a later date, as well it might, then it would be bound to result in a huge row between them.

She was pretty tolerant, but he suspected that even Karyn had her limits. She was bound to be upset, probably lose her temper with him, but at least she wouldn't throw a fit and have a heart attack like his mother had done, he thought grimly.

The showdown between Karyn and Tudor happened by accident. It was a wet morning. There had been a depressing drizzle as Karyn set off to take Delia to school, but by the time she started to walk back to Adeline Street afterwards, the rain was coming down sharp and slanting, not only driving into her face, but soaking her right through to her skin.

She felt annoyed when she found Tudor was still at home, lolling back in the armchair, smoking a cigarette and dropping the ash all over the place.

'Haven't you got any work to go to?' she asked irritably. 'One of us should be earning some money and so far I've not managed to find a job.'

'Why don't you go and get out of those wet clothes,' he laughed. 'Go on, dry off and I'll have a cup of tea ready to warm you up.'

As she pulled off her dripping wet clothes and towelled herself dry she felt as if the whole world was conspiring against her. She had thought it would be easy enough to find a job when she could work any hours they wanted, but so far she hadn't managed to do so.

What angered her almost as much was the fact that Tudor seemed to be working less and less. The strange thing was that he was still giving her plenty of money each week to buy their food and pay the rent.

Even the cup of hot tea that Tudor had waiting for her failed to make her feel any calmer. Instead, she demanded to know what it was that his mother had known that had upset her so much it had caused her to have a heart attack.

Taken unawares, Tudor began blurting out things he had never intended to tell her.

Karyn listened in silence as he told her about the men he had met while he had been in Cardiff jail. He told her about how he had run a card school and in the four months while he had been inside he had managed to win almost fifty pounds.

'Is that how you managed to buy the handyman business?' she asked.

'I didn't buy it, cariad. I won it!' he said triumphantly.

'How could you do something like that?' She frowned.

'The chap who owned it ran up such a big betting debt and owed me so much money that it was the only way for him to pay. A bloke called Huw had been carrying on doing the work for him and he wrote a note telling Huw that he was to hand the business over to me.'

Karyn stared at him wide eyed. 'You mean completely?' she gasped.

'Well, not exactly. The two of them worked together so I had to agree to keep Huw on.'

'So he's your partner in the business now, is he?'

'No, not really. I'm the boss so he does most of the work and I share the takings with him.'

'So that's why you are at home so much. You do less and less and he does more and more?'

'Put it like that if you want to.' Tudor shrugged. 'He's happy with the arrangement. He agrees with me that I'll never be any good as a handyman. When we work together the customers are more interested in hearing me sing. He gets on with doing their painting or repairs and I entertain them.'

'How long do you think that is going to last?' she asked sceptically. 'He'll soon get tired of that sort of arrangement and what happens then?'

'Don't worry, cariad.' Tudor smiled reassuringly. 'It's not my only way of earning money.'

'No, stealing is another sideline isn't it?' she retorted bitterly. 'Upstairs I've got a drawer full of pawnbrokers' tickets to prove how good you are at that.'

'Bringing all that old stuff here and letting you pawn it was a stupid mistake on my part and it's all finished and in the past,' he promised.

'And what about your gambling?'

He pulled her into his arms and rested his lips against her forehead in a long, tender kiss. 'From now on I'm going to concentrate on my singing,' he told her. 'I'd give the business to

Huw except that if I give up betting as well then how will I give you any housekeeping money?' he chuckled.

Karyn had the feeling that he was laughing at her and that he wasn't really taking the situation seriously.

'If we both worked hard and saved every penny we could, then we could move away from here and put all of it behind us. I'd like a house of our own, not a couple of rooms in someone else's place.'

'That's your dream, is it?' He smiled. 'Mine's to be a famous singer and one day both of them will come true. Remember how we talked about it when we were still kids at school?'

'You've been trying for years, Tudor, but it doesn't seem to be happening, does it?' she said gently.

'That's because I didn't go about it the right way when we first came to Cardiff. I know differently now. I talked to a chap while I was inside who knew the ropes and he was able to tell me how to go about promoting myself and the right way to get auditions and all that sort of thing.'

'If he knew so much about how to be famous, then what was he doing inside?'

'He couldn't sing, cariad. When he heard me warbling away he was absolutely astounded that I hadn't been discovered. He said it was only a matter of time and I'd be topping the bills up and down the country.'

'So what have you done about it since you came out? Have you taken any of the advice he gave you?'

'No, I've done nothing so far, cariad. It takes time to set up the necessary meetings. They said it was better for me to wait until I was ready to do a presentation.'

'What on earth is that?'

'Perform a carefully planned programme in front of a genuine talent scout or someone who is auditioning because they are planning to put on a show.'

'I see! So where do you have to go to find one of these people, then?'

'Well, that's the difficult bit because most of them are in London. You have to write to them and ask if they'll let you come down and meet them and do a presentation to show them what you can do. This bloke gave me the names and addresses of one or two people that I should get in touch with.'

'And have you?' Karyn asked impatiently.

Tudor looked at her blankly. 'Have I what?'

'Have you been in touch with any of them and asked if you could go and see them?'

He shook his head. 'I haven't felt like it . . . not with Mam dying like she did. That shook me up pretty badly, see. I felt I needed to get over that first. But I will. I've got the list of names and I mean to write to every one of them.'

'It could take months before you hear from

them, that's if any of them bother to reply.'

'I know, but that's what it takes. You have to believe in yourself and that you have talent and you need to have endless patience. This bloke I met in there said he knew chaps who'd been struggling for years to get recognised and to get themselves established as actors or entertainers.'

'And in the meantime they commit crimes to get by,' she said cynically.

'I thought you would be the one person who would believe in me?' Tudor said sourly.

'I do! I think you have a wonderful voice. I could listen to you for ever, and I think you do stand a chance of one day making a living from singing.'

'There you are, then. You'll just have to be patient, the same as I am being.'

They'd talked of nothing else until it was time to go and collect Delia from school, but Karyn still had no clear idea about what the future held. She did realise, however, that the chance of them moving to a house of their own was so remote that she might as well forget all about it.

She hated the idea of Tudor gambling because she knew how his moods could change and how depressed he became when he was on a losing streak. And there always seemed to be far more of those than there were of winning ones, she thought grimly.

Yet if she insisted that he went on working

as a handyman, then that might be putting another temptation in his path. It was encouraging him, indirectly, to continue stealing!

Chapter Twenty-One

Karyn had virtually given up all hope of finding work when a job fell into her lap. She had called into the Fish Parlour where she'd once worked on the off chance that they might need a waitress, and had been told that although they didn't need anyone there might be a job going in a small corner shop a few streets away.

'The middle-aged couple who own it, Rhys and Cara Williams, are friends of ours and Cara has to go into hospital for an operation. Rhys was only saying yesterday that he'll have to get someone to give him a hand, so they might consider you if they haven't found anyone else yet.'

'That sounds wonderful,' Karyn agreed, her eyes lighting up with enthusiasm.

Rhys Williams was in his late fifties, balding and overweight. His wife looked older because her face was drawn with pain and as she told Karyn, 'I've not been well for the past couple of years.'

They were happy enough to employ her especially when she told them that she'd worked in a general shop once before when she lived in Pen-y-llyn.

'That's first class, you'll soon get the hang of

things here,' Cara said with relief. 'I've got a week or two to show you the ropes before I go into hospital, so by then you'll be on top of things.'

'Is it only to be a temporary job?' Karyn asked tentatively.

Cara shrugged. 'The doctor says that I'll need to rest up for at least three months after my operation and he advised that I ought to take things easy for another six months or so. I'm not sure if you call that temporary or not. We'll have to see how things go, it might even be longer.'

'That sounds fine to me,' Karyn told her. 'When do you want me to start?'

'Would tomorrow be too soon? I'd like to think you could handle things and knew all the prices and where everything is kept. I don't want to be lying in hospital worrying about things, now do I?'

'Tomorrow it will be, then,' Karyn agreed.

'We open at eight o'clock in the morning and close at six or seven except on Fridays and Saturdays, when we usually stay open until about nine. You won't be expected to work that late, though,' she said quickly as she saw the worried look on Karyn's face. 'Got young kiddies, have you?'

'Only one. A little girl. She's just started school.'

Now it was Cara's turn to look worried. 'Does that mean you will want to finish by four o'clock every afternoon? And what is going to happen on Saturdays?'

'No, that will be all right,' Karyn assured her. 'My husband will collect Delia from school and he'll look after her on Saturdays.'

Cara nodded understandingly. 'I'll tell you what, shall we say that you'll start work at nine in the morning, and that you'll come here straight after taking your little girl to school?'

Karyn's eyes lit up. 'That would be wonderful. It would mean my husband could get off to work early to make up for having to finish before four o'clock to pick Delia up after school.'

'There you are, then,' Cara Williams said with a sigh of relief. 'Everything seems to be settled. We shall look forward to seeing you tomorrow.'

Karyn walked home on air. She liked both Rhys and Cara Williams and looked forward to serving in their shop.

Tudor seemed equally pleased by the news.

'Quite an achievement.' He grinned. 'You've even made sure that I won't be late getting to work in the morning; that was a clever move.'

'Not really.' Karyn frowned. 'It was Mrs Williams's idea. She said I could come to work straight after dropping Delia off at school. I said you would be able to meet her from school in the afternoon and that I would be able to work until six o'clock.'

'Is that the time they close? It seems early for a corner shop.'

'They live over the shop and that is when she finishes. She goes up and starts cooking their evening meal while Mr Williams spends another hour clearing up in the shop. If anyone comes in while he is doing that, then he serves them.'

'And what happens on Fridays and Saturdays when most corner shops stay open until nine o' clock, or even later?'

Karyn shrugged. 'Mrs Williams said I could finish at six o' clock, so I didn't ask.'

Tudor inhaled thoughtfully. 'There's only one problem, then, who is going to collect Delia at dinner time?'

'No one! She can take some sandwiches with her and sit at her desk and eat them.'

Tudor blew out a cloud of smoke. 'She won't like having to do that.'

'I don't think she'll mind. Lots of the other children take their midday meal along with them and then they play together afterwards.'

'And I collect her at four o'clock?'

'That's right. You said you'd have no problem arranging your day so that you could finish in time to do that.'

'Yes, so you can go ahead and start work tomorrow,' he agreed affably.

Karyn found she had no difficulty in adapting to working at the Williams's corner shop. Both Rhys and Cara were warm and friendly and they seemed to be pleased by the way she

270

handled the customers and the speed at which she learned where the different items of stock were kept.

'I won't have a single worry about this place while I'm in hospital,' Cara said, smiling. 'I can't believe you've mastered everything so quickly, it's a load off my mind.'

Inspired by Cara's confidence, Karyn did her very best. The customers were very varied and many of them dithered for ages about what to buy and how much it cost. They ranged from newly married young twenty-somethings, who sometimes were not even sure what they needed, to very old ladies who were living on their own and had to watch their pennies very closely. A great many of the customers in the late afternoon were youngsters sent along by their mother with a list of what they needed written on a scrap of paper.

Tudor seemed quite happy with the new arrangements. He and Delia always enjoyed each other's company and now they seemed to have so many secrets that at times Karyn felt a twinge of jealousy. It sometimes seemed to her that she wasn't needed, except to carry out the mundane duties of cleaning their two rooms and doing the washing and ironing.

Karyn still had dreams about moving to a small house of their own and from time to time she brought the matter up with Tudor, but he always pooh-poohed the idea.

'We'll have to move soon,' she protested,

'Delia is getting too old to be sleeping in the same room as us; it's not right.'

Perhaps we should ask Josiah and Sophia if they would rent us another room, then. There's the box room.'

'That's only a slip of a place, I don't think you'd even manage to get a bed in there.'

'I'll ask them and see what they have to say about it.'

'Do you think that is such a good idea?' Karyn said worriedly. 'They're bound to want us to pay more rent and that will mean we will save less—'

'Does it matter?' Tudor interrupted impatiently. 'We've nowhere near enough put aside to even think about moving to anywhere else. You'll have to wait until I get a proper singing contract before we can think about doing that.'

'That's like waiting for a miracle,' she snapped. 'You are no nearer managing to do that than you ever were.'

'I've got plans,' he said huffily, 'you'll just have to be patient for a while longer.'

Karyn said no more. She didn't want to stir up any discord. At the moment things were going smoothly enough. They had a routine worked out that suited her fine. She didn't earn big money, but it was there waiting for her every Friday night. In addition, Mr Williams gave her a generous discount on her groceries and he was always willing to let her have any left-over bread or cakes or stale biscuits for a fraction of their real price.

Cara was out of hospital and seemed to have made a splendid recovery from her gall bladder operation. Already she was pottering around in her kitchen.

'I need to take things easy, mind,' she insisted whenever Karyn asked her when she was coming back into the shop. 'As long as you are there I don't need to hurry, or worry. It's been a godsend having you working here and no mistake.'

Karyn was pleased that they found her work so satisfactory, but she was also a little concerned about Delia. She was happy enough and Tudor seemed to be enjoying taking care of her after school. That was partly the trouble, Karyn thought unhappily. By the time she arrived home at six o'clock each evening and they'd eaten their evening meal, it was time for Delia to go to bed. She was with Tudor all day on Saturday so it was only on Sundays when she really saw anything at all of her. Whenever she suggested going to the park Delia would say that she and her dad had been there the day before.

'I tell you what we will do,' Cara Williams suggested, when she confided in her, 'we'll arrange for you to have the afternoons off once your little girl breaks up for the school summer holidays. What do you think of that? Could your husband manage to look after her until one o'clock each day?'

'You should have told her that wasn't necessary,' Tudor scowled when she told him. 'I can manage.'

'I'd like to have more time with Delia, though,' Karyn protested. 'I don't see nearly enough of her. Anyway, it will give you a chance to let Huw have a few days off, I'm sure he'd be grateful for a break.'

Karyn certainly enjoyed her afternoons off. Most days it was fine enough for her and Delia to go out together to Victoria Park or Roath Park. Karyn varied the routes they took so that she could find out more about other parts of Cardiff. She looked longingly at the street of small two-up, two-down houses quite near Roath Park and wondered if the day would ever come when they would be able to rent one of them. She was sure they could afford to do so now, but Tudor seemed to be reluctant to make any change.

They were almost halfway through the school holidays when Delia remarked that they hadn't been to the cemetery to see Granny's grave for a while.

'It must be full of weeds by now, unless my dad has found time to go and see to it.'

Karyn was puzzled. Surely the grave didn't need constant attention. Tudor hadn't ever mentioned the matter to her; in fact, she'd had no idea that he had been visiting it.

Delia was so persistent that in the end she agreed they'd pay it a visit. She hadn't been

274

near Cathays Cemetery since the funeral but Delia knew exactly where the grave was. The moment they got off the tram at the junction of Crwys Road and Fairoak Road she led the way past the wall and railings into the cemetery.

'It's this way,' she said confidently. 'We come here nearly every week after school,' she went on.

'It looks in good order to me,' Karyn commented as she looked down at the plain grass mound. There was no headstone, simply a container of flowers set in the middle of it.

'My dad always brings a trowel with him so that he can make sure the sides are neat and tidy,' Delia told her. 'We should have brought one as well.'

'But why? There's nothing at all that needs doing,' Karyn pointed out.

'Dad always brings some flowers and then he takes out that tin box thing there in the middle and sends me to the tap over there to wash it out, fill it with clean water and bring it back here,' she said importantly. 'Then he arranges some fresh flowers in it.'

Karyn bit her lip. She knew it was Tudor's mother who was buried there, but to be putting fresh flowers on her grave every week did seem extravagant when she was trying so hard to be economical and save every penny she could.

Delia was so near to tears because they hadn't brought any flowers that Karyn decided that as a compromise they could refresh the water.

Carefully she took out the bunch of flowers already there and lifted out the container.

'Right, where do we go for clean water?'

'I'll do it, I'll do it,' Delia insisted. 'I'm the one who always goes to get the water.'

She almost snatched the container out of her mother's hand. 'You straighten up the sides of the hole it has to go back into, I won't be a minute.'

She set off at a run towards the far side of the cemetery, her hair flying. Karyn looked at the bunch she'd removed. They looked as fresh as if they'd only been put there a couple of days ago and she wondered if Tudor had been back to see to his mother's grave without Delia.

She felt humiliated by her own meanesss in begrudging him the money he spent on the flowers. She'd had no idea he felt so sentimental about his mother. He had certainly kept it to himself, she thought with a wry smile.

She knelt down to make sure that the hole was tidy enough for the container to fit back in when the glint of metal deep down at the bottom caught her eye. Her curiosity aroused, she reached down to see what it was. As her fingers closed round a piece of chain she tugged at it. As she pulled it out of the hole she saw that it was a gold chain with a pretty pendant on the end of it.

She stared at it with a mixture of disbelief and horror as unpleasant memories crowded her mind. As she heard Delia coming back she slipped it back into the grave out of sight.

They rearranged the flowers and left the cemetery hand in hand, but Karyn barely listened to Delia's chatter on the way home; her mind was too preoccupied with thinking about what she had found and wondering why it had been lying there. Had it dropped into the grave by accident, or had it been buried there deliberately?

She didn't really want to face up to the suspicions buzzing about in her mind yet she knew she had to tell Tudor and to find out what he knew about it. Deep down she knew perfectly well that the necklet couldn't possibly have fallen in when someone had been bending over the grave.

Suddenly there were dark storm clouds shutting out the happy summer sun of the wonderful summer she had been enjoying so much.

She felt as though she was on the edge of a precipice and she didn't know what she would do if her suspicions were confirmed. Remembering the collection of pawnbrokers' tickets that she had amassed when Tudor first came out of prison and started working as a handyman, she shuddered. Was it a piece of jewellery left over from then? Or – and the thought sent a feeling of dread through her – had he started thieving again?

There was only one way she could set her

mind at rest, she resolved, and that was to come back on her own to check whether or not there was anything else hidden away in Bronwen's grave.

She waited for three days, growing more and more impatient and apprehensive, before she had a chance. She made the excuse that she wanted to go and make sure that Cara was all right because she hadn't been feeling too well that day. Instead she went off to Cathays Cemetery, this time armed with a small trowel and fork.

Her heart thundered as she approached the grave and saw that there were different flowers in the container. She realised that Tudor must have been there. She hesitated for a few minutes by the side of the grave, trying to convince herself that taking the container out and checking what was down there was something she must do.

Dropping down on to her knees, she lifted out the flowers and laid them carefully to one side. Then she prised the metal container out of the hole. The soil beneath it was loose, as though it had been disturbed quite recently.

With a sense of dread, her heart thundering, she loosened it even more with the prongs of the hand fork and then, using the small trowel, lifted some of it clear of the hole. In no time at all she had uncovered a canvass-wrapped package.

She paused to sit back on her heels and open

it up and the blood rushed to her head when she saw that inside was a motley collection of rings, necklaces and bracelets.

For a moment she didn't know what to do. Should she replace them and hope that Tudor would never notice that his cache had been discovered? Then her heart hardened. That would only be condoning his crime, she told herself.

His mother had died because she had been so upset to discover that he had done such things, she reminded herself. Unless she faced Tudor with the proof she now had in her hands, how could she ever convince him that she knew and make him stop doing it?

By rights she ought to hand over what she had found to the police and give them a chance to trace the owners. Some of the pieces probably had sentimental value as well as being worth a lot of money. If Tudor was caught again, he would go to prison for years.

She knelt there for several minutes, feeling sick with fear as to what the outcome could be. There were tears streaming down her cheeks as she wrestled with her conscience about what was the right thing to do.

Chapter Twenty-Two

Tudor was pacing the room like a cat on hot bricks when Karyn arrived home. For a moment she thought he had guessed where she had been and what she had been doing, but before she could speak he caught her round the waist and whirled her round, his handsome face glowing with excitement.

'I've done it, cariad! I've broken through; my singing career is on its way!'

Karyn looked bemused. 'What are you talking about?'

'I didn't say anything to you before in case it came to nothing, but I went for an audition a couple of weeks ago and now I've heard from them and they want me to appear at the Abacus Music Hall in Rhymney Street. The show will be on there for the whole week and I'll be on stage singing every night. My name will be on the billboard. It's all happening at last.'

He twirled her round, hugging her so tightly that she thought he would crush her ribs.

'When did you hear about this?' she asked breathlessly.

'Tonight, after you went out to see Cara Williams. Sophia brought the letter in to me. It seems that it was delivered earlier today when we were both out. Sophia had put it on their mantelpiece and forgotten all about it until Josiah spotted it and wanted to know what it was.'

He was so excited that Karyn hadn't the heart to question him about her find at the cemetery. All the way home she had rehearsed what she would say and how she would cross-question him, determined to get the truth out of him, but seeing the jubilation on his face, how could she do that now?

'How long did you say you were going to be in the show for?' she asked cautiously.

'Only for a week. It's a sort of trial, an experimental run. If they like my act, then they could sign me up for six weeks or even longer.'

'You'd be singing all that time at the same theatre?'

'No, of course not, don't be twp. We'd be touring. Newport, Merthyr, Porthcawl, Penarth, Swansea, probably even further afield, if the show is popular.'

'So this one week at the Abacus Theatre is a sort of try out for you, is it?'

'Yes, but I'm sure they'll give me a longer contract once they've heard me sing,' he said confidently. The audience are bound to be won over by my repertoire; you know how they loved my singing back at Pen-y-llyn and at the Voyager.'

'Yes, and the crowds in Morgan's Arcade!'

Tudor pulled a face. 'Do you have to keep reminding me about that? I made a mistake and I paid for it; now it's all in the past.' He waved the letter in the air jubilantly. 'This is the future and what I've been waiting for all this time.'

'It certainly sounds a great opportunity,' Karyn agreed. 'When do you start?'

'Tomorrow! Rehearsals begin at ten o'clock. There's a matinée and an evening performance each day. Will you iron my best white shirt and press my suit for me?'

'Hold on! What about Delia? You are supposed to be looking after her every day until one o'clock when I finish at the shop.'

His face clouded, and then his smile was wide and beaming. 'Tell Cara Williams you don't want the job any longer. I'll be earning enough for both of us.'

'I can't simply walk out and leave them in the lurch like that, not when they've been so very good to me,' Karyn exclaimed aghast.

'I'm not missing out on this chance, not after all the time I've waited to be discovered,' Tudor blustered. 'You'll have to take Delia with you. Explain to them what's happened. If they don't like it, then walk out. You won't be letting them down if you offer to work and they turn you down.'

Cara Williams was far more helpful than Karyn had ever dreamed she would be.

'Of course you can bring Delia along to work

with you,' she agreed without a moment's hesitation. 'It's less than a week before they go back to school, isn't it?'

'Thank you so much. You're quite right; school starts again next week.'

'There you are, then, that's all settled.'

'If you're certain that she won't be in the way, or that Mr Williams will object to her being in the shop? I'll bring along some crayons and a colouring book and sit her in a corner.'

'Oh no you won't!' Cara Williams said sharply. 'Delia can come upstairs and keep me company.'

'Are you quite sure? She's a terrible little chatterbox,' Karyn warned her.

'Good, she'll liven up my morning. It's only until one o'clock and then you'll be taking her out somewhere. What are you going to do when she goes back to school? Will her father still be able to meet her in the afternoons?'

Karyn shook her head. 'Not if this theatrical company decide to keep him on and they start touring. If that happens, I'm not sure when he will be at home.'

'Then we'll have to make some sort of arrangement. If I am feeling well enough, I'll go and collect her, otherwise you can nip out and do it. Then she can stay upstairs with me until you finish at six.'

'It sounds all right, but you should have told her you won't need to work there any longer now that I've got this singing contract,' Tudor boasted when Karyn told him of the arrangement with Cara Williams.

'Well, let's see how it all works out, shall we, before I burn my bridges,' she said cautiously.

'You mean you haven't any faith in me? You don't think that this will lead to other bookings and that in next to no time I'll be topping the bill, not one of the names near the bottom?' he said sulkily.

'I'd like to think that would happen, cariad, but we both know that anything to do with show business can be pretty precarious,' Karyn said cautiously. 'Anyway, what are you going to do about your other business?'

'I've already handed that over to Huw. He was doing most of the work anyway and the chap I won it off will be out of jail any day now so he'll probably want it back.'

'Not exactly a gift then, was it!'

Tudor shrugged disinterestedly. 'They are old mates so they can sort it out between them. I'm fed up with it and I don't want anything more to do with it.'

Karyn wondered if this was the right moment to mention the cache of jewellery she had found at the cemetery. She would like to know if he had been back there since and discovered that it was missing or whether his time had been taken up at the theatre. Now, if he went on tour, then he mightn't even be in Cardiff for several weeks.

The thought that the things she had found were still in the house worried her a great deal. She still didn't know if all of it had been hidden away there by him or whether perhaps this chap Huw who worked with him was in some way involved as well. Or, of course, Tudor might even be hiding it for the chap he met in jail, as part of the deal when he had been given a share of the business.

It was a problem that haunted her. She wished there was someone she could turn to for advice. She toyed with the idea of talking to Cara Williams about it then common sense told her that would be rather foolish.

She knew that the right thing to do would be to go to the police, but if the hoard of jewellery had been put there by Tudor, then they would arrest him. If that happened, then he would be back inside and his career as a singer, as well as everything else, would be scuttled before it had a chance to start. Now that Tudor had, at long last, been discovered that would be so frustrating for him especially if he was only hiding it for somebody else.

Since she hadn't been able to bring herself to discuss the matter with Tudor she decided that while he was away on tour she would go back to the cemetery and check to see if anyone else had been to the grave.

The next day she was holding her breath, she felt so tense, and when she reached Cathays Cemetery with Delia her knees were knocking as she walked towards Bronwen's grave the suspense was so great. When she saw that flowers in the holder were so old that most of them had shrivelled up, she let out in a long sigh of relief. That was surely an indication that Tudor hadn't been back there, she told herself. Could that possibly mean that he didn't know anything at all about what was hidden there?

Deep down she knew that it was highly unlikely after what Delia had told her, but it had been pointless asking him. From the moment he woke up in the morning until he went to bed at night every fibre of his being was involved with singing. If she had mentioned it, she knew he would either have dismissed it by saying he didn't know what she was talking about, or flown into a temper and said that she was accusing him of a crime that had nothing to do with him.

At the end of the first week he had come home overjoyed that the show was being retained in Cardiff for a second week and was being transferred to the Sherman Theatre.

Karyn was so relieved that she felt guilty about even thinking so ill of him. As a way to salve her conscience she resolved to take Delia to the Sherman Theatre to see him on stage.

She said nothing to him about her idea, but she told Delia that if she promised to keep it a secret, then she would take her there as a birthday treat.

'You mustn't tell your dad, though,' she emphasised, 'or it won't be a surprise.'

'Will it be all right to tell him I've got a secret?' Delia asked eagerly.

'It might be better if you didn't do that in case he tries to find out what the secret is,' she warned.

Delia nodded solemnly. 'When will we be going to the theatre? Will it be on my birthday?'

'Yes, and we'll go to the matinée.'

'Can I wave to him when he comes on stage, so that he knows I'm there?' she asked excitedly.

'Of course you can, but he mightn't see you, there will be a lot of other people there in the audience as well, remember.'

When she saw the disappointed look on Delia's face Karyn's heart softened. 'I tell you what,' she promised, 'we'll have another secret as well.'

'Another one!' Delia's dark eyes widened and she waited expectantly to be told more.

'After the show finishes,' Karyn promised, 'we'll go round to the Stage Door and ask if we can go in and see him.'

In the days that followed Karyn was thankful that their visit was less than a week away because she was quite sure that Delia would be unable to keep it a secret for very much longer. She was constantly giggling to herself and making so many remarks about 'her treat' and 'their secret' that she was surprised Tudor hadn't picked up on the fact that there was something going on which he didn't know about. She was sure he would have done so normally, but he was so wrapped up in what was happening in his own life that he didn't seem to be able to think of anything else.

He'd talked so much about the show, and the other people on the bill, that she was almost as keyed up as Delia was about their forthcoming outing.

To take some of the pressure off Delia she allowed her to tell Sophia and Cara about her forthcoming treat. By the time Saturday morning arrived both of them were almost as excited about the matinée as Delia was.

Sophia was willing to look after Delia until Karyn finished work at one o'clock, but Cara Williams had already offered so that she could see Delia in the new dress which Karyn had bought her for her birthday and which she would be wearing for the first time.

'I'm not wearing my new dress to the shop,' Delia told Sophia, importantly. 'I'm going to take it with me and change into it after my mam stops work because I don't want to get it dirty or to spill anything down it.'

Cara insisted that both Delia and Karyn had a ham sandwich and a cup of tea before they set out. She also made Delia promise to remember everything that went on and then she could tell her all about it after school on Monday.

Rhys Williams was waiting for them by the

shop door as they came downstairs ready to leave. He admired Delia's pretty dress and gave her a bag of toffees to take with her, adding even more excitement to her special birthday outing.

They arrived at the Sherman Theatre in good time and joined the queue at the box office to buy their tickets. Delia was looking around all the time in the hope of seeing Tudor and was disappointed when she didn't. Karyn explained he would already be inside the theatre getting ready to go on stage along with all the other actors.

Karyn was afraid that sitting still during the opening acts would be too much for Delia, but she was quite wrong. She sat entranced as a troupe of girl dancers did the opening routine and then a juggler followed by a stand-up comic performed.

When the compère announced that the Cardiff baritone, Tudor Morgan, would be next she wriggled and squealed with excitement. In an attempt to quieten her down Karyn warned her that unless she was quiet they would be told to leave.

Karyn's own heart was in her mouth when Tudor strode out on to the stage. She thought he had never looked more handsome – tall and so good-looking, with his dark head held so proudly. It made her legs turn to water simply to see him standing there.

When he began to sing, his magnificent baritone voice soared up into the rafters and seemed to fill every corner of the theatre.

Karyn had never seen him on stage before and as he put his heart and soul into his performance it brought tears to her eyes and she found it tremendously impressive.

She felt Delia's little hand creep into hers and squeezed it tightly. As she turned to smile at her she saw that the child's mouth was slightly open, so immersed was she in what was happening.

Tudor performed twice. In between there were several other acts and the troupe of chorus girls danced twice more as well. The last time was to bring the show to an end. Then there was a line-up on the stage of all the performers to rapturous applause from the audience.

'Come on!' The moment the curtain came down for the second time, Karyn took Delia by the hand and edged her way out of the row where they were sitting. Once outside the theatre she hurried her down the side of the building to the Stage Door.

There was an anxious moment while Karyn explained to the doorman who they were. Then they were inside and following his directions to the dressing rooms in search of Tudor.

For a moment, Karyn thought they had been sent to the wrong place because all she could see in the room were the chorus girls, some still in their scanty costumes. Then she spotted Tudor; he was sitting on a chair and was surrounded by girls who were all laughing and talking and vying with each other as they tried to attract his attention.

For one moment a streak of pure jealousy stabbed through her. Even though she was wearing her best dress she felt drab alongside so many pretty young girls. Then, as she felt Delia squeezing her hand and heard her complaining plaintively that she couldn't see her dad, she pushed her way through the gaggle of girls so that they could reach Tudor's side.

He was quite startled when Karyn tapped him on the arm and he turned round and saw her. 'What are you doing here? Is something wrong with Delia?'

'No, I'm here,' Delia piped up as the girls made way for her. 'We've been sitting in the theatre listening to you singing,' she told him excitedly.

'Was I good?' he asked, picking her up and holding her high in the air.

'You were wonderful. Everyone in there was listening to you!'

'I should hope so,' he told her laughingly.

'So are you going to come home with us now?' Delia demanded.

'No, cariad, I'm afraid I can't. I have to stay here because I have to sing again this evening.'

Delia pulled a face. 'Once or twice?'

'Twice, the same as I did this afternoon. All these pretty ladies have to stay as well because they have to dance and I have to sing.'

Delia let out a deep sigh and nodded as if she understood.

'Come on, then, we must be going home.' Karyn held out a hand to her. She felt she couldn't get out of there quickly enough because watching the way the chorus girls were fawning over Tudor she felt the sharp spike of jealousy stabbing at her again.

Chapter Twenty-Three

Karyn knew that she should be bursting with happiness. She had a handsome husband who had achieved the singing career which he had longed to have ever since he'd been a schoolboy. She had a daughter who was growing taller and prettier by the day. She was also fortunate in that she had a part-time job, despite the fact that the depression resulting from the miners' strike the previous year was affecting most people and a great many businesses.

The only thing she had to complain about was that she felt neglected. Not only was Tudor away far more than he was there with them, but when he was at home he could talk about nothing else other than the show he was appearing in.

It wasn't that she was lonely, she had Sophia and Josiah to talk to when she was at home, and she had Cara and Rhys when she was at work. In addition, a great many of the customers now stopped to chat to her as if they were old friends. She also had Delia, who never stopped chattering.

Despite all this her mind was filled with concern about what Tudor might be doing when he was away on tour. The memory of him when they'd gone backstage at the Sherman Theatre, surrounded by showgirls who were all vying with each other to claim his attention, haunted her. So much so that she commented to both Cara and Sophia about it.

'He's a handsome-looking man, but he can't get into much mischief when there are so many of them around him all the time,' Sophia laughed.

'If you are all that concerned, my dear, then you ought to have a quiet talk with him and tell him how much it is worrying you,' Cara advised. 'He might even be prepared to change his job if he knew how much it was worrying you.'

'I doubt it, he's never been happier. Singing is something he's dreamed about doing all his life.'

Even so, having a talk with Tudor and telling him how she felt was uppermost in her mind the next time he came home. She decided to wait for the right opportunity when they were on their own after Delia was in bed, but Tudor forestalled her.

He was there when she came home from the shop with Delia and she could tell the moment she walked in that he was very upset about something.

'You're early! Has the show come to an end?' she asked in a conciliatory voice, even though, deep in her heart, she thought that would be the perfect solution to her problem. Touring might be something he wanted to do and which made him happy, but it certainly wasn't doing the same for her.

She felt ashamed of her jealousy, but she kept telling herself it was only because she loved him so much that she couldn't accept his new way of life and that it was breaking her heart.

She had planned it all in her mind; they'd have a nice meal and then, as soon as Delia was in bed, settle down to a cosy chat. She'd tell him how lonely she was without him. If that didn't work then she'd lead the conversation round to his mother, and visiting her grave, and then, if he didn't say anything, she'd face him with the facts about what she'd found and perhaps even hint that she'd go to the police if he didn't give up touring.

Now, with him in this uncertain mood, she felt her resolve weakening and suddenly she wasn't at all sure that it was the right way of dealing with the matter. It would be a form of blackmail and, knowing Tudor, he might see it as a challenge – which would make him all the more determined to do what he wanted to do.

All her plans were shattered when, almost before she had her hat and coat off, Tudor asked if she had been up to the cemetery while he had been away.

'Yes, Daddy, we've been up there and we put

some new flowers on Granny's grave,' Delia chimed in.

'When?' His voice was as curt as a whip and his eyes had a hard, icy glare.

'Ages ago, I think it was the first week you went away,' Karyn said quickly.

'You've not been there since?' He directed his gaze towards Delia, as if knowing that she wouldn't lie.

Delia shook her head. 'No, sorry! We forgot all about it. Can we all go there together tomorrow, Daddy? I want to get the water for you like I used to do while you tidy the hole up and my mam can watch or else she can arrange the flowers.'

Tudor didn't answer, but stared hard at Karyn, his eyes questioning. 'And what about you?' he asked softly.

'Me?' She frowned as if unable to understand what it was he wanted to know.

'Have you been up there on your own to tend my mam's grave?' he asked in a steely voice.

For one second she thought of denying it, then at the same moment she realised that this was her opportunity to confront him about what she had found and to ask for an explanation.

The tension between them was tangible. She was sure that Tudor not only knew about the hidden cache, but also that he had been the one responsible for putting it there. That being the case, it was obvious that he suspected that she had been the one to remove it.

'Let's talk about it later on, after Delia is in bed,' she suggested.

'Talk about what?' Delia looked from one to the other, her face alive with curiosity.

Tudor's mood changed like quicksilver. Whisking Delia up in his arms and singing to her, he began to dance around the room. She squealed with happiness and, for the next hour, the pair of them indulged in an interpretation of what she had seen when Karyn had taken her to the theatre. Tudor sang his entire repertoire, and in between each item Delia danced, pretending that she was one of the chorus girls. All Karyn could do was sit and applaud, despite the fact that her own mind was seething with anxiety about what Tudor might tell her after Delia had gone to bed.

As he watched Delia pirouetting and imitating the way she had seen the chorus girls dancing, Tudor's own mind was also in turmoil. He had been both shocked and alarmed when he realised that Karyn had been to the cemetery. Yet, at the same time, he was relieved that it had been her and no one else who had discovered his hoard. He was rather put out that she had been the one who had taken it from the grave, and he hoped that it was hidden away safely. At the back of his mind he had been apprehensive in case Huw had been spying on him and had discovered his haul and taken it for himself.

After their meal, he offered to put Delia to bed and spent almost half an hour talking to her and singing to her until she was so sleepy that she was willing to let him go. Then he braced himself for the confrontation with Karyn.

As he walked back downstairs he was undecided whether to let her be the one to tell him what she knew or to launch straight in with his account of what had happened.

'So you've been looking after my mam's grave!' he said, lighting a cigarette and looking at her expectantly.

'Not really. I went there a couple of times, once with Delia and once on my own. Since then I've been too afraid to go near the place in case I found I wasn't alone.'

'I never knew that you were afraid of being on your own in places like that; surely you know there's no such thing as ghosts,' he commented sarcastically.

'There *were* ghosts, Tudor, ghosts from the past, and I was very afraid,' she told him quietly.

For a moment he looked shamefaced then he tried to turn the tables on her. 'You took the stuff that was hidden there, didn't you?' he accused. 'Do you realise what that did to me? Duw anwyl, I've been to hell and back worrying about it. Why couldn't you have said something?'

'I was afraid to do so; scared of what you might tell me when I asked you how it got there.'

His eyes narrowed. 'You'd already made up your mind, though, without giving me the opportunity to tell you my side of the story,' he blustered.

'Go on, then, tell me all about it now,' she said quietly.

'I want to hear what you know first,' he prevaricated. 'Have you still got the stuff?'

She nodded.

He drew hard on his cigarette. 'Safely hidden away?'

She nodded again, her head teeming with a vision of a drawer full of pawnbroker slips.

'Can we cut out this cat-and-mouse behaviour,' he said irritably. 'That hoard you found was my nest egg, a safeguard against the future, something for us to fall back on if times became hard while we were waiting until my name was up in lights.'

'You've already achieved that, haven't you?'

His face darkened, but he made no reply as he ground out his half-smoked cigarette.

'Go on.'

'No, *you* go on!' Tudor curled one hand into a fist and smote it down on the open palm of the other hand. 'Have you any idea what you've put me through? I thought someone had stolen the lot and yet all the time you've had it tucked away quite safe and never said a word to me about it. That's hardly being supportive, is it?' he exploded.

'I wanted to ask you to explain. I hoped you'd

say that you knew nothing about it. I didn't want to believe that you had started stealing again, not after all that has happened. Betting and stealing, they're the only things you are really good at, aren't they? To use your mother's grave to conceal your loot was so wicked, especially since it was your behaviour that caused the heart attack that killed her.'

Tudor shrugged. 'I did it for you.'

'For me!' She almost screamed the words at him. 'Have you ever thought about the people who owned those rings, bracelets and necklaces and how much they meant to them? They were probably presents given to them by people who loved them.'

'That's sentimental rubbish,' he said dismissively. 'Anyway,' he added when she remained silent, 'there's not much that can I do about it now, is there?'

'I don't know, and I don't know what to do about them either. They should be handed over to the police.'

'We can't do that! Duw anwyl!' He ran a hand through his hair. 'Do you want to see me back inside again?'

'Of course I don't, that's why I've done nothing, or said anything to anyone.'

'If I get rid of them all, then can we put it all behind us?' he asked hopefully.

'How would you do that?' she asked, frowning.

'Return it to the man who asked me to take

care of it for him. I didn't steal it,' he told her quickly, 'it belongs to the chap I met up with in jail, the gambler I won the business from, and he's out now so he'll be very happy to have it back. With my being away so much I haven't seen him and I didn't want you to know that he was out of prison and that he might come looking for it.'

Her relief was so great that she was speechless. Then doubts began to creep in. She looked at him bemused. 'That's not what you said a little while ago. You said it was a form of insurance in case we had any bad times . . .'

He looked shamefaced. 'Well, it was – in a way. I would have made use of it if I'd had to; anything rather than see you and Delia go short.'

Could she believe him this time or was this just a trumped-up story to placate her? Immediately her doubts were followed by remorse that she had ever thought that it had been Tudor who had hidden the stuff there.

If only the other problem she wanted to resolve could be dealt with so easily, she thought ruefully.

She had intended to ask him if he would stop touring, but now she didn't feel she could. If he was telling the truth, then she'd been so wrong about the jewellery that she was probably just as wrong to be jealous about the attention he seemed to be enjoying from the chorus girls.

It's because he still means so much to me, she told herself. She knew she was still in love with him. He was so good-looking that it was easy to see how other women were attracted to him.

Saying nothing and letting him enjoy the career that all his life he'd longed for so intensely was the only way she could make up to him for what she had been thinking, she decided.

Watching her closely, Tudor understood her so well that he had a pretty clear idea of what was going through her head. He knew she was back in the palm of his hand and would agree with almost anything he might suggest. Even so, he didn't know whether to drop his bombshell now or to keep her on tenterhooks for another week or two.

He was eager to get on with his new plan, but when he found his secret hoard had been discovered and, even worse, that it was missing, he hadn't known what to do.

He been afraid that when he told Karyn about his new plans she would oppose him because, to some extent, it was a tremendous risk. Without the money he hoped to be able to get for the jewellery he'd hidden away it would probably be impossible.

He turned everything over in his mind, wondering whether or not he had said enough to persuade her to simply hand the haul over to him so that he could return both the jewellery and the business. Had he convinced her that he was going to give it all back to Huw and his jailbird mate?

In Karyn's eyes that was bound to look good, he told himself. It would convince her that he really was making a complete break with the past and starting afresh.

Then, afterwards, when he had told her about meeting Marcus Webb and about his new plans for the future, would she give him her full support. He knew he had to be very careful about what he said and how he handled things. He had to be diplomatic, and it might be better to play on her sympathy by telling her that he couldn't stand touring because it meant being away from her and Delia so much and that he could see she was very concerned about it all.

She would probably be even more upset if she knew the full value of the hoard she'd hidden away somewhere.

He wouldn't be able to get a quarter of its true value, but, even so, he was counting on it being enough for them to live on for the next few months until his career was established.

This time, he reflected, his name really would be up there in lights. Films were something revolutionary and they were going to be the big thing in the future. No more prancing around on the stage and then the entire company packing up at the end of the week and moving on to more dreary digs and more cold, draughty theatres.

Film making was still in its infancy, but not so new that he'd be taking any great risk. Marcus Webb knew what he was about. He'd come over from America looking for new talent, that's why he'd been in the theatre that night when they'd played in Newport.

He'd said afterwards that he'd spotted Tudor's prospects at once because his wonderful voice had made him stand out from all the other acts.

'They're run-of-the-mill, but you are pure gold with a voice like that,' Marcus had told him when they'd gone for a drink together afterwards. 'If you can afford to put some money up front, then I can get you a lead part in a new musical that is about to be made.'

The money up front, he explained, was for promotional purposes and nothing to do with the making of the film. It was to make sure that it would not only be Tudor's voice drawing people's attention, but also his looks and personality as well.

'You need a portfolio of pictures of yourself that will impress the casting director and the people who'll be publicising the film,' Marcus told him. 'All that sort of thing costs money because, even though you are very good-looking, you need a top-notch photographer to produce the right sort of professional shots. You'll also need the smart suits, the right shoes and all the other clothes that can transform a good-looking guy like you into a real heart-throb.'

Tudor had been highly impressed by Marcus's knowledge of the film world. His confidence was boosted when Marcus assured him that in a matter of months the name Tudor Morgan would be one that film producers would fight over.

When Marcus talked about the sort of money the big singing stars could earn, Tudor had been thunderstruck. Even when he was warned that to achieve that sort of reward he might have to move to America he was not in any way apprehensive; in fact, it only added to his determination to succeed.

'The first step, of course, is to find a good agent to represent you,' Marcus advised. 'You need someone who not only knows the ropes, but who is also on good terms with all the top brass in the film world.'

'What about you becoming my agent?' Tudor suggested the following evening when he met Marcus for a drink after the show.

Marcus had looked interested. 'It's a great idea, and I think we could work well together because I am confident you have a terrific career ahead of you,' he said enthusiastically.

'Great!' Tudor held out his hand to shake on the deal.

Marcus paused and looked uncertain, 'Are you sure you can afford all the preparation and build up when you've got a wife and child to support?'

He'd gone on to say that until the film was

underway, and there were advanced bookings to prove that it was going to be a winner, the stars wouldn't receive any money at all. 'That's the way things work,' he had explained.

Tudor had still been eager to go ahead. Remembering the stash of jewellery he'd hidden away in his mother's grave he'd said confidently, 'I can't hand over any money to you right this minute, but when the show ends tomorrow, and I go back home, I can have it ready for you within a matter of days.'

Marcus had agreed to the arrangement and said he would meet him in Cardiff the following week.

Tudor had been utterly devastated when he arrived back and found the grave empty. The only person other than himself who even knew he visited the cemetery was Delia. She couldn't possibly have known anything about it because he had always made sure that she was well away from the grave, fetching water for the flowers, before he extracted any of the jewellery.

He had been so careful, only ever taking out one piece on each visit, and he always made sure that he went to a different pawnbroker each time as well as always giving a different name and address. He'd done everything he possibly could to make sure that no one knew his secret and that whatever happened he could never be located in case the item was ever traced by its original owner.

It was unbelievable that, of all people, it had

been Karyn who had stumbled on his secret, and that the hoard was now in her safe keeping; it was either sheer bad luck or good fortune, depending on how easy it was to persuade her to hand it all over to him.

Chapter Twenty-Four

Karyn took an instant dislike to Marcus Webb from the first moment she met him. He was of medium height, slightly tubby, and he had a prominent nose, receding chin and cold, dark blue eyes. In his flawlessly cut charcoal-grey suit, spotted bow tie and black homburg hat his appearance was so flamboyant that she found him off-putting even before she had spoken to him.

She had heard a great deal about him from Tudor. Ever since the day he'd first met him in Newport he seemed to have placed him on a pedestal and not only believed every word the man uttered, but also was prepared to slavishly follow his advice about how he should further his career.

Marcus had told her that Tudor was far too good to be singing in a revue show and that he deserved a far wider, more appreciative audience.

'I've told your husband that he deserves to be auditioned for a lead singing part in one of the talkie films that are taking the world by storm,' he pronounced.

Karyn could see how excited Tudor was by

the idea, but she was more cautious because she was sure that there must be a great many drawbacks. Talkies were so new that very few people knew anything about them or what was involved in making them.

There were one or two outstanding actors who had become household names like Al Jolson in *The Jazz Singer*, but that had been made in America and she thought Tudor was aiming rather high if he thought he could do anything like that.

She tried to show an interest in what Marcus Webb was suggesting because she hated the idea of Tudor being on tour. She decided, though, that she would prefer it if he continued to be away rather than risk starting all over again by trying to do something so new and risky.

She'd had high hopes that once Tudor had handed back the cache of jewellery she'd found hidden in his mam's grave that their lives would once more be straightforward.

She had a job, Delia was happy and settled in her school, and he was making a living singing which was what he had wanted to do all his life.

If they made any further changes, then she hoped it would be to move into a house of their own. She liked both Sophia and Josiah Earl and appreciated how kind and helpful they were, but she longed to have a home that was completely hers where she could run things in her own way. She wanted to know that when she shut her front door no one could come in unless she invited them to do so.

On New Year's Eve, Tudor dropped the bombshell that he wouldn't be doing any more touring because he had finished with the company for good.

'You mean they've taken your name off the bill?' she said worriedly. 'Does that mean you are out of work?'

His eyes twinkled. 'What do you think?'

Karyn chewed at the nail on her forefinger; she felt confused and uneasy. On the one hand, she was pleased to learn that he wouldn't be on tour and going away from home all the time. On the other, she was scared that it meant he would be going back to being a handyman again and all the temptations that entailed.

She had never completely believed his tale that he hadn't been the one who had stolen all the jewellery she had found. Not that it mattered, she told herself, since it was no longer in their keeping. After she'd given it back to him he'd returned it all to Huw and asked him to deal with it.

'So if you have finished with the revue company, then what are you going to do now?' she asked as calmly as she could. She walked over to where he was sitting in the armchair and slid an arm around his shoulder and kissed him on the brow. 'Never mind, perhaps you can make a completely fresh start in 1930,' she said encouragingly.

'What's that supposed to mean?' he challenged.

'New year, new sort of job . . . perhaps even a new home,' she said brightly.

'Duw anwyl! Are you on that tack all over again? Forget it, will you!' He shrugged her away. 'We can't afford to move, not yet anyway. Perhaps in a few months' time . . .'

Her face brightened. 'Have you ever thought that perhaps we should take on a shop and live up over it, like Rhys and Cara Williams do?'

'Shop! What are you talking about? I've never worked in a shop in my life.'

'I have, and I was thinking that it would be great for us to work together in a little corner shop of our own. Think what a lovely secure background it would be for Delia. She could even work there with us if she wanted to when she was old enough.'

'That's not the right sort of future for her,' he laughed. 'She wants one where her dad is famous.'

'Famous?' Karyn sensed that he was leading her on. 'What have you got in mind this time?' she questioned anxiously.

'I've been thinking about what Marcus Webb had to say. He thinks I have a tremendous voice and that I should be in one of these new musical pictures that are being made to show in cinemas. He said it's only a question of having the right agent.'

Karyn's mouth tightened. 'He's the right agent that he has in mind, I suppose.'

'As a matter of fact that's exactly right,' Tudor agreed in a surprised voice.

Her heart pounded. 'How much is it going to cost to let him represent you?'

'We haven't got as far as finalising any of the business details yet,' he said evasively.

'Why ever not! After all, you've decided you're going to do it haven't you?'

'I wouldn't dream of making a serious commitment like that without talking it over with you first,' he told her with a disarming smile.

Karyn shrugged and gave a rueful smile of acceptance. She suspected that no matter what she said he was determined to do what Marcus Webb suggested.

'Perhaps you ought to meet him again and hear what he has to say,' Tudor went on. 'Do you think Sophia would listen out for Delia if we went out for a drink with Marcus after she's in bed one night?'

'Probably, but why do we have to go to all that trouble? Your mind is already made up.'

'I want you to be completely sure that I am doing the right thing. I think you will be when you really listen to what he has to say about the sort of a future he thinks I could have.'

Karyn didn't want to meet Marcus Webb again, but Tudor was so persistent, and kept on talking so excitedly about his own future if

Marcus acted as his agent, that in the end she capitulated.

'I can see there won't be a moment's peace until I do but I'm warning you he'll have to be pretty convincing to make me change my mind.'

Tudor was so anxious that she looked her best and impressed Marcus that he made her nervous, and she told him she'd changed her mind. When she admitted it was because she had nothing smart enough to wear, Tudor insisted that she should go and buy herself a new dress.

'Choose something eye-catching, not one of those sensible jobs you usually wear,' he ordered. 'Go to Howell's or David Morgan's for it. Don't buy something cheap from one of the stalls on the Hayes, mind.'

'Whatever I buy he won't see it until I take off my coat, and I've had that ever since we left Pen-y-llyn.'

'Then you had better get a new coat as well. How about something slinky, with one of those big fur collars that are all the fashion?' he suggested as he handed her two crisp, white, five-pound notes.

'You really are trying to impress him. Is it all right if I get some new shoes as well?' she challenged.

''Buy whatever takes your fancy, if you've enough money. Do your best, make me proud.'

'Even if it means we have to live on bread

and whatever scraps I manage to bring home from the shop for the next couple of weeks?' she challenged as she waved the fivers in front of his eyes.

She felt so angry that he was prepared to go to such lengths in order to impress Marcus Webb that she threw caution to the wind and went ahead and did what he'd told her to do.

Shopping with so much money to spend was such a novelty that she found she was enjoying every minute of it. The dress she fell for was in pale pink georgette with the waistline at hip level and a short skirt that skimmed the top of her knees. She had never owned a dress like it in her life. It was the sort of dress a young flapper would wear and so highly impractical that she could see why it was knocked down to a fraction of its original price.

She found a coat that also brought a smile to her lips. It was in a bright red wool cloth, and was trimmed around the hemline and at the cuffs with broad bands of black fur. To complete the look she picked a little black cloche hat to wear over her newly shingled hair and finished it all off with some flesh-coloured artificial-silk stockings and high-heeled black patent court shoes.

If this outfit doesn't stun Marcus Webb then nothing will, she told her reflection as she twirled round slowly in front of the shop's full-length mirror while the black-garbed assistant murmured encouraging words of praise.

Not only was Marcus Webb impressed, but Tudor couldn't take his eyes off her all night.

There was nothing really new in what Marcus had to tell her because she had already heard most of it before from Tudor, so she found it easy to confound him with countless questions.

Marcus, answered most of them very adroitly. By the end of the evening she had still not managed to find out exactly how much money was involved or how much security there was for Tudor in the propositions he was putting forward.

A week later when Tudor told her that he and Marcus had signed some sort of agreement, she felt dismayed.

'You mean you've signed a contract with him?' she asked anxiously.

'Not only that, but Marcus is going to compile a publicity portfolio for me and he is also going to arrange for me to take dancing lessons.'

'Dancing lessons!' She looked at him in disbelief. 'You're supposed to be a singer, you don't need to prance around on stage like a chorus girl!' she flared.

'It's not like that,' Tudor said heatedly. 'Marcus says that if I can dance as well as sing then it will open up all sorts of new opportunities for me,' he explained.

'That's Marcus's opinion is it! Do you have to believe everything he tells you?'

'He knows what he's doing, cariad. Now that I'm signed up for him to act as my agent then it would be foolish not to take his advice, now wouldn't it?'

Karyn shrugged dismissively. There seemed to be no point in arguing. Tudor's heart was now set on becoming a singing film star so all she could do was support him to the best of her ability, just as she had always done.

When she saw the portfolio that Marcus put together for Tudor her heart turned over and she thought she would burst with pride. She had to admit that this was one instance where Marcus was right and knew what he was doing. Tudor was extremely photogenic. His profile was outstanding and the full-facial shots, especially those in which he was smiling, were so compelling that she found herself wondering why he had never been discovered long before this.

From then on the dancing classes took up most of Tudor's day, although he usually managed to get back in time to collect Delia from school. If he wasn't able to, then either Karyn or Cara collected her and she waited in the corner shop until Karyn finished work and they could go home together.

Even when he was at home, dancing seemed to dominate Tudor's time and interest. He seemed to be always practising new intricate steps. To do it properly he needed a partner and, since Karyn was too busy with household chores, Delia spent most of her evenings and weekends dancing with him. Tudor found that she was as nimble-footed as he was.

He constantly sang her praises to Marcus, telling him how well she danced, until in the end Marcus suggested that Tudor should bring her with him to the Studio the following Saturday morning.

At the end of the session Marcus showered Delia with praise. He'd had numerous shots taken of her dancing both on her own and with Tudor, which he said were so outstanding that he might include them in Tudor's portfolio.

Their dual performance was now so accomplished that a week later Marcus encouraged Tudor to sing not only 'Ol' Man River' and 'Honeysuckle Rose', the songs most suitable for his voice, but to try some of the newer ones like 'Baby Face', and 'Yes, Sir, That's My Baby', which were so popular.

'Try singing them while you are dancing with Delia,' Marcus instructed.

He even provided Delia with a glamorous dress to make her look like a young flapper, so that she would look the right sort of partner for Tudor.

When Karyn heard what was going on she was furious. 'Tudor, how could you agree to Delia doing something like that?' she said angrily. 'She's still only a baby.'

'Baby! Duw anwyl! You should see her when

she's dressed up in her glad rags. She's no baby, I can tell you; you'd think she was at least fourteen.'

'Tudor, she's only seven, she shouldn't be doing this sort of thing, she should be out playing in the street along with children of her own age.'

'I'd sooner be dancing with my dad than playing with anybody else,' Delia smirked. 'Marcus says that if I practise my dancing, then one day I'll be a film star like Greta Garbo or Mary Pickford.' She sighed dramatically. 'When that happens then I shall live in a great big house. I'll have dozens and dozens of lovely dresses and I shall lie on a pink velvet couch and eat sweets and ice cream all day.'

This made Tudor laugh, but it annoyed Karyn, who told her quite sharply not to be so silly.

Delia pouted and then sulked for several days because Karyn had told her off. The following Saturday, when she and Tudor went to the Dance Studio, she came home with a large glossy photograph in which she was wearing one of the dresses Marcus had given her.

Karyn was outraged when she saw it. In her estimation it made a mockery of her little girl. She looked like a child impersonating a grown-up; even her lips had been reddened and there was powder and rouge on her cheeks hiding the fresh, natural bloom of her young skin. It was as if Delia was turning from an innocent, happy child into a precocious little madam in front of her eyes, she thought in alarm.

She also hated the way Marcus was filling her little girl's head with ideas of being a film star. It would end in tears for all of them, she was quite sure of that, and she couldn't understand why Tudor was so oblivious about the harm it was doing to Delia.

Chapter Twenty-Five

Karyn was busy putting together an order for a customer when Tudor called into the Williams Corner Shop to tell her that Marcus Webb wanted him to go for an audition and that he wouldn't be home until the next day.

'I can't stop, Marcus is waiting for me,' he told her hurriedly when she started to ask questions about where the audition was being held and why he had to stay away overnight.

'I'll tell you all about it when I get back,' he promised. Raising his hat to her and to Mrs Phillips, who was patiently waiting for the rest of her groceries, he was gone.

'Is that your fella?' Mrs Phillips asked. 'Nice-looking chap, isn't he? What does he do for a living, then?'

It was on the tip of Karyn's tongue to say, 'As little as possible', because she was so angry, but loyalty made her explain that he was a singer.

'Singer, eh! He's handsome enough to be one of these new film stars,' she cackled.

Karyn merely smiled. She wondered what Mrs Phillips would say if she told her that was exactly what Tudor wanted to be.

As the morning went on Karyn felt more and more irritated that Tudor had taken off at such short notice. It meant that she would either have to take time off to go and collect Delia after school as she'd promised to do, or she would have to ask Cara to do it.

They were so busy in the afternoon that Cara said she would go and meet Delia. Half an hour later, when things began to slacken off, Karyn was suddenly aware that she hadn't seen them come back and she wondered if they had gone for a walk.

No matter how busy the shop might be, Cara usually told Delia to run and give her mam a kiss before she went upstairs for a biscuit and a cup of milk. She was on the point of nipping up to see if they were back when Cara came into the shop looking so distressed that Karyn thought she was about to collapse.

'Mr Williams, can you fetch a glass of water, your wife isn't feeling too good,' she called out. Rushing round the counter, she took Cara's arm and guided her to the wooden chair placed there for the customers to sit down on while being served.

Rhys was out at the back of the shop weighing up sugar, but he came hurrying through to see what was wrong and he was as concerned as Karyn at the state Cara was in.

'Duw anwyl, you look like death warmed up!' he exclaimed. He held the glass out to her, steadying her hand because it was shaking so much that she could barely hold it to her lips. 'Now, don't rush, cariad, but as soon as you feel up to it, try and tell us what's the matter.'

'It's Delia. I couldn't find her,' she gasped. 'I waited by the school gate as usual, but when her class came out she wasn't with them. I thought she'd been kept in.'

'Did you ask her teacher?' Karyn said worriedly.

'Yes, and she said Delia had already gone! She said that her dad had come to the school and collected her early this morning. I couldn't believe it. I was sure she'd made a mistake so I went on standing there until the very last child went home. I know it was silly, but I was sure that sooner or later Delia would come running across the playground, her hair flying and her coat hanging off her shoulders, just as usual.'

Karyn shook her head in disbelief.

'Well, when she didn't, then I knew that her teacher must be telling the truth,' Cara went on, 'so I thought the best thing to do would be to come back here and tell you. I don't know why I was so worried because I remembered Tudor had been in here this morning to tell you something.'

'He came to tell me that he was going away, but he didn't say that he was taking Delia with him,' Karyn said with mounting alarm.

She took the glass from Cara's hand and gulped down a mouthful of water herself. She knew she was shaking almost as much as Cara was. Her head was in a whirl and she was almost too scared to think about what could be the reason behind Tudor's action.

Without asking permission she pulled off the white apron she wore to protect her clothes while she was serving and was out through the door and running along the road to the school as if the devil himself was behind her.

The school looked thoroughly deserted, but she knew that the teachers often stayed on for another hour, discussing things in the staff room, or preparing lessons for the next day, so she hammered on the door until someone answered.

'Why did you let her go with him,' she sobbed when Delia's teacher, Miss Sherman, appeared.

'Well, really, Mrs Morgan, I don't know why you are speaking to me like that,' she said stiffly. 'I knew it was her father, so why should I question his request, even though I don't approve of children being taken out of school like that?'

'Didn't you think it strange that he should be coming to collect her when he'd only just brought her to school?'

Miss Sherman shrugged. 'I wasn't very pleased about it, but he said it was a family matter and very important.'

Karyn sighed and ran a hand over her forehead. 'I'm afraid you don't understand,' she said bitterly.

'And what is it that I don't understand?' Miss Sherman asked coldly.

'My husband came into the shop where I worked this morning to say he was going for an audition for a part in a film,' Karyn explained. 'He said he would be away overnight so I don't understand why he would decide to take Delia with him . . . and without saying a word to me about it.'

Miss Sherman frowned. 'I can see why you are so concerned, Mrs Morgan. It certainly is rather strange, but I can assure you that it was her father who collected her. He said he was in a hurry because he had someone waiting for him . . .'

'Did you see who it was, can you describe them?' Karyn asked eagerly.

'No, not really. It was a man and he was waiting in a car so I couldn't see him very clearly. I'm sorry, Mrs Morgan. I'm sure there must be a perfectly logical explanation and I'm sure that you are worrying unnecessarily and that Delia will be quite all right,' she added lamely.

Sitting in the back seat of the big black car with her Uncle Marcus driving and her dad sitting in the front beside him, Delia felt she must be dreaming.

She had no idea where they were going, but she didn't really mind because her dad said that it was all going to be very exciting when they got there.

It had already been a lovely surprise when

her dad had come into school and asked Miss Sherman if it would be all right for her to have the rest of the day off so that she could go with him.

There was only one thing that bothered her; she wondered if her mam knew what was happening. If not, then she might be worried when she found that she wasn't at school because she had specially asked her to come and meet her at four o'clock.

Her dad had said it would be all right, but she couldn't understand why he hadn't told her mam at breakfast time that he was going to pick her up from school later in the morning.

She wished her dad would come and sit in the back and cuddle her, but he was so busy talking to Uncle Marcus that he wasn't taking any notice of her at all. She was glad when they stopped, although she had no idea where they were.

'Come on,' Tudor opened the car door and held out his hand to her. 'This is it!'

Holding his hand she skipped along happily at his side as together with Uncle Marcus they went into a building, down some long passages and then into a room which looked like the studio where they went on Saturday mornings for dancing lessons. This room was much bigger, though, and there was a group of men at one end, one of them sitting at a piano and the others holding various musical instruments as if waiting to play.

There was also a photographer busily setting up a camera on a tripod and arranging lights on stands so that they shone down on to the centre of the floor where a large circle had been marked out in white chalk.

'Here you are, Delia, here's your dress. Pop behind that screen over there and put it on,' Marcus told her, handing her a large brown paper bag. 'Come along, get changed as quickly as you can, there's a good girl.'

She took it and made her way across the room to do as he'd told her. Inside the bag was the prettiest dress she'd ever seen. It was in white voile with a pattern of pink and red rosebuds printed all over it. It had tiny puff sleeves and was trimmed with pink ribbon.

Quickly, she pulled off her white blouse and grey gymslip and cardigan and in next to no time she was transformed from a drab little schoolgirl into a fairy princess. She stuffed her school clothes into the paper bag, but not before she had taken out the silky white socks and the dainty white satin shoes trimmed with pink rosebuds and which matched her dress perfectly.

She tried to tidy her hair, but she didn't have a brush or a comb so she simply pushed it back behind her ears.

'Come along, Delia, we're waiting.'

As she appeared from behind the screen she found her father waiting for her. A lady was standing talking to him and she beckoned her over and began brushing her hair and twisting it into ringlets. Then she tied it back from her face with a pink ribbon the same shade as the rosebuds on her dress.

To Delia's delight the lady also began to powder her cheeks and put rouge on them, then to outline her lips with pink lipstick.

'How does that look?' the lady took her by the hand and led her across to the other side of the room so that she could look into the full-length mirror that was fixed to the wall.

Entranced, Delia twirled round in delight.

Marcus suddenly appeared and he looked her up and down very critically, making her feel quite frightened.

'You'll do.' He smiled as his eyes met hers in the mirror. 'Now, I want you to dance for us.'

Delia nodded and looked round anxiously for her father.

'You can dance with your dad later, I want you to dance on your own first,' Marcus told her briskly. 'Stay inside that white circle and keep going until the music stops.'

He made a signal to the band and as the music filled the room she tried to obey. Slowly she glided around, twisting and twirling, in time to the beat, unaware that Marcus had also signalled to the photographer to start work as well.

When the music stopped she flopped down on the floor exhausted.

'You can go and sit with your dad and have a little rest and then I want you to dance again. This time it will be with your dad and you'll be wearing another pretty dress,' Marcus told her.

Karyn was so on edge for the remainder of the afternoon that she found it was impossible to concentrate on serving customers and kept making mistakes and giving them the wrong items.

'Go upstairs and have a cup of tea with Cara and talk it all over with her and see if she can think of anything we can do to help,' Rhys suggested.

Cara was full of sympathy and insisted on both of them having a nip of brandy to steady their nerves.

'I'm feeling as guilty as if I was the one who'd whisked Delia away,' she confessed.

'Oh Cara, it wasn't your fault, you and Rhys have been wonderful,' Karyn told her.

'What on earth can Tudor be thinking of to go to the school and take her away like that without a word to you about where they were going?' Cara asked, bemused.

'I don't know and even though Miss Sherman told us that is what happened I still can't believe he would do such a thing.'

'Do you think that perhaps you'd better go home and see if he has left a message there for you?' Cara suggested. 'You never know, he might even be back,' she added brightly.

'Surely if he'd returned home, then he would have come here to the shop and let me know they were back safe and sound. He must know by now that I'd be worried out of my mind when I found out what had happened.'

Karyn felt quite scared as she went back to Adeline Street. She half hoped that when she walked into the room she'd find them both there. She prayed that Delia would be at home, babbling on about where they'd been and what they'd been doing all day.

Instead, she was met by utter silence. She walked into their living room and it was exactly as it had been when she'd left that morning. She went up to their bedroom but nothing had changed there either. All Tudor's clothes and all of Delia's were still there, apart from what they'd been wearing that morning.

She knew she was shaking again. Her mouth felt dry and her head ached. She went back downstairs and out across the yard to the scullery to get herself a drink of water.

Sophia was in there and as Karyn opened the door her cheery greeting died on her lips as instinctively she realised that there was something wrong.

She listened in mounting anger as Karyn related what had happened.

'Tudor left here around mid-morning,' she confirmed, 'but he never said where he was going. Come to think of it,' she frowned, 'someone came to the door to see him and a few minutes later they went off together.'

'Can you try and remember who it was, Sophia?' Karyn begged. 'Was it Marcus Webb who called to collect him?'

'Yes, I'm pretty sure that's who it was. He had a car waiting outside.'

'I was afraid of that,' Karyn shuddered. 'I don't like Marcus Webb, I don't trust him,' she added worriedly.

'I don't understand what you mean,' Sophia probed. 'Marcus Webb seems to be a real gentleman. Such nice manners! He always looks so smart, too, and he has his own motor car. You don't see many of those in Splott!'

Karyn smiled. Yes, she thought, Marcus had a motor car, that was what he had taken Delia away in by all accounts. Even though she was confident that Tudor wouldn't let any harm come to his little daughter, she was still worried about what might happen to her; happen to both of them, in fact.

Karyn found it was impossible to sleep. She sat in an armchair until long after midnight, until she was so cold and unhappy that she could stand it no longer. She sought comfort beneath the sheets and blankets of Delia's bed because she couldn't bear the vast loneliness of the double bed.

It was barely daylight when she awoke next morning. Tudor and Delia were still not back. She didn't know whether to stay home and wait for them to return, or whether to go to work.

'You're not going to do any good sitting around here,' Sophia told her when she knocked on her door to find out how she was. 'You go to work and if they do turn up, then I'll send that husband of yours to the shop to let you know that they are safe and sound, or I'll come down there myself.'

Cara and Rhys were full of concern when she arrived at work. They plied her with so many questions and so much good advice that her head started spinning.

She explained that Sophia Earl would make sure she knew the moment they returned home.

'I agreed with her that I'd be better off here working than sitting at home worrying about what might be happening,' she said, smiling wanly.

Although Rhys and Cara both nodded in agreement she was aware that there was an uncomfortable atmosphere between the three of them all morning. A few of the customers who had an inkling about what had happened gave her curious looks, or asked Rhys in a whisper whether there was any news.

When four o'clock came, Karyn asked for a few minutes off so that she could go to the school gates and make sure that Delia hadn't somehow mysteriously returned and was there waiting to be collected.

She waited until the last child had left and the playground was empty and silent, before she returned to the shop. When she finished work she went home and spent another night alone in their rooms, worrying about her daughter and not able to sleep.

Chapter Twenty-Six

The next day dragged by. Karyn couldn't settle, and every time the shop door opened she hoped that it might be Tudor and Delia walking in, but it never was.

A few minutes before four o'clock she caught Rhys Williams's eye and at his silent nod, she whipped off her apron, struggled into her coat and, ramming her hat on her head as she went through the door, she ran as fast as she could towards the school.

As the children streamed past her Karyn felt a lump rising in her throat. Delia wasn't there. They still hadn't come back.

Her footsteps dragged as she returned to the shop. Rhys didn't ask any questions, there was no need; he could tell from her dejected air that once again her trip had been fruitless.

'I think you'd better get upstairs and have a cuppa with Cara,' he said gruffly.

Karyn hesitated.

'Go on,' he said, 'don't keep her waiting. She's as worried as you are about young Delia, cariad, and she thinks it's high time that you took some positive action.'

* * *

'Now listen to me, cariad,' Cara told her firmly as she poured out the tea and passed a cup across to Karyn, 'you can't let things go on like this any longer. Delia's been gone for three days now and there's not been a word from that husband of yours to say where they are. Let's face facts; you don't even know for sure that Delia is still with him.'

'Oh, don't say that!' Karyn exclaimed, a strained look on her face.

'Well, I am saying it! That Miss Sherman said it was her father who came and collected her, but was she sure?'

'Of course she was; she knows Tudor! He used to collect Delia most afternoons,' Karyn pointed out.

'Yes, that's true,' Cara agreed grudgingly. 'Even so, who was the other man there with him? Where was he taking them?'

Karyn shook her head. 'I don't know for certain, but I am pretty sure that it must have been Marcus Webb. Tudor said he was going with Marcus for an audition and he'd be away overnight.'

'Yes, and three days have passed and not a word. Really, Karyn, there's no doubt about it, you've got to act and you've got to do it right away if you want her back.'

'How can I when I haven't any idea what to do? I don't know where to start looking.'

'I know you don't, that's why you must go to the police and tell them what has happened and ask them to help you find her.'

'The police!'

'That's right, Karyn. They'll be able to track him down,' Cara assured her.

'No!' Karyn almost shouted she was so frightened at the thought of involving the police. If she did that, the moment she mentioned Tudor's name they'd know all about him being in prison and then everyone would know.

'No,' she said in a calmer tone, 'I'd rather not do that . . . not yet, anyway.'

'Well, it's up to you, of course, but I talked it over with Rhys last night and we think that's what you should do. The longer you leave it the more difficult it will be for them to trace where they've gone, remember.'

Sophia and Josiah said much the same thing when she got back to Adeline Street. 'You can't let it go on any longer. How can you be sure that he is taking proper care of Delia? She's only seven, far too young to look after herself.'

'No, she's nearly eight; her birthday is less than two months away.'

'Seven or eight, she's still too young to have to take care of herself. She still needs someone to do her hair and make sure she washes properly and so on.'

'Tudor will look after her, he knows how to take care of her.'

'Yes, that's all right if Tudor is still with her.'

'What on earth do you mean? He wouldn't go off and leave her.'

'You can't be sure about that.' Sophia hesitated,

335

looking uncomfortable. 'Karyn, have you thought that he might have been *made* to take Delia along with him. What do you know about this Marcus Webb? Exactly who is he?'

Karyn wanted to tell Sophia to mind her own business, but she knew how fond of Delia she was and realised that she was only trying to help.

'He's some sort of theatrical agent,' she explained. 'He's supposed to be representing Tudor and finding him a singing and dancing part in a film.'

'Do you know the name of the film or where it was going to be made?'

Karyn shook her head. 'No, I've no idea. I don't think Tudor has ever said.'

Sophia frowned. 'So you have no idea where to start looking for them?'

'If I had, then don't you think I would have done so before now?' Karyn said exasperatedly.

'Exactly! So you need help and the right people to help you are the police.'

'You're the second person to tell me that,' Karyn admitted wearily. 'Cara Williams said much the same.'

'There you are, then, so when are you going to do something about it?' She stood up determinedly. 'Let's do it right now. I'll come down to the station with you.'

'No, no!' Karyn held up her hand. 'Not tonight. Leave it until tomorrow. If they aren't back by then and there is no letter from them in the morning, I'll go to the police, I promise.'

'I think you should go now, tonight, not put it off until tomorrow,' Sophia argued.

Karyn shook her head. 'Tomorrow. I feel completely whacked. I didn't sleep last night for worrying about it all. I want to have an early night and then I'll feel better and up to talking to the police.'

Sophia shook her head despairingly.

'I mean it!'

'I can't make you go down to the police station but if you change your mind and want to go later on this evening, then let me know and I'll come with you.'

'Thank you, Sophia. I do appreciate it.'

Although she'd said she wanted to have an early night, sleep eluded her just as it had on the previous two nights. This time, it wasn't only worrying about where Tudor and Delia were, but the thought of what might happen if she went to the police and what she ought to say to them if she did.

No one in Adeline Street, not even Sophia and Josiah, knew that Tudor had been in prison. Nor did Cara and Rhys Williams. She didn't know how they would react once they found out. The Earls might well turn them out and she was quite sure that the Williamses wouldn't want her serving in their shop any more.

No one at the school Delia went to knew about Tudor's background either, and, once one person knew it, in next to no time there would be a whispering campaign and everyone would know. She wouldn't be able to stop the gossip, the looks from customers, or the insinuations and snide remarks. She wasn't sure that she could stand up to that, not without Tudor being there to provide support and a shoulder to cry on.

At the same time she would never be able to forgive herself if anything happened to Delia. She knew that both Sophia and Cara were quite right when they said that Delia wasn't really old enough to take care of herself.

All these dancing lessons with Tudor over the last few months had made Delia so precocious, Karyn thought unhappily. Sometimes she spoke and acted like someone twice her age. She wished she'd stepped in and stopped her going for the lessons. She should have been out playing with her little friends on Saturdays, not having dance lessons.

Her head was aching and she felt physically sick next morning as she waited for the postman to do his rounds. There was no letter.

She saw Sophia watching her expectantly, but she still couldn't bring herself to take such an irretrievable step as going to the police. She couldn't bear the thought of seeing that warm, solicitous look on Sophia's face change to a look of disbelief or even distrust.

She wished her mother was here, someone who understood her and who would stand by her whatever happened. She even wondered if she should go back to Pen-y-llyn, but then she wouldn't be here in Splott if Tudor and Delia suddenly turned up.

Delia would need her. By now she must be upset and wondering what was happening to her. How could Tudor do something like this – and why?

It was late afternoon before Karyn capitulated and went to the police. Before she did so she told Rhys and Cara about Tudor having been in prison and explained that this was why she was so reluctant to involve the police.

'We can understand, cariad, but your little girl's safety is more important than your husband's pride,' Cara told her.

'Now go down to the police station and tell them all you know and find out what they can do to help you,' Rhys told her firmly. 'Your job will still be here when you come back,' he added, patting her shoulder awkwardly.

Karyn was almost too choked by tears to thank him.

'Do you want one of us to come with you?' Cara asked hesitantly. 'I'll come if you don't want to go through with it on your own.'

'No, it's all right. I'll have to tell Sophia Earl what I've told you and I think she will come with me . . . that's if she doesn't turn me out,' she added with a tremulous smile.

'Of course she won't,' Cara assured her. 'Half the people in Splott have been picked up by the police at one time or another, the same as folks in Tiger Bay. Tell the truth and shame the devil, that's what my old mam always used to say. You can't hide things like that for ever. It's bound to come out sooner or later. Now run along before you lose your nerve, cariad.'

Sophia Earl was taken aback when Karyn explained why she was so reluctant to go to the police and, for a moment, Karyn was afraid that she had made a mistake in confiding in her.

The suddenly Sophia's arms were around her, and she found herself being pressed against Sophia's ample breasts and hugged as if she was a little girl who needed comforting.

'You poor child,' Sophia said consolingly. 'Such a burden on your young shoulders and now this has to happen.' She sighed deeply. 'You must go through with it, cariad. For Delia's sake, you must go to the police.'

'I know, and I will . . . I'm going to go there right now.'

'Wash your face and tidy yourself up, then, and I'll get my coat and come with you,' Sophia told her.

'Thank you!' Once again Karyn found she had tears in her eyes and a lump in her throat. No matter what happened now she felt more confident that she had good friends behind her and wouldn't be going through it on her own.

The police listened to what she had to tell them and then they started questioning her. When she told them about Tudor's imprisonment they checked their records and were satisfied that what she told them was accurate and then more or less dismissed the matter. They were far more interested in details of Marcus Webb.

They already had a file on him and they kept referring to it and then questioning her further.

When Karyn went on to explain that not only her husband, but also her little girl was missing, their attitude changed immediately.

Their professional concern startled her.

'You don't think he would harm Delia, do you?' she asked in alarm.

They were evasive, but so obviously concerned that it sent shivers through her. More and more she wished she'd listened to Cara and Sophia and come to the police as soon as she knew Delia had been taken away by Marcus and Tudor.

The police seemed to be very much of the same opinion.

'If you had come to us right away we would have found them by now and you would have your little girl home with you safe and sound,' the sergeant told her sternly.

'So what happens next, do you think you will be able to find them?' Karyn asked anxiously.

'Don't you worry, Mrs Morgan, we'll find your husband and your daughter. How long it will take is something I can't predict. As I said before, if you'd come straight to us . . .' he let his voice trail off, leaving her feeling guilty.

'So what do I have to do?'

'Keep us informed if you hear any news of

them, otherwise leave matters in our hands. We'll be in touch with you the moment we have anything to report,' he promised, checking over the papers in front of him to confirm her address.

'Will it be all right if I go to work?' she asked hesitantly.

He frowned. 'Where will that be?' He drew a pad towards him and wrote down the details she gave him.

'So if you are not at one address, you'll be at the other?'

'You can always contact me at the Adeline Street address,' Sophia told him.

'And you are?'

'Sophia Earl. It's my house and the Morgans rent two rooms from me.'

'There you are, it wasn't so bad, now was it?' Sophia murmured as they left the police station and started to walk home.

'They were very helpful,' Karyn agreed. 'I was surprised because I didn't think they would be when I admitted that Tudor had a prison record.'

'He committed a crime and he was punished and now it's all over and done with, so you should forget about it,' Sophia stated. 'Now, are you going to come in and have a cuppa before you go back to work?' she asked.

'I wonder how long it will be before we have any news,' Karyn mused as they sat in Sophia's living room going over everything that had been said.

342

'Have patience, give them time, they're on to it and they'll do their best,' Sophia said confidently.

After listening attentively as Karyn told them all about what had happened at the police station, Rhys and Cara once again echoed what Sophia had said.

'It sounds as though that Marcus Webb could be a bit of a villain,' Rhys commented. 'I wonder what sort of details they have on file about him. They didn't tell you?'

'No, I wish they had. I didn't like to ask.'

'They probably wouldn't have told you even if you had,' Cara laughed, 'you know what they're like.'

'Well, don't worry about it. They'll tell you all about him when they're good and ready,' Rhys agreed. 'They know who he is so no doubt they know the places where he is likely to be found,' Cara said thoughtfully.

'Cara's right, but these things take time. At least you've done the right thing by going to the police,' Rhys assured her. 'Try not to worry any more about it. If you want to spend some time at home we understand.'

'No, no. I'd sooner be at work. I've given the police this address so they know where to find me when they have some news.'

'Well, if they do call to see you, I think you should ask them about Marcus Webb's background,' Rhys reminded her.

*   *   *

Karyn thought over all that Rhys, Cara and Sophia had said and felt she had been foolish not to have questioned the police about Marcus Webb. The trouble was she had been so nervous that she had been scared stiff and anxious not to put a foot wrong. That night, her mind was more settled and feeling thoroughly exhausted after three disturbed nights, she slept solidly and woke the following morning feeling rested and much calmer.

If they hadn't been to see her by mid-afternoon next day, she would ask Rhys if she could take some time off and go to the police station and ask them, she resolved as she got ready for work.

Rhys agreed with her that it was a sensible thing to do.

She asked for Sergeant Carew, and explained that she'd talked to him the day before and, after a short delay, she was shown into his office.

'We've no news for you yet, Mrs Morgan,' he greeted her.

'No, I realise you haven't had time to find them yet. I was wondering, though, if you could tell me what you know about Marcus Webb?'

She saw his face tighten and was afraid he was going to refuse her request. 'Please,' she begged. 'I have to know. Is he the sort of man who might hurt Delia?'

Sergeant Carew pursed his lips. 'I don't think so,' he said thoughtfully, 'not with her father being there with her.'

'So why is he on your records?' she persisted.

'You said he was acting as some sort of agent?'

'Yes.' She frowned, unable to follow his reasoning. 'He said he would get my husband a part in a film. My husband is a singer, you see. He appeared here at the Sherman Theatre last September.'

'Not since then?' Sergeant Carew asked sharply.

'The company went on tour afterwards and he went with them. They went all over the place. Penarth, Swansea, Pontypridd, Merthyr and Newport. It was while they were at Newport that he met Marcus Webb.'

The sergeant nodded as if mentally confirming something he already knew. 'That's where we first heard of him,' he explained. 'He was hiring young children and filming them dancing ...'

He stopped speaking as Karyn drew in a sharp breath and the colour drained from her face. 'What is it, Mrs Morgan, have you remembered something?'

'Marcus Webb persuaded my husband to take Delia to dancing lessons,' she explained. 'Is that what is happening now? Has he taken her away somewhere so that he can make a film of her dancing?'

Chapter Twenty-Seven

Delia Morgan was a very unhappy little girl. She had no toys to play with, no pencils to write with, no paper to draw on, and not even a book to read. All she did all day was dance and it made her legs ache and her feet feel sore.

Although she knew that at almost eight she was much too old for the dolls and teddy bear that Nana Pryce had given her it would have been nice to have them there to cuddle and talk to.

She didn't like the sort of dancing she was being asked to do and she didn't like any of the new dresses that Uncle Marcus had told her to wear. She'd never worn any dresses like them before and she wondered what her mam would say if she could see her in them. When she asked her daddy if he liked them, he'd simply smiled and said, 'You look lovely whatever you are wearing,' but she knew that meant he didn't.

The dresses she had to wear after the first one with the rosebuds weren't even in pretty colours. She'd never worn black before and she'd never worn a dress that was so short. It barely covered her bottom! The top was so tight she could barely breathe and then it was row upon row of frills from the waist down.

When she stood in front of the mirror and looked at herself, she thought she looked like a tea cosy; a black tea cosy on very long, skinny legs with a little white face on top and a black bow as big as a parasol perched on top of her head.

It was horrible, and so was the dance that Uncle Marcus made her do. There was no band, only a gramophone. Her daddy had the job of keeping it wound up all the time so he couldn't dance with her like he usually did.

Not that he'd want to do the sort of dance Uncle Marcus told her to do. It was all kicking her legs up into the air and doing silly handstands and balancing on a cushion and waving her legs in the air. It wasn't proper dancing at all.

There was another man in the room all the time, but he had his head covered over with a big blanket because he was taking pictures. She couldn't see his face and that frightened her. It made her think of the bogey man, only she was too old to be frightened by the bogey man because she was nearly eight now.

She wished her mam was with them. Her dad had said that she hadn't been able to come because she had to work at Mr Williams's shop.

She kept telling him that Miss Sherman would be cross because she wasn't at school, but he told her that he'd explained everything to her teacher and she understood.

He'd told her, 'Miss Sherman said that she thought you were a very lucky little girl to be able to go and dance instead of going to school.' She didn't really believe that, though; it didn't sound like Miss Sherman. She was very strict about them always being at school on time, behaving themselves, and paying attention to the lesson she was teaching.

She missed seeing Cara after school every day and the cakes and biscuits she always had waiting for her. She wished she could go home every night so that she could have a cup of hot milk and a cuddle and have a story read to her before she was tucked up in bed with her teddy bear.

She didn't like her bed here at all. She had to sleep in a tiny bunk bed up over the one where her dad was sleeping. It was hard and narrow and every time she turned over she was afraid she was going to fall out. Whenever she looked over the side it seemed to be a long way down to the floor so she knew that if she did fall out in the middle of the night, she would hurt herself.

After they'd had their meal, which was usually fish and chips straight out of the newspaper they were wrapped in, she was sent to bed and her dad and Uncle Marcus sat at the little table and drank beer and played cards. The whole place was so full of smoke that it tickled her throat and made her cough.

They'd already been away from home for three days and she kept asking when they would be going back. When she looked out of the window it was all woods and trees so she didn't even know where she was.

She was missing Aunt Sophia and Uncle Josiah as well. Aunt Sophia always gave her a biscuit or a sweet whenever she saw her and said funny things that made her laugh. Both Aunt Sophia and Uncle Josiah had black skin and tight black curly hair and they were both big and fat and jolly and laughed a lot as though they were very happy all the time. Uncle Marcus wasn't like that; he was impatient and bad tempered and frowned a lot. She couldn't remember ever hearing him laugh.

Her dad wasn't very happy either, at least not since they'd come away with Uncle Marcus. She wondered if it was because she was being asked to dance and he wasn't. He liked dancing and singing, and he liked dancing with her.

When she said that she wanted to go home her dad kept telling her that they would go home as soon as she'd done all the dancing that Uncle Marcus had asked her to do.

She said she didn't like having to wear the black frilly dress because it made her feel sad, so the next day Uncle Marcus said she could have a different one.

She'd hoped that it would be pretty, perhaps blue or bright yellow, but it was a very pale pink. It didn't have any frills, but it was in a soft, silky material and fitted her so tightly that it was like a second skin. When she looked at herself in the mirror it looked as though she had nothing on at all.

The dancing Uncle Marcus wanted her to do was even sillier. She had to pretend she was a big sleeping doll and then wake up and stretch and turn somersaults and then start dancing. He made her do it over and over again until she felt so tired that all she wanted to do was curl up and sleep.

Karyn was working in the shop when the police came to tell her that they thought they had a lead. A man answering Marcus Webb's description had been seen in Treforest. They said he'd been accompanied by a younger man and a little girl and that they seemed to answer the description she had given them of her husband and Delia.

Karyn looked bewildered. 'Where's that and what on earth are they doing there?' she asked.

'You don't have relatives in that area?'

Karyn shook her head. 'I don't even know where this place Treforest is. Both Tudor and I come from Pen-y-llyn and that's nowhere near there, is it?'

They shook their heads solemnly and made entries in their little black notebooks. 'If there is anything further you remember, then let us know,' they told her before they went away. 'Remember to ask for Sergeant Carew.'

Karyn couldn't sleep again that night for wondering and worrying. If they'd been seen in Treforest, then what were they doing there?

The next day, she asked Rhys Williams if he knew where it was because the police hadn't told her. He said that it was not far from Cardiff, midway between there and Pontypridd. That left Karyn even more bewildered than before.

When she went home and told Sophia and Josiah they insisted that they went down to the police station right away to ask them for more information.

'I'm sure the police will come and tell me as soon as they know anything else,' Karyn demurred.

'Oh don't you count on it, cariad, not for one minute,' Sophia told her. 'They only came to see you today because they wanted to find out if you knew anyone living there, any relatives or friends that Tudor could have been visiting. Come on, put on your hat and coat and I'll come with you.'

They asked for Sergeant Carew but he wasn't available and no one else was willing to tell them anything about it, so they were told they would have to wait until he was free.

Sophia was very annoyed and suggested that they went back home and asked Josiah if he would go to Treforest with them and see if they could find Delia themselves.

'I don't think Sergeant Carew would be very pleased if we did that,' Karyn protested. 'We might ruin whatever investigation he is on. You never know, he might be planning to arrest Marcus Webb or something.'

'Listen to yourself,' Sophia said scornfully. 'What if he isn't? Marcus Webb still has Delia with him.'

'Tudor's there as well, remember, he wouldn't let Marcus hurt her.'

'We're pretty sure that it is them,' Sergeant Carew told her when he eventually came to talk to them. 'What is more, the three of them are living in a caravan. Do you know anything at all about that?'

Karyn shook her head; she couldn't understand what was going on.

When Sophia suggested they were thinking of going there themselves Sergeant Carew was most emphatic that they must do nothing of the sort.

'We are keeping them under observation and the moment we are sure of our facts then we will move in and interrogate them. If you go there you will ruin all our hard work. Do you understand?'

Karyn felt desperate. It didn't help when Miss Sherman came to the shop after school the next afternoon to ask why Delia was still absent.

Karyn burst into tears and it was Rhys Williams who explained what was happening. 'The police are looking into it,' he told Miss Sherman firmly.

'This is very distressing for all of you,' Miss

352

Sherman said in a shocked voice, 'Please let me know as soon as you have any more news. I shall have to report this to the authorities, of course. Normally the school board man would be visiting you, but I'll see what I can do to prevent that happening. I'm sure you don't want any more officials coming to see you.'

Another two days passed before the police made a positive move. During that time they had not only kept watch on the caravan site, but they'd checked on the movements of Marcus Webb, Tudor Morgan and even little Delia.

They knew that each morning all three of them, with Marcus Webb driving a large black car, went from the caravan site to a building site some short distance away that looked as though it might be a factory. Several other people joined them there at about the same time each day as if reporting for work.

The police had also amassed a great deal of background information about Marcus Webb and established that he claimed to be a film producer, but so far the only sort of films he had made were of a very dubious nature. Mainly they featured young girls in unnatural poses or doing unusual dances while wearing very brief, exotic costumes.

'According to our information he has even taken pictures of very young girls who were completely nude,' Sergeant Carew said, frowning heavily.

'Oh no!' Karyn's hand flew to cover her mouth to quieten her cry of horror as her imagination took over and filled in all the details which the police weren't telling her.

'Surely he wouldn't do anything like that with Delia, not with her dad being there with them, would he?' she asked tremulously, her eyes filled with distress.

Sergeant Carew didn't answer, but his mouth tightened into a grim line of disapproval.

'You must stop him, prevent anything like that happening to my little Delia,' Karyn sobbed. 'You must do something right away, or else I'll go to Treforest myself,' she threatened despairingly.

She knew she was talking rubbish, however. The only people who could really do anything were the police, and no matter how distressed she might be, she had to wait for them to act in their own good time.

Sergeant Carew seemed to understand what was going through her mind and his voice softened slightly as he advised her to go home and be patient.

'Believe me, Mrs Morgan, we are as anxious as you are to catch this fiend. If you do anything rash now, you'll completely ruin any chance we have of doing so.'

She nodded, but she found it hard to comply with his request. All she wanted was to have little Delia back in her arms and to know that she was safe and sound. She loved her so much

354

that she couldn't bear the thought of her little girl being harmed in any way. She'd never forgive Tudor if she was.

The rooms in Adeline Street seemed so desolate without her. The empty single bed made Delia's absence all the more poignant so that she found she was unable to go into the bedroom. She certainly couldn't spend another night there on her own. Instead, she slept curled up in the armchair, alert for every sound, until her nerves were not just on edge, but raw and jangling.

Cara and Rhys Williams were as supportive as they could possibly be, but the strain of waiting for news was affecting them as well. They seemed to be incredibly busy in the shop; people were calling in for just one item in order to ask if there was any news.

Sophia and Josiah were almost as worried about Karyn as they were about Delia. They made sure she ate something before she went off to the shop each morning and they insisted that she shared their evening meal with them even if she barely touched the nourishing food they put in front of her.

It was inevitable that the story was picked up by the newspapers. They splashed huge headlines across their pages, playing up the fact that there was a little girl involved. They also dug up all the previous murky history about Marcus Webb and his exploits. Most of the papers also emphasised that the little girl's father, Tudor Morgan, had been in prison.

355

Sophia tried to keep the newspapers away
from Karyn, but it wasn't easy. She and Josiah
also tried to fend off the newshounds who were
constantly knocking on the door hoping for
more details about what had happened. She
tried not to let any of them know where Karyn
worked, but somehow they found out and
began pestering her at the shop.

When this happened, Rhys Williams took
matters into his own hands and immediately
sent for the police. They warned off the
reporters and cautioned Karyn that she must
say nothing to any of them under any circumstances.

'I'll do everything you say,' Karyn promised,
'if only you will bring my little Delia home.
That's all I want,' she sobbed. 'It's all I ask,
bring her home to me, I want her back . . . safe
and sound.'

Chapter Twenty-Eight

It was early morning, the sun wasn't even high enough in the sky to warm up the world, but Delia Morgan was already awake and feeling restless.

She didn't know what time her dad and Uncle Marcus had stopped drinking and playing cards and come to bed, but they were now both snoring so loudly that she knew that must have been what had made her wake up.

She lay there listening to them. Her dad's snores were long and soft, Uncle Marcus's were much noisier and sometimes ended in a whistling sound.

Delia knew she wouldn't be able to get to sleep again, so she decided she might as well get dressed. If she did it very quietly she wouldn't waken them. All she had to do was to pull on her school blouse and grey gymslip and cardigan and she'd feel nice and warm again. She didn't have a nightie on because they hadn't brought one with them so she had to sleep in her knickers and vest.

She crawled to the end of her bunk where she had hung her clothes so that they would shut out the light coming in through the window. As she went to pull them towards her she saw a movement outside. She stayed very still, making sure that most of the window was still covered by her clothes and watched to see who it was. Two men were hiding behind the trees as if trying to make sure that no one could see them, but, step by step, they were creeping towards the caravan.

She watched for a second longer and then she guessed that they were looking for them. She felt a moment's excitement. If she waved to them and they saw her, then would they come and get her and take her home to her mam?

Before she could make up her mind as to what to do, she saw another figure behind them. This man was wearing a policeman's uniform and he had a fierce-looking brown and grey Alsatian dog with him on a long leash.

Delia's feeling of excitement died away. The last time the police had come to their house they had taken her daddy away and he hadn't come home again for months and months. Suddenly she was afraid that might happen again.

Leaning over the side of her bunk she tried to waken her father. She felt frightened and so she threw caution to the wind and shouted to him. It didn't matter if it woke Uncle Marcus as well, or if he was cross, because she was sure they were in some sort of danger.

'Quiet, Delia, go back to sleep,' Tudor grunted as he turned over and pulled the blanket up over his ears.

'No, Dad, you must listen. There're some men outside, they're policemen, and I think they're looking for us . . .'

'What did you say!' Tudor was out of bed, clutching the blanket round him and peering cautiously out of the window in the direction Delia indicated.

'Duw anwyl, you're right, cariad!' He went over to where Marcus was sound asleep and shook him by the shoulder. 'Come on, get up.'

'What the hell for? Leave me alone,' Marcus grunted irritably.

'The police are outside; we've got to do something.'

Marcus was instantly alert. 'Bloody hell! Get some clothes on before they get here, then!'

The two men scrambled into their trousers. Both had been sleeping in their shirts and hastily fastened them at the neck and smoothed their hair into place.

'I'd better get dressed as well,' Delia said as she pulled on her blouse and took her skirt away from the window.

Marcus grabbed her by the arm. 'I want you to get back into your bunk and hide under the covers and keep perfectly still and not make a sound. Understand?'

'Why?' Delia looked at him puzzled.

'Those two men and the policeman have probably been sent here to find out why you are not at school.'

'Then I can tell them that I've been here dancing.' She smiled brightly.

'No, I don't think that's a very good idea,' Tudor told her. 'You're not supposed to stay away from school for something like that.'

'You said that it was all right because Miss Sherman knew. You said she'd told you that she thought I was lucky to be able to dance instead of going to school.'

'Look, Delia, don't argue,' Marcus Webb said impatiently. 'Tudor, tell her to do as I say. Now! Quickly.'

'Come on, Delia; do as you've been asked.' Tudor helped her back up on to the bunk and as he arranged the covers over her he whispered, 'It's like a game, cariad. Lie as quiet as a little mouse until I tell you when it's all right to come out. Don't move or peep out and whatever you do, don't giggle! Now promise.'

The next moment there was a loud banging on the door and Marcus went to open it.

She could hear their voices even though what they said was muffled by the blanket. She heard Marcus and then her dad tell a policeman that they were having a few days' holiday, nothing else.

'We've come here to do a spot of fishing,' she heard him say.

'We were told that you had a little girl staying here with you,' one of the policemen commented. 'Can we come in and have a word with her?'

'Little girl?' Marcus sounded so surprised that Delia almost choked, trying hard not to laugh.

She felt the caravan shake as the policemen came inside and knew they must be looking for her. She had only to wriggle and make the slightest noise and they'd know she was there. If she did that, then they'd find her, but would they take her back home to her mam, she wondered?

It was very tempting, because she hated being there and she missed her mam so much. It was only the fear of what might happen to her dad that stopped her doing so.

She could hear them all talking to each other and it seemed the policemen were about to leave. Then she heard another voice and the sound of a short, sharp bark and suddenly the caravan was rocking violently from side to side. She screamed in fright as she felt the covers being tugged off her as the huge brown and grey Alsatian she'd seen out of the window poked its face into hers.

There was nothing she could do now, she told herself. Slowly, she climbed down from the bunk and stood there shivering, looking from one to the other of them.

When the policemen started asking her all sorts of questions she didn't know what she was supposed to say. They kept telling her to tell the truth and one of them stood so close to her that she couldn't see her dad's face so she had no idea what he wanted her to say.

By the time they stopped questioning her, Delia was in tears. She was so muddled that she didn't know what she was saying or understand what was happening. All she knew was that all three of them were being taken away to the police station.

As they went outside, she saw that a crowd had gathered and they started shouting out questions and trying to take pictures.

'Duw anwyl! Can't you do something to stop all this?' Tudor protested.

The policemen didn't bother to answer, but hurried the three of them towards a dark blue van that was waiting nearby.

Inside the van there were seats down both sides and two of the policemen accompanied them into the van and sat facing them so that they weren't able to talk to each other without whatever they said being overheard. Delia felt frightened because the dog was also in there with them and sat panting, with his tongue lolling out and his eyes fixed on her the whole time.

When they reached the police station, the dog was taken away somewhere and the other policemen took her, her dad and Marcus Webb inside.

They were taken into a room and a sergeant arrived and began asking them questions and writing down all the answers. They asked so many that she felt dizzy; they wanted to know where she'd slept in the caravan and what she'd done each day while she'd been there.

She told them all about the dancing and about the dresses, especially the ones she didn't like having to wear and about how she'd had to sleep in her vest and knickers because she didn't have a nightie. She didn't understand all their questions, but they said it didn't matter and that she'd been very clever to remember so much.

Afterwards, one of the policemen took her into another room where a lot of people were working. He gave her a toffee and told her to sit quietly until her father came for her.

Only he hadn't come to find her. When she asked if she could speak to him, she was told he had to stay where he was. Then she over-heard people in the room saying that they were going to lock him and Marcus Webb up.

She felt very frightened and started crying, but when they told her that they would take her home to her mam, she stopped crying and felt quite happy again because that was where she wanted to be more than anything else in the world.

The newspapers had a field day. There were special editions with banner headlines followed by all the latest news of the case. Marcus Webb and Tudor Morgan had both been arrested, taken into custody and charged with abduction.

There was a great deal about Marcus Webb.

It was not the first time that he had been in trouble for taking and distributing unsuitable pictures. They also speculated on the sort of films he was planning to make. They described him as a villain, an entrepreneur, a man-about-town, and made a great deal of the fact that he had been involved several times before on different charges.

In much smaller print they said that the little girl who had been abducted was safe and well and that she was now back home with her mother.

Karyn was so overjoyed when the police arrived at the Williams's corner shop early in the after-noon bringing Delia with them, that she burst into tears.

She was shocked by Delia's appearance. She looked tired and dishevelled. Her white blouse was grubby and her grey gymslip was creased and dirty. Her hair was greasy and scraped back behind her ears. It was the look of fear and weariness in Delia's eyes that worried Karyn the most, though.

The moment they were inside the door Delia flung herself into Karyn's arms and began sobbing her heart out. In between her sobs she said how frightened she'd been, especially at the police station when they'd separated her from her father and refused to let her speak to him.

'Hush, cariad! You're back with me again now,

so you've nothing to worry about. I expect they only want to ask your dad some more questions. Once he's answered those, then he'll be home again and we'll all be able to forget what has happened,' Karyn murmured soothingly.

Karyn did all she could to pacify Delia, but the child went on sobbing, as if all the pent-up fear of the past few days was being drained from her.

'Why don't you bring her upstairs and let's see if we can find her a biscuit,' Cara suggested. 'Rhys can manage down here in the shop on his own for half an hour.'

'Yes, yes, do that,' Rhys urged. 'Go on quickly, out of sight before any reporters turn up and start hounding the poor little thing with all their questions.'

Delia calmed down eventually, but both Cara and Karyn were in tears themselves by the time they'd listened to her account of all that had happened to her.

'That Marcus Webb should be jailed for life for putting a little child through such an ordeal,' Cara declared angrily. 'Taking such pictures indeed! No good would have come of it, it's fortunate they caught him before he had a chance to do anything with them or anyone else saw them.'

'What I can't understand is why Tudor went along with such an idea. He should have put a stop to it right away and brought her straight back home,' Karyn said angrily.

'Easy to see why he didn't,' Cara said scornfully. 'He was in it up to his neck. He's as thick as thieves with that awful man, as you well know! The pair of them had only one thing in mind and that was money. They were taking those pictures so that they could sell them as postcards or something like that.'

'I still can't understand Tudor not putting a stop to it all,' Karyn protested.

'He probably had very little choice in the matter,' Cara commented sagely, her lips tightening. 'Perhaps he was talked into doing what he did by that Marcus Webb.'

'What on earth do you mean?' Karyn asked looking puzzled. 'No one can make Tudor do anything he doesn't want to do! I should know that!'

'Your Tudor was probably only going along with all this picture business because Marcus Webb had told him that in return for letting him film Delia dancing, he'd give him a star part in the film that he was making.'

Karyn shook her head in disbelief. She didn't want to hear any more. Cara was possibly right and it frightened her to think of the danger that Tudor had put Delia in just to achieve his ambition. Even so, she wanted to hear what Tudor had to say before she passed judgement.

'I think I ought to take Delia home now and give her a bath, and let her get some sleep. Do you think Rhys will mind?'

'Of course Rhys won't mind,' Cara agreed.

'In fact, we both think that you should take tomorrow off as well. Stay at home with Delia and help her to forget about what has happened. She certainly shouldn't go back to school for a day or two.'

'You are probably right and I would like to be able to spend some time with her.'

'Good! We'll be able to manage perfectly well, so don't give it another thought.'

Sophia and Josiah were overjoyed to have Delia back. They both hugged and kissed her and made a tremendous fuss of her. Sophia tried to reassure her that everything was all right now and that she had nothing to worry about.

'You do as your mam says and let her give you a nice hot bath, and while you're doing that I'll cook a really special meal for you, how about that?'

'Can I be the one to choose what we have to eat, then?' Delia begged.

'Yes, of course, cariad. You can have anything you like. Unless you would rather have a surprise?'

Delia weighed up the idea for a minute. 'I'm too tired to choose so I'll have a surprise,' she yawned.

'Good, off you go, then, and have that bath. I bet you haven't had one all the time you've been away. Your hair looks as though it hasn't been combed for days as well.'

Delia sighed. 'I used to think it must be nice not to have to wash every day or have my hair brushed every night, but now I really wanted my mam to do it,' she admitted.

An hour later, pink from her bath and with her hair newly washed, towelled dry and combed back from her face, Delia looked much more her old self.

'Come on, then,' Sophia greeted her, 'up to the table and see what Josiah has cooked for you. Something very special; things we know you always love to eat.'

Chapter Twenty-Nine

It was three weeks before the case came to court; three weeks of mental torture for Karyn and considerable anxiety on the part of the Williamses and the Earls.

Delia seemed to recover from her adventurous ordeal incredibly quickly. After a few days of being pampered she was back into her normal routine and she no longer even mentioned what had happened. She was, however, becoming bored at being at home with nothing to do.

Karyn had stayed home with her for two days, but she felt she was being unfair to Rhys and Cara Williams to stay away from work any longer. Also, at the back of her mind, there was the fear that if she didn't go back soon, they might decide to replace her.

At the moment, Cara was helping out in the shop, but she was not in good health and Karyn knew that the sole purpose of them taking her on in the first place had been so that Cara could get more rest and not have to be in the shop every day.

'I think you are ready for school again, don't you?' Karyn said, smiling when, for the umpteenth time, Delia asked what could she do.

Delia pulled a face, but she didn't object and, five minutes later, Karyn found her looking for her satchel and asking what treat would be in her lunchbox.

'We'll walk along to the shop and see what Mr Williams can suggest,' Karyn told her. 'At the same time I can tell them that I will be back at work tomorrow,' she added.

Cara and Rhys were delighted by the news. While Delia was talking to Rhys and trying to decide what to have as a special treat, Cara pulled Karyn to one side. 'Have you heard when the case comes to court?' she asked in a whisper.

'No.' Karyn shook her head. 'I hope it will be soon. Worrying about what the outcome will be is driving me mad, even though I know that it is Marcus who is to blame. Tudor wouldn't hurt a hair on Delia's head, he loves her so much.' She dabbed at her eyes with her handkerchief. 'I still feel angry with Tudor about what he's done, but I want him home; it's so lonely without him.'

'Yes, my dear, I'm sure it is.' She patted Karyn's arm consolingly. 'Try not to worry, though, I'm sure he'll be back with you very soon.'

'I'll be glad to get back to work,' Karyn confided. 'If I'm kept busy, then perhaps I won't think about it so much.'

Miss Sherman also said that Karyn was doing the right thing in letting Delia come back to school.

'The only trouble is I'm afraid that some of the other children may ask her awkward questions and I want her to forget all about it,' Karyn explained.

'I quite understand, but I think your fears are groundless,' Miss Sherman told her. 'Children don't take the same interest in these sorts of things as grown-ups do. By now, most of them will have forgotten all about what happened. I shall keep a close eye on Delia and if I suspect there is any chattering about what happened, I shall nip it in the bud, never fear.'

'Thank you very much!' Karyn smiled gratefully. 'I'm going back to work myself today, so if there are any problems you know where to find me.'

'And you will be here to collect her at four o'clock?'

Karyn hesitated. 'I'm not too sure, Mrs Williams may come some afternoons. Does it matter?'

'Not in the least,' Miss Sherman told her briskly. 'It's just that we will keep a close watch on Delia and we don't want her disappearing with the wrong person.'

Karyn stiffened. 'My husband is still in custody and so is Mr Webb.'

'When is the trial being held, have you heard?'

'No, not yet, but I will let you know when I do,' Karyn promised.

For the next few weeks everything seemed to be back to normal. If they were busy in the shop, then Cara went to collect Delia and took her straight upstairs. Occasionally, Karyn walked to the school herself, but even then Delia always went upstairs to stay with Cara until Karyn finished work.

Back at Adeline Street, Josiah and Sophia kept an eye on both of them and made sure that everything was all right. They made a great fuss of Delia, hoping that it would help to compensate for her father not being there.

At first Delia missed Tudor almost as much as Karyn did, but then other things took over. She liked to spend time with the Earls playing snap with Josiah or listening to Sophia telling her stories about the way people lived in Africa, rather than playing outside with any of her school friends.

'Not that I've ever been there,' Sophia told Karyn. 'I was born and brought up in Tiger Bay and we moved here to Splott after I married Josiah. My mam and dad used to tell us stories about Africa when we were little, but I never knew if they'd ever been there or not. My dad was a merchant seaman so he may have done, because he sailed all over the world – or so he used to tell us.'

'The boat he was on was torpedoed during the war and sank with all of them on board.

Not one survivor!' She wiped a tear from her eye. 'My mam was heartbroken, but she had six of us to bring up. I was the oldest, so even though I was working I had to help her as much as I could when I got home at night. I was working in Curran's along the embankment. That's where I met Josiah and when he asked me to marry him I was in heaven. I've never regretted it, I've had a wonderful life ever since.'

'And what about your mam, what happened to her after you left home?'

'She married again soon after I left home and she still lives down the Bay.'

'Do you see much of her?'

Sophia laughed and shook her head. 'Josiah and my mam don't get on one little bit. She's a Catholic and when I married Josiah I gave all that up and started going to the Gospel Hall with him. I liked that a lot better.'

'You took Tudor's mother to one or two of their meetings, didn't you?' Karyn smiled. 'She seemed to love it. All the singing and music, so different to the grim services she was used to in the chapel back at home.'

Sophia beamed. 'I think it's the same God up there, so why not enjoy singing his praises in the way you think is the best? Some people need all the incense and pomp that the Catholics use in their services, some need the brimstone and fires of hell that Tudor's mam had in her chapel. Me, I like the happy clappy cheerful fun that we indulge in at the Gospel Hall. You're welcome to come with me anytime you like,' she invited.

'Thank you! But not at the moment, though.'

'It's a standing invitation,' Sophia told her. 'Anytime you feel like coming along then you have only to say. I won't pester you about it, in fact, I won't even mention it again, but the invitation is there whenever you are ready.'

Karyn didn't attend the court when the trial started because she couldn't bear the thought of seeing Tudor having to stand up in the dock and then having to listen to all the things he was accused of having done being read out. She even refused to read about it in the newspapers.

Rhys Williams said he understood how she felt and that he would keep an eye on what was happening. He promised to save all the newspapers so that she could read it all for herself later on if she wanted to do so.

Some of the customers expressed surprise at finding her still working behind the counter, but Rhys was quick to intervene before they could start asking her questions or making comments on how the trial was going.

Every day Karyn hoped that he would tell her that the trial was over. Once that happened she was positive that Tudor would come home.

When the trial finally did end and she learned that the outcome was that Tudor had been given three years, while Marcus Webb had got off with only a six-month sentence, she was utterly devastated.

'How could such a thing happen? There must be some mistake!' she wailed. 'I should have followed the case or even gone to court and spoken up for Tudor.'

'They probably wouldn't have let you do so because you're his wife,' Rhys placated her. 'Funny thing, the law, you know,' he added lugubriously.

'I should have told them what a good father he was, how he looked after Delia even when she was only a tiny baby so that I could go to work.'

'It wouldn't have done any good at all,' Rhys repeated. 'What you must remember is that Marcus Webb had a barrister to speak up for him.'

'What difference could that have made to what I told them?' Karyn argued stubbornly.

'He would have cross-questioned you and twisted anything you said to further his own argument.'

'Even though I was telling the truth?'

'You'd better go upstairs and ask Cara to make you a cup of tea and sit down and read the summing up of the case very carefully,' Rhys told her, passing her a copy of the *South Wales Echo*.

Karyn read the report three times and still refused to believe what was written there.

'It says that it was Tudor's idea to take the

pictures. That he asked Marcus to take them. It says that it was Tudor who was planning to sell them as postcards. That's a whole load of rubbish. Tudor had no such scheme. He wouldn't know how to go about selling them, so whatever made them say something like that?' she protested.

'Well, cariad,' Cara pointed out patiently, 'the last time he was caught by the police and sent to prison it was for exploiting little Delia, if you remember.'

'Yes, but it was nothing like this! They were only singing in Morgan's Arcade. I know it was wrong and he shouldn't have done it, but he was there with her and she couldn't come to any harm.'

'He was there with her at Treforest as well and he did nothing to stop it happening,' Cara pointed out.

'You believe all this rubbish don't you?' Karyn flared, jabbing angrily at the paper. 'You think he's guilty and that he deserves that sort of sentence!'

Cara didn't answer.

Karyn was dismayed to find that most other people seemed to think the same as Cara. Because he'd been guilty of exploiting Delia once before, Tudor's reputation was already tainted.

When she went to see him in prison after he'd been sentenced she tried to convince him that she didn't agree with the verdict because she knew he wouldn't harm a hair on Delia's head.

She told him what Cara had said about Marcus Webb coercing him into letting Delia have her picture taken and promising that in return he would be given a lead part in the film Marcus said he was going to make.

'She's right, up to a point,' Tudor agreed bitterly, 'except that there was never going to be a film. He's admitted that now. It was all a scheme to get me to let him take those pictures of Delia.'

'So really you are completely innocent of all the things they've accused you of doing,' she exclaimed in relief. 'Can't you appeal and ask to have the case retried?'

Tudor shook his head. 'It would be a complete waste of time. Marcus has the money to hire a barrister, like he did this time, and between them they'd convince the judge and jury that I was the one in the wrong.'

'I still think you should try,' Karyn insisted stubbornly.

'No, the only thing I can do now is to serve my time and hope that if I am on my very best behaviour then perhaps I'll be let out early.'

'Three years is such a long time, though!'

'Don't you think I know that?' he said bitterly. 'There's nothing I can do about it though.'

'Delia will be eleven. It's a long time for her to have to be without her dad. It's going to be a long time for me to be on my own, as well,' she added softly.

Tudor covered his face with his hands as if trying to shut out what she was saying. 'You could always go back home to your family in Pen-y-llyn. You'd have your dad there; let him take my place in Delia's life.'

Karyn shook her head. 'And I'd have your Olwyn living next door going on and on, night and day, about what's happened to you.'

'Why on earth should she do that?' he asked in surprise.

'Your mam always blamed me for getting pregnant and you having to marry me when you were so young. She said I'd brought you trouble and your sister agreed with her. Olwyn even said that it was my fault that your mam died because if she hadn't been down here in Cardiff visiting us, then it would never have happened. Mind you,' she added with a wry laugh, 'at the time she was glad to have the house all to herself.'

'So what are you going to do?'

'I'll stay on in Adeline Street, I suppose. Luckily I still have my job at the corner shop. Rhys and Cara Williams have been very understanding.'

'And Sophia and Josiah? What have they had to say about what has happened?'

'They've been good friends, too. I think they understand and they're very fond of Delia.'

'You'll still be fending for yourself though. It's not going to be easy for you.'

'Delia is a lot older now than she was last time. She'll soon be able to come home from school on her own . . . well, to the shop at least. It's only a couple of streets away. For the moment I will still collect her. If I'm too busy to do it, then Cara will fetch her, and she'll take Delia upstairs until I finish in the shop. It works very well. Cara is teaching her to knit and she loves it. It will soon be the school holidays, so perhaps I'll take her to stay with my mam and dad for a few weeks. It will get her away from Adeline Street, and from Cardiff, until all the publicity dies down. It won't take long for all this to be forgotten.'

'True! You know what they say; today's news is tomorrow's fish and chip paper.'

'Sophia and Cara will turn the reporters away and in a couple of weeks' time things really will be back to normal. Well, as normal as they can be with you locked up in here,' she added wryly.

Tudor nodded. 'I know, I'm sorry I got into this mess.' His face looked haggard as he ran his hands through his hair. 'I . . . I would understand if you wanted to end things between us for good.'

'End things?' She frowned, puzzled. 'What do you mean? What are you talking about?'

'I mean, after the way I've let you down, if you want to cut your losses and split up,' he declared bluntly.

Karyn stiffened, her face flaming. 'Are you trying to say that is what you want?'

'Duw anwyl, of course not! What do you take me for! Of course I don't want that to happen, but I realise that this is the second time you've had to face up to something like this.'

Quickly, she stretched out her hand and let her fingers touch his. 'I love you, Tudor. I always have, all my life for as long as I can remember.'

'And I love you.' His fingers squeezed hers then he let go quickly as an officer advanced towards them.

The bell indicating that visiting was over sounded and reluctantly Karyn stood up. Leaning as close to him as she possibly could she declared in a hoarse whisper, 'I love you, Tudor Morgan, and what's more I always will until my dying day.' She sniffed back her tears. 'When you get out of here I'll be waiting for you, cariad . . . I promise.'

Chapter Thirty

Karyn found that it was extremely difficult trying to manage on the money she earned at the Williams Corner Shop even though there was only herself and Delia to cater for.

Tudor's earnings had always been erratic, but he had always managed to give her a decent amount towards the housekeeping and over the years she had learned not to ask whether he had earned it by singing or gambling.

The money she earned had always been used for extras; little luxuries, and for clothes for herself and Delia. Now she had to spend every penny of it on basics and no matter how economical she tried to be it was never enough and she didn't know what she was going to do.

She toyed with the idea of trying to earn more money by finding an evening job. She wondered if Llew Parker at the Voyager would take her back as a barmaid. If not, he might be able to tell her where there was a vacancy and even put in a good word for her.

The problem about doing that was what she would do with Delia. She couldn't leave her on her own and she could hardly expect Sophia to keep an eye on her every night since she often went out in the evening to her Gospel meetings.

The only other solution would be to ask her mother if Delia could stay with her for a while. She didn't like to do that in a letter so it would mean a trip to Pen-y-llyn to see her. That mightn't be such a bad idea, she reflected. She had mentioned to Tudor she wanted to go and see her mother. Even a few days away from Cardiff would be a nice break for both her and Delia and would help her to put all the miserable things that had been happening behind them.

Delia was overjoyed at the prospect and needed no encouragement to get her clean clothes packed and ready for their trip. She was so excited that she had told the Earls about it before Karyn had a chance to do so.

'How long will you be away?' Sophia asked.

'Not long, only a few days. Will it be all right if I pay my rent when I get back?'

'You mean you want to leave it this week and give us two weeks next time?'

'That's right. You don't mind, do you? I have to pay the train fare and—'

'No, no, that will be all right, I understand,' Sophia said quickly, but Karyn detected a note of annoyance in her voice.

Cara also showed signs of disapproval. 'I hope you're not going to be gone for very long, Karyn. You know I find it a strain to have to be down in the shop. We can't afford to take on extra staff and pay your wages at the same time.'

It was so unlike Cara to be so outspoken that Karyn felt quite worried. If she lost her job at the shop she really would be in a pickle. It was so convenient; only a sort distance both from where she lived and from the school Delia attended. What was more, Cara was always willing to let Delia stay upstairs with her until she finished work.

She was suddenly very aware of how much time she had taken off lately and knew that she must stop doing so. It also made it even more important that she found a second job, something to fall back on if she did lose her job at the shop.

She wondered if she should write to her mother again and tell her that they wouldn't be coming to Pen-y-llyn after all. Delia would be so disappointed, though, and Karyn did very much want to see her own mam and dad. They would have read all about Tudor's case in the papers and she wanted them to know the truth, the real story of what had happened.

Rain was sleeting down when they arrived at Pen-y-llyn and the surrounding countryside looked grim and foreboding. Owen Pryce was waiting for them, his coat collar turned up and the brim of his flat cap pulled down as protection against the weather.

His greeting was so curt that Karyn felt

piqued, but things were even more strained when she reached Clydach Street. Olwyn Baker was on her doorstep waiting for them, despite the driving rain.

'So you've come, then,' she greeted Karyn. 'Duw anwyl, I wonder you have the nerve to show your face back here in Pen-y-llyn, girl, not after what you've done!'

'What on earth are you on about, Olwyn? I've done nothing wrong.'

'Get inside the pair of you, standing out here shouting the odds at each other like a pair of alley cats,' Owen Price said heatedly. 'And you go on in and find your granny,' he told Delia as he opened the door and pushed her over the threshold.

'I would rather stand out in the rain than be under the same roof as her,' Olwyn told him defiantly. 'Ruined my brother, she has, and taken my mam from me. My mam would still be alive and well today if she hadn't gone galli-vanting off down to Cardiff because Karyn needed her to help look after young Delia. Left me here on my own to get on with things even though I have three youngsters to bring up not just one spoilt little brat.'

'That will do, Olwyn Baker! At the time, if I recall, you were all in favour of Bronwen going there.'

'No, Dad, let her have her say. Let her get it off her chest. After all, if she doesn't say it to me, then she will go round saying it to everyone

384

in Pen-y-llyn even though it's her own brother's name that she's blackening.'

'I don't need to blacken his name, you've done a pretty good job of that already,' Olwyn sneered. 'Letting him get you into trouble and then the pair of you clearing off to Cardiff and ending up living in Tiger Bay of all places.'

'I said that was enough and I meant it. Go in and look after your youngsters, Olwyn, and you, Karyn, get inside the house and let's shut this door.'

Karyn had never heard her father so angry. Much as she wanted to have things out with Olwyn she knew better than to defy him. There would be plenty of opportunities to talk to Olwyn later on, she resolved. For the moment it was far more important to see her mam and have the cup of tea that she was sure would be waiting for her.

The bad start was only the beginning. Everyone in Pen-y-llyn, even her own mother, seemed to have strong views about what had happened. Delia was petted and pampered and given little treats by all and sundry, but Karyn found herself treated with so much hostility that she wished she hadn't come home.

After a couple of hours there she was pretty certain that it was going to be no good asking her mother if Delia could stay with them for a while and she was quite right.

'I don't think it is a very sensible idea at all, not at the moment,' her mother said evasively, 'and I'm sure your dad would say the same thing, if you asked him.'

'I thought it would do Delia good . . .'

'Another time, perhaps; wait until all the gossip and bad feeling about what has happened has had a chance to die down. Olwyn is that hopping mad at the moment that it wouldn't be fair on Delia. She'd make her little life a misery, take my word for it!'

'Surely Olwyn wouldn't take her spite out on Delia!'

'Even if she didn't, then those children of hers would,' her mother told her. 'They'd tease the life out of her, I can tell you! Poor little thing, she's been through quite enough lately so you don't want her to have to put up with that sort of treatment, now do you?'

'No,' Karyn agreed wearily. 'I suppose you're right; I don't want anything else happening to her.'

'Then get yourself back to Cardiff, cariad. It might be better if you didn't come here again until all the gossip has died down,' Enid added gently.

Karyn nodded in agreement, she felt too choked to speak. This wasn't at all the sort of homecoming she'd expected. Even her own mam and dad seemed to think that what had happened was so terrible that they didn't want to talk about it. She'd never forget her mam's accusing voice saying, 'Couldn't you have done something to stop it?' as though

386

she held her partly to blame for what had happened.

When she'd asked, 'Well, what could I have done?' her mam had been very forthright about a woman's place being in the home and that if she had been at home looking after Delia, instead of out working, then Tudor could never have taken her away.

After that she hadn't tried to explain anything to either of them. She felt it would be a waste of time. The only thing she could do was to go back to Cardiff and manage her life the best she could.

She'd have to buckle down and make sure she didn't lose her job at the shop or she really would be in trouble. It would have been more sensible if instead of coming to Pen-y-llyn she had paid the rent to Sophia as she should have done, and gone to work every day, she thought unhappily. From now on she'd have to do what she could to live on what she was earning. Three years would soon pass, she told herself.

Cara and Rhys were very surprised to see her back so soon. 'From what you said we thought you'd be away at least until the end of the week,' they told her.

'So did I.' Karyn smiled. 'Then I came to my senses and realised what a lot of time I'd had off lately and I didn't think I was playing fair, not when you've both been so good to me.'

She saw them look at each other and an unspoken message pass between them.

'Well, to tell you the truth,' Cara said, 'we weren't even sure if you would be coming back at all. What with all the gossip and the fact that Sophia told us you hadn't paid your rent and one thing and another ...' she stopped, too tongue-tied to go on.

'What Cara is trying to say, my lovely, is that we have someone else coming in part time. Only for a few hours a day, see. Just to give Cara a chance to rest. She gets very worn out if she has to be down here in the shop for very long, as you very well know.'

Karyn looked from one to the other of them in dismay. 'You mean you don't want me here, that my job has gone?'

'No, no! Nothing like that. We're more than pleased to see you back. We have promised the other girl, Morag Hughes is her name, that she can have a couple of hours work each day, though, so we can't back out of that now.'

'Tell you what,' Cara suggested. 'If Morag comes in every afternoon from four o'clock until six and then she also does Saturdays, it will mean you'll have more time to be with Delia and you'll be able to look after her yourself.'

'Yes, that sounds fine,' Karyn agreed, a mixture of relief and doubt in her voice. 'What about my wages, though, will it make any difference?' she asked anxiously.

Rhys pursed his lips. 'Well, naturally we have

to pay Morag and since you won't be here . . .'
his voice trailed off.

Karyn stopped listening. What did it matter
what excuse he made about cutting her wages.
She couldn't manage on what she was getting
now, so she certainly wasn't going to be able
to manage if he paid her less.

Tudor Morgan found that his second term of
imprisonment was nothing at all like his
previous one. He had not found that easy, but
this time, right from the very first day, it was
gruelling.

Most of the warders were the same ones
who'd been there when he'd been inside before,
but although they knew who he was, they
treated him in a completely different way.

When he had been serving time before they
had all laughed about his exploits, thought it
highly amusing that he'd been done for singing
in Morgan's Arcade. They'd seemed to
completely overlook the fact that his little girl
had been involved as well. This time, however,
there was no such leniency.

Some of them dubbed him 'queer' or 'barmy',
while others said he was 'downright evil' to
allow those kinds of pictures to be taken so that
he could sell them.

His punishment was far greater than merely
being imprisoned. He was always given the
dirtiest jobs. He was shouted at, made to wait
for his food, and always given the smallest

portions possible or the scrapings from the bottom of the pan.

Even the other prisoners regarded him with contempt and either ignored him or picked on him whenever possible.

When he was involved in any fights, the warders usually turned a blind eye, even if several men attacked him at the same time. They ignored his injuries, or else they said that he'd been the instigator and meted out even more punishment. His life was such hell that he actually welcomed it when he was given solitary confinement; except that when he was completely alone he was haunted by what had happened.

Looking back he knew he should never have listened to Marcus Webb. The glittering prospect of achieving his life-long dream of being recognised as a singer had been such tantalising bait that he'd simply done whatever he asked.

At the time he'd seen no harm in Marcus arranging for Delia to be photographed dancing. He'd thought it would be done on Saturdays when they attended the dancing classes that Marcus had arranged for both of them.

Even when Marcus had suggested spending a whole day at another studio that had much better facilities, and that it was just outside Cardiff, he'd still not seen any harm in it.

He realised now that he shouldn't have

agreed to take Delia out of school for the day, but at the time even that hadn't seemed to be all that important.

He'd been a bit worried when Marcus had said that the pictures weren't as good as he'd hoped they would be and so they would have to be redone and suggested that as he had a caravan nearby they could stay there overnight and take them again first thing the next morning.

He should have called a halt right there and then. Things mightn't have got out of hand if he'd had the sense to do so. He should have known that Karyn would have been half out of her mind with worry when he and Delia didn't come home and that sooner or later someone would come looking for them.

Yes, he admitted he'd been a fool. He hadn't meant to worry anyone and he certainly hadn't intended to cause so much trouble.

He hadn't approved of the clothes Marcus had made Delia wear. He thought the posturing and dancing Marcus asked her to do was strange, but he'd never considered them to be depraved. He most certainly hadn't intended to profit from them – except in so far as he would be rewarded with a lead part in the film Marcus kept talking about. Now he didn't even have that to dream about; in fact, he had very little to look forward to, he thought glumly.

When he'd heard the way the evidence piled up against him, the way the barrister acting for

Marcus was able to twist things so that he was the guilty one and make it appear as if he had coerced Marcus into taking the pictures for him, he was shocked to the core.

It was too late now to do anything about that, but his mind was still troubled by the harm it might have done Delia and also by the problems he had caused Karyn.

He worried constantly about how she was going to manage. Her wages wouldn't be sufficient to pay the rent and leave enough for her and Delia to live on. She might manage it for a few months but certainly not for three years.

No matter how much Karyn tried to economise, Delia would grow out of her clothes and also need bigger shoes. From what Karyn had told him about her visit to Pen-y-llyn to see her parents it looked as though there would be no help coming from them.

He was surprised that Owen and Enid Pryce hadn't been more understanding and let Delia stay there with them. Saying that she'd be tormented by Olwyn and her children had simply been an excuse. He knew Olwyn had always been jealous of him because he'd been his mother's favourite, but he didn't think she would vent her spleen on an innocent child.

The last time he'd been in prison he had organised a card school and he'd won money and all sorts of privileges with his gambling skills. This time none of the other prisoners were even willing to include him in their card games because of what he had done. They treated him almost as if he was a leper. Thieves, vagabonds, cheats and swindlers all looked down on him and treated him with contempt. No matter what crime they'd committed, they were regarded as being more acceptable company than he was.

When he'd asked to see the Governor to petition a move to another prison, one where he wasn't known by both the warders and inmates, his request was turned down.

'No good bleating to him,' one of the warders sneered, 'because he's a family man like the rest of us and he thinks that anyone who meddles with children should be hung.'

He'd said he wanted to see the prison chaplain, but nothing came of it. He was probably a family man too, Tudor thought bitterly. It was a pity he hadn't said he was a Catholic, at least Fr Bunloaf wouldn't be able to admit to being a family man, he thought sourly.

There seemed to be no one he could turn to who would intercede in any way, so it meant he had to face three long years of harsh treatment. The last time he'd been in solitary confinement he'd even considered topping himself. He'd ripped the Hessian bedcovering into strips and knotted them together in readiness. The only thing that kept him from going through with it was his feelings for Delia and his pride in her. She was so pretty with her dark curls and clear, hazel eyes. She was as light on her feet as a little fairy and as bright as a button, and so affectionate that it grieved him that he had put her through such an ordeal.

Karyn's declaration of her love the last time she'd visited him had been more than he could ever have hoped for, especially when he'd given her the chance to walk out of his life if she felt she couldn't tolerate any more upsets.

Karyn had told him that she had always loved him and always would as long as she lived . . . and he believed her. It was the only encouraging news he'd had since the day he'd been sentenced. With no family willing to help her out and a child to support, it meant that Karyn would be enduring a three-year sentence of her own, he thought morosely.

Chapter Thirty-One

Karyn couldn't believe what had happened. Things seemed to be going from bad to worse. She tried to work out how much less she was going to find in her wage packet at the end of the week, but her brain was so fogged by the news that another assistant had been hired that she couldn't do it.

Neither Rhys nor Cara seemed prepared to help her by stating exactly how much she would be earning.

What was even worse was the chill in the air between them. Furthermore, in her absence Cara had taken a stand, or perhaps it had been Rhys, and had decided that Cara would no longer look after Delia.

She wished she knew how long they had felt like that and why they hadn't said anything before now if Cara found it so onerous. It worried her because she'd thought that they were all such good friends that they could talk freely to each other about such things.

She wasn't sure whether or not to confide in Sophia about what had happened. She was bound to wonder why she was back home at four o'clock each afternoon and why she didn't go to work on Saturdays.

But if Karyn told her what had happened, and that her wages were being cut, Sophia might be afraid that she wouldn't be able to pay her rent and turn them out. She had been rather short with her when she'd asked her if she could leave the rent for a week because she needed the money to go to Pen-y-llyn.

The thought that she was still a week behind with her rent only made her feel even more despondent. If only Tudor wasn't in prison. She needed him; together they could cope. She didn't mind working, she enjoyed it more than he did, but she couldn't be in two places at once. Delia needed looking after and it was her duty to do just that.

Other women who went out to work left their kids to fend for themselves but Delia wasn't eight yet and after what she'd been through recently she couldn't possibly do that to her.

Sophia seemed to be very surprised to see her back after such a short time and quick to notice that she was looking glum. She immediately wanted to know why.

'You'd both better come and have a cuppa and a biscuit with me,' she invited the moment Karyn and Delia came in through the door.

'Come along and then you can tell me all about your trip and why you are back so soon. You look so down in the dumps there must be something up,' she persisted when Karyn tried to shrug her questioning away.

'Reaction, I suppose, it's only really sunk in these last few days that Tudor won't be home for three years.'

'You said that you were going to stay with your family for at least a week, so what's brought you scurrying back after only a few days?' Sophia probed.

'I thought perhaps I shouldn't take too long off from work because the Williamses mightn't like it. If I'm not there, then it means that Cara has to come down and serve in the shop. In fact, I dropped in to let them know I was home and that I would be in to work again in the morning.'

'I heard that they'd got Morag Hughes in there helping out,' Sophia said, stirring her tea and avoiding looking at Karyn. 'Going to be a regular thing, I hear?'

Karyn said nothing, but she felt annoyed that there had been gossiping and that Sophia already knew.

'Does that mean you'll be picking Delia up from school at four o'clock and then coming home with her every afternoon?'

'Yes, it will be much better, won't it,' Karyn said evasively.

'And is it right that this Morag Hughes is going to work at the shop on Saturdays as well?' Sophia pressed.

'I'm not too sure about that,' Karyn hedged, stirring her tea.

'Well, I heard that she was! Funny that Cara Williams didn't tell you so, cariad.'

'They did say something about it,' Karyn admitted.

'I heard that Cara was finding things too much for her,' Sophia added, nodding her head in Delia's direction. 'The reason they took you on in the first place,' she added, 'was so that Cara Williams could rest more.'

Karyn took a drink of her tea before answering. 'She finds serving in the shop too much for her when she's not feeling too good,' she agreed.

'Bit hard on you, though, cariad,' Sophia sympathised. 'It's going to mean a lot less in your pay packet if you are only working there part time.'

'I'll be working every day the same as ever,' Karyn said stiffly.

'Yes, but only until four o'clock. That's not the same as a full day, now is it? And then there's the question of Saturdays,' Sophia went on, harping back to the subject. 'Morag says she will be working all day on Saturdays, so are they going to employ both of you then?'

'No, I'll be off all day on Saturdays,' Karyn admitted wearily. She was worried enough about what was happening without having to go into details with Sophia.

'Oh dear! That means less in your wage packet each week; how are you going to manage?'

'What you're really asking is am I going to be able to pay the rent for my rooms, aren't you?' Karyn snapped.

'Well, I did wonder. You know we depend on it, otherwise we wouldn't be letting our rooms out in the first place.'

'I'll see you get your money,' Karyn promised.

'I know you'll try, but you had to put off paying me this week in order to have enough money to go and see your folks, now didn't you? If you haven't got it, then you can't pay it, now can you!'

'Frankly, at the moment, I don't know how I am going to manage, but don't worry, I will think of something,' Karyn declared, pushing back her chair and holding out her hand to Delia.

'Hold on, cariad. Don't be in such a rush. Listen to what I have to say first of all. What about giving up one of your rooms? Now that there's only you and Delia you could turn the downstairs room into a lovely bedsitter for the two of you and then we could let out your bedroom separately.'

'How could you do that? They'd have to come through your living room every time they wanted to make themselves a cup of tea or cook a meal. And it would mean that there would be three of us all trying to use that poky scullery.'

'No, not the sort of lodger I was thinking of

taking in,' Sophia explained quickly. 'I was thinking of a young single man, see. I'll be supplying all his meals so there will be none of the problems you've just raised.'

Karyn stared at her bemused. 'You and Josiah have already decided about all this, haven't you!'

'Well, as a matter of fact, you're right.' Sophia's round black face beamed. 'We've a lovely surprise for you; wait until you see the beautiful new couch we've put in your living room! Come on, I'll show it to you. It's not simply a couch, it's a bed as well! It's called a put-you-up,' she went on excitedly. 'It looks like a couch, but it opens out and you can use it as a bed at night. Then in the morning you shut it all up and it's a couch again. Now isn't that a marvellous idea?'

Karyn couldn't trust herself to speak. After what had happened at the corner shop this was yet another blow. Living and sleeping in one room sounded almost as bad as being shut up in a cell like Tudor. Yet what option did she have but to accept what Sophia was offering her?

'I'll try it out and think about it,' she told Sophia. 'When do you want to know?'

'I'm afraid it has already happened,' Sophia told her, shrugging her plump shoulders. 'We've already let your bedroom. We fixed it all up while you were visiting Pen-y-llyn.'

'I was only away for three days! Are you

telling me that there is already someone else using my bedroom?'

'Yes, cariad, it's already let. To a young relative of Josiah's called Oliver,' she explained. 'You'll like him,' she added enthusiastically, 'he's about your age.'

'So what's happened to all our clothes and bits and pieces that were up in our bedroom?' Karyn demanded furiously.

'Don't worry; they're all safe and sound. I took everything out of the room before Oliver moved in. I'm sure you and Delia will be as cosy as can be down here,' she added with a beaming smile.

'And what about the rent? How much am I going to have to pay if I've only got one room?'

'That's the really good news for you, instead of twelve shillings a week it will now only be seven shillings.'

'Seven shillings! For one room? If I only have half the accommodation I had before then it should only be six shillings,' Karyn protested hotly.

'You have more than one room. You have the use of the scullery as well,' Sophia reminded her. 'And don't forget that you have a brand new Put-you-up.'

'That was your idea, not mine!'

'Would you sooner have an iron bedstead in the room, then?'

Karyn shook her head. She was well aware

that would be even more insufferable than the arrangements Sophia had already made.

'We could have had bunk beds like me and Daddy slept in when we stayed in Uncle Marcus's caravan,' Delia piped up.

'Really! You must come and have tea with me and tell me all about it,' Sophia invited.

Karyn sighed. That was a matter she certainly didn't want discussed under any circumstances, so it seemed that the best thing she could do was to say nothing more about the new arrangements. She'd accept them without further comment even though she didn't like having to do so.

Miss Sherman also had a great deal to say about Delia being off school yet again.

'She's only been away for three days,' Karyn pointed out. 'I thought it would be a good idea to take her to see her grandparents and that it would help her to forget all that had happened.'

'Yes, I can see it has probably been an unpleasant ordeal for her, but children are very resilient, you know. If you didn't mention it, she would probably have forgotten all about it in a few days. Making a fuss about what happened only makes her feel important and the centre of attention,' she said severely.

'Well, in that case, then, I hope you can keep the promise you made earlier and make sure that the other children don't say anything to her about what happened,' Karyn said firmly.

Miss Sherman looked rather taken aback and quickly changed the subject.

'You will be here to meet her yourself each afternoon from now on, or so I understand?'

'Yes, I will be, but how did you know?' Karyn frowned.

'I heard it mentioned,' Miss Sherman said vaguely.

'You mean Cara Williams told you . . . or was it Morag Hughes?'

'I'm not sure,' Miss Sherman told her. 'One of them mentioned it, I believe.'

'While I was away?'

'It must have been. I haven't seen them since you came back,' she pointed out.

'Quite! So it must have been Morag Hughes, because she has a child at this school and Mrs Williams would hardly have come to the school if she wasn't meeting Delia, now would she?' Karyn said abruptly and turned on her heel and walked away.

She felt so angry, knowing that they had all been talking about her behind her back. Talking and scheming, making decisions that changed her life round completely and leaving her no choice but to accept their plans for her whether she wanted to or not.

At the moment there was nothing she could do to alter anything, but one day in the future, when Tudor was once more a free man, then her life would change, she vowed.

All she had to do, she told herself, as she

squared her shoulders and raised her head proudly, was to remember that when you reached bottom there was only one way you could go after that, and that was up.

One day she'd walk away from Adeline Street and never come back there ever again. They'd buy a posh house in Roath, or somewhere like that, and all their troubles would be behind them.

The new arrangement in Adeline Street signalled a transformation between her and the Earls. They were still quite civil, but the close friendship they had enjoyed seemed to have vanished.

On the next visiting day, when she asked Sophia if Delia could stay with her while she went to visit Tudor, Sophia hesitated. 'Isn't Cara Williams well enough to look after her?'

'I didn't ask her. I thought Delia would be happier here with you and Josiah. If it's not convenient, then—'

'No, of course it's all right,' Sophia said quickly. 'Visiting is only once a month after all.'

Karyn didn't know whether to tell Tudor about the new arrangements at work and the atmosphere at Adeline Street or not. There didn't seem to be much point in doing so since there was nothing he would be able to do about it. If he knew how difficult she was finding it to survive, then it would only worry him.

He looked thin and unhappy and after she'd listened to his bitter account of the way he was being treated she decided that it was better to say nothing. He was suffering many more hardships than she was.

He had a haggard and gaunt look as though he hadn't slept well for weeks. There was even a sprinkling of grey hair at his temples, shining amongst his jet-black close-cropped hair like threads of white cotton.

He sounded bitter as he told her of some of the punishments that had been dealt out to him and the way the other prisoners were treating him because of what had happened to Delia.

'I would never have let anyone harm little Delia,' he assured her. 'I had no idea what was in Marcus Webb's mind or the sort of pervert he was. You must hate me, Karyn.'

'No,' she assured him, 'I could never hate you. I love you too deeply to ever hate you. We'll get through this. The time will soon pass and then you'll be out and we'll all be together again.'

'Marcus Webb will be out in about six weeks,' he said bitterly. 'Just think of that! He was the guilty one, not me, and all he gets is a six-month sentence and I get three years!'

'It's no good dwelling on it,' Karyn told him sharply. 'You've learned your lesson and with any luck you'll never see or hear of Marcus Webb ever again.'

'I'll make it all up to you when I get out,' he promised. 'We'll make a fresh start and there'll be no more singing. I'll get an ordinary sort of job and we'll try and lead a normal life.'

'There's been a man here asking for you,' Sophia told Karyn the moment she walked in the door.

'Really, who was that?' She frowned as she picked Delia up and hugged her. Fear suddenly gripped Karyn. 'It wasn't Marcus Webb, was it?' she asked, her voice sharp with fear.

'No, it wasn't Uncle Marcus,' Delia piped up. 'It was a different man altogether.'

'Was it a reporter?' Karyn asked, looking at Sophia over the top of Delia's head.

'No, no! At least I don't think so. He was ever so posh. Smartly dressed, and he had a swanky voice. Not the sort of geezer you see around Splott.'

'Didn't he tell you his name?'

'Well, he left a card. Here it is.' She reached out and picked up a small piece of card that was on the mantelpiece. 'It says Samuel Pettigrew. Does that ring any bells?'

Karyn held out her hand for the card and read the name aloud for herself. 'No, I've never heard of him.' She frowned.

'He said he would be calling again. He seemed to be very keen to talk to you,' Sophia persisted.

'Really! Well, I don't know what it can be about. Are you sure that it was me and not Tudor he wanted?'

'Definitely you! He didn't even mention

Tudor's name. He seemed to recognise Delia, though.'

Karyn shook her head, completely puzzled.

'You want to be careful, mind,' Sophia warned. 'Look at the mess Tudor got himself into getting mixed up with a man he knew nothing about.'

Karyn's lips tightened, but she didn't answer.

'Well, now you're home I can get on with my cooking. With Oliver here I have an extra mouth to feed every night so there's more to do.'

Karyn nodded, but she wasn't really listening, she was still wondering who Samuel Pettigrew was and what he wanted with her. Sophia had said he'd seemed to recognise Delia and she wondered if that was from the reports in the newspapers or because he had something to do with Marcus Webb and it made her feel very uneasy.

Chapter Thirty-Two

Karyn looked at the business card that Samuel Pettigrew had left with Sophia at least a dozen times during the course of the evening. Apart from his name and an office address in Mount Stuart Square there was nothing to indicate what his business was.

Mount Stuart Square brought unpleasant memories of the cellar where they'd once lived, but she also remembered all the big, prosperous offices dotted around the Square and tried to remember if there had been any newspaper offices. Samuel Pettigrew might be some kind of newspaper reporter and she knew only too well from previous experience how those sorts of people hunted you down.

She was tempted to tear the piece of card into pieces and throw it on the fire, but something stopped her doing so. If she did that it still might not be the end of the matter because he knew where to find her and might call again. Perhaps she should wait until the next prison visit and ask Tudor if he knew anything about him and what he thought she ought to do.

She left the card on the table and it was the

408

first thing she saw the next morning when she woke up.

She still had no idea who Samuel Pettigrew might be, but if she ignored it, then it was more than likely that he would turn up at Adeline Street again. Next time he might discuss whatever it was he wanted to know with Sophia and she certainly didn't want that to happen.

At one time she wouldn't have minded, but since Tudor had been in prison she found too many people, including Sophia, were making changes in her life and deciding things that affected her without saying a word to her first.

She knew the only thing to do was to go and see this man herself, but she wasn't sure when she could do it. If she waited until Saturday it might be too late and, what was more, most offices were closed on a Saturday.

Her mind made up, she decided she would have to go to Mount Stuart Square as soon as she picked Delia up from school at four o'clock. It meant taking her along as well, but Sophia had said the man seemed to know Delia, which was also very odd.

Karyn worried all morning about whether or not she was doing the right thing or whether to ignore it all together. Several times she was on the point of asking Rhys Williams what he thought, but drew back at the last minute, telling herself that since she didn't like other people making decisions for her then it was better to deal with this herself.

Delia was quite excited at the thought of going to Mount Stuart Square, but Karyn felt nervous about doing so. She was relieved that the office building they had to visit was on the far side from the area she knew.

She felt very apprehensive when the moment they entered the building a liveried doorman approached and asked if he could assist her. She gave her name and asked for Samuel Pettigrew, then sat down nervously on the edge of one of the padded benches that were along one wall.

By the time a smartly dressed young man in a navy pin-stripe suit and gleaming white shirt came to escort them up to Mr Pettigrew's office she was wondering what on earth she was doing there and was on the point of leaving.

The office they were shown into was a large, airy room with a high ceiling. There was a massive mahogany desk in the centre of it and three or four leather chairs facing it.

'Mrs Morgan!' A tall, angular man in a light grey suit and with the largest, floppiest cravat in a medley of colours that she'd ever seen rose from behind the desk and advanced across the room towards her, hand outstretched.

'Mrs Morgan!' He shook Karyn's hand warmly, almost as if he was a friend, then turned to smile at down at Delia. 'Hello, Delia.' He patted her on the head.

'What is all this about, why do you want to see me, Mr Pettigrew?'

'Mrs Morgan . . .' He paused and looked from her to Delia rather hesitantly. 'Mrs Morgan, would you mind if my assistant took care of Delia for a few minutes?'

Fear at being separated from Delia, even for a few minutes, made Karyn's heart race. She wanted to refuse but choked on the words.

'I'm sure he'll be able to find her a biscuit and a glass of sarsaparilla? You'd like that, wouldn't you, Delia?'

Without waiting for an answer he walked over to his desk and pressed a bell. Within seconds the young man was back. He listened attentively to what Mr Pettigrew told him, and then held the door open for Delia.

Karyn waited until the door closed then she demanded, 'What's all this about? Why can't you say whatever it is you have to say in front of Delia?'

'I felt it was better not to do so since it affects her and I wanted to discuss it with you first,' he said gravely.

'I don't understand,' Karyn said, frowning. 'I don't know you, so what is it you want to talk about?'

'I followed your husband's trial with interest. I think he was wrongly punished because I know all about Webb's dubious career in show business. You must be finding things very hard . . . three years is a long time.'

'You mean you are some sort of solicitor and you want him to appeal? Or are you another of these reporters trying to get a story for your newspaper?'

'No, no. Nothing at all like that,' he assured her with a smile.

'So who are you, then? A friend of Marcus Webb's?'

His face grew stern as he shook his head emphatically. 'Most certainly not. I think what he did was extremely reprehensible.'

'Yet you followed the case?'

'I did and I also saw the photographs of your daughter which were shown in court.'

Karyn stiffened and looked uncomfortable. 'She's not going to pose for you, if that's what you're hoping.'

Mr Pettigrew remained silent. He leaned his elbows on the desk, forming his hands into a pyramid and resting his chin on the top of it.

'I can see that you are very sensitive about what has happened and that is quite understandable. I would like you to listen to what I have to say, though.'

'Go on!'

He leaned back in his chair, looking up at the ceiling, as if searching for the right words. Karyn clutched at her handbag, her knuckles white, her heart thudding. She didn't know what to make of this man. He was smartly dressed and yet with his foppish cravat he didn't really look like a businessman, so what was he?

'As I said, I understand that your daughter

can perform in front of the camera. She can dance and I believe she enjoys singing. I suppose she has inherited both these talents from her father.'

'Possibly. Tudor has a wonderful baritone voice,' Karyn told him proudly. 'He's always wanted to earn his living singing on the stage. Marcus Webb had promised him a part in a musical film he was going to make.'

'I doubt if that would ever have materialised,' Samuel Pettigrew smiled wryly. 'Marcus Webb's main interest was in taking specialised pictures which he sold to collectors, mostly on the Continent and in America.'

'All these theatrical types are the same,' Karyn declared bitterly, 'you can't trust any of them.'

'No, that's not quite true, Mrs Morgan. Not all of us are bad eggs!'

Her eyes narrowed as she stared at him. 'So you are also in show business, are you? I should have known!'

'Yes, as a matter of fact I am, but I don't make films, I put on plays and musicals that are performed in top theatres all over the United Kingdom; in London, Brighton, Birmingham, Liverpool and Manchester, as well as here in Cardiff and right the way up to Edinburgh. My shows are staged at top theatres in all the big towns.'

'So what has that got to do with me? My husband is in prison, so you can't hire him until he comes out and that won't be for three years. Yes,' she repeated angrily, 'they sent him down for three years and he was innocent. It was Marcus Webb who should have been given that sentence, not my Tudor.'

'I agree with you, Mrs Morgan. It's not your husband that I'm interested in hiring, though, it's your daughter. No,' he held up his hand to stop Karyn speaking as her face flamed and it was obvious she was extremely angry. 'It's not to take pictures of Delia like Webb did. I want her to play the part of a young girl in a new musical I am about to produce.'

'This is utter rubbish, I wouldn't dream of letting her do it,' Karyn declared. She stood up ready to leave. 'Where is Delia?'

'One minute, Mrs Morgan. Before you walk out let me tell you a little bit more. There would be a period of six weeks' rehearsals here in Cardiff and then we would go on tour to all the places I've mentioned and possibly many others as well—'

'Like I've already said, it's all rubbish you're talking. Delia's too young to do something like that. She still needs me to take care of her.'

'Of course she does,' he agreed. 'You would come with her. You would be paid a wage for looking after her and you would be provided with accommodation both here in Cardiff and in every town we eventually visit. You would be expected to accompany Delia to and from the theatre and remain backstage to help her dress and get ready for her performance.'

'What sort of performance?' Karyn's voice was sharp with suspicion.

'I've already told you; playing a part in this musical I am producing,' he repeated patiently. 'She will sing and dance. A very delightful song and the dancing will be very proper.'

Karyn shook her head in bewilderment.

'I'm sure you will want time to think all this over,' Samuel Pettigrew observed. 'It's a big decision, but it could make a star of your little girl.'

'A star!' Karyn laughed a little hysterically. 'It's not Delia who wants to be a star; it's her dad. And look where it has got him!' she added bitterly.

'This is quite different. Why don't you think very carefully about what I've told you and come back on Wednesday afternoon and let me know what you have decided.'

Karyn shook her head. 'I need longer. I would have to talk to my husband about it and get his permission before I could agree to Delia doing anything like that.'

'He's in prison, Mrs Morgan, so surely it's up to you to make the decision. You are responsible for her wellbeing – and your own.'

'He's Delia's dad and I certainly wouldn't let her undertake anything like this without him agreeing to it,' she said stubbornly.

'Very well.' He drummed thoughtfully on the blotter in front of him with his fountain pen. 'How soon can you see him?'

'Not for another three weeks.'

Samuel Pettigrew frowned. 'I was hoping you'd give me your answer sooner than that! If I am going to give Delia this part then it is very important that she starts rehearsing right away with the rest of the cast.'

'No!' Karyn shook her head again. 'There's such a lot to be considered. If I accepted your offer, then it would mean giving up my home here in Cardiff.'

'Yes, that's probably true, but you are only living in rooms, I understand.'

'Who told you that?'

'The lady whose house you are sharing in Splott.' He ran a hand over his chin. 'She told me that you owed her rent and that you were finding it hard to make ends meet because your husband was in prison and you only had a part-time job in a shop.'

Karyn's face flamed. 'It is nothing to do with her; she needs to watch her tongue. It's none of her business . . .'

'No, it's not,' he agreed softly. 'That's why I said the decision was up to you. Three years is a long time. You can either spend it living a hand-to-mouth existence like you're doing now or you can live comfortably and earn a good wage. Delia will also be earning a regular fee which will be retained until the end of the play's

416

run and then paid to whoever is responsible for her in a lump sum.'

'How much will she be paid?'

He shrugged. 'It depends to some extent on what sort of box-office returns we get. She will get a percentage of the takings so it could be quite substantial. It will certainly be enough to help you and your husband to make a fresh start when he comes out of prison.'

'And I'd get wages quite separately from that?'

'You would. What is more, your accommodation would be in a good-class boarding house in each of the towns we visit and it would all be paid for by my company. That means the money you earn would be entirely yours. Now are you tempted?' He smiled benignly.

Karyn stared at him for a moment, trying to make up her mind, but it was impossible. He had a proper office and staff and he certainly sounded very professional, not blustering and flashy like Marcus Webb had been. It was a wonderful offer but why was he so sure that Delia could fulfil the part he had in mind for her when he hadn't even seen her dance or heard her sing?

'Yes, I suppose I am', she agreed reluctantly. 'Even so, I need more time to think about it all.'

'Right. Wednesday afternoon. Shall we say four-thirty?' He pressed a bell on his desk. 'I'll leave it to you to explain it all to your daughter,' he said as Delia came running back into the room.

'What is it that you have to explain to me, Mam?' Delia asked as they walked out into Mount Stuart Square.

'Not now, cariad. I need time to think about what Mr Pettigrew said and then I'll tell you all about it.'

'He said you have to explain it to me,' she persisted. 'What is it you have to explain?'

'Nothing, nothing very much. Leave it for now. I'll tell you all about it tomorrow.'

Delia pouted, but she didn't persist. 'Could we go and have a milk shake?' she asked hopefully.

Karyn stopped and counted the change in her purse. 'If we do, then we'll have to walk home.'

'I don't mind, I'm not a bit tired, but I am ever so thirsty.' Delia grinned.

'I thought you had a drink of sarsaparilla while you were waiting for me?' Karyn teased.

Delia pulled a face. 'I did, but I think that is what has made me thirsty!'

'All right, well, as a special treat, then, but first you must promise me something. You are not to say anything to Sophia or Josiah about where we've been this afternoon. Do you understand?'

Chapter Thirty-Three

Karyn couldn't sleep. She couldn't stop thinking about her meeting with Samuel Pettigrew. One minute it was as if he was offering her heaven on a plate, the next her mind was full of suspicion. How could such good fortune be coming her way? Was it some sort of trap? Was he as evil as Marcus Webb?

Whom could she trust? Whom could she ask? If only Tudor was there to talk it over with her; tell her what he thought about it all. Would he know any better than her, though? After all, he'd been taken in by Marcus Webb.

Delia's welfare and her future depended on her making the right choice. If she refused this offer, then she was condemning both of them to a hand-to-mouth existence for the next three years. In fact, probably for a lot longer because with a prison record behind him it would take Tudor a long time to get back on his feet and find work.

If she accepted Samuel Pettigrew's offer, then she and Delia would both be well fed, comfortably housed and have money for clothes. She might even be able to save up some of her wages for when Tudor was released so that they would have enough to live on until he decided what he wanted to do or found work of some kind.

She tried to think of someone who could advise her. At one time she could have talked it over with Rhys and Cara Williams, but these days there was no rapport between them. She was just another employee. The cosy chats with Cara had ended abruptly and her conversations with Rhys were limited to him giving her orders about what he wanted her to do.

Sophia and Josiah had stopped asking her to join them for a cuppa or a meal. Now they were completely absorbed with their lodger Oliver who was a Jamaican, like them. They all went off to the Gospel Hall together and acted like one big family. Anyway, she didn't want to confide in her. She knew Sophia was curious to know if she was going to contact Samuel Pettigrew, but she didn't want to let her know that she'd already been to see him or to tell her what he'd said.

That left only her mam and dad, but there had been such a marked coolness between them the last time she'd gone all the way to Pen-y-llyn to see them. In fact, thinking about it now, she wasn't sure whether they were the more relieved that she'd left so quickly or whether she was.

None of this was helping her to make a decision, she thought exasperatedly. Her mind was buzzing and she knew she had no hope of sleeping so she might as well get up before her restlessness disturbed Delia.

As she pushed away the bedclothes she heard a noise and although it was pitch dark in the room she sensed the door was opening and that someone was coming in.

Holding her breath, she stayed perfectly still, desperately trying to work out who the intruder moving towards the bed could be, but she couldn't make out their features. Then she caught the gleam of teeth and the glint of eyes and knew it must be one of the Earls. She couldn't see the face because there was no light in the room.

'Who is it, what do you want?' Her voice was shaky, she felt so frightened.

There was no reply and when she felt a hand touch her shoulder it took all her self control not to scream.

'Stay quiet!' It was an order, not a request, and she recognised Oliver's voice.

'What do you want? Go away,' she hissed.

He laughed. A rich, dark sound, yet to her ears there was something threatening about it that sent shudders through her.

'What do you think I want?'

'I don't know. Go away before you wake Delia. We'll talk about it in the morning.'

Again he laughed. This time louder and to her ears it sounded even more sinister.

'Come on, you've been fluttering those eyelashes at me ever since I arrived here, so I

421

know what you want. With your old man inside you're crazy for me. No one else need know about it. It can be our little secret, honey.'

'Go away! You must be mad. If you don't get out of my room, then I'll scream for Sophia and—'

His hand clamped down over her face stopping her from saying another word. As she felt his other hand moving over her body she tensed then began to struggle wildly.

The punch at the side of her face brought tears to her eyes. 'Shut up before you wake the kid.'

He was too late; Delia was already stirring and calling out her mother's name.

With an oath Oliver let go of Karyn and began backing away. 'There'll be another time,' he warned.

She held her breath until the door closed, and then she concentrated on hushing Delia back to sleep.

It took several minutes, but eventually Delia's breathing deepened and became regular. Gently Karyn eased her back on to the pillow and freed her own arm which had been underneath Delia and was already numb.

Her thoughts were now in even greater confusion. She had only tried to be pleasant to Oliver Earl because Sophia had said he was a distant cousin and wanted to make him welcome. She had no idea that he had thought she was trying to flirt.

422

She shuddered. She didn't like him in the least. First thing next morning, she'd tell Sophia about what had happened. It was the only way because she was sure that he would try it on again.

To her surprise after such a disturbed night she did sleep. A deep, blank sleep, almost as if her brain was unable to cope with any more problems and had shut down completely.

They were both so late waking up that it was a mad dash to get Delia to school on time and not be late for work herself.

She was so busy all day that she had to push all the events of the previous day and night from her mind. They surfaced with a vengeance after she'd collected Delia from school and was on her way back to Adeline Street.

She knew the first thing she must do was talk to Sophia about Oliver's behaviour the previous night. She'd also make sure that she barricaded the door to her room before she went to bed so that whatever happened he couldn't get in there again while she was asleep.

She waited until Delia was in bed and asleep before she went along to see Sophia and tell her about what had happened. She found it highly embarrassing because Sophia refused to believe that Oliver was capable of doing such a thing.

'Either you have been encouraging him or you told him to come to your room and then changed your mind,' Sophia declared.

'What utter rubbish!' Karyn was so taken aback that she was almost speechless.

'Well, that's what it looks like to me,' Sophia insisted indignantly.

'Why ever should I do that?'

Sophia shrugged expressively. 'You're used to having a man in your bed, cariad, so it is only natural that you must be missing him now he's locked up.'

'How dare you say something like that,' Karyn blazed, flushing hotly.

Sophia was quick to take offense. 'That's how it looks to us! In fact, we have been so concerned that I was going to speak to you about it. I feel responsible for Oliver and I don't want him led astray.'

'And I'm telling you that he crept into my room last night and tried to get into my bed, even though I had Delia sleeping there with me. What sort of a man does that?'

'I think you've said enough, Karyn Morgan. I think it would be a good idea if you found somewhere else to live.'

'Don't worry, I will. I don't feel safe here any longer.'

'Good!' Sophia faced her angrily. 'You can leave tomorrow then . . . after you've paid me the rent you owe me.'

Karyn was trembling so much that she stumbled and had to put out her hand to support herself as she made her way across the passageway to her own room.

She sank down on the edge of the bed wondering what she was going to do now. She wasn't sure if Sophia had meant what she'd said about her leaving or not, but at least it focused her mind about what to do about Samuel Pettigrew's offer. She had no choice now but to accept.

It would be like jumping into the unknown, but probably it would be no worse than what she was enduring now.

She looked round the room and realised that none of it was hers. Their only possessions were Delia's toys and books and their clothes.

Before she settled for the night, Karyn dragged a chair across the room to block the door so that if Oliver Earl did decide to pay her another visit he wouldn't be able to get in.

They were still eating their breakfast when Sophia banged on the door and attempted to come straight in without waiting for an answer, but found her entry blocked by the chair.

'Hah!' she exclaimed angrily. 'You didn't take my word for it that you had no call to worry, then. Well, I've just come to remind you about what I said last night. I want you out of my house, but I am prepared to be reasonable. You can stay until the end of the week, but I want every penny of the money you owe me. Do you understand?'

'I'm going. I wouldn't want to stay on here,' Karyn told her, squaring her shoulders and looking Sophia in the face.

After taking Delia to school she started to walk towards the corner shop, and then stopped. Perhaps it was more important that she went to Mount Stuart Square and made sure that Samuel Pettigrew's offer was still open than it was to worry about inconveniencing Rhys and Cara Williams. If she went along with Pettigrew's offer, she'd be giving up her job anyway.

She hesitated. Samuel Pettigrew had said the same time as her previous visit, she reminded herself, and that meant half past four in the afternoon.

Slowly she resumed her steps towards the corner shop. She might as well go to work and be paid for it. She certainly needed the money; she owed two weeks' rent and she intended to make sure that Sophia had every penny that was outstanding so that she could leave with a clear conscience.

Karyn's heart was thumping and her palms felt damp by the time she and Delia reached Mount Stuart Square. Her mind was in turmoil because she was so anxious to do the right thing. It was Delia's future as well as her own that had to be resolved.

'Mr Pettigrew is expecting me,' she told the doorman.

Her knees were knocking, but holding Delia by the hand, she held her head high as she walked into his office once again.

'Well?' This time Samuel Pettigrew didn't rise

to greet her or offer her a seat. 'You've come back to see me, so I hope that means you've decided what you want to do, Mrs Morgan,' he said brusquely.

'Yes, I have.' Despite her nervousness she managed to keep her voice level. 'There are, however, one or two other things that you will have to agree to.'

'Oh yes?' He frowned, drumming his fingers on his desk impatiently. 'Go on; tell me what they are.'

'I want to move out of my present rooms in Adeline Street immediately, tomorrow, if possible. And . . . and I want a small advance so that I can clear my outstanding rent.'

'I see!' He stared at her thoughtfully for a moment. 'I think that can be arranged.'

He pulled open the top drawer in his desk and drew out an official-looking document, scanned it briefly, then passed it across the desk towards her.

'Sit down, Mrs Morgan,' he indicated a straight-back chair. 'This is a contract setting out all the details I outlined when I spoke to you before. I want you to go through it very carefully and if you agree with everything that's in it, then please sign it at the bottom.'

Karyn took the document from him and tried to read it, but the words blurred so much that for a moment she couldn't understand a word of it. Then she took a deep breath and concentrated.

'Satisfied?' He asked when she looked up.

'It seems to be exactly as you told me,' she agreed.

He handed her a pen. 'Will you please sign it, then, right here at the bottom,' he said, pointing with his forefinger.

'And does this mean that we can move away from Adeline Street immediately?' she asked as she passed the signed document back to him.

'Yes, I'll make all the arrangements for you to do so tomorrow. Is that soon enough?'

Karyn nodded. 'That will be fine. Where will we go?'

'If you come back here tomorrow, any time after eleven o'clock, my assistant will tell you the address and you will be able to move in there right away.'

'Will it be here in Cardiff?'

'As I've already told you, rehearsals will take place here,' he said a little impatiently. 'For the moment we'll find you a respectable boarding house in Cathays or Canton, will that be all right?'

'What about school? Won't Delia get into trouble if she doesn't go to school?'

'I'll take care of all that. Someone will be employed by the company to tutor her,' he explained. 'There are other children, so a tutor will travel with us. Like the others, Delia will spend a certain number of hours each day doing lessons.'

'Yes, I'm sorry to be asking so many questions, Mr Pettigrew. I'm a little bit confused by all this. It's a very big step, you know. There is just one other thing,' she went on hesitantly, 'the advance; could you see your way to letting me have that now to clear my overdue rent? If I don't pay it now, Mrs Earl may stop me from taking my possessions.'

As soon as they left the offices in Mount Stuart Square, Delia wanted to know what they had been talking about and what was going on.

The idea that she would be singing and dancing in a real musical frightened her at first until Karyn carefully explained that it had nothing at all to do with Marcus Webb.

'There will be other children taking part,' she assured her, 'and I'll be in the theatre with you all the time. You'll do lessons every day as well as learning to sing and dance.'

Delia bombarded her with so many questions that Karyn's head was spinning. To quieten her down Karyn took her to a milk bar and bought them both a drink and something to eat.

'I suppose we have to walk all the way home now,' Delia sighed when they came outside.

'No, cariad, we can take the tram.' Karyn smiled.

'Even though we had buns as well as a drink!' Delia exclaimed in surprise.

'Yes, tonight we can do both,' Karyn laughed. Suddenly she felt light-hearted. She had money in her purse; she was going to move out of

Adeline Street and away from Splott and Tiger Bay as she'd always longed to do.

She still had to break the news to Tudor when she went to visit him in three weeks' time, so she hoped that he would agree that she had acted for the best, because once she and Delia joined the theatre company she would probably not to be able to visit him unless they were in Cardiff.

Chapter Thirty-Four

Tudor Morgan walked out of Cardiff Prison and strode towards Adam Street before he slowed down, took a deep breath and looked around.

Fishing in his jacket pocket he pulled out a crushed packet of Woodbines and stuck one in the corner of his mouth, then searched for a match. Taking a long pull on the cigarette, he allowed himself a small smile of satisfaction before striding out briskly towards Wood Street.

It was three years to the day since he'd been sent down. He'd not been given any remission for good behaviour even though he'd tried hard never to put a foot wrong.

In those three years, a great portion of the time had been spent in solitary confinement and had given him ample time for retrospection. If it had been possible to turn back the clock he'd like to have started again, right back in the days before his father had been killed and he'd left Pen-y-llyn to come to Cardiff.

Marrying Karyn was something he'd never regret. His love for her was as strong as it had ever been. He admired her stamina and the way she had turned life around for herself and Delia while he had been inside without any help or advice from him. Everything had already been arranged and a contract signed by the time she was able to come and tell him about it.

At first he had felt enraged that Delia should be achieving the sort of career that he so dearly wanted for himself. It seemed so unfair when he had been striving to sing on stage ever since he was a schoolboy and yet at the age eight she had been offered a prime role with a well-established company and a director and producer who were household names.

Karyn had been unsure if she could do it, even though she'd agreed that Delia seemed to have inherited his vocal talent and that she loved the idea of singing and dancing.

Looking back, he thought with an inward smile, it had been ridiculous how jealous he'd felt; now, though, he was very proud of her and what she had achieved.

He knew they were putting on a show at the Prince of Wales Theatre in Wood Street and he couldn't wait to get there and see what the publicity posters said about her. There might even be some stills as well and he was eager to see what she looked like now.

She'd been barely eight when he'd gone down. Three long years since he'd set eyes on her. She'd been on stage for all of that time so she would probably be self-assured, and poised. And she'd also be pretty; he was sure about that.

As he drew nearer to the theatre his heart beat faster. He would only be able to look at the bill boards now, but tonight he'd go and see the show. On his own, so that he had no distractions. He wanted to concentrate on her completely, on every movement she made on stage.

He remembered the way she danced when they'd both gone to the classes Marcus Webb had organised for them on Saturdays. She'd moved like a little dream.

There were no pictures of Delia outside the Prince of Wales Theatre, but the posters were lavish in their description and their praise:

CHILD WONDER – THE VOICE OF
AN ANGEL

AS LIGHT ON HER FEET AS
THISTLEDOWN

COME AND BE ENTRANCED

AS SEEN AND ACCLAIMED IN
BRISTOL, SWANSEA, LIVERPOOL,
MANCHESTER, NEWCASTLE AND
EDINBURGH

He felt overwhelmed by the praise meted out to Delia; it brought tears to his eyes. His little girl, his Delia. It seemed unbelievable that she had become a star while he had been shut away in prison.

Once again he recalled the first time Karyn

433

had told him what she was planning to do. The thought of them touring the country had scared him stiff. Anything could happen to them in strange towns and cities. Karyn had calmed his fears and explained that wherever they went they would stay at a reputable boarding house and that there would be other members of the cast staying there as well.

She'd allayed his fears still further by assuring him that she was also being employed by the company.

'I have to make to make sure that Delia gets from our lodgings to the theatre safely and on time,' she explained. 'Then I stay at the theatre to look after her and to help behind the scenes with the clothes that are being worn in the show.'

Even Delia's schooling while she was on tour was taken care of because a tutor travelled with them. He couldn't have asked for a better future for her; it was certainly far above anything he would have been able to provide.

The fact that the show Delia was appearing in was returning to Cardiff exactly three years after Tudor had been sent to prison was a happy coincidence. Karyn had written to tell him that they would be there on that date and hoped that he would be free by then.

She had expected him to be released at least six months earlier because there was always remission for good behaviour. In his case it seemed to have been overlooked; unless he had done something she didn't know about and lost such special favours.

It was over two years since she had last seen him. Once the company had set out on tour it had been impossible to get back to Cardiff on the one day a month when she was allowed prison visiting rights.

He said he understood, but as time passed their letters became more and more brief, almost limited to a catalogue of where she and Delia had been and where they would be going next.

The letters from him were even terser. There was nothing to report, he told her. Life was virtually the same, day after day, as the weeks became months. He couldn't even write about the weather because he didn't know what it was like most of the time.

At first Delia had missed him a great deal and suffered from spells of depression when she didn't want to learn her part or do anything that was asked of her. Gradually, though, her interest in her new life filled all her waking hours. Tudor faded into the background and his name was rarely mentioned. Karyn wondered how she was going to react when they were once more reunited.

Optimistically, she hoped everything would go smoothly because Delia had matured so much. She was tall for her age and already developing slight curves. Her glossy dark curls reached almost to her shoulders and her skin was soft and peachy. As a solo singer and

435

dancer she had acquired tremendous confidence and was able to handle situations, which would confuse or distress most grown-ups, with complete aplomb.

Tomorrow, Karyn resolved, when their first night in Cardiff was over and their nerves were once again settled, she would find out what was happening and the exact date when Tudor was due for release.

She had explained all this to Samuel Pettigrew and he had been very understanding. He had even agreed that Tudor could stay with her and had even booked them into a separate boarding house from the rest of the cast.

She was now completely used to this nomadic style of life, and so was Delia, but she wasn't sure how readily Tudor would accept it.

Her own parents thought it was shameless to drag Delia around the country in such a manner and in their letters they never failed to reprimand her because she never brought Delia to see them. They refused to accept her explanation that it was not possible because of the way they worked. Instead, her mother claimed that they were deliberately staying away.

Remembering how reluctant both her mother and father had been to have them stay in Pen-y-llyn after Tudor had been sent to prison, and their refusal to even have Delia stay with them until she could sort things out, she simply hardened her heart and refused to let her mother's comments make her feel guilty.

Her own life had been fulfilling and rewarding. She had more money saved up than she had ever had before. Their contract was now almost at an end, and a new one was being arranged. She had taken a firm stand, however, and stipulated that before she signed anything she needed to discuss it all with Tudor.

She had hoped that at this point Samuel Pettigrew would have definitely said that he would also hire Tudor, but although he'd hinted several times that this was a possibility, he had still not actually committed himself. She wasn't sure whether it was because he didn't want to employ him or whether he thought it was best to talk to him direct.

In some ways, she thought that would be preferable since it would restore Tudor's self-confidence to know that someone of Samuel Pettigrew's standing wanted him.

As the performance ended and Delia returned three times to take a curtain call, Karyn waited in the wings, proud of her daughter's achievement and popularity and wishing that Tudor could be there to see her.

He would be out very soon, she told herself. They were playing in Cardiff for two weeks and he must be released any day now.

Laughter and clapping brought her out of her reverie and she peered more closely to see what was happening on stage and saw that

437

someone had thrown a posy of rosebuds, aiming it so that it fell at Delia's feet.

Delia had picked it up, held the bouquet to her face then kissed her fingers and waved them towards someone in the audience.

Karyn frowned, slightly worried when she saw that they'd come from a tall, shabbily dressed man who was standing in the aisle right at the front of the auditorium. Then her breath caught in her throat. There was something vaguely familiar about him. As the lights went up she could see him more clearly. Tall and handsome, his thick dark hair greying very slightly at the temples. She couldn't believe her eyes. Forgetting that she was supposed to remain out of sight in the wings, she darted forward on to the stage, calling out his name.

'Tudor, Tudor! Oh, Tudor!'

Pandemonium reigned. One of the theatre attendants moved towards the man and Karyn was so afraid that he was about to be thrown out that she pleaded, 'Leave him, leave him.' Clasping Delia's arm she exclaimed, 'It's your dad, cariad! Don't you recognise him?'

The audience cheered and clapped. A dozen hands pushed Tudor forward and helped him climb up on to the stage.

For one terrified moment Karyn thought that Delia still didn't recognise him, then she rushed towards him, and he swept her into his arms, hugging and kissing her. Over the top of her head their eyes met and as Karyn moved towards him, one of his arms went out to envelop her and draw her close. As their lips met in a long, hungry kiss that said far more than words ever could, the audience broke into fresh applause.

The first meeting between Samuel Pettigrew and Tudor after the curtain went down and they were all backstage was extremely cautious. Both men seemed to be wary and very guarded about what they said to each other.

When Samuel Pettigrew suggested that Tudor might like to join them for the celebration they were holding afterwards, Karyn felt on tenterhooks in case he refused.

Delia solved the problem. Clinging on to Tudor's arm she pleaded with him to do so. When he still hesitated, looking questioningly at Karyn and then at Samuel Pettigrew as if to assure himself that they really wanted him to be there, Delia pouted prettily and said it would spoil her evening if he didn't come.

'Everyone wants to meet you,' she prattled on. 'Mr Pettigrew said he'd heard you sing at the Sherman Theatre and when I told him that you could dance as well he said then we might be able to do a double act and—'

'Delia, hush!' Karyn exclaimed. Her face flushed with embarrassment. 'You shouldn't presume something like that—'

'Why not? It's what he said,' Delia interrupted. She gave an elaborate sigh. 'I suppose it is too much to expect; grown-ups are always saying things they don't really mean.'

'Not always,' Samuel Pettigrew told her, 'but we'll have to wait and see. Your dad mightn't want to join our company and do a double act with a little minx like you since you are bound to be the one who will get all the applause.'

Karyn felt deflated by the sternness of his voice. Like Delia she had hoped that there might be a possibility of Samuel Pettigrew offering Tudor an opportunity to sing, but now it looked as though Delia might have ruined this by over-stepping the mark with her outspoken comments.

She tried to put it out of her mind and to enjoy what was going on as champagne corks popped and glasses chinked, but it cast a cloud over her evening. When they were all saying goodnight she could hardly believe it when she heard Samuel Pettigrew invite Tudor to call and see him in his office so that they could discuss the possibility of a double act some time in the near future.

As Tudor accompanied them back to the boarding house where she and Delia were staying she felt as if she was walking on air. Not only were the three of them together again, but it looked as though there was a promising future for Tudor as well as for Delia.

One day quite soon, she told herself, she'd see them on stage together and Tudor's name, as well as Delia's, would be up in lights as she'd always known it would be.